Yellowstone
The Bears of Caldera

Written and Illustrated by

Chad-Michael Simon

Text copyright © 2019 Chad-Michael Simon
Illustrations by Chad-Michael Simon copyright © 2019

IN THE GARDEN. by Emily Dickinson
from *Poems by Emily Dickinson, Second Series*,
edited by T. W. Higginson and Mabel Loomis Todd,
first published in 1891

Exerpt from *Democracy in America* by Alexis de Tocqueville
G. Dearborn & Co., 1838.

All rights reserved. Published by Hyphenated Press
The STAMP DESIGN and associated logos are trademarks
and/or registered trademarks of Hyphenated Press.

John, Millicent, and Miriam Laskow and all related characters and elements are
trademarks of Hyphenated Press.

No part of this publication may be reproduced in whole or in part, or stored in a
retrieval system, or transmitted in any form of by any means, electronic, mechanical,
photocopying, recording, or otherwise, without written permission of the publisher.

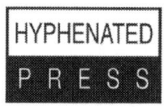

Hyphenated Press paperback printing
Amazon/Kindle

ISBN-13: 9780615759982
ISBN-10: 061575998X

Printed in the U.S.A.
First printing, February 2019

Acknowledgements

Natalia,
You've been my best friend
and partner as I've brought this to life.

Libbey,
You were my first fan
and are a constant inspiration.

Evan and Aidan,
I drew so much detail from your
thoughtfulness, intelligence, and humor.

My parents,
You always encouraged me to draw
and listened to every silly little story.

Contents

Part I: Too Silver for a Seam

One - 1
Into the Other

Two - 25
Lights, Caves, and Unreachable Trees

Three - 39
The Two Hosts

Four - 55
The Bighorn Sheep

Five - 67
The Mammoth and the Mesa

Six - 83
Concerning the Habits of Animals

Seven - 109
What Happened at the Geyser

Eight - 121
Hide and Seek

Nine - 149
Good Night

Part II: Where Nature's Temper Reaches

Ten - 161
Contraption

Eleven - 179
Ze'eva

Twelve - 189
Curious Minds, Curious Caves

Thirteen - 209
Dust Is the Only Secret

Fourteen - 229
If I Could Bribe

Fifteen - 255
Two Journeys

Part III: War Is Oblique

Sixteen - 301
Abatakai

Seventeen - 331
The Battle of Doyadu-khani

Eighteen - 361
Tumo Nataquinde

Nineteen - 397
The Asaquatzi

Twenty - 439
Aftermath

Appendix I: Glossaries

454
Locations

455
Arthur's Phrasebook

Appendix II: The Yellowstone Sketchbook

458

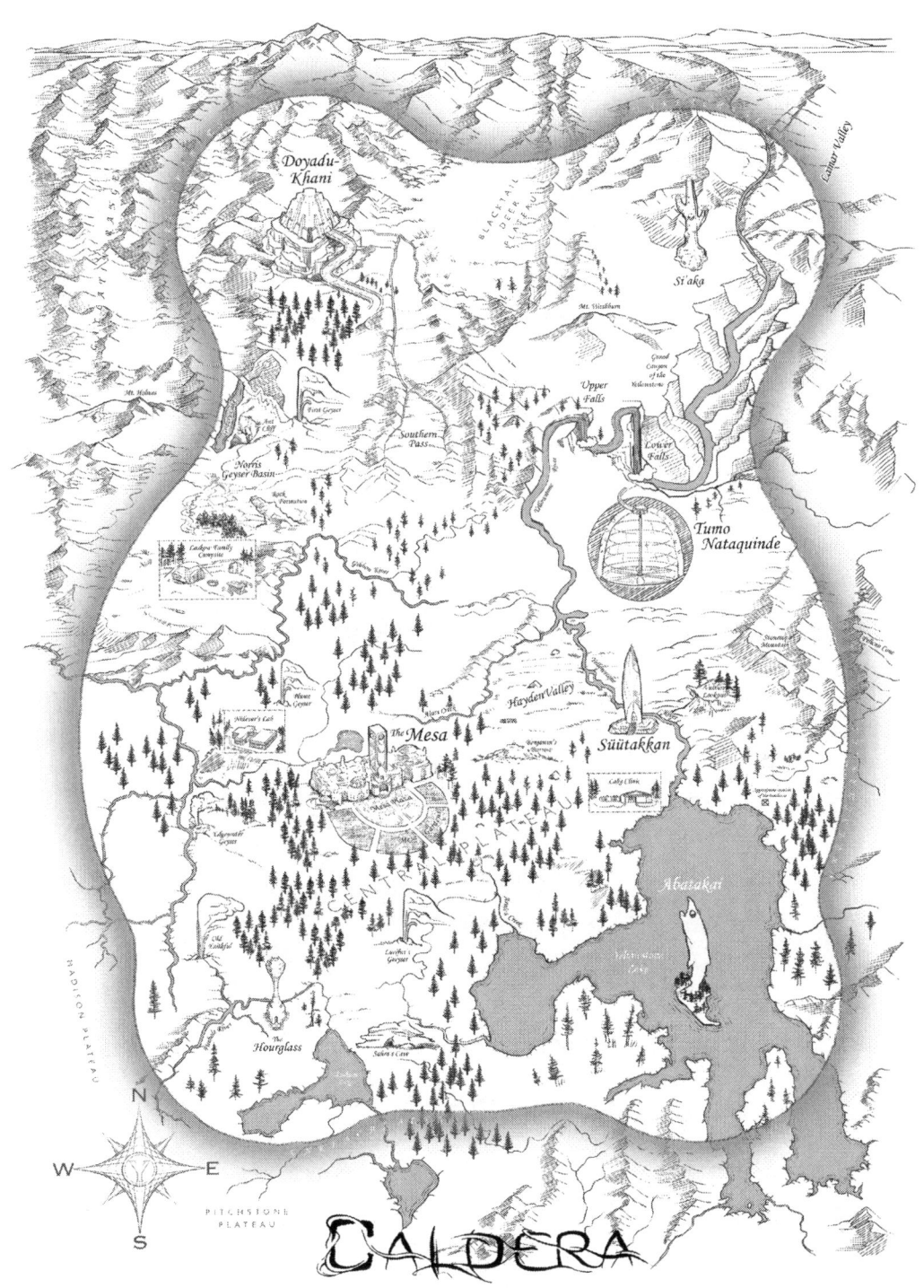

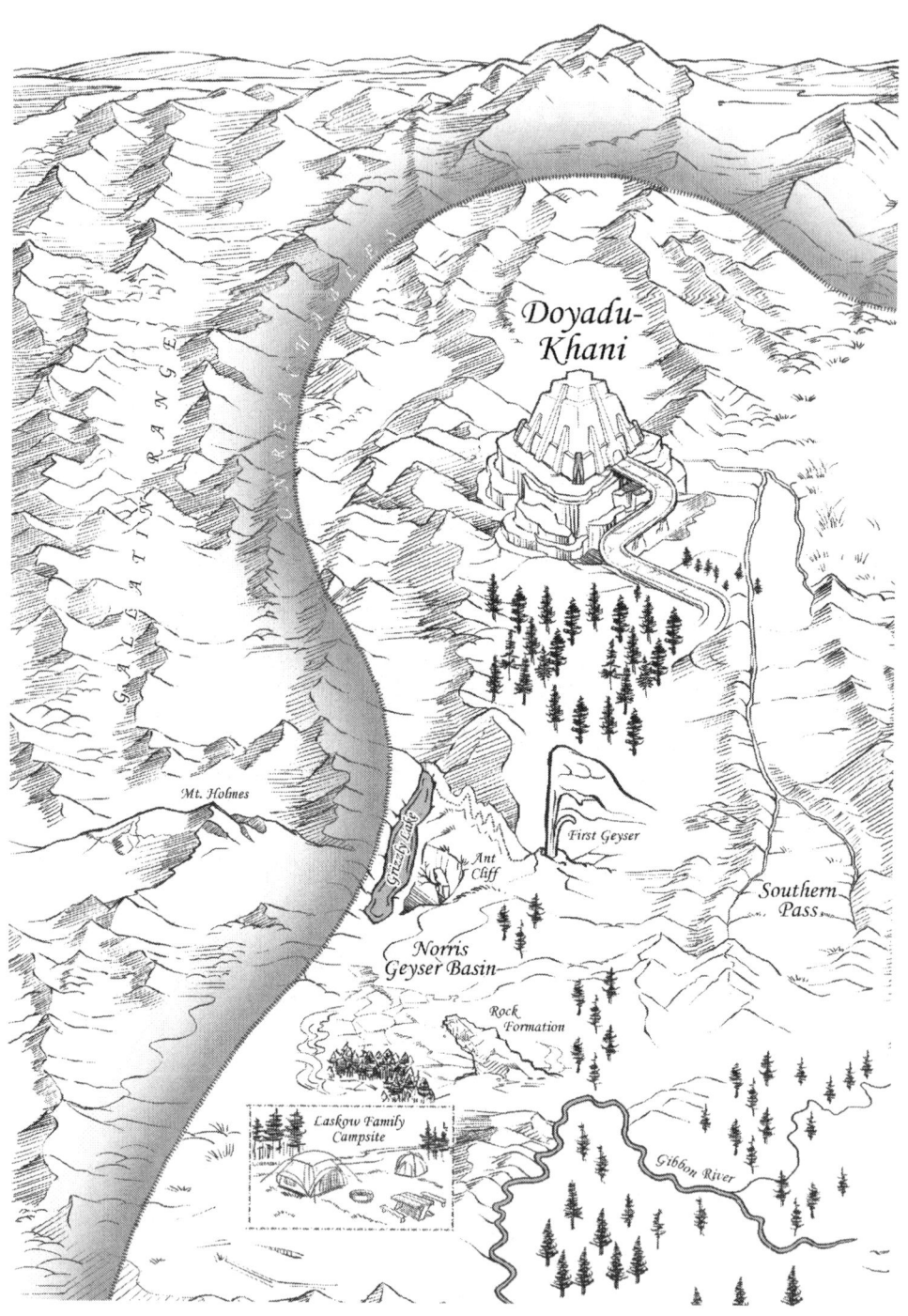

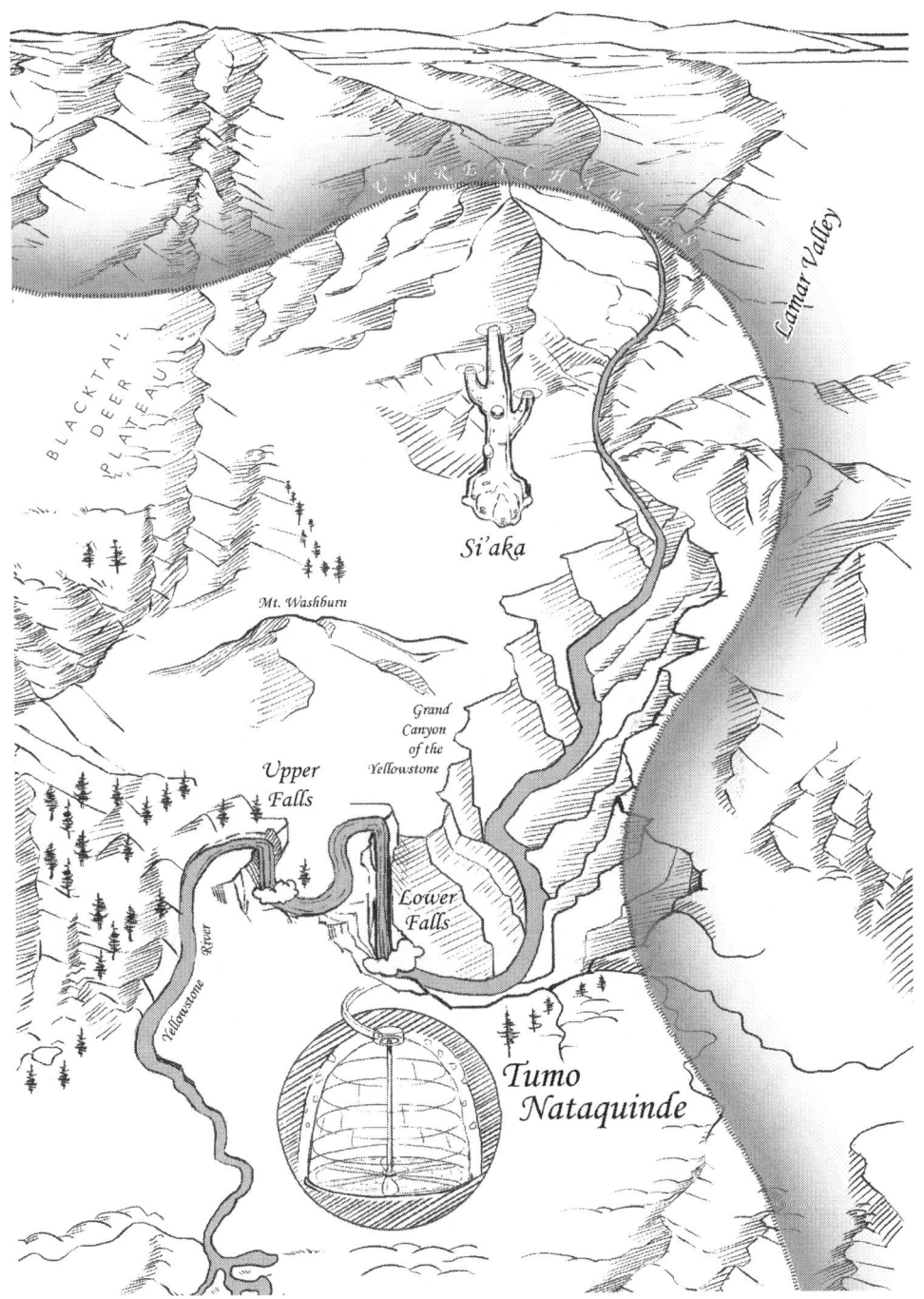

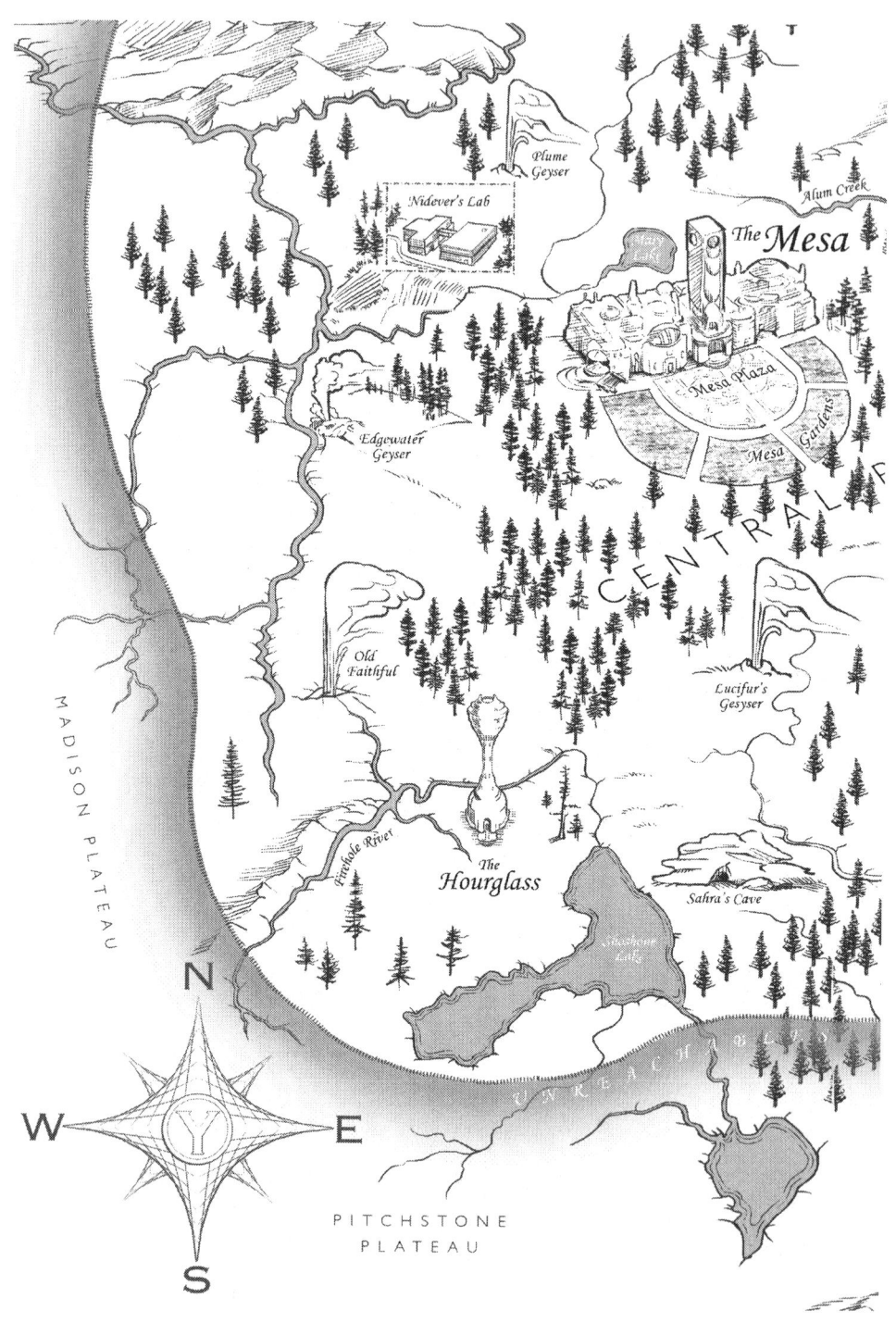

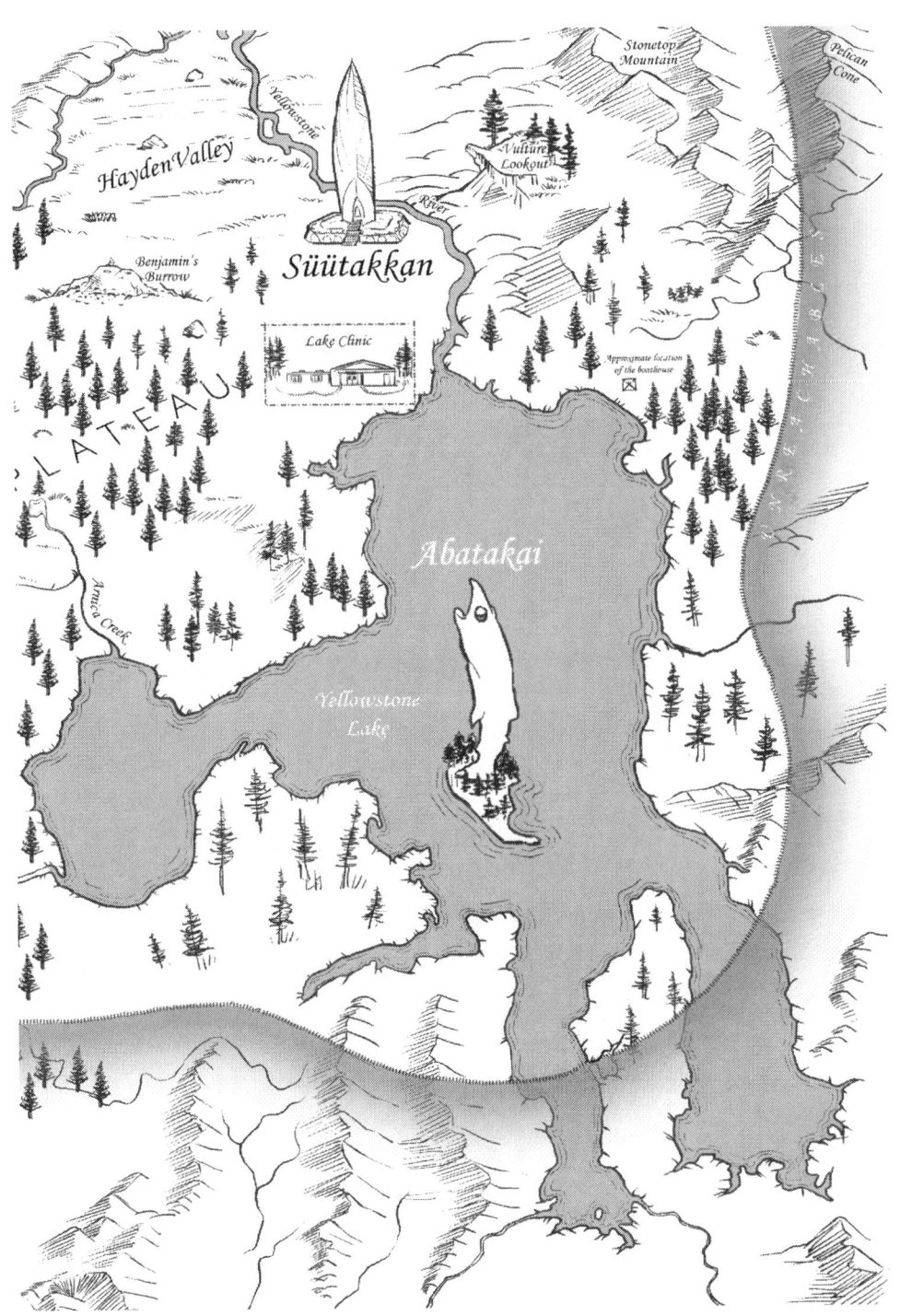

PART I
Too Silver for a Seam

ONE
Into the Other

John Laskow thought Yellowstone National Park would be far enough away from home to forget about his problems. All it took was one stupid sentence from his sister — his *little* sister — to send him into a rage.

You're too wimpy to hunt for bears.

Miriam's mouth ran ahead of her brain, and her fists ran ahead of her mouth. A trio of bullies had picked on John throughout the schoolyear, and Miriam was the one who stood up to them. She never let him forget that fact.

Why don't you learn to defend yourself, John? she asked in front the gawkers after she clocked and tackled the leader of the pack. It was humiliating. At least it happened on the last day of school, but he held no hope that the situation would defuse itself over the summer. No, these boys would remember, and they would be there in the fall when he started eighth grade.

The great irony, he thought, was that his defender was a tiny 11-year-old with sunshine in her hair who was just as guilty of bullying him as often as she defended him, though she would never admit this. It was Miriam being Miriam, cocky and bouncy.

So, early the first morning at their campsite, she laughed at him when he said he was going on a bear hunt with their mother. It wouldn't be a real bear hunt, of course; they would just be hiking, but John wanted to make an adventure out of it.

She started by mocking his collection of equipment.

Ha! Are you going to lure the bear with the cookies and then bonk it on the head with your thermos?

Chapter One

Cocky and bouncy. That was Miriam, oblivious to how much her words could hurt.

To add insult to injury, his other sister, Millicent, was already in a foul mood because she'd lost the book she'd been reading the day before. The family searched the campsite. After she scoured their van a third time, she slumped into their hammock and made the offhand remark that she wouldn't go after John if he were attacked by a bear during this bear hunt of his.

The sibling bond stops at bears, she said.

Great. Charming. Millicent thought she was being very clever, but as usual her delivery was acrid and laced with a vocal fry, that creaky voice some girls use, that guttural croak that made John's skin crawl. She'd acquired the trait over the last school year, and he was shocked that their parents hadn't corrected it.

Dark and moody. That was Millicent.

Cocky and bouncy. Dark and moody.

That's how he described his sisters to the school counselor when she asked about his support network. *My support network? Wow, that's a therapeutic term,* he thought, something Millicent would have known about, but not him. Not John Laskow.

I don't need therapy, he told his father.

Just try it for a little while. It might help.

He went twice a week to the same therapist Millicent saw for her anxiety. It was embarrassing, and he couldn't understand how either of them would need it. They didn't have any problems. No real ones.

"You're too wimpy to hunt for bears," said Miriam.

He yelled and threw his father's old thermos at the ground.

"Just shut up, Miri!"

"Hey!" said their father, whose name was Barry. He rushed over from hanging their laundry bag and stood with his hands on his hips. He was quite a fun dad, but he could turn serious in a heartbeat when necessary. "What's going on?"

"She won't stop picking on me!"

Into the Other

"All right. Miri, what did I tell you? In the tent."

"But —"

"You heard me."

Miriam groaned and walked away. "I don't see how this is fair."

John gave her a scowl while their father picked up the thermos, but he got caught making the face.

"John, that's enough." He shook the thermos. It was weathered and gray, and he'd had it for many years. Its glass liner rattled inside, broken. "You do *not* throw things when you're upset. I don't care how mad you get. This is *never* okay. Do you understand me?"

John heard him, but his father was talking about a normal kind of mad. He couldn't possibly understand this level of mad-mad, which perfectly justified the throwing of things.

Their mother, Ana, came out of the big tent (John's little pup tent was set up next to it) and crossed her arms. She never yelled, but her Stern Voice could tame a lion.

"We haven't been here for 24 hours, and this is how you're behaving? Really?"

John didn't blink.

"You never, *ever* throw something out of anger. I don't care how annoyed you are. You're not a toddler."

Why does one parent always repeat what the other just said?

"I'm not sure if I want to go hiking if this is the way you're going to be."

Ouch. That's a low blow, Mom.

"No, please, Mom, no! I really wanna go."

His dad shook the thermos again, and then he shook his head. "You're getting too big for this, buddy."

Quick! Apologize before they ask you to!

"I'm so sorry that I broke your thermos, Dad."

His father gave him a smug and skeptical look. "Mm-hmm. Never again. Do you hear me?"

John nodded. It's not like they could send him to his room. Maybe

Chapter One

to his pup tent? He'd just read his comic books . . .

His father put an arm around him. "Look, I know it's been a rough year. But part of growing up means learning how to control your temper, right?"

John nodded against his shoulder. "Right."

They pulled apart. The broken glass sloshed inside the thermos.

"Man. I loved this thermos. What was in here?"

Man. Guilt.

"It's milk. For the cookies."

"Looks like you're stuck with cookies and water."

Yuck!

His parents exchanged looks. John knew this series of looks and was relieved, because it meant the talk was almost over.

His mother zipped up her jacket. "All right. Finish packing what you need, and we'll go."

The morning hike was a planned one-on-one trip with his mother, and it couldn't have come at a better time. They drove twenty minutes north to a pull-off that had barely enough room for five cars. This was the trailhead for the Grizzly Lake Trail, and the area was empty compared to the amusement-park-like atmosphere around Old Faithful, which they'd visited the day before.

"This feels like a completely different park, doesn't it?" she asked with a cheerful tone to coax him away from his bad mood.

"I guess so."

The trail led them first across a broad, grassy meadow dotted with wildflowers and pine trees, and, once they were away from the Grand Loop Road, it did feel like they'd been transported to a different world. The landscape was full of bleached, fallen trees that were victims of a huge fire, according to an informational sign.

John adjusted his backpack and rolled his shoulders and lifted his chin. He was mighty, darn it, and no little sister could tell him otherwise. But the cold, thin air made him tire, and, less than a mile into the hike, a wheeze rattled deep in his lungs as the trail tipped upward.

"Mom, can we stop for a second, please?"

Not so mighty now, are you, wimpy boy?

"Sure. There's no rush. Catch your breath and take a drink."

His skin tingled from the blood rushing to his head, and he was already sweaty under his layers of clothing. By contrast, his mother looked around like she was deciding where to go for a jog. She went for morning runs, took spin classes, and played volleyball with her coworkers and had to pry John from his PlayStation or sketchbook to get him to exercise. She often told people that she was amazed by how skinny he was despite his lack of movement. This hike was already a lot more work than he'd anticipated, and he felt like he'd been duped into one of her routines.

"Wow," she said. "Isn't this amazing? Just breathe it in."

"Breathe what in? It smells like rotten eggs around here!"

She gave him a dour look. "How long are you going to keep this up?"

"What? It stinks!"

"You know what."

"No, I don't! Tell me what I'm doing."

She rolled her eyes. "If you don't know, then I'm not going to tell you."

"Fine. I'll just keep quiet then."

"Yes. Keep quiet then."

They continued along the trail through a series of switchbacks that descended a steep, forested mountainside to the shore of Grizzly Lake. They strolled along the water's pristine edge and watched a few early-morning fishermen.

"How are you feeling?" she asked.

It was a simple question, but he launched into complaining about everything that was bothering him. His sisters. Bullies. Fall coming at the end of the summer and the beginning of eighth grade. His frustrations bubbled into tears, and he even used the word *friggin'* a few

Chapter One

times.

His mother simply listened.

He wiped his cheeks with brisk swipes and glared at his reflection in the smooth surface of the lake. He was fair-skinned — though his face was ruddy at the moment — with dark, brown hair that was a little shaggier than usual. He inherited bright, blue eyes from both parents, and they were fiery from crying.

His mother rested her hand on the top of his backpack and caressed the back of his neck. "You're scaring me, looking at yourself like that. Come on. Miri was just being sarcastic."

"And Millicent, too. They're always ganging up on me, and I hate it."

"Look. Your Dad was going to talk to them after we left. They'll apologize when we get back."

He hated that, too. He knew how he felt when they made him apologize to his sisters for some stupid thing or another. He never *meant* it when he said he was sorry, and they wouldn't mean it, either. They would just play nice, so they could return to a peaceful vacation.

His mother held out her hand. "Come on. Let's start climbing."

Halfway up the switchbacks, she stopped and pointed back the way they'd climbed. From there, the lake looked like a long shard of blue glass lying in a bed of trees.

"Look at that view."

He admitted it was gorgeous. And now he felt bad for ruining their morning together. He loathed teenagers and had long feared the day he'd become one, and he hated that it was near and inevitable for him.

"I think it's time to update your log," she said.

He nodded. She always knew what to say and when to say it. *Enough with the crying*, he thought, and he proceeded as though none of it ever happened.

Me? Cry? Surely you're thinking of somebody else.

He'd received a digital recorder as an early birthday present, something to enjoy while they were on vacation. It was a throwaway, dollar-store toy and was already one of his favorite belongings. He lifted it to his mouth and pressed the record button.

"Grizzly Bear Update! Our expedition to the low ground was a failure, I'm sad to say. After two hours of searching, we haven't seen a single bear. So, we're heading back to base camp for lunch."

Pleased with himself, he tucked the recorder into his vest pocket. He unscrewed the cap of his canteen and took a swig of water that trickled down both sides of his chin. A stray drop caught in his windpipe and made him cough and spit.

His mother touched his backpack again. "Easy there, ranger."

Cough-cough!

She laughed. "Every time. You do that every single time! I'm going to make a bet with you that you can't go a day without choking on a drink."

Cough! "I can't help it! I'm thirsty." *Cough-cough!*

"Everyone else is capable of drinking without choking . . ."

Grumble.

She tussled his hair. "What was that? Grumble-grumble? I'll give you grumble-grumble! Rawr!" She wrapped her arms around him and rocked back and forth.

He giggled and groaned and pulled away and stood on the tips of his toes, which made him almost as tall as her. He smirked and lifted his chin to be even taller.

"You're not going to be able to do that much longer," he said.

She fixed him with an *oh really?* look and pressed his shoulders down to shrink him back to normal size. She pressed her forehead against his and stared intently.

"I will *always* be able to do that to you. Even when you're six feet tall. And my goodness, you need a haircut."

He crossed his eyes to look at the strands of hair that fell across his forehead. It wasn't *that* long. It was barely to his eyebrows. But through protests and timing, he'd postponed a trip to the barber until it was too late. He was proud of that.

Chapter One

His mother took a drink from the canteen and handed it back to him. "I'm so glad we did this. Aside from this morning, are you having a good time?"

He put on a serious face. "Mom, I have to be honest with you. I'm not having a good time." She gave him a look, and he raised his hands over his head. "I'm having a *great* time!"

Water spilled down his arm from the canteen. She corrected his grip.

"You are so *clumsy*. You're not allowed to be clumsy anymore once you turn thirteen."

"Ha-ha! So, I can be clumsy for another week!"

"Great."

They traversed the remaining switchbacks to climb out of the valley. John swung his walking stick like a sword and made crashing sounds like *crsshh!* and *pitsch!* and *booshhh!* He fished the recorder out of his vest pocket to continue the report.

"Having climbed out of the valley, I'm sorry to say we haven't seen any signs of bear activity, either. No scratch marks or poop — "

"Ahem," said his mother. "A professional guide would call it scat, and so should you."

He continued as though he hadn't heard her. "No scratch marks or scat. No clumps of fur or tracks — "

He stopped. Large paw prints drew a path across the trail in front of them.

Unaware, his mother walked into the back of him, turned her ankle, and stumbled. "Ouch, John! You can't stop like that!"

"Um, Mom?"

He pointed at the tracks, which were crisp in the sunlight, each the size of his face, and each with five claw marks gouged into the ground at the end of each toe.

"Oh, my goodness," she said as she crouched for a closer look. "Wow, these are huge! Did you see these on the way down?"

"No."

"Neither did I." She bit her bottom lip and scanned the woods.

Fascinated by their size, he squatted beside her and placed his palm in the middle of one. He could have fit five hands in it.

"Wow. Maybe I should switch to hunting mice."

She pulled him up. "I'm sure we're okay, but we should get back to the trailhead." She untied the bear bells from his backpack and fastened them to the end of his walking stick to be noisier. "Do you know any songs we can sing?"

"Oh yeah! The website said bears'll stay away if you're making noise — "

He froze at the sight of a massive grizzly bear with deep red fur. It stood twenty feet away, behind his mother, where the trail descended to the switchbacks. The bear's head jutted low, and it locked bitter, watery eyes on him.

"M-mom."

She turned and went rigid. She stepped backward and pushed John along with her.

"Move slowly. Don't run. Just — "

"NEED!" said the bear.

"What?" asked his mother.

He stomped his huge front paws. He charged and shouted, "I NEED THE BOY!"

John's mother grabbed him and dove into the brush. The bear bells jingled as he dropped the walking stick, so he could wrap his arms around her. The bear hooked his forearm around her waist and hurled her out of John's reach and opened his mouth above his face. He could only see teeth and wet and black.

"No!" said his mother.

The bear turned and roared at her, but she was ready with a can of pepper spray from her belt. He shielded his eyes with his forepaw to avoid the sickly, white stream until the can hissed empty.

The bear turned back to John. His eyes lit up yellow like there was fire behind them.

Chapter One

"RUN!" said the bear.

The word cut through John's mind, and, without thinking, he ran into the woods. He couldn't stop. The trees rushed by like he was a passenger in someone else's body. He cleared the thicket and clambered over a heap of boulders. He hoped to double back to his mother.

Why did I run?

The bear burst from the forest, spotted him, and ran toward him again.

John sprinted to the next stand of trees. His backpack slid off his shoulders as he jumped over a snare of roots. He hurdled a fallen lodgepole pine tree into an open basin and dodged long cracks that zigzagged across the ochre ground. The land vented steam and the stink of rotten eggs.

A geyser was erupting at the center.

"SLOW DOWN!" said the bear, and John slowed down. "GO LEFT!" said the bear, and John pivoted to run straight at the geyser.

A flash of blue light engulfed his body as he hit the column of scalding water.

He pinched his eyes shut.

But the geyser didn't hurt him, and he kept running. He shouted and ran until the ground vanished from beneath his feet.

His stomach dropped. His eyes flew open, and all he could see were the distant mountains as he plunged over the edge of a cliff. He landed in the branches of a hardy dogwood tree that grew from the face of the cliff. His new recorder tumbled out of his vest pocket and plummeted to the treetops below.

He clung to the branches and bobbed up and down. Behind him was a ledge, so he inched backward, sure that the tree would snap before he reached it. Panicked, he rushed the last two feet to safety and panted with relief on the solid ground. It was a narrow landing with barely enough room to stand comfortably. There was no place to climb back up.

Nasty scrapes stung his forearms, and pain shot across his side under his ribcage, like he'd been stabbed there. He touched the spot without looking, and his fingers glistened with blood. Terrified, he pressed his elbow against his body.

What if I bleed to death here?

What if Mom can't find me?

What if this ledge breaks?

He threw himself against the wall, felt the cold rock against his cheek, and called for his mother.

"Mom!"

A squeak — a voice — sounded in his head.

"Hey!"

He searched the edge of the cliff above him. "Mom?"

"Down here!" said the squeak, but instead of sound in his ears, the voice came like a thought in his mind. "Look to your right!"

John strained his eyes to the right. There was nothing there but the drop-off and an unremarkable, black carpenter ant on a pile of rocks.

"What have you done?" asked the ant. He gestured with his front legs.

John dropped to all fours. It must have been an installation from an attraction or maybe a toy, so he looked around the rocks for a speaker or mechanism.

The ant sighed. "I'm right here, dummy. You've disturbed the nest, and the queen is outraged! What happened?"

John didn't want to talk to an ant. "I — I fell."

"How did you manage to do that?"

"A bear attacked me and my mom."

"Oh, my! What did it look like?"

The voice disoriented his brain and turned his stomach. All he wanted was to find his mother and know that she was safe.

"Mom!"

The ant cocked his head. "Your mother's up there?"

John clawed at the cliff. He wished he could climb it. Chunks of rock crumbled from the sandstone, which terrified him.

Chapter One

His voice cracked. "MO-OM!"

Another ant arrived, and they greeted each other by rubbing their antennae. "What's the noise?"

"Noise? This human was attacked by a bear!"

"A bear? Oh no! Do you know if it was–"

"Was about to ask! Hey, human-boy, what color was the bear?"

John's face was ruddy and wet with tears. "It was red!"

The ants froze. "Stay here!" they said, and they dashed underground.

He grimaced and kicked the cliff.

Miriam Laskow sat alert on a couch in the waiting room of the Lake Clinic and tugged the button hook of her overalls. She wished she was wearing something more comfortable. Her sister, Millicent, was curled on the couch beside her with her head in Miriam's lap. The wait lasted forever. After John and their mother left to go hiking, she and Millicent dueled with sticks in a breathless, giggling battle around the campsite. Miriam was about to change into lighter clothes and help their father prepare lunch when an SUV skidded up to them.

A bear attacked your wife and son, the ranger told their father.

Her memory after that was blurry. Panic. There was a rush to douse the campfire and jump into their van to follow the ranger's truck to the clinic. There were raised voices. Her father was distressed. After the hour-long drive, it turned out that the people at the clinic had no idea where their mom and John were.

And on top of everything, she was hot and itchy in overalls. Meanwhile, her sister's gangly, bare legs stuck out of her shorts and were covered in goosebumps.

Why did they go alone? Miriam didn't ask when they left, but she wished she would have. She could have protested and demanded they go as a family. But the morning was already tense, and John needed the time alone. And their dad had talked to them about being nice.

Blah, blah, blah.

Into the Other

She sighed and stared at Millicent's very curly hair, which was barely tamed into two pigtail buns. Miriam's hair was straight, which didn't make sense because they were identical twins. She liked to keep it short for soccer and karate and Morning Striders (her before-school running club) and chalked up the difference in their hair to a genetic oddity. Maybe they weren't identical, after all, but the doctors insisted they were. They definitely shared the same face. Their parents joked that Millicent's curliness was her imagination spilling out of her head. It was funny, but Miriam found it distasteful after hearing it a few times because it implied that she had no imagination by comparison.

It didn't matter. Not now. She wrapped one of Millicent's curls around her finger and gave a gentle tug.

Their father talked to a nurse in blue scrubs and the old ranger with a kind face who'd retrieved them from their campsite. His Smokey-the-Bear hat sat on the registration desk.

Their father was angry but restrained. "I don't understand. How can you not know where they are? Why did we come all the way to this side of the park if they're not here?"

Miriam shook Millicent's shoulder. "Did you hear that? They still don't know where they are!"

Millicent nodded. Her face was tight with worry, and she rolled to whimper into Miriam's tummy.

Miriam had never seen him like this. He was always positive, smart, logical, and funny. *He's a professor of physics, for Pete's sake!* She looked around the room for something pleasant, something she could show him to make him smile when they finished talking. She squinted to read the printing on some T-shirts that were for sale on a tiny gift counter.

> Enjoy your stay in our nation's first National Park. Our National Parks belong to everyone! You have every right to indulge yourself. So, feed the bears, walk up and pet the moose, let your children ride the bison, swim in the boiling hot mineral pools, drive fast and pass on curves. These messages from the folks who

Chapter One

really care: Yellowstone Park Medical Services. We want your business!

How could they print that! She looked away in horror and shifted her focus to a poster of a few bison grazing in a misty valley. Their short horns and dark eyes looked peaceful, but a yellow piece of paper tacked to the wall warned that bison could weigh a ton and sprint at up to thirty miles per hour.

**These animals may appear tame
but are wild, unpredictable, and dangerous.
DO NOT APPROACH BISON.**

She closed her eyes. *Okay. That's not helping, either.*

The nurse in blue was gone. The ranger touched their father's shoulder again, and, with a final word, picked up his Smokey-the-Bear hat and left.

Dressed for camping in a maroon sweatshirt and khaki cargo shorts, their father carried an uncharacteristic slump in his shoulders and cupped his hand over his mouth.

Come over here, Dad, thought Miriam, and he looked at her as though he'd heard.

He approached and opened his arms for a hug. Millicent buried her face in his sweatshirt and sobbed.

"Mom and John might be at another hospital," he said, "and we're waiting to find out for sure. Okay?"

Miriam nodded and lifted her chin. "These messages from the folks who really care," she said. She knew he didn't understand the reference, but he smiled anyway. He kissed the top of her head and pulled her close.

John curled up on the ledge. His voice was hoarse from calling for help. He coughed and swallowed dust. He rested his head on his folded

Into the Other

arms, closed his eyes, and imagined that he was back at the campsite. He smelled the fire and saw his dad's maroon sweatshirt. He heard his sisters' laughter. He saw his mother — felt her hugs and kisses and felt guilty for any time he'd told her to stop because it was gross. The daydream was so strong that he thought he could open his eyes and be inside his pup tent. He could unzip the flap and tell everyone about the nightmare he just had.

Voices interrupted him. He opened one eye to discover a group of ants whispering on the rocks near his head. Their antennae waved like a parade of windshield wipers.

"Is he dead?"

"Dead isn't breathing."

"Breathing is a must!"

"Must be sleeping."

"Sleeping out here?"

"Here comes someone!"

"Someone above!"

A stone hit John's foot, followed by a rock on his head. He stood to look and winced, reminded of the gash in his side.

"Hello?" he called with his creaky voice.

A grizzly bear stood silhouetted by the sun at the top of the cliff. John flattened against the rock while the ants talked in circles.

"It's Sebastian!"

"Sebastian, yes!"

"Yes, he'll help you!"

He shushed them, his eyes pleading, but they kept talking. He kicked the rocks.

"He's killed Harvey!"

"Harvey's dead over here!"

"Here lies another Harvey!"

The remaining ants, apparently all named Harvey, scurried out of sight.

His heart pounding, he peeked at the tufts of grass at the top of the

Chapter One

cliff. The bear was gone. He waited to see if it would poke its head out again, and when it didn't, he slumped against the wall with a renewed worry for his mother.

Where are you?

Are you looking for me?

Did he . . . hurt you?

The temperature was dropping. He wished he had his backpack with his sweatshirt, canteen, and bag of homemade cookies. He slid to sit with his back against the cliff and watched the sun creep toward the horizon.

Millicent Laskow tugged on her puzzle toy. It was a jumble of metal rods and plastic balls she'd been trying to untangle — without resorting to using the solution sheet — since they left Naperville, but she was convinced that it was unsolvable. She eyed a milk crate full of preschool toys in the corner of the waiting room. Her curly pigtails sagged.

"Super. We can either play with baby toys or a puzzle we can't figure out." She slipped it into her hoodie pouch and yawned.

Miriam yawned in reply. "Stop it. I don't wanna be tired."

They hadn't eaten in hours, and Millicent always turned into a monster when she was hungry. Her stomach growled.

"Dude. You're either tired or you're not. Don't blame me."

The phone rang. The ranger glanced to the ceiling to give a silent thank you.

"This is Kolb.

Yes.

What can you tell me?

To where?

Okay, now, whose call was that?"

As he spoke, the tension in Millicent's tummy tightened like someone was twisting a wooden handle attached to her guts. That's how she described it to the counselor, who taught her tricks for dealing with anxiety. But the puzzle toy was annoying, squeezing the pressure points in her wrists wasn't working (it never did), and she was already lightheaded from taking deep breaths. She pressed her elbows into her sides to keep from shaking.

Miriam put her hand on her back. She knew. Her sister always knew.

"What's happening, Miri?"

Miriam gave her a squeeze and hopped to her feet. "I'll find out." She tugged the back of their father's sweatshirt. "What are they saying, Dad?"

"Oh, Miri. You're being so good."

His blue eyes were vivid from weariness, and his face looked different to her, longer and pale. They'd never been through something like this.

"The ranger is talking to someone, so hopefully soon."

"Okay," she said, studying the ranger. It looked like he was on hold, and it looked like he wasn't happy. She chewed on the inside of her cheek. "Um, we're hungry. It's been a while, and Millicent needs to eat."

"Is the monster coming out?"

"Just starting to. She's shaking."

"You're a good big sister."

They called her this to John's chagrin (because he was a year older) and Millicent's annoyance (because she was only a few minutes younger), but Miriam knew it was true. Looking out for her siblings was a full-time job.

He thumbed through his wallet. "Here. See if you can find anything in the vending machines. Come right back, okay?"

"Thank you. We will. Do you want anything?"

"Something small. Surprise me."

In a tiny cafeteria, the girls found three vending machines, two old card tables, and a microwave with fingerprints smudged on the handle. The vending machines stood like sentinels, and the light from their cases spilled odd shapes across the floor. Millicent leaned against Miriam's shoulder and moaned about her immediate need of sustenance, lest she

Chapter One

perish.

Miriam chose a can of root beer for them to share (and to boost Millicent's blood sugar) and grabbed two beef sticks with cheese, three apples (one for their dad), and a pack of trail mix. She balanced the armful, put her other arm around Millicent, and turned to leave.

The red grizzly bear blocked the doorway. With him, a thick smell of rotten eggs flooded the room. His eyes glowed yellow.

"Don't scream," he said without opening his mouth.

Miriam dropped their snacks and shoved Millicent behind her. The can of root beer cracked and rolled and sprayed fizz across the tiles. She opened her mouth to yell for their father, but her voice caught in her throat.

"PERFECT!" said the bear. "You perfect!"

Night fell, and John was terrified of rolling off the ledge if he were to fall asleep. He nestled into the corner against the cliff and built a barrier of rocks. The cold wind was relentless, and the wound on his side stung from shivering. He still refused to look to see how bad it was.

He was relieved when the clouds opened, when he could see in the moonlight, but then they rolled in thicker and left him in darkness.

A rustling came from above with a dusty stream of pebbles. A bright light, like someone was waving a flashlight, descended toward him. He gasped with hope.

"Hello?"

A dark shape the size of a housecat lowered on a rope to his eye level. It wore a small miner's cap, and the glare from the head lamp hid the creature's face. It spoke in the same manner as the ants, into his mind, and the voice was deep but thin, like a man who'd inhaled helium.

"Hello!" he said as he hopped off the rope onto the ledge. Tied to the line behind him was something that looked like a yellow pool noodle.

John screamed.

Into the Other

"Chip-chip-chip!" said the animal. His miner's cap tipped back to reveal the beaver-like face of a yellow marmot. "I'm here ta help ya!" He smiled with gruesome incisors.

"Get out of here! Go away!" said John, and he kicked erratically. The marmot ducked and bobbed to avoid the flying feet.

"Now you listen to me! If you wanna get off this cliff, you're gonna hafta to do what I say!"

John froze. "How — how are you talking?"

"That's a bigger question than we have time to answer right now. Here, put this harness on."

He offered the yellow pool noodle, but John didn't move.

Did I hit my head on the way down? Yes, I must have hit my head. This is crazy!

"Human-boy! If you put this harness under your arms, the folks up top will pull you outta here, and voila! You're rescued!"

His mind was a whirlwind, but he knew he couldn't stay on the cliff. With his eyes on the marmot, he slipped the harness under his arms and felt like he was about to float down a lazy river.

"All right, Sebastian!" said the marmot. "He's ready!"

The line pulled taut and lifted John from the ledge. He twirled until his feet anchored against the cliff and could walk up the surface. The marmot hopped onto him and hooked their harnesses together. He was uncomfortably close.

He grinned again. "I'm Benjamin, by the way. Nice to meetcha!"

A new voice entered John's mind, deep and handsome like notes from a cello.

"You're quite the diplomat, Benjamin."

John looked up to discover that he was being lifted toward a grizzly bear. He yelled and kicked against the cliff and spun in place. He looked down to see how far a drop it would be if he were to slip out of the harness, but it was already too far.

Panicked, he looked up again as a gray wolf appeared next to the bear. Before he could reach for the clasp, the wolf spoke into his mind

19

Chapter One

with a gentle, female voice. Her eyes glowed yellow.

"Sleep, human-boy. Sleep."

His motivation evaporated, and his vision faded to black.

The red grizzly didn't hurt Millicent and Miriam. He led them out of the clinic through a side door and ordered them to climb onto his back. They didn't want to, but his voice compelled them to do as he said. Miriam sat in front, so Millicent could cling to her from behind.

The bear marched into the woods and rocked the girls side to side with each step. Millicent looked back at the clinic, which receded out of sight through the trees, and wanted to scream for their father. The bear's earlier command locked her voice.

Miriam held handfuls of his bristly, red fur, which was awful because patches of it were missing, and his exposed skin looked raw and painful. The smell of rotten eggs sickened her.

At the base of a steep hill, he extended his neck and clawed at the ground to climb. Millicent lurched backward. She lunged for a better grip but fell off his back, still unable to scream, and tumbled down the stony slope. She scraped her bare knees and an elbow along the way and landed on her bottom with a spray of pine needles.

"OFF!" said the bear, and Miriam slid from his back. "STAY!" he said with a yellow flash in his eyes, and she couldn't move her feet.

Millicent cried at the bottom of the hill. The bear bounded down to her and snarled in her face, and with the snarl came the light in his eyes again. She fell silent.

"Follow! FOLLOW!" he said. The light flared when he repeated the word.

Millicent felt like she'd been skewered, like a sharp vine pierced through her brain and down into her gut. She hated climbing but had no choice under his command. She slipped and stumbled in the dark.

No speaking, no crying, no stopping.

"Get on my back!" he said when they reached the top. This time, Miriam was able to assert enough control to put Millicent in front, so she could secure her from behind.

Into the Other

The bear walked for an hour. He was like a machine with a singular purpose, though they had no idea what that purpose could be. It was a cold and endless march.

Miriam stayed upright and alert the whole time while her sister kept her arms around her and rested her head against her back. She wanted to ask the bear where he was taking them, but she couldn't find the gumption to speak.

The bear stopped where the forest opened to a vast plain. A halo formed around the edge of the clouds, brighter and brighter, until the moon appeared. Apparently satisfied, he continued.

A sound like a locomotive hissed in the distance. Millicent squeezed Miriam's forearms. A few minutes later, the sound came again, louder and closer, and the bear quickened his pace.

Ahead of them, a forty-foot tower of water and steam arced and fell in sheets across a rocky basin. As the eruption ended, its final blast hit the ground in great, wet plops. The smell of sulfur was so strong they could taste it.

The bear stopped at the geyser opening.

"Off now!" he said, and the girls slid from his back to stand shivering. He grabbed the front of Miriam's overalls with his teeth. She screamed and beat her fists against his snout. She pushed and kicked as he positioned her beside the geyser spout.

He pulled Millicent by her arm, so she faced Miriam with the spout between them. She collapsed to her knees.

His eyes strobed yellow. "STAND!" he said, and she jumped to her feet.

He walked between them to straddle the spout. "Hands!" he said, but they didn't know what he meant. "REACH! HOLD HANDS!"

Miriam reached over his back. She strained to pull her hands down, but invisible strings held them in place like she was a marionette puppet. Millicent sobbed, because holding hands forced her to press against the bear's side.

A bubbling crackle came from below. They screamed as the

21

Chapter One

fountain of water and steam hit them. Heat from the eruption rose to a crescendo but vanished with a burst of cool air just when they feared it would burn them.

The red bear bellowed in pain. He arched his back against their hands, and blue ribbons of light coiled around their arms and locked them together.

In a flash, they fell to the ground as the eruption ended. Miriam wanted to grab Millicent and run and hide and get away, but she was suddenly losing consciousness.

No, not here! she thought. She watched Millicent slump onto her side with her eyes closed, and though she urged her limbs to crawl forward on her hands and knees, she collapsed face down and fell asleep next to the bear.

Two

Lights, Caves, and Unreachable Trees

Miriam woke with a pounding headache. Millicent and the red bear lay near her, and she watched to see whether the bear was asleep or awake — or dead. His ribcage, covered with wet, messy fur, expanded.

A sheet of blue light rippled across the sky from end to end like a swift aurora. The hues were rich and faded from deep and royal to pure cyan. It took her breath away like when a powerful bolt of lightning streaks through a cloud and turns the night into day.

Wow, what was that?

The black, starry sky returned, and she noticed a glow on the horizon. She found the Big Dipper, traced a path to the North Star, and placed the glow to the East.

It's already morning!

She knew her father would have been searching for them all night and wondered if he was nearby.

But how can he find us? We need to go, go, go!

Her legs felt fused to the ground because of the cold. She shivered as she stood and sneaked around the sleeping bear in a wide circle toward Millicent, and she held her mouth open to keep her teeth from chattering.

"Millicent!" she whispered.

Millicent stirred. Her curly pigtails crunched with frozen dew. "Wha — ?"

Miriam shushed her. It was always a difficult task, waking Millicent. She didn't want to linger, so she shook her shoulder and whispered.

Chapter Two

"Wake up! We can get away!"

Millicent's eyes opened wide. She looked at the bear through a cloud of her breath that hung in the cold. "Is it dead?"

"No, it's still breathing. Let's go, let's go!" She wrapped her arm around her shoulders and led them away. The sky shimmered again, followed by distant thunder. When they walked far enough, she pulled Millicent by the hand and ran.

And they ran, and they ran.

Miriam looked over her shoulder often to see if the red bear was coming after them. They ran until the cold air burned their throats and then walked until their strength returned and could run again. Millicent always slowed first, her skinny legs pink and splotchy red from the exercise she detested, and Miriam tugged her arm to keep moving.

Light moved through the woods ahead of them.

"Look!" said Miriam.

Millicent tripped on the word "look." She dusted off her bare knees, which already sported raspberries, and grunted. Somehow, she'd acquired a small twig in her hair and plucked it out.

"What?" she asked with a bit of venom.

"I think there's a car!"

Headlights moved along the hillside below them. Miriam waved her arms and yelled.

Millicent tutted at her. "There's no way they can see us from here."

"Well, come on then!"

Millicent groaned and ran after her. She hated running more than she hated climbing.

The light receded and vanished, so the girls looked for the road to wait for another car. Miriam stopped and looked around and scratched her head.

"I don't get it. It didn't look this far away."

Millicent coughed with a stitch in her side. "At least it's getting light out. It'll be easier for them to see us."

Miriam bit her fingernails and turned in a circle. A new set of lights

Lights, Caves, and Unreachable Trees

approached from the way they came.

"Over there!"

Millicent whirled to look. "Wha — ? How did we miss the road?"

"I don't know, but let's go!"

The promise of a rescue boosted Millicent's strength for another run. They slowed when it looked like the car would pass nearby, but there was no road to be found. The headlights and taillights swooped by without a vehicle between them, without engine noise or the sound of its tires along the ground. The lights floated away along a road that didn't exist.

Miriam was dumbfounded.

Millicent was spellbound.

Another car appeared across the valley. Its headlights strobed toward them through the trees, and Millicent's desire to understand the phenomenon overrode her senses. She stepped for a closer look. Another set of lights sped from the opposite direction and passed through her. Nothing solid struck her, but her tummy fluttered, and air blew across her skin.

Miriam screamed and yanked her away from the invisible road. "Get back here! Are you crazy?"

Millicent examined her arms and body. "I just wanted to — "

"What? Jump in front of an oncoming car?"

"No! I wanted to be closer! I'm sorry! I don't know what I was thinking." She was always quick to tears, and sometimes the smallest, most random things could set her off. This was neither small nor random.

Miriam had a lifetime of experience dealing with Millicent's peculiarities. She'd learned when to argue and when it was best to not provoke her. More often, though, she understood when it was time to comfort her. She rubbed her back and studied the side of her face. Tears formed in the corners of her eyes and threatened to brim over.

Uh oh. Losing her, losing her. Avert! Avert!

"No, don't cry. Hey. It's okay. I'm glad you're okay. Are you okay?"

Chapter Two

Millicent shook her head no. Miriam kept rubbing.

"You just scared the heck out of me! Ya know?"

Millicent held her tears in but deflated against Miriam's shoulder. "What do we do?"

Miriam cringed with the fear that they'd stayed in one place too long, and the red bear could be sneaking up behind them. They weren't far enough away yet. She looked both ways as new lights appeared in the distance.

"I think we should follow them. What do you think?"

Millicent nodded.

Okay. Crisis averted.

They debated which way to go, as the invisible cars were heading in both directions. Millicent searched the horizon to find Mount Holmes. Their campsite was in that direction. The geyser and the red bear were behind them. Away from the bear seemed to be the best criteria, so she pointed at the mountain range.

"That way?" asked Miriam.

"That way," said Millicent.

It was warm. That's the first thing John noticed when he woke up. He lay in a heap of blankets on the ground in a rocky nook surrounded by a curtain. The air was thick with a strange, sweet smell, and purple light shimmered across the earthen ceiling. Odd, padded footsteps approached. He held his breath to keep quiet and noticed bandages over the scratches on his arms.

The rich voice from the cliff spoke into his mind.

"Are you awake?"

He slid into the corner away from the curtain and pulled a blanket around him. "Yes?"

"How are you feeling?"

"Where am I?"

"You're in a safe place. We brought you here, so you could recover. You had a lot of excitement yesterday!"

Lights, Caves, and Unreachable Trees

"Where's my mom? Is she okay?"

"We don't know yet, but I'll tell you as soon as we do. My friends told me you and your mom were attacked by a bear?"

John didn't like talking to a stranger through a curtain. He was afraid to move. "Are you a doctor?"

"No, just a concerned bystander. My name's Sebastian. Can you tell me what you remember about the bear?"

"Not much. It happened so fast. I mean, it attacked us, me and my mom, and then it chased me."

"Did it hurt your mother?"

John shook his head. He didn't know, and the worry swelled up in his belly and chest and throat.

"I don't know. I don't think so."

There was a grumbly sigh. "I can't imagine how scared you were. Can you describe it to me, the bear?"

"It was huge and red. And it looked old."

"Deep red, like blood?"

"Yes."

There was a pause. "Thank you. You've been very helpful. And very brave. What do you remember after the bear chased you?"

"I didn't want to leave my mom, but I ran anyway. There was a clearing that I didn't want to go to, but I couldn't stop. It was like he controlled me. There was — "

He didn't want to mention the geyser or blue light.

"Well, then I fell over that cliff." The rest of the story involved talking ants and a marmot with a miner's cap, so he stopped.

"Did you talk to anybody on the cliff?"

Surely, Sebastian would think he was crazy.

"Did any ants talk to you?"

"No." *How does he know?*

"Did you go near a geyser?"

"No."

"It's all right. You won't be in trouble."

Chapter Two

John was startled to discover a bandage around his chest under his shirt and examined it. It was clean and white except for a spot under his arm where the blood soaked through, but it was already dark and dry.

"I think you did come close to a geyser. The friends who told me about you were the ants you talked to on the cliff. You see, something amazing happened when you touched that geyser. You left your homeworld and came to a place where animals can speak telepathically."

Though this was bizarre news, Sebastian's candor and tone were disarming. And the word *telepathically* made John's stomach flutter, because while this must have been how the ants had spoken, he believed telepathy was impossible and assumed there was a plainer explanation.

"I remember a beaver."

Sebastian chuckled. "That was my friend Benjamin. He's a marmot, but they do look a little like beavers. I know all of this is hard for you to believe, but I want you to know that I would never, ever hurt you."

Though he couldn't explain why, John believed him.

"Are you a grizzly bear?"

"Yes, I am."

John's heart pounded as Sebastian pulled aside the curtain with his teeth. The bear was enormous, much larger than he was expecting. He squeezed the blanket with his fists. Sebastian's brown fur gave him some comfort, though. At least this wasn't the bear that attacked him. At the center of the chamber was an iron pit ablaze with purple fire. He watched the odd-colored flames, unsure of what to do and afraid to speak or make eye contact.

"Hey. It's okay," said Sebastian, and John dared to look. The bear regarded him with golden-brown eyes set into his broad, round face. His snout was long and handsome, capped with a black, spongy nose.

Something clattered in the distance, and Sebastian peered down one of the hallways that led into the room. "Ah, here comes Benjamin with some food." It was unsettling to process his telepathic voice and seemed odd the way his mouth didn't move.

Lights, Caves, and Unreachable Trees

Benjamin entered carrying a small platter that spilled over with fruits and vegetables and set it on the ground. "Hello again!" he said, also without moving his mouth. John's brain tingled every time they spoke. He was nervous about taking food from them, so he didn't reach for anything, though his stomach tightened at the sight of it. Benjamin fed a long, green leaf into his mouth like a log through a chipper.

"I've been thinking while you were asleep," said Sebastian, "and I have an idea about how to get you home."

This was unexpected news. "Do you mean back to my parents?" His voice resonated off the walls of the cave and sounded unfamiliar to him. He was, after all, the only one speaking aloud.

"Well, we can't do that," said Sebastian.

John blinked. "Um, why can't you?"

Benjamin reached across the platter, caught a grasshopper, and crunched it in half. "Have fun explainin' it to him!"

John scrutinized the plate. The food was crawling with insects. Grasshoppers hopped, crickets chirped, and what he thought was a legume was a woodlouse that unrolled and walked across an apple. His hunger faded.

"Hush, Benjamin," said Sebastian. "What's your name, kiddo?"

"John."

"John, this will be difficult to understand. Will you follow me? I want to show you something."

Do I have a choice? The two animals waited for his response, so he stood, sore and unsteady.

"Okay," he said, and he followed them out of the room with the blanket wrapped around his shoulders. He stayed several paces behind Sebastian through a stone hallway. He'd never been this close to a bear before (not including the one that had attacked him) and was surprised to see how he walked flat-footed, more like a person in a furry suit than a dog.

The stone walls had no sharp corners. Every surface seemed molded together like it was cast in melted wax except for friezes along the wall

Chapter Two

that were filled with bas-relief sculptures of nature scenes. There was a grassy meadow, a rocky lakeshore, and a towering forest. Some of the tableaus featured carved animals frozen in action.

John cleared his throat to find his voice. "Is this a castle?"

Sebastian turned his head, which was an unnecessary gesture for a telepath, John thought. "It's more of a city, really. We call it the Mesa."

"Oh. Um, where are you taking me?"

"We're going to a storage room to pick up a radio. When I escaped from the scientists, I kept the collar they made me wear, and it has a radio built into it."

Benjamin scampered from behind them. "I don't know why you kept those things!"

John veered toward the wall to avoid stepping on him. "What do you mean about scientists? And the radio? I'm confused."

"I'm sorry," said Sebastian. "I'm getting ahead of myself. We're going to use the radio to contact your people."

"Okay?" *And the scientists?*

They came to an enormous wooden door covered by a metallic sculpture, a diorama of fish floating on wires, metal sheets cut to look like trees, reptiles and mammals posed to scurry around, and higher animals like bears, elephants, and horses standing on the top layer. The sculpture was falling apart. Some animals were missing limbs and hung out of place. Bare wood showed through at the center.

Benjamin scuttled past them to reach into a hollow in the wall and pull a lever, and a burst of steam vented from a hole in the ceiling. The walls echoed with clinking and clanking.

How big is this place? John wondered.

There was a loud crack, and the doors opened down the middle, splitting the copper sculpture in half.

The next chamber was vast with a ceiling as tall as a cathedral. Beams of sunlight slanted through openings in the high walls and crisscrossed off large metal plates that hung on wires like a mobile. Massive piles of stuff — chairs, pots and pans, pieces of lumber, lengths

Lights, Caves, and Unreachable Trees

of fabric — filled the room, and it reminded John of a dragon's lair full of junk instead of gold.

"Wow, what is this place?"

Sebastian seemed to smile. "This is where the rodents keep everything they've foraged over the years. I call it the Den of Antiquities."

John saw a pattern forming. Each of Sebastian's answers prompted at least two more questions. "Rodents? Foraged from where?"

"Well, I'm embarrassed to say it was all stolen from campers. They pull through objects from your homeworld."

That's impossible. The largest heap was as tall as a two-story house.

Sebastian directed him to racks of clothing. "See if you can find something warm. It's going to get cold soon."

"Okay . . ."

With the words *stolen from campers* hanging in the air, be browsed and found a baggy, green, hooded sweatshirt. After a moment of hesitation, curious about who lost it — *maybe this was somebody's favorite hoodie* — he slipped it on. The soft, warm lining convinced him not to dwell on the theft.

A tiny bird with a bright, white belly and black, speckled wings flew in and landed on a broken table lamp near Sebastian. It twittered urgently. Beneath the birdsong, John heard a girl's whispering voice.

"Sebastian! Ze'eva sent me to tell you that Lucifur has returned!"

"What? How?"

"We're not sure, but the sky has been flashing ever since. Word has already spread. He's searching for the human-boy and asking all around!"

"Thank you, Windy." He turned to Benjamin. "Ben, take him home with you."

Benjamin stomped his tiny, brown foot. "Not on your life, bear!"

Sebastian moved toward the door. "If he's back — if he's still after the boy — we need to know why. Take him to your family. Keep him safe!"

Chapter Two

John struggled to follow their change of plans. "Wait! What's happening? What about the radio?"

"I'm sorry, John. I truly am. My brother knows this place and will come looking for you here. Please do as I say and go with Benjamin. I promise I'll come as soon as I can." He bounded out of the room with four mighty strides.

The silence that followed was awkward. John cleared his throat again. "I take it Lucifur is the red bear?"

"Unfortunately," said Benjamin.

"And he's Sebastian's brother?"

Benjamin lowered his head. "Yes. His real name's Genesius. Lucifur's just a nickname he picked up."

Lucifur. That's a perfect name for him.

Benjamin twiddled with his fur. "We should get a move on. We can talk once we're in the burrow."

John blinked at him. *The burrow?*

"Yes, my burrow."

The sun rose over the forested valley, and Millicent and Miriam could no longer see the headlights of the invisible cars. They lost track of where the road should be, stumbled upon a wide river, and followed it with the hope that it would lead to a bridge or campground. Their mouths were parched, but they remembered their parents warning not to drink from the lakes and rivers because the water could contain bacteria that would make them sick. The sun climbed higher and beat down on them.

Miriam was about to suggest they switch clothes when Millicent said, "Grr! Cold then hot, cold then hot! Can't this place make up its mind? I'm boiling!" So, she tugged her overalls away from her skin and let the sweat trickle down her legs under the denim. She always made sacrifices for her sister. Many went unnoticed, but she didn't care.

In the distance, steam vented from the ground and fouled the air with the scent of rotten eggs.

Lights, Caves, and Unreachable Trees

"There's that smell again."

"I think half the park smells like this," said Millicent. "It's just the sulfur."

There were no paths to follow, and though they tried to find clear patches of ground for walking, Millicent's bare legs scraped against thistles and thorns. This gave her something new to complain about.

Another line of trees invited them to walk farther, as though civilization could be over the next ridge past the grove. They hoped to find campers. They imagined spotting a ranger and calling their parents. They talked about seeing their family again.

Miriam stopped walking. "This is weird . . . "

"Everything feels weird now," said Millicent. "I'm, like, all buzzy."

"No, those trees — look how far away they are."

Millicent was keeping her eyes to the ground to save her legs from more scratches. She looked up to discover that the trees ahead appeared as distant as they had a few minutes ago.

"Well, things are huge around here. Maybe it's an optical illusion."

"But they're right there!" said Miriam, jabbing both hands toward them.

"I have to stop anyway. My legs are killing me."

"All right. You rest. I'm going to walk toward *that* tree." She pointed at an isolated pine about a hundred feet away.

Millicent sat on the ground and dug a finger under her knee. "Gar! I'm so itchy!"

Miriam marched. The trees bobbed up and down in her field of vision with each step, as they should have, but the treetops stayed at the same level — by now, the taller, closer trees should have towered overhead.

"I don't understand this!"

Millicent gasped. Miriam was where the trees should have been, and the trees appeared twice as far away. Her vision bent around her sister like she was looking through a fisheye lens.

"Miriam!"

Chapter Two

They ran to meet halfway and were shocked to close the distance sooner than expected and crashed into each other. The trees, on the other hand, hadn't moved.

"This is nuts!" said Miriam. "Have you heard about this?"

"No."

"Are you sure?"

"Yes, I'm sure! I read the books and studied the maps. You were listening to music the whole way here."

"I know! That's why I'm asking you!"

"Then why are you mad at me?"

Miriam waved her hands over her head. "I don't know!"

Millicent turned away.

The trees mocked them with silence.

Three
The Two Hosts

Millicent and Miriam experimented with the unreachable trees. They walked hand-in-hand toward them, moved away from each other in wide arcs, and, out of desperation, threw sticks and rocks at them. Nothing they did brought them closer. They gave up and walked away into a forest that behaved normally. They were thirsty and hungry, and it was getting late.

"Why did we waste so much time?" asked Millicent. The hungry monster had come and gone. She was fading and shuffled or tripped with every step.

Miriam frowned at her sister's legs covered with cuts and scrapes and declared it was time to switch clothes now that it was cold again. They should have changed a long time ago, she thought, and she cursed herself for not doing it sooner. She could handle a few scrapes. Millicent hooked the straps of the overalls and stood like a proud farmer glad of the warmth. Miriam stretched her leg muscles and enjoyed the open air against her skin.

They found the swollen river again and followed its bank. The land ahead looked treacherous, jagged with rocks and dead-looking trees. Miriam plucked a low-hanging pinecone. "Do you think we can eat these?"

Millicent stopped. "Go ahead. Eat it."

Miriam lifted the long, gray cob toward her mouth, not expecting it to be tasty, but perhaps as a form of wilderness survival. Millicent sighed, blocked her arm at the wrist, and said, "No. We can't eat pinecones."

Miriam threw it down. "Well, we need something!"

Chapter Three

"What you need," said a silky female voice, "is to watch where you're walking."

The girls jumped. Something like a snake swished in front of their faces, and they screamed and grabbed each other. A lean, golden mountain lion sat above them on an outcropping of rock. She leapt into their path with her tail dancing behind her, long and sly.

"And just where do you think you are going?" she asked, though her mouth didn't move when she spoke. Her yellow eyes compelled them to stare at her, like a hypnotist swinging a gold watch on a chain.

Miriam stepped backward and squeezed Millicent's hand for her to follow, but the cougar slinked behind them.

"Oh, no-no, kittens. You can't go off alone." Her long, white whiskers tickled their arms. She sniffed and nipped at one of Millicent's pigtails.

Millicent broke into tears. After all they'd been through, this was her breaking point. This cougar was going to eat her, and she would never see her mom and dad again.

"Silence!" hissed the cat. "I don't do well with children. I'm here because Sebastian wishes it. I don't know how well I can protect you in the open, so if you want something to eat, then cease this blubbering and follow me."

Yellow light flashed in the cougar's eyes, and she seemed to vanish. They watched an impossible blur streak back to the perch on the rock where she reappeared, as though she teleported before their eyes.

"Let's go."

With another blink of light in her eyes, she blurred to a higher ledge. Seeing that they weren't moving, she snarled.

"I feel rage! Listen to me! An angry, red grizzly bear is ranging nearby, thanks to the two of you. A brown, friendly bear wants to protect you. Now, I don't care whether you get eaten or not, but I will give my best attempt at this because Sebastian has been kind to me."

The Two Hosts

Miriam relaxed. It was clear that the cougar wasn't going to eat them, at least not yet. But what was that light? How did she move so quickly? It seemed supernatural. That and the fact she was *speaking*.

The sky rippled with blue light. Miriam shuddered with the suspicion that the cat's eyes and the sky were somehow connected, but she didn't know what it could mean. The cougar seemed to be intrigued by the light in the sky and watched it flicker past. Once it was gone, she arched her back, spread her front claws, and rolled her tongue in a hearty yawn. She searched the horizon and licked her chops. She vanished again and reappeared in front of them.

Millicent gave a sharp scream as the cat nuzzled Miriam's chest.

"Speak, kitten! Open your mouth and share your words!"

This cat is crazy! thought Miriam, and she was glad it was her and not Millicent being harassed. Miriam hated bullies, even large, carnivorous ones. She shoved the mountain lion's head aside.

"Stop it!"

The cat vaulted back a few feet and crouched. "Ah! I knew you could talk! Now, follow me!"

"We don't want to!"

Her eyes narrowed. "You'd rather face Lucifur than come with me to safety?"

Why is she talking about the devil?

"How about this: come with me if you want to see your brother again."

Miriam gasped. "John?"

"Whatever."

"How do you know about John?"

"He's with another animal. He's quite safe."

She walked to the lower rocks and paused.

"Last chance, kittens. Here I go."

This time she climbed at a normal pace and didn't look back.

Miriam felt compelled to climb after her, but she knew Millicent would protest.

41

Chapter Three

"I think we should follow her."

Millicent shook her head.

The cougar was out of sight, and Miriam didn't want to lose track of her. "Milly, we can't stay out here all night." She pulled Millicent's arm, half expecting her to collapse and go limp, but she walked without a saying a word.

As they climbed, the cougar reappeared at the top to check their progress and, satisfied, continued ahead. Her face looked enough like a housecat to seem cute, almost funny in the way she popped in and out of view, and it gave Miriam a smirk in spite of the situation. Her mother once told her that she was a good judge of character, though at the time she was too young to understand what that meant. Those words came back to her, and she nodded to herself. This cat could be trusted. As surreal, frightening, and unbelievable as this day was, this cat would protect them. She climbed faster and pulled Millicent along.

When they reached the top, Miriam hurried to catch up but stayed far enough back not to be intrusive.

"Umm, ma'am?"

"I am Sahra."

"SARR'ra," Miriam repeated, overenunciating to get her name right. "Where are you taking us?"

"To my cave. Fidget and Earl will have prepared your food and a place to sleep."

Fidget and Earl sounded like odd names for mountain lions. "What about our brother?"

"You will be reunited tomorrow. It's getting late, and I will leave you to hunt."

The hike wore on for twenty minutes. It was a long, held breath that got colder and colder as they stumbled through the dark. Miriam's hope faded with a sinking feeling that she may have been wrong. Why was the night so still and crisp? Why was every sound amplified, every scrape of Millicent's shoes across the rocks and every swish of grass? It was like they were trapped in a repeating dream until, at last, they arrived at an opening in the side of a cliff.

"Here is the cave," said Sahra, and she vanished into the woods without saying goodbye.

Miriam stood baffled as Millicent sniveled and leaned against her. An odd, purple light emerged from the cave. A raccoon carrying a tiny lantern crawled out to greet them, followed by a twitchy squirrel.

"Come in please," said the raccoon. His voice in her head sounded like that of a young boy.

Miriam adjusted her arm around Millicent to hold her up. The fact that they'd just conversed with a cougar was still sinking in, and now here was a talking raccoon.

"Won't you come in?" he asked. He waved with his free hand and held the lantern toward the cave.

I can follow a mountain lion but not a raccoon? Come on. Figure this out.

"Are you Fidget and Earl?"

"Yes, I'm Fidget. This is Earl. We have food for you. And water."

Those were the magic words. The raccoon had a simple charm about him. With Millicent about to fall over, she nodded at the cave entrance.

"All right. Lead the way."

From the Den of Antiquities, Benjamin led John through a series of tunnels that exited into the forest. He walked for an hour and lingered only for John to keep up. They stopped before an isolated bluff, bathed in light from the sunset. A marmot atop the tallest rock beeped several times.

That's a strange noise for an animal, thought John.

Benjamin chirped in return. "Don't mind him. We marmots tend ta be nervous. Now, let's get a look at'cha."

He put a paw under his chin as he scrutinized John's height and frame and shook his head in disapproval. "Well, you'll never fit through the main entrance, that's for sure, so what we'll do is improvise! Follow me."

Chapter Three

He climbed to the top. John followed and sank into the talus slope at the base of the mound but managed to find his footing and hoist himself up.

Benjamin held open a blue-glass skylight. "It'll be a tight fit, but you'll manage." The other marmot backed away as though John was a giant iguana.

John peered into the dark hole. "Oh boy." He gritted his teeth and climbed in feet-first. Polished metal throughout the tunnel bounced what sunlight remained into a room below. Scents of musk, flowers, and the sweet purple oil wafted to meet him. He dropped through the end of the chute onto a down-stuffed patch of fabric.

"He's here! He's here!" cried a young girl's voice.

Oblong shapes about two feet tall loomed from the shadows and swayed like buoys. Benjamin covered the opening with a large, copper bowl, which cast the sunlight across the low ceiling. Seven marmots gawked at John with beady eyes and jittery whiskers. The younger ones looked like guinea pigs, and they drew close with a disturbing fascination.

"Don't be afraid," said a tiny marmot with her paws up. "I'm Sheba! And you're John!"

Two of the small marmots hid behind an older, scowling one. "What are ye about, Benjamin?" she asked in a craggy voice. "Your father would rise to die if he could, bringing a human here." Her furry jowls shook as she moved her head.

"Oh, he's a darling," said a slender marmot next to Benjamin. "I'm Rebecca, Benjamin's wife." The young marmots ran and bounced around.

"How long does he hafta be here?" asked the old marmot.

Benjamin scoffed. "Mom, mind your manners. This is Sebastian's ward, and you'll treat him kindly." To John he said, "Don't mind her — she's pure squeal but no real deal, ya feel?"

John smirked. *Okay, that was strange but funny.* He looked around the bare room. The presence of family, even though it wasn't his, was calming. Two of the children plopped on either side of him and stared as though they expected him to perform magic tricks.

Rebecca offered water in a plastic cup. "Here you go, dear. Are you hungry?"

His stomach cramped. "I'm starving." He didn't care if he got sick. He gulped the water and was dizzy from how cold and clean it tasted.

"The table is full. Help yourself," she said, busying back to their pantry. In the corner was a flat mound of earth laden with leaves and small branches.

"Don't eat my cambium!" said Benjamin's mother.

"I don't know what that is."

Sheba patted his hand and giggled. "You don't know what cambium is? It's soft wood from under the bark, ya goof! You can have some of mine. It's okay."

Benjamin waved for him to join them. "Lots to choose from!"

John tried to be polite, but the thought of chewing on soft wood wasn't appealing. He scrutinized their offering, and, as he feared, it was teeming with insects. He sorted through the pile and shooed away a few crickets and a spider before taking a handful of leaves to nibble. It tasted like spinach. He hated spinach.

Sheba burst with news. "You fought Lucifur and visited the Mesa! You came through a geyser! And ya brought more humans with ya!"

"Sheba!" said Benjamin. "Mind yer noise!"

"Humans don't belong here!" said the old marmot. She grumbled and waved her fist.

The room grew quiet. A peculiar presence tickled the base of John's brain, and the marmots' emotions poured into his body. He experienced Benjamin's fear and bravery, Rebecca's protectiveness, and Sheba's crush on him as though they were his own feelings. He swooned. The burrow closed in on him.

"Please, you're no bother," said Rebecca. "You're a guest in our home."

Chapter Three

The emotions stopped. Was this something marmots could do here, transfer their feelings? He shook his head and rubbed his eyes. Something Sheba said stuck out to him.

"Did you say I brought more humans with me?"

"Yah! It's all over the network!" She gestured as though she was presenting a headline in a newspaper. "Lucifur returns to Caldera! Three human children enter with him!"

"That's enough, Sheba," said Benjamin.

"What other children? What's going on?"

Benjamin wiped his hands on a piece of cloth and stood tall. "Your sisters are here, too."

"My sisters? They're here?" He bumped his head on the ceiling.

"No, no! They're not here in the burrow. They're safe with another friend. They're enjoying dinner like you, half-a-day south of here."

The mention of his sisters destroyed the last of his patience. "WHAT'S GOING ON HERE? Answer me! What happened to my mom? Why do I feel so strange? How are all of you talking?"

The marmots cowered.

In Sahra's den, Millicent and Miriam sat close together on a blanket. A purple fire burned in a shallow pit in the center of the cave. Sahra's bed of blankets, which they were forbidden to touch, lay on the opposite side. Their dinner was more appetizing than John's with nuts, fruit, berries and a helping of raw rabbit meat piled on top of leaves on the ground. They ate everything except the rabbit meat.

Fidget, the raccoon, scampered away and returned with a variety of putrid objects to replace the raw meat. He threw the latest offering (a headless mouse) into an empty corner and ran out of the den. Earl, a ground squirrel with a tan belly and white stripes, entertained them with strange jokes about foraging. Fidget returned with two boney fish. The carcasses were disgusting.

Miriam lost her patience. "Ugh, please! We don't eat any of these things!"

The Two Hosts

Fidget covered his face with his tiny hands as his fear leapt into her. Millicent felt the emotion fly between them like an arc of electricity.

"I'm so sorry," said Miriam. "I didn't mean to scare you. Don't be afraid."

"Thought you like fish . . ."

She petted behind his ear. "Yes, I do when they're fresh!"

She noticed Sahra watching them from the entrance tunnel.

"I return from my evening's hunt to I find that I'm most interested in this exchange between human and raccoon. You experienced Fidget's fear, did you not?"

Miriam noticed a flicker of emotions coming from the big cat and dared to coax them out. She felt Sahra's pride, annoyance, and . . . fear. The fear surprised her.

Sahra broke the connection between them by closing her eyes and turning her head with a hiss. "Fool kitten! Naughty kitten!"

Miriam cringed, expecting the lioness to strike her. Instead, she turned her attention to Millicent.

"And you? You seemed intrigued. What did you feel?"

"I don't know. I just wanna go home!"

Miriam wanted to keep the cat's attention away from Millicent. Feeling her fear gave her a modicum of confidence and curiosity. How could this giant predator be afraid of them?

"Sahra?"

"I can't get a straight answer out of either of you! What?"

"Could you explain what's happening, please? I think it would help if we knew what was going on."

Sahra padded over to her bed, sniffed it to verify they hadn't touched it, circled twice, and reclined with her tail playing along the ground.

"Fine. You have questions? Ask away, kitten."

In the burrow, the nervous marmots huddled together and watched John. Benjamin kept his chin up.

Chapter Three

"Remember when ya asked why we couldn't take ya to your parents?"

"Yes," said John. Their fears blew around the room like ghosts. He tried to ignore them.

"We can't take ya to them because they don't exist here." John opened his mouth, but Benjamin kept talking. "Now, before ya let that bother you too much, they're okay. At least, we think they are. No one's fer sure about that part. Anyway, the point is, when you touched that geyser, you should have been hurt by it, right?"

"It couldn't have been a geyser."

"Well, what do ya remember?"

"I was running through the woods. There was an open space, and I was running . . . and then . . . the light."

"Light?"

"I thought it was a geyser, but when I ran through it there was a flash of light. Then I fell over that cliff."

"And the rest is history," said Benjamin. "That light? It was a gateway. That's when you left your homeworld and came to ours."

"But I'm still in Yellowstone."

"Exactly! Only you won't find any roads or buildings here, or humans for that matter."

"I don't understand."

"Hold on a sec."

Benjamin bobbled out of the room. Sheba rested her paw on John's hand and looked up at him dreamily. He gave a weak smile. Benjamin returned with two sheets of paper and a chunk of black rock.

"Say you have two pieces of paper, and each of 'em is a map of this place." He stuck his tongue under his incisors and drew identical sketches with triangle mountains and a blobby lake, but only one included roads and houses.

Not bad drawings for a marmot.

The Two Hosts

Benjamin gave him the picture with the roads. "When you came through the geyser, ya jumped from your piece of paper to our piece of paper. Same place, same trees, but no human stuff. We call it Caldera."

John shook his head. "How — how do I get back to my piece of paper?"

"That's what Sebastian's workin' on, besides keeping track of Lucifur."

John compared the drawings again. It was impossible, what Benjamin was describing, yet he was sitting in a burrow with a family of talking marmots. Benjamin's piece of paper and the empty space between their drawings gave him chills.

Sahra relaxed with her eyes mere slits. The purple fire flickered between them. Fidget and Earl curled beside Miriam while Millicent studied the whiskers above Sahra's eyes, at how long and white they were like the ones on her snout. She fantasized about how angry Sahra would be if she were to pluck one.

"How big is Caldera?" asked Miriam.

"A fine question. Yellowstone is situated in the geographic caldera. Our border is similar to the caldera's boundary and was named thusly."

"Your border . . . Is that where we couldn't walk to the trees?"

Sahra's eyes widened for the briefest moment. "Precisely. The Unreachables surround us. Trees, mountains, horizon — no one has ever reached them. The only way in or out of Caldera is through the geysers."

"So, all the animals come from our world?"

"No, almost all of us were born here. But a few years ago, humans started testing Caldera with animals from your world, like Sebastian and Genesius. We set them free. They were normal when they arrived, simple, stupid animals, but they became intelligent and learned to speak as we do."

"We're changing, too, aren't we? That's why we've been feeling so strange."

Chapter Three

Sahra purred. "You are correct."

"What's going to happen to us?"

"I don't know, and that's the truth. Certain animals have special abilities. Some can heal. Some can read emotions. You've already seen what I can do."

Miriam's heart jumped. She was surprised that the cat was being so candid. "Yeah . . . What was that? Can you teleport?"

"No. Short bursts of speed. We call it phasing. My point is, judging by what happens to other animals here, I imagine you could gain several abilities."

Millicent hadn't spoken a word and squeezed Miriam's hand. She was tired and scared and wanted to go home before anything else happened to them.

Sahra seemed to notice this. She turned and laid flat on her bed with her back to them. She stretched her limbs and pawed the ground.

"Get some sleep, kittens. Tomorrow you'll reunite with your brother, and then you're going home."

"Through a geyser?" asked Millicent, startled into finding her voice. Her brow tightened and wrinkled up her forehead.

"Yes. It's the only way."

While Millicent panicked, Miriam looked around the cave at the fire and blankets. The emotions were calm. She whispered into Millicent's ear. "She won't hurt us. I can feel it."

Millicent watched Sahra's torso rise and fall. "But the geyser?"

Miriam hugged her. "I know. It didn't hurt before. Hopefully it won't hurt when we go back." She gathered a few blankets, rolled two into pillows, and pulled another over them. They lay facing each other and held hands. Miriam stroked Millicent's hair until she fell asleep.

She lifted her head to check on Sahra. The big cat lay facing them again and stared back at her. She gave a slight nod. Miriam's tummy fluttered. She nodded back.

Please don't eat us in our sleep.

The Two Hosts

In the marmot burrow, the younger animals fell asleep as John continued to ask questions. And just like when he asked Sebastian, he found that each new fact carried several new mysteries. It was wearisome. Unreachable Trees? He couldn't imagine the phenomenon no matter how Benjamin tried to describe it.

"So, I can't walk out of here because there's a magical barrier?"

"I know. It sounds crazy, but it's true."

"If all the animals can talk here, then what do the carnivores eat?"

"I see where your mind's goin', but don't wory. We all live by a rule that says no thinking animal can kill another. We call it the Code of Cognizants. The carnivores capture their prey from your homeworld."

"Huh?"

"They sense when an animal is near in your world and reach right through. Just like the rodents steal objects? They steal food."

John tried to imagine a cougar snatching a rabbit out of thin air, but it seemed — again — impossible. "So, in my world the prey animals just disappear?"

"Yep! They vanish in a flash of light!"

"Wouldn't somebody notice?"

"Well, the chances of a someone catchin' it happenin' are slim, but Sebastian thinks it's how the researchers found out about Caldera."

John was finished with this crash course in implausible things. It was too much. He expected someone to pop up and reveal that he was being pranked, that the burrow was a set on a stage, and that a camera crew was sitting just outside with puppeteers controlling the marmots. His mother was safe and laughing with his father and sisters.

He clenched his fists. Several moments had passed since he'd thought about his mom. She was all that mattered, and this was a huge waste of time. She was out there either worried and searching for him or —

No, she was searching.

Then he remembered the ants and how he killed a few of them.

"Oh no, wait! I broke your Code! I squished those ants!"

Chapter Three

How do they punish murderers here?

Benjamin chuckled. "Don't worry. They may be intelligent, but they're ants. You hafta understand. Think of us as animals mostly. I'm a marmot and proud of it! This burrow may be a little fancy, but it's still just a hole in the ground. In the same way, the ants live by ant rules. They get killed by the dozen every day because it's their nature. Folks would only get upset if you wiped out an entire colony."

"Oh. That doesn't make me feel any better."

Benjamin finished tidying the pantry. "Maybe next time you'll be more careful."

John tried to put each piece of the puzzle into place. He didn't like depending on the animals. He'd heard enough and didn't want to talk anymore, so he faked a big yawn, which worked better than he hoped and turned into a real one.

"Where will I sleep?"

"This way. Follow me."

He crawled after Benjamin through a tunnel past rooms housing other marmot families to a cubby full of blankets. It was cramped but big enough for sleeping. Another copper bowl hung from the ceiling, and he guessed there was a tunnel leading to the roof behind it.

"Here ya be." Benjamin glanced at the bowl and hesitated. "All right then. Good night."

"Good night."

John lay on his back, put his hands behind his head, and stared at the ceiling, at the bottom of the copper bowl, and fantasized about removing it and climbing out onto the roof. Benjamin said that Millicent and Miriam were a half-day's journey south of the burrow, but that was for a marmot. It would only take a couple of hours for a human, he hoped. He would get some sleep and then go find his sisters.

Four

The Bighorn Sheep

John was having a nightmare. The red bear shouted for him to run, and his feet pounded against the ground out of his control. No matter how strong the desire was to turn around and see his mother, he shot forward toward an erupting geyser. The moment replayed over and over, each time drawing him farther away from her. He woke in a panic in the tiny sleeping room, rolled to prop on his elbow, and caught his breath.

Mom...

A hopeful idea occurred to him: if Lucifur *had* returned to Caldera, then his mother might be okay. Maybe she escaped while they were at the geyser. Maybe she found his dad and mounted a search party.

Please, let that be what happened. Please, please.

The plan to find his sisters popped back into his mind, and the nervousness from the dream was replaced by the fear that Benjamin would arrive before he could sneak away. In a rush, he tossed his blanket aside, rolled up to a crouch, and unfastened the copper bowl from the low ceiling.

He climbed out onto the roof where rain hit his forehead with annoying splats. His breath joined the fog covering the meadow as he crawled across the top of the bluff, and his soles slipped and squeaked along the wet rock. He slid down the talus slope and grumbled as water seeped into his supposedly waterproof hiking boots. He pulled up his hood, stuffed his hands in the pouch, and sulked because the foul weather spoiled his ability to use the sunrise as a guide. How would he know which way was south?

Chapter Four

Something moved behind him. Sheba skipped down the bluff and ran toward him with a vine of wildflowers around her head and a posy of blue larkspurs in her paws.

"John! John!" she said, and she tripped and spattered the flowers across the ground.

"Sheba, shush!" he said. He knelt to steady her and watched to see if other marmots would follow.

"Where ya goin'?" she asked.

"For a walk. By myself."

"I was pickin' flowers. Do you like my tiara? I picked these for you!" She scooped up the flowers and threw them over him like confetti, and, as he ducked, she sneaked in and licked him on the mouth.

He spat and tumbled backward. "Blech!"

"Can I come with ya on your walk? Where ya walkin' to?"

He dragged the back of his wrist across his mouth to erase the wetness. "I'm going to find my sisters, and I'm going by myself. Alone!"

Her eyes widened. "You can't! You'll be killed!"

"Oh, and a groundhog's supposed to protect me from a grizzly bear?"

"Marmot," she said, looking sad. "We're marmots. Groundhogs don't live around here. Yes, we're s'pposed to protect you! That's why Sebastian sent'cha here."

"Ha! Sebastian? Where is *he*? He tells me he's gonna get me home and then just disappears."

"You should trust him, John," she said, pulling off her tiara. "Just wait here with us."

He didn't have any reason to trust Sebastian. He imagined the dark, cramped spaces inside the burrow and knew that his mind was made up.

"Which way is south?" he asked.

Sheba stared.

"Okay, where does the sun rise in the morning?"

The Bighorn Sheep

She raised her tiny paw and pointed to what he hoped was east. He pointed his left arm like a compass needle at a pine tree in the direction she was pointing and pivoted ninety degrees. In front of him were more pine trees. And south, he hoped.

"Thank you," he said, and he walked toward the forest in the rain. Sheba whimpered behind him but didn't follow.

He marched until the burrow was out of sight. He kept up a deliberate pace until he was sure nobody was running after him to convince him to stay. He hoped the sun would show itself. He was nervous about correcting his course as soon as possible, if he needed to, because it would be difficult once the sun was too high in the sky.

His throat ached with every inhale of the cold, damp air. He wished he could just exhale for a while, because his outgoing breath was warm and soothing. He cupped his hand over his mouth to relieve the sting and wished he had a scarf. Meanwhile, the rain washed away his body heat. His muscles tensed like his body wanted to fold in on itself to keep warm.

His feet slowed as he left the trees behind and arrived at the edge of an endless prairie. Every step felt meaningless. It was as though he could walk forever without the landscape ever changing.

He walked.

And he walked.

And he walked.

I might as well be walking on a treadmill!

The idea of finding his sisters among the miles was foolish, but he refused to let this fact sink in.

A new meadow rolled downhill into a valley filled with sagebrush and patches of buckwheat. Everything looked gray under the clouds. The sky darkened with heavier rain that soaked him, while shrubs and a meandering stream prevented him from keeping a straight course. So, he didn't know which direction he was walking anymore.

The bandage around his chest was wet and sloppy. He dug under his shirt to remove it. To his surprise, the gash in his side was almost

Chapter Four

healed despite only being a day old. He ran his fingers back and forth along the scar, bewildered and nervous.

How did this happen?

A clutch of trees stood tall and rugged in his way. He missed the round, leafy maple and oak trees at home, and the flowering dogwood tree outside their kitchen window, and the giant weeping willow at the park down the street. That was his favorite. The trees here were rugged with sparse greenery on top and old branches that curled like dead fingers along the skinny trunks.

When he cleared the grove, he saw in the center of the field ahead a line of bushes covered with black dots. *Berries!* he thought, and he ran to them. He plucked one to test, and it burst sweet and sour over his tongue. He stuffed his mouth as fast as he could pick them. Sunlight warmed the side of his face, and blue sky peeked through gaps in the clouds. He decided his luck was changing.

He unzipped his sweatshirt and folded up the bottom of his t-shirt to carry a load of berries to a nearby cluster of boulders, so he could sit down. The mountains looked closer (*maybe?*), though he didn't know which range they were. *Millicent would know,* he thought. Beneath them stretched endless, rolling hills broken by clusters of trees, bare blotches of tan earth, and silver streaks of water. Steam rolled from the ground in several places. A bendy creek wound through the mudflats toward the sun. This was Hayden Valley. He was almost sure of it. From here he could see for miles, and from here he would spot his sisters.

Turkey vultures circled high overhead, gliding on the air currents. Smaller birds zipped and fluttered low to the ground along the rise of the valley. And a pair of long-legged cranes with gray feathers and bright, red crests hunted at the side of the creek. They paused to look at him and then returned to their feeding.

He was puzzled by dark, brown dots speckling the landscape across the river until he realized they were bison. The enormous animals appeared tiny from where he was sitting.

Okay. Maybe it wouldn't be so easy to spot Millicent and Miriam.

The Bighorn Sheep

He pressed his hand flat on the rock, already dry and warm from the sun. "Isn't it beautiful?" he could hear his mother asking. His nerves fluttered. He gritted his teeth. His chest rose and fell. A tear slipped down his cheek before he realized he was crying.

He used the bottom of his shirt to wipe his face, smearing berry juice on his chin, and scanned the valley again. Was it true? Was he really lost in a strange copy of Yellowstone? If he walked far enough, would he find the unreachable trees that Benjamin described?

That Benjamin described . . .

Marmots can't talk. Bears, ants, and birds can't talk. Convinced that he was in the middle of a long and strange dream, he lay on the rock and closed his eyes.

"I'm sorry to catch you kipping this morning," said a voice with an effete British accent.

John fell to the ground between the boulders. He bonked his head and scraped his knee through his jeans. The berries scattered and sprinkled around him. He looked up to the face of a bighorn sheep, a ram of impressive size. His massive horns twisted in ridged curls on either side of his head, and he his eyes were bright and golden. Gray hair covered his body except for his white underbelly. He bowed and swung his horns around as a greeting.

"Are you all right, my good man?"

Another talking animal, John thought as he pulled himself from between the rocks. "Who are you?"

"I am Rodney, Dombul of Groscorn, representative of the Northern Bighorn Sheep. And you, if I may presume, are John who is called, well, John, unless you have a formal title which you wish to disclose."

"Um, just John, I guess. John Laskow."

"Welcome, John Laskow," said the ram, bowing his head. "I shall be your guardian."

"My what?"

Chapter Four

"I've been sent by a mutual acquaintance to fetch you hither and ensure your safety. I shall act as your guide and protector during the remaining passage."

Who knew animals were so chatty? "I'm sorry, Domcorn, but — "

"Rodney, Dombul of Groscorn. If you're requesting a common form, you may call me Rodney."

"I'm sorry you came from . . . wherever you came from, but I'm going to find my sisters and go home." He stood and discovered he was slightly shorter than the ram.

"Tell me, learned squire, how do you aspire to this?"

"Huh?" *I can't understand this guy.*

"Oh, really now? Tis the proper tongue! Perhaps if you increased your reading, your vocabulary would expand!"

"I don't need your help," said John, and he walked away. Rodney followed close behind. John groaned. "Please, leave me alone!" He walked faster, but the ram trotted in step.

John sprinted. He dodged sideways to confuse Rodney, but the ram pranced next to him, and the distance between them never wavered. John leaned and ran as hard as he could, with strides wider than ever before.

He had to stop. The air was too thin. He dropped his hands to his knees to pant and cough. Rodney stood in place next to him and looked over the meadow as though they'd never moved.

"I merely asked how you were planning to accomplish this task."

John coughed horribly.

"I see!" Rodney replied, as though the cough was intelligible. "Well, yes, traveling south is a fine plan, especially when one hasn't the foggiest notion where one's going. The marmot said south, so tally ho! I'll head south!" He waited a few seconds and then continued as though had John replied. "Right, right. Top notch. You'll find your siblings in no time flat."

He lowered his head to nibble the grass but paused as he was about to eat. "There is one problem with your little scheme, however — a hole in your plot, so to speak. You see, your destination — wherever *that* could be — doesn't lie due south from the marmot's burrow."

John pretended not to listen.

"In fact, I would say — and this is purely a guess, mind you — that the stalwart traveler would be better served by bearing west-by-southwest. And upon reaching the destined area, how would he recognize the cougar's den?"

John's eyes shifted. *Cougar?*

"It's not as though he could summon them by bellowing through the dale now, could he? Not at all. If I were him, I would be most appreciative of any bears, marmots, or sheep who sallied forth to my aid, otherwise I'd end up walking five kilometers out of my way and be at the mercy of the Unreachable Trees. Oh, what grace it would be to find such allies!" Rodney squinted, looking wise. "But that's just me."

John wanted to block his words. He thought again about how he treated the ants, how he hadn't trusted Sebastian, and how rude he'd been to the marmots.

He tried to wet his lips, but his mouth was too dry. "I'm sorry. I'm just so tired. I'm scared."

"Cheer up, young Laskow. We understand. You've endured two exhausting days. All we ask from you now is — "

Rodney plunged his muzzle between John's knees and flipped him over his horns, and John landed as though he was riding a gray horse. He clawed at Rodney's neck and shoulders to find something to hold onto.

"On guard, John — Lucifur is here!"

John looked around Rodney's stout neck. The massive, red grizzly bear stood twenty yards away at the edge of the meadow, shrouded in steam from the boiling pits. He reared onto his hind legs and stood ten feet tall.

Rodney braced. "Hold on to my neck, son. I don't want to lose you."

"Look around, sheep," said Lucifur across the field. His voice surprised John. No longer the gruff and monosyllabic shouting, it was

Chapter Four

low and precise, and it sliced into his mind like a razor. "There are no cliffs for you to spring to for an easy escape. The boy must come with me. I won't harm you if you leave, but I'll kill you if you interfere. Decide now."

Rodney's body tightened. "Why do you mean to harm the boy? How has he offended you?"

Lucifur dropped to all fours and charged at them.

Rodney pawed the ground and lowered his head and stomped his hind legs. At the last second before Lucifur reached him, Rodney bolted to the side. John's chin hit the back of his fuzzy neck, and it felt like his arms were being yanked off.

Lucifur swiped and missed.

John reset his grip and tasted blood in his mouth. He pinched his eyes shut and focused on the heat from Rodney's neck.

Water splashed on his legs as they ran into the river. John held on but floated up, so his legs trailed behind him. Afraid Lucifur could grab him, he bent his knees and pulled against the water to curl his body forward. When they reached the other side, Rodney climbed onto the shore and dipped his head to sling John onto the ground.

"Let go! Run!"

But John couldn't run. Scared and exhausted, he froze in place and watched as Rodney rammed into Lucifur's skull as he emerged from the water. Lucifur staggered. Enraged, he swatted Rodney across the muzzle and wrapped his arms around him.

"You should've listened. You've chosen a senseless death!"

Rodney's scream pierced John's brain.

Then Sebastian's voice broadcast into his mind from across the valley.

"GENESIUS!"

Four grizzly bears and a mountain lion raced toward them.

Lucifur threw Rodney's limp body to the ground and stepped toward John. The ram's horns sank into the mud of the riverbank.

The Bighorn Sheep

The mountain lion streaked across the plain ahead of the bears in successive bursts of speed and vaulted through the air with a wild screech. She landed between them with her head low, ears back, and fangs gleaming. Her eyes glowed yellow, and her tail bristled behind her.

Lucifur snarled. "Sahra? My, my. Don't *you* look fierce?" His eyes glowed yellow. "Stand down. This isn't your fight."

Sahra's eyes flashed in response. She showed her fangs again and grunted. "You dare use your power against me? Attempt to control me? I'm not afraid of you. Attack and meet both tooth and claw!"

Lucifur's muscles tightened, which raised the fur on his shoulders and back to make him appear larger. "Ignorant cats neglect to withdraw their tongues after licking. Don't die needlessly like the sheep."

The four bears arrived and surrounded Sahra. Sebastian stepped to the fore.

"Brother . . . what have you done?"

Though he was larger than Sebastian, Lucifur stepped back now that he was outnumbered. He wavered and looked like he was ready to run, but he never took his eyes off John.

"I need this boy."

"No! I mean, *what have you done to Rodney?*"

"I made my intentions clear. I need the boy and his sisters."

John couldn't breathe. Why on Earth would he need them?

"Why on Earth do you need them?" asked Sebastian.

Exactly! thought John.

"You said my pursuits were a waste of time. Now you're interested. I'm sorry, brown bear, but you're too late. I don't need you anymore. My followers are legion."

"Your . . . followers?" asked Sebastian.

"Human history is comprised of nothing but conquest. You know this. How many of the poems and stories you love so much are devoted to war? They'll breech the boundary. And they'll be unstoppable once they get in."

Chapter Four

"Look at him!" said Sebastian, gesturing toward John with his snout. "Is he such a threat to you?"

"Yes. He is. And I know how to protect us. The secret of Caldera."

"Then tell me!"

"Ha. I don't think so."

Rodney turned his head and dragged his horns from the marsh. He was shaking, but he stuck his chin up and limped to stand beside Sebastian.

"Clearly, we are at an impasse," said Sahra, "unless you're prepared to fight?"

"You," said Lucifur, lowering his stance. "I thought *you* of all creatures would understand."

"I'm neutral, but I would never break the Code as you have."

"Predictable. Sebastian commands and you obey. It's shameful. You're a strong leader for your species, yet you don't know that your own kind plots against you. Copernicus will betray you. The Code no longer matters to him."

Sahra growled.

"Why are you talking like this?" asked Sebastian. "You're not a killer!"

Rodney groaned and teetered with blood covering his throat and chest, and John was horrified by the irony of Sebastian's words. *Not a killer? Do you see all this blood?*

Sebastian stepped forward, followed by the other bears. "The boy stays with us."

"Then Sahra is right," said Lucifur. "There will be no agreement here." He looked at John. "Are you sure you won't come with me, boy?"

His eyes flashed. But Sebastian's burned with yellow fire in response.

John shuddered. *Go with him? Is he insane?* He shook his head and inched closer to Sebastian.

The Bighorn Sheep

"I see," said Lucifur. He stared for several beats. "Of course. I see. So be it. My friends, this is the last time you'll find me alone. Remember this chance, Sebastian. You could have stopped it before it began."

He ended the conversation by turning and walking away. He didn't hurry. He strolled along the riverbank.

John's heart beat furiously.

"We let him go?" asked Sahra.

Sebastian's voice was stern. "What would you have us do? We need to get Rodney to the hospital, and we need to secure the children. Ze'eva will deal with him now."

She cocked her jaw. Her eyes flickered like she was about to phase after Lucifur, but she relented.

"Fine. We'll play it your way. But be warned; I don't expect the Lady Wolf will treat him kindly after this."

FIVE

The Mammoth and the Mesa

"Easy, cousin," said Sebastian to Rodney. "We'll have you to the healers soon."

"Yes indeed, old friend. Better days ahead, eh?"

Sebastian leaned to keep him propped up. "I need some help here."

Sahra sniffed the spot where Lucifur had stood. "Foul stench of sulfur! When the humans named him after the devil, I don't know if they were very smart or very dumb."

"Sahra, please."

"Yes, yes."

They pulled Rodney onto one of the other bears, so he draped over his back. The bear adjusted his shoulders to balance the weight.

Sebastian nodded at him. "All right, Dorami. Take him as quickly as you can. We'll meet you back at the Mesa."

Without a word, the bear named Dorami ran north with Rodney. John watched after them. He felt numb. The tingling in his brain from their voices was overwhelming.

"Are you okay?" asked Sebastian.

He nodded.

"Are you sure?"

He frowned and nodded again.

"All right. We're heading south first. Your sisters are hiding up ahead."

John snapped to attention. "What — they are? Are they okay? Where are they?"

67

Chapter Five

"Yes, they're fine. About a mile from here. We had them hide as soon as we picked up my brother's scent. Hop on my back."

This invitation was terrifying. John shook his head and took a step back. *First, the red one wants me to go with him, and now this one wants me to ride on his back? No way!*

"All right, then walk with me."

John wanted to run ahead and find his sisters as he'd planned, but he looked again along the river. Dorami was already out of sight. Lucifur was gone, too. He didn't like the idea of turning his back him. He followed Sebastian and kept looking over his shoulder.

"Will that ram be okay?" he asked.

"Rodney? I think so. He's losing blood, but the healers are quite talented."

Through the cotton of his shirt, John touched the rise of scar tissue on his side. "Did they do something to me?"

"Yes, they did, when you were sleeping."

"How?"

"I'm not sure how they do it, but it's one of those things I don't really question, you know? It's their special ability."

He was afraid to ask. "Who are they?"

"The wolves. They run the hospital in the Mesa."

John pictured a pack of wolves tending to him while he was unconscious and cringed. Why did they have to be wolves? Why couldn't the healers be field mice?

He sensed that their conversation was irritating Sahra — her annoyance radiated from her in waves that thrummed into him. But he felt no emotions coming from Sebastian. He pushed a little but couldn't feel anything.

"So, it's true," said Sebastian. "You're already reading emotions."

John looked sideways at him.

"It's okay. I wondered if it would happen to you. Bears can do it, too — one of *our* special abilities. I suspect you could become a powerful empath, being human."

The Mammoth and the Mesa

"Okay?" John said plainly. He wasn't sure what the proper response to this information could be. He looked at himself — bruised, scratched, and dirty — and didn't feel powerful at all. He swallowed blood from his tongue where he'd bitten it and wished he could use a mirror to see how bad it looked. He looked over his shoulder and shuddered again.

"Where do you think he's going? Lucifur, I mean."

"Genesius, John. My brother's name is Genesius. I'm not sure where he's going or what he wants with you, but word of what he's done will fill our network. His options will be limited. He certainly won't be allowed back in the Mesa unless he's willing to turn himself in."

John looked ahead this time, hoping to spot Millicent and Miriam. He wanted this to be over. He feared what would happen once they were together again. Would they be allowed to go off by themselves, he and his sisters, or would the animals continue to — how did the ram put it? — act as their guides and protectors? He wasn't sure which option he preferred. After Lucifur's attack, the thought of being alone was dreadful.

Sebastian and the two other bears walked quietly. Sahra's eyes glowed yellow, and she streaked ahead of them in a blur.

"Wow!" said John. "What was *that?*"

"As I was mentioning," said Sebastian. "Bears read emotions, wolves heal, and the cats can, well, do that! It's called phasing. Pretty cool, huh?"

It was pretty cool. And scary. And impossible. It struck John that Sebastian was leaving something out. He hesitated before clearing his throat to ask.

"Um. What about your brother? He controlled me, and I think he just tried to control that cougar, too. His eyes glowed like hers."

He felt an emotion from Sebastian that the bear couldn't seem to hide. It was sadness, and it grew like a bubble, broad and round, and threatened to pop.

Chapter Five

"Yes, well . . . bears can also control other animals. It's actually an extension of our empathic powers, but it's unethical to use it. I'm very sorry Genesius did that to you."

"We could never do this," said one of the bears walking with them. "It's a violation of the Code of Cognizants."

Wow, thought John. "So, may I ask why the two of you are fighting?"

"It's a bit of a story."

"Well, you said we have a mile to go, right?"

Sebastian smiled. It was a hint of a physical smile, like when a dog looks like it's smiling, but it was mostly a pleasant sensation in John's mind.

"You're right. We do. Well, let's see. Where to begin? He and I were born in your world — did I tell you that?"

"No."

"We were normal bears. I remember our mother. I remember roaming the countryside and doing all the things normal bears do. I was happy, sad, playful, curious . . . It was a wonderful life.

"About three years ago, after we left our mother, a group of research scientists caught us. They have a lab at the center of the park with the sole purpose of studying Caldera. Humans can't get in here, but animals can. So, they sent us in on tethers to see how it affected us."

"What? What do you mean humans can't get in here?"

Now he's going to tell me that I'm not human?

"Yes. I'll get to that in a second. Being in Caldera changed us. Our intelligence grew the longer they left us in, but when they took us out, we reverted to normal over a couple of days. I can't remember not speaking before I was captured, but I sure could afterward when it slipped away. It was scary!

"Well, the leader of the wolves freed us from our tethers two years ago, and I've been here ever since. Rodney taught us how to read. Genesius gravitated toward history while I read literature — the poems and stories he was referring to. He became obsessed with learning about

The Mammoth and the Mesa

Caldera. He couldn't understand why there was no mention of it in all of human history. And he began questioning why the carnivores weren't in control here. That's when this started. I didn't agree with him. Couldn't understand his fixation. He, on the other hand, ridiculed me for wasting time with silly poems.

"As part of his new . . . *mission*, he started freeing any animals the scientists sent in. Well, the they didn't like that very much, as you can imagine We're worth quite a lot to them. Two weeks ago, they trapped him while he was rescuing a dog and pulled him back to your homeworld.

"Somehow, he escaped them, but — and this is the important part — he couldn't get back into Caldera. He hurt himself trying. He became desperate for a way to return before he lost his intelligence, so he decided to use you, a human child, to open the barrier and force himself through. Now, I don't know where he got the idea, but you managed to slip through without him.

"I spoke with our council. We think he found a loophole. Our guess is that while human adults can't get in, maybe human children *can*. That's why he went after your sisters."

John stopped walking. "What?"

"Yes. That's how they came to be here. He used them to open the barrier and was able to return."

John panicked. Millicent would have collapsed and gotten eaten. Miriam would have fought the bear and gotten eaten.

"And they're okay? You said they're okay!"

Sebastian smiled again. "Yes, they're fine."

"Ohmigosh! How much farther?"

"Not far. Just over that bluff."

John searched the rise ahead for any sign of them. The anticipation grew painful as they approached a stand of trees at the edge of the next meadow.

Chapter Five

Sahra sat near a fallen tree. When she saw John and the bears, she nodded, and Millicent and Miriam climbed out of the husk of the tree. John opened his mouth but couldn't speak. It was as though no words could convey what he was feeling. Their clothes were filthy, their faces were smeared with dirt, and it seemed like they'd stumbled through a crack in the air to suddenly join him in his crazy dream.

Miriam cheered and ran toward him. Millicent gasped and ran after her, and they tangled in an awkward, three-way hug. Seeing each other made everything real, proof that they weren't dreaming after all.

Millicent hugged John more than she ever had in her life, and the surreal swirl in her tummy made her cry. She pressed her cheek against his sweatshirt and squeezed his ribcage. She never shared this much affection with him, so he felt at once like a complete stranger and a long-lost friend.

John hugged her head and scrunched one of her pigtail buns in his fist. "What are you doing here, Millipede? I thought you said the sibling bond stops at bears!"

She let out an ugly guffaw between tears. "I really thought it did! I think it still does!"

Miriam wiped her eyes and stepped back. "So, what *happened*? What happened to Mom? Is she hurt?"

"I don't think so," said John. "Lucifur — um, Genesius — shoved her, but I don't think he hurt her. You never heard anything?"

"No! All we ever heard is that you were attacked, so . . . It was awful! The people at the medical place didn't have a clue where you were."

John hoped they'd have more news than this. He pictured their mother lost in the woods or lying somewhere hurt.

Millicent pulled away with a sobering look on her face. "Oh, no. Dad . . ."

John felt a rush of fear that she had bad news after all.

"What, Mill? What about Dad?"

The Mammoth and the Mesa

Miriam put both hands to her mouth as she caught up with Millicent's thinking. She paced away and then back again as her eyes scanned her imagination.

"He's all alone! Think about it. First we hear that you and Mom were attacked by a bear, and then we disappear! He probably came to look for us in the cafeteria and then freaked out when we weren't there. All just like that — *snap!* — we're all missing!"

John felt sick thinking about it from their father's point of view.

"Kids," said Sebastian. "We need to get moving. I don't like being out here in the open. The sooner we get back to the Mesa, the sooner we can try to get ahold of somebody in your world, okay?"

The three of them nodded. The happiness of seeing each other vanished into worry.

During the long hike, they shared everything that happened over the past two days, every unbelievable detail and inexplicable phenomenon. John was jealous when he heard that the girls saw Caldera's boundary and experienced the Unreachable Trees. He asked if they might see it along the way, but Sebastian explained that they were heading in the opposite direction toward the center of the region, as far away from the boundary as they could be.

John kicked a rock and said, "Friggin' muck!"

That was his way of swearing without swearing. He couldn't remember where or when he'd picked it up, but his parents allowed it and usually laughed when he said it. It was okay as long as he didn't overdo it, so he used it strategically.

Millicent's anxiety crept into her guts again. She didn't like walking with these bears as they plodded along. Her stomach flipped every time she looked at Sahra. She couldn't understand how John and Miriam conversed with these animals as though it was normal. So, she kept her eyes to the ground and mulled over everything to keep her mind occupied.

"Let me get this straight," she said not looking at anyone. "We're going to contact some scientists on your radio, and they'll send a tether

Chapter Five

through a geyser to pull us home, but the geyser won't hurt us because it's magical?"

"Yes," said Sebastian.

Yes? His bluntness left her stunned.

"Don't worry," he said. "If all goes well, you'll be back with your parents this evening."

She couldn't believe it, and no explanation or reassurance would convince her that touching a geyser was ever a good idea.

Miriam tapped John's arm. "Hey. Have you been feeling strange?"

"Yes. My brain won't stop buzzing."

"Ours too. Hold on. I want to see something." She grabbed his and Millicent's hands.

As soon as they touched, a current flowed through them and stopped them in their tracks. Their emotions surged. They felt each other's feelings as clearly as if they were speaking. Millicent's stomach fluttered. Miriam laughed aloud from the thrill of it, and her laughter became contagious. They laughed until their bellies and faces hurt and they couldn't breathe. It was exhilarating.

Millicent pulled her hands away and clutched her tummy. "Enough! Enough! Ohmigosh, that was insane!"

Sahra gaped at them, an expression they caught a glimpse of when they looked at her. But she hid it and slipped back into her usual, apathetic demeanor.

"That's two shocking events I've witnessed today. First your brother's betrayal, and now this. What if he's right, Sebastian? What if the humans do get in? You see how powerful these children are already? Something is happening, changing here. There's that blue ripple in the sky and an anger in the air."

Sebastian sniffed the wind. "I only smell brimstone. Just relax and look at them."

The children stood embarrassed and looked back at them.

"Have you ever seen anything so magical? Did you hear their laughter? No matter what happens, I'll never forget that sound. The

The Mammoth and the Mesa

timing of their arrival — I don't know, Sahra — it feels like helping them is something I'm supposed to do."

She gawped again, this time as though she'd never heard him speak before.

"You were born here and never left," he said. "You know what my life was like before. Sometimes I envy normal animals! But we're not normal. We came here. Once we can think, understand humor — contemplate death — we can explore what it means to be alive and what to do with all this time we have."

Sahra's ears curled back. She hissed. "I don't think such thoughts! I am a lioness. I hunt, I eat, I sleep. That is my life! I don't need anything else. I don't *want* anything else, and I don't want talk like yours to change what I have. Can't you see? You're sides of a coin, you and your brother. Something *is* happening, and you're going to be too busy thinking your lofty thoughts to notice before it kills you."

She walked ahead in silence.

Sebastian approached the kids. "I'm sorry about that. We, ah, I tend to disagree on a few things, too."

"You don't say . . ." said John.

"Come on. Let's keep moving. Six miles to go. We can rest when we get to the Mesa."

Millicent wanted to fall to her knees. *Six miles?*

Miriam scooped her arm around Millicent's lower back to pull her along. "Ten-hut, trooper. Hup, two, three four. Hup, two, three four."

Millicent swore under her breath. Nobody would guess it by looking at her, but she could swear like a sailor when no adults were around.

"Come on," said Miriam. "You love me."

"No, I hate you. I really hate you right now."

John smiled and felt the tears sneak into his eyes again. Yes, they were truly his sisters.

Chapter Five

When Benjamin took John to the marmot burrow, they'd left the Mesa through tunnels. He never saw what it looked like from the outside. As they hiked the Central Plateau, he saw a bright object through the treetops. He tapped Miriam's shoulder.

"Look!"

Miriam gasped and tapped Millicent. "Look!"

Millicent squinted to see through the pointy branches. An enormous yellow wall grew taller as they approached.

"What is that?"

They arrived from the forest onto a grazed lawn half-cultivated with flower and vegetable gardens and more plants and colors than they'd ever seen in one place. A worn path led down the center of the gardens to the Mesa. It was a city of rock, a colossal shock of stone with steep walls two-hundred feet tall. Splashes of green and white decorated its terraces and towers. Long rectangles, octagons, and circles of blue-green glass windows dazzled in the sunlight. Behind the Mesa, with its tree-lined shore visible to the side, lay a mountain lake.

"Wow!" cried Miriam. "It's a giant sandcastle!"

"Look at that!" said John, pointing out the tallest tower. "It looks like the clock tower at Dad's college." There were even giant, circular openings where the clock faces would be.

"I've never heard of this," said Millicent, puzzled.

"It doesn't exist in your world," said Sebastian.

"What?" she asked, startled by his sudden speech in her mind.

"Humans have buildings that don't exist here, and vice versa."

Her face twisted. "But this isn't a building, is it? It looks like a mountain! Somebody *built* this?"

They continued walking. "We don't know. We guess that it's thousands of years old. There are several structures like it throughout Caldera, but this one is by far the biggest."

As they approached, the Mesa was the only thing they could see. It was teeming with animals that appeared in a multitude of doorways, high and low. Hundreds of birds lined the tops of the towers or flew out

The Mammoth and the Mesa

of rock chimneys. Red and white chickadees streaked past. There were finches, buntings, and sparrows. Eagles soared with falcons and hawks. A hummingbird zipped to Sebastian's ear to whisper hello and then whisked away faster than their eyes could follow.

Animals of all sizes arrived from tunnel entrances to greet them. Beavers scampered out of the way of a cluster of voles, who ran from the hooves of pronghorns and elk. A waddling parade of merganser ducklings admired their parents with shiny eyes. "Hello! Hello! Hello!" they said.

The two bears that accompanied them said goodbye to Sebastian and blended into the crowd. Millicent watched them, relieved that they were leaving but still curious as to why they'd been so quiet during the walk. They felt *simpler* than Sebastian, she decided.

John thought they'd stepped into a bizarre cartoon full of talking animals. "Look at all those rabbits! There's a shrew. An otter. A badger!"

Miriam nodded and wore a slap-happy smile.

Millicent felt his amazement, too, but was unnerved by the chorus of voices in her head. "There are so many of them . . . "

Sebastian and Sahra stopped them in the center of a grand, cobblestone plaza laid in a semicircle around the main entrance. Eight small lynxes, wildcats with tufts of hair growing from the tips of their giant ears, pranced out of the doorway at the top of the steps. They stood in a line, four on either side. All the animals quieted. Even the birds stopped chirping. Four bison arrived with white flowers around their horns and colorful blankets over their humped backs. Slow and precise, they moved into formation next to the lynxes.

On a balcony over the main entrance, thirty feet above them, sunlight spilled on long, curved, white tusks with ornate metal caps and then a broad, hairy forehead. It was a Columbian mammoth. Shaggy with auburn fur, it was dressed in embroidered silk regalia and wore thin, gold chains on its trunk and a crown of woven branches laced with flowers on the furry, bony crest at the top of its head. Four more mammoths arrived beside it.

Chapter Five

Every animal bowed.

The lead mammoth trumpeted, and the sound echoed across the plateau to the surrounding ridge, leaving only the wind and a spare scrape of hooves.

Sebastian turned to the children. "That's Emily, our Honorary Mother."

Sahra yawned.

Millicent forced air from her lungs to speak. "H–how is that possible?"

"Surprising, right? I know they're extinct in your world, but there are hundreds of them here! The Mesa is their home. Now, please pay your respects."

He bowed his head. Uncertain, the children bowed their heads, too. The Honorary Mother lifted her chin. Her voice was like that of an adolescent girl, light yet throaty in their minds.

"You have traveled far, young humans, and I welcome you. Here you will be embraced by all creatures. So long as you are in my presence, you shall be safe from harm. Please rest and eat before your journey home."

Eat. It was a wonderful word. John listened to everything she said, but now all he could think about was food.

She continued, louder, to the assembly. "My friends, we must be on guard. Lucifur has broken the Code. Rather than return here, he has gone into exile. Rumor has it that he's recruiting animals to his cause of worry and fear, and I've received reports of strange things happening throughout Caldera. There are missing loved ones. There is activity around Süütakkan* after being vacant for many years. And I assure you that we're investigating the blue shimmer in the sky."

She pointed down to Sebastian with her trunk. "We welcome Sebastian grizzly bear, whose bravery in rescuing the human children will long be remembered. We weep with you in thinking of your brother and this dark path he has chosen."

*See *glossary and pronunciation on guide for place names on page 454.*

The Mammoth and the Mesa

Sebastian bowed again as a sign of appreciation, but Miriam watched his claws grip the soil. She furrowed her brow in sympathy.

"We salute the cunning Sahra for guiding the humans to safety, though we all know that she would rather be napping!"

The animals laughed. Sahra froze.

"May she accept our gifts!"

Two elk pranced from the entrance with blankets nestled in their antlers. Sahra's fur stood on end, and her eyes bulged as though they were about to pour boiling water as they flung the blankets over her. Everyone laughed again.

"We applaud Good Sir Rodney, Dombul of Groscorn, of the Northern Bighorn Sheep, who risked his life to protect the human boy, John Laskow."

John gulped. That was his name being broadcast to thousands of strangers. Animal strangers, no less.

"Gratitude to Dorami grizzly bear for bringing Rodney to the wolves, who have assured me that he will soon be well."

The crowd murmured politely. John could still hear the echo of his name and wished he could slip away and hide.

"Enough pleasantries! Let us retire. Thank you to those who traveled out of curiosity and to pay homage. You may remain here as long as you like. Thank you to those who have volunteered to secure the Mesa against attack. I bid you all strength and happiness."

She lifted her trunk, planted a forefoot, and trumpeted. The crowd relaxed. The air filled again with chirps, bleats, whistles, and telepathic chatter.

Millicent concentrated on the voices beneath the animal noises. She closed her eyes and could tell which animals were near and which were walking away. Listening without hearing sound made her ears feel itchy.

Without saying goodbye, Sahra walked to the eight lynxes near the entrance, who sniffed and rubbed against her. She nodded, and two of them ran inside while she sat and surveyed at the crowd.

Chapter Five

"She sure likes being in charge, doesn't she?" asked John.

"Cha! Try spending the night with her," said Millicent. "I can't believe I slept at all."

Miriam frowned. "I know she's glad to be rid of us, but I'm going to miss her."

Millicent coughed and wondered how they could possibly be related. How could anyone miss that cold, giant carnivore?

"Psst!" said Emily, interrupting them. She'd come down from the balcony and somehow sneaked closer to them than they imagined possible for a mammoth to sneak. "Let's go inside! I wanna change real quick and have some time to talk to you before you leave!"

The children craned their necks to look up at her. She was ten feet tall, and her long, curved tusks splayed around them like arms closing for a hug. She was a startling sight at first, but her eyes were bright, and her mouth seemed to curl into a pleasant smile beneath her hairy trunk. The image of her as an important, articulate, and regal leader conflicted with how she moved with restless energy and bopped her head.

Millicent noticed a thin, white cord under Emily's chin that led to each of her ears. She was listening to music. Millicent made a bewildered, *well-that's-not-something-you-see-every-day* face.

"Um. What are you listening to?"

"Huh? Oh, Madonna."

Madonna?

"Yeah, she helps with my nerves when I have to speak in front of the crowd."

Sebastian sighed. "All right, kids. Let's go."

They followed the bear and mammoth into the Mesa.

Six

Concerning the Habits of Animals

The foyer of the Mesa was a long cavern with sunlight streaming through countless openings and dark, green ivy climbing the walls. Nearly every surface was covered with bas-relief carvings of animals and nature.

Emily excused herself to change clothes and said she would have food prepared for them before they left, if all went well with the radio.

How does a mammoth change clothes? wondered Millicent.

John gazed at the vaulted ceiling. "I haven't seen this part of the Mesa!"

"You've seen very little of it," said Sebastian. "But I'm taking you to a place you're familiar with."

"Ooh! The Den of Antiquities?"

"You got it."

"Yes!" He turned to Millicent and Miriam and beckoned them forward as they gawked at the foyer. "You two are going to love this!"

They followed Sebastian down the length of the foyer to a wide stairway. He took them up two levels and into a hallway that glowed with the purple, burning oil. The artwork throughout the Mesa seemed endless. Some of the friezes were small, about the size of a textbook, while others covered entire walls.

"Who carved all of this?" asked Miriam.

"We assume it was the work of rodents a long time ago, but the artists didn't sign their names."

"It's overwhelming . . ."

"Yes. Sometimes I'll stroll the halls just to look at it, and I still see something new every time. I have a lot of favorites."

Chapter Six

John breathed the sweet scent in the air. "Mm. I missed that smell."

"Yeah," said Miriam, "this is what Sahra's cave smelled like. Where's it coming from?"

"It's the purple fire . . . " said Millicent, thinking aloud. She kept her distance from Sebastian, wary of having a grizzly bear as a tour guide. Her anxiety worsened now that they were in an enclosed space.

"It's called grelyxir," he said. "As far as we know, it doesn't exist in your world."

"Really?" asked Miriam. "That seems strange."

"If you think that's strange, then you'll love this. You know how you and Millicent saw the headlights of the invisible cars?"

"Yes?"

"Well, the light from grelyxir *doesn't* shine through to your world. It's invisible there."

Millicent had a headache from processing the steady stream of odd facts. They weren't adding up, and she prided herself at being able to add things up. She liked to ace online IQ tests and, for a time, boasted about her intelligence because of her scores. Her father was a physicist and professor at Northwestern University, the smartest person she'd ever known, and he told her to cool her jets.

IQ tests are useful tools, but all they really tell us is that you're great at taking IQ tests. It doesn't equate knowledge, and it certainly doesn't equate wisdom. You're a smart kid. Nobody denies that. But part of being super smart is being just as openminded. If you lose that, then your intelligence counts for nothing.

So, she tried hard to keep an open mind.

"Where does it come from?" she asked nervously. "The grelyxir."

Sebastian pushed opened a tall door at the end of the hall. "It wells up from underground. The researchers who sent me in here were keen on studying it, so I collected it for them."

More odd facts. "What did they learn about it?"

"I wish I knew! I was freed before I could find out."

Concerning the Habits of Animals

They walked into the Den of Antiquities. The chamber and its piles of collected items loomed even larger than John remembered.

"Wow!" said Miriam. She enjoyed the echo. "What is all this stuff?"

John stood with his hands on his hips, as though he was responsible for the chamber because he'd been there before. "Yeah, isn't it amazing? Sebastian said rodents stole it all! You should see the clothes on the other side."

Miriam gazed up at the largest mountain of stuff. "Can we climb it?"

Sebastian looked up at it, too. "Hmm. You know, the thought of climbing this has never occurred to me . . . but the cub in me thinks it's a brilliant idea. Sure. Be careful. It's stacked well, but it could shift. You wouldn't want to get buried in there."

"Okay!" she said, and she dashed to a row of chairs and climbed hand over hand, up rolls of rugs and small, wooden crates.

Not to be showed up, John raced to pass her. "Beat you to the top!"

She charged faster as they sank into chains of necklaces and bracelets, shoes, and cardboard boxes. With a rush of adrenaline, she burst past and reached the top before him. She yelled in triumph with both fists over her head.

"A-ha!"

Darn it, thought John as he came in second.

"Look at this place!" she said.

From the summit, it was easy to see the how the chamber was arranged. There were rows of wooden objects, a collection of metal pieces, including a car bumper, and a row of plastic items with buckets and bottles. There were sleds, slipcovers, and colorful old toys. The mountain they stood on seemed to be an assortment of everything.

Millicent followed but took her time and inspected a few items along the way, like a silver platter here and a book bag there. There was a set of keys and a thermos, a manila envelope and a box of photographs taken decades ago, judging by the clothing and hairstyles in the pictures. She reached the top and panted from the effort.

Chapter Six

"Rodents stole all this stuff?" she asked. "Why do they bring it here?"

"I don't know," said Miriam. "Maybe they build nests with the clothes?"

"But there's so much! I mean, a car bumper?"

Coldness crept into their feet like they were standing in ice water. Their smiles faded. It was an emotion from John. He looked around at the collection with a serious look.

Miriam shivered and pushed his shoulder. "Hey, I was finally in a good mood! What's up with you?"

He wished they had more time to explore every item to see where it all came from and how old everything was. If Sebastian's plan worked, they'd never be able to. He realized that they'd gotten swept up in the excitement and felt bad for forgetting about their parents and home, even if it was for a second.

"I dunno. It's like we're in the car, and Mom points at the biggest, most amazing toy store in the world, but then she just keeps driving. I wanna go home — I really do — but it's so amazing here! I wonder if we can ever come back."

The girls never heard him talk this way. For the first time, he reminded them of their father.

"I guess I'm just scared."

Now Millicent was sad, too. She didn't care about the stuff. The supernatural things that were happening to them were more intriguing and amazing to her. She looked at her hands, turned them to see her palms. Her body buzzed with energy, and it frightened her.

"Do you think all of these feelings will go away once we leave?"

"Empathic resonance," said Sebastian from below them. He'd climbed to the top of the rugs and crates. "That's what we call it, anyway."

They blinked at him.

"Empathic resonance?" asked Millicent. "I like that."

"Come here, the three of you."

86

Concerning the Habits of Animals

They climbed down to his level. Miriam walked straight up to him with John behind her. Millicent lingered as far away as she could.

"I know you're afraid," he said, "and I can't say I blame you, but don't worry too much. Going out through the geyser doesn't hurt. It just kinda tickles. And you'll get to see the sparkling, blue light again. That's something to look forward to, isn't it?"

Miriam smiled and nodded. His eyes and voice were comforting.

"What happens after we're out?" asked Millicent. She still felt the cold from John's melancholy mood and hugged herself.

"I don't know. I only know of one other human in Caldera, but he's never left. I imagine — "

"What?" said John.

"Wait — there's another human here?" asked Millicent.

"Where is he?" asked Miriam.

"Why didn't you tell me about him before?" asked John.

Sebastian's eyes flicked around in embarrassment under their flood of questions. "I — I don't know. I guess it never came up. His name is Robert. The animals call him the Fisherman because he fishes all day on Yellowstone Lake. I just call him Bob. He lives in a giant tower shaped like a fish."

"A what now?" asked Millicent.

"It's called Abatakai. I wish you could see it."

"Doesn't he want to go home? To our world?" asked Miriam.

"I've never asked him! I will the next time I see him; I'm curious to hear what he says. He likes to fish and sleep and spend time with his birds. Thousands of birds live there with him. There are eagles as tall as grown men, one in particular. Some animals think he's crazy, but I think he just likes being a hermit."

John laughed. "A crazy bird man who lives in a giant fish, huh? I guess we'll never get to meet him."

Sebastian nodded, and his sadness poured into them. It was the first time they felt his emotions unguarded.

"Oh, ouch," said Miriam. "Can I give you a hug?"

Chapter Six

He paused and then nodded, and she wrapped her arms around his giant neck.

John was jealous — after all, he met Sebastian first — but Miriam was the social butterfly who initiated conversations and got involved in things a lot more often than he did. He hadn't even dreamt of touching Sebastian, let alone hugging him. He ran his fingertips across his fur. Then he plunged his fingers into the coat and felt the warmth and thick, downy undercoat.

Millicent kept her distance.

"I've been wanting to hug you since we got here," said Miriam. "You're quite cuddly!"

"Well, I've never been called cuddly before, so that's a first."

"Oh yeah? Well I think you're *super* cuddly!" she said, pouncing onto his back and landing on the word "super" with her arms and legs draping over him like he was a bean bag chair.

Another wave of jealously hit John. Why did she always think of the best ideas? He laid his palm flat against Sebastian's cheek and tugged on one of his ears, which was thick and warm, not flimsy like a teddy bear's.

Millicent took an analytical approach and pretended that he was a tranquilized bear in the field and that she was a researcher. From where she was standing, she studied his paw, which was turned with its bottom toward her, and noticed the pattern of rough pads on his palm, and the curve of each two-inch claw — and her lungs seized. She stared at the five, black crescents of flesh-ripping death and decided this immersion therapy wasn't working.

He tucked his paw away to stand on all fours. "Yes, you'll be leaving soon, and I'm going to miss you."

"We'll miss you, too," said Miriam.

"So . . . Where is this radio?" asked John.

Millicent stood upright. "And, hey, how can we talk to someone at home with it?"

Concerning the Habits of Animals

"It's nearby. And just like you can see light from your world, it's the same with other forms of radiation, like radio waves."

She sucked in her cheeks, not wanting to be impressed by him. "You sound like a scientist."

"I love science. Reading about astronomy changed my life. Imagine it: we're all stuck to a ball floating through space! Normal animals have no idea."

Imagining this giant brown bear reading both tickled and boggled her mind. "You can read?"

"Yes," he said proudly. "I told John. Rodney taught me after I was freed."

"What do you read around here?" asked John.

Sebastian began climbing down. "Come on. I brought you here to get some warm clothes, but I suppose we can stop through the library before we use the radio."

"A library! Can we see it?"

"Where is it?"

"Is it here in the Mesa?"

"Are there a lot of books?"

Emily's boisterous voice sounded in their heads from below.

"There are more books than you could read in a lifetime! I swear, no camper in the past fifty years has gone home without missing a book. The rodents steal them."

Her royal clothes were gone. She'd changed into an outfit that could be considered stylish by human standards: a pale blue tank top, a brown sweater thrown over her shoulders, and a crinkled peasant skirt, all mammoth-sized.

Miriam gawked. Emily must have stitched them together from many articles of clothing. *But how does a mammoth sew?*

John snickered.

She slugged his side. "You look beautiful, Emily!"

Chapter Six

Millicent shrieked, which made everyone jump. "My book! A rodent stole my book — I just know it! I had it at the campsite and then couldn't find it! We looked everywhere! Argh, it was driving me crazy!"

"That's very likely," said Sebastian. "Come on. Pick out some clothes, and we'll get going."

They browsed with Emily, who was delighted to join them on their shopping spree. Millicent and Miriam zipped into hoodies and stuffed knit caps into their pockets for later. Miriam found sweatpants to slip over her shorts and said thank you to the girl who had lost them, whoever she was.

Millicent kept her overalls on under her sweatshirt and found a fleece vest to put over it. Her outfit was a mishmash of colors and fabrics. She also found a pair of mini moon boots that she thought would be more comfortable than her soggy, old sneakers, and at Sebastian's suggestion, she picked out a green backpack to carry food and supplies.

Miriam gave her a bemused look.

"What? I need layers! I get cold easy."

"Okay, you're either a weirdo or a trendsetter."

Millicent hooked her thumbs in her vest pockets. "I'll accept weirdo trendsetter, thankyouverymuch."

John was happy with what he was wearing, so he inspected the tags on shirts, pants, and jackets. He was impressed. They were organized by size, color, and style like it was a department store.

"I don't understand why the rodents go through all this trouble."

"Don't people do things like this in your world?"

He considered the question. Not only did he have an answer, but he was acutely aware that he couldn't have articulated it before coming to Caldera. His mind was working faster.

"I guess we do like collecting things. Some people collect a lot of weird stuff, like ceramic elephants or bottle caps. I have a whole binder full of cards, but I hardly look at them once I put them in there."

"See? You get it. Thinking and talking is a wonderful gift, but in here, squirrels can't seem to be happy just climbing trees. They get bored and gossip and argue. I think raiding the outside is a way for them to feel useful."

"It's gotten a little out of hand, don'tcha think?"

"Heh. A little bit."

Sebastian tousled John's hair with one of his massive paws, which made his heart skip. The massive paws carried massive claws, and they hovered out of sight as the calloused pads rubbed against his head. Quieting the whirl in his tummy, he decided that befriending a grizzly bear was as terrifying as it was amazing.

One corner of the Den of Antiquities housed the electronics. There were old DVD players and handheld video games, junked circuit boards, gears, and electric razors. One shelf held radios, some old and dusty and others looking like they might have been obtained that morning. Next to the normal radios sat several white collars. Though a few of them were big enough to fit a bear, Sebastian nosed at one the size of a dog collar.

"These look cool!" said John.

"Take that little one. Don't drop it."

"It looks like a little astronaut belt," said Millicent.

John resisted the urge to push any buttons, though he did brush a clasp that opened a small, empty compartment. He snapped it shut and offered a goofy smile.

Sebastian shook his head. "You are a clumsy boy, aren't you? Let's head outside. We won't get any reception in here."

"Are you sure someone will answer?" asked Miriam.

"Oh, yes. Someone will answer."

They followed Sebastian with Emily down a new hallway and up a short flight of stairs where the purple burning oil flowed in tracts where handrails would be.

"Emily . . . " thought Millicent aloud. "Sebastian . . . Benjamin and Rodney . . . "

Chapter Six

"What are you thinking about?" asked Emily. "Oh, I wish we had more time to talk!"

"I was wondering about your names. You all have human-sounding names."

"My mom named me after Emily Dickinson. I guess she predisposed me to love her work, because I devoured it as soon as I learned how to read. Here's one of my favorites."

A BIRD came down the walk :
He did not know I saw ;
He bit an angle-worm in halves
And ate the fellow, raw.

And then he drank a dew
From a convenient grass,
And then hopped sidewise to the wall
To let a beetle pass.

He glanced with rapid eyes
That hurried all abroad,--
They looked like frightened beads, I thought ;
He stirred his velvet head

Like one in danger ; cautious,
I offered him a crumb,
And he unrolled his feathers
And rowed him softer home

Than oars divide the ocean,
Too silver for a seam,
Or butterflies, off banks of noon,
Leap, plashless, as they swim.

Concerning the Habits of Animals

"That was lovely," said Sebastian.

"Wow," said Millicent. "Too silver for a seam."

"What?" asked Emily.

"She described the bird's wings pushing through the air like rowing a boat through water, but air is invisible. It's 'too silver for a seam,' too thin to make ripples. It reminds me of this place."

"Wow! You're a smart cookie! How does it remind you of this place?"

"Well, we're right where we want to be but still can't get there. It's like all we need to do is take a step to the right to be home again, but we have to find some invisible door first." She adopted a deep, melodramatic voice. "'And the children left Caldera through the silver seam.'"

"My goodness," said Emily.

"Milly always gets As in reading comprehension," said John.

"I bet she does!"

Miriam was mesmerized by Emily's tall, hairy legs as they crossed back and forth. She thought it was lucky that most of the hallways in the Mesa were large enough for her — maybe the Mesa was built by the mammoths?

"How did you get to be Honorary Mother, Emily?"

"My mother was Honorary Mother, her mother was before her, and so on. Mom retired and handed the title over to me. I'm not sure what all this business is all about, but it's fun to dress up and give speeches."

Sebastian stopped before a heavy wooden door. He looked at each of them with a gleam in his eye and waited till he had their full attention.

"Animals search for different things in this library. Bison, elk, and sheep enjoy science and history. Beavers and other rodents always look for home improvement books."

Millicent smiled at the image of a squirrel wearing a canvas apron and safety goggles.

"When the animals learned that the mammoths are extinct in your homeworld, they thought having them here was a miracle. They

Chapter Six

decided there should be an honorary position among them, the triumph of Mother Nature personified. That's what that business is all about."

"Oh," said Emily. "That's beautiful! No one's ever bothered to explain it to me like that!"

"Well, they certainly should have."

He opened the door. It was a tight fit for Emily, but she ducked her head and squeezed through. They stood on a broad balcony with stairs that led off both sides, all hewn from the rock. Beyond the rail, a cavernous hall glowed in crisscrossing beams of light that streamed onto the stone floor. Thousands of books hung in clusters attached to ropes, which in turn hung from the ceiling, row after row, to the back of the hall.

"Oh my gosh!" said Millicent. "All these books are from our world? That's impossible!"

"Oh, it's possible," said Sebastian. "Give enough rodents enough time, and they can do just about anything. These aren't all from visiting campers — I mean, who brings encyclopedias on vacation? Some of them came from the park offices."

A plump gray opossum carrying a coffee cup flopped in from small tunnel. He froze at the sight of the visitors and dropped the cup. Its handle snapped and sent ceramic chips across the floor.

"Oh, relax, Pete!" said Sebastian. "It's me. These are the humans you've heard about."

Pete Opossum gathered the broken bits of cup. His whiskers twitched while he sniffed the air. "They need a bath!"

"Yes, they do," said Sebastian. "Millicent, did you want to ask him about your book?"

His thoughtfulness took her by surprise. She hiccupped and tripped over herself in her excitement. "Yes! It's *Over Sea, Under Stone* by Susan Cooper. It has my name and address inside the front cover, and someone stole it a couple days ago from the Norris campground. I'm sure of it!"

Pete shuddered from her rush of words.

94

Concerning the Habits of Animals

Sebastian added, "Oh, and please get my favorite art history book, if you don't mind."

The opossum sniffed again, shook his head, and slipped back through the tunnel.

John pressed his palms against the thick banister and rubbed them over the smooth, lumpy stone. He puzzled over the library's design. The ropes full of books reminded him of the columns of a strange cathedral. And the walls throughout the Mesa didn't look like stacked stones or bricks, more like frozen fluid, like putty, molded and smooth.

"Millicent, what's that building in Rome called?"

"The Colosseum?"

"No, no, the other one with all of the columns."

"The Parthenon?"

"Yeah! That's it."

"That's in Greece."

"How do you *know* that?" he asked, annoyed and impressed at the same time.

"Because the Parthenon is in Greece? I don't know what else to tell you."

"Well, this is like a Parthenon of books!"

Sebastian cooed. "That's a perfect name. We have a Den of Antiquities. Why not a Parthenon of Books?"

John smiled. Sebastian's delight tickled his gut and made him chuckle with empathic resonance.

Empathic resonance, he thought. *Parthenon of Books.* Not only was knowing Sebastian terrifying and amazing at the same time, but Caldera was, too. He ached to see his parents again, so he could tell them about it, but it somehow felt wrong to enjoy anything while they were there.

They'd want us to enjoy all this, right?

While he contemplated, Millicent tried to count just one cluster of books, then how many clusters hung in each column, and then how many columns were in each row, but her vision blurred and skipped

Chapter Six

and made her lose count. She guessed the library held a hundred-thousand books.

A squirrel skittered across the floor far below.

"Look down there!" she said, pointing.

The squirrel climbed one of the ropes, jumped onto a high cluster of books, and plucked one free. It slipped the book into a red cloth bag and lowered itself with the bag to the ground by pushing another rope.

"Hmm. This must all work with pulleys?"

"You are correct," said Pete Opossum from behind her, carrying the book. "This chamber was constructed before recorded history, and several modifications — "

"Hey! How'd that get here so quickly?"

"Ahem! *Several modifications* have been made to the mechanisms over the years, allowing us to store and retrieve books with tremendous efficiency."

He handed the book to her. She opened the front cover and read an inscription from her mother.

Dear Milly,

I almost forgot about these books. I spent hours reading them when I was your age and hope you'll enjoy them as much as I did. I also hope you don't mind when I borrow them on a rainy Sunday when we can curl up under a blanket and read together.

Love,

Mom

Concerning the Habits of Animals

She closed the book and clasped it to her chest. She didn't care that the rodents stole it now that she had it back. It was a piece of home. Her chest caved in around it like she could absorb it into her body, and her mouth tightened, and her tears fell.

Miriam was there to rub her back and give her a hug.

"I miss her so much!" said Millicent.

Miriam nodded and made a face like she'd tasted a lemon. She hated crying and didn't want to start now.

With a scrape and a thump, two beavers arrived through another tunnel, hefting a large book, and gave it to Sebastian. He laid it open on the banister and used his nose to flip the pages with surprising skill.

"Are you okay, Millicent?" he asked.

She wiped her eyes with her hoodie sleeves and put her book in her backpack. She straightened her back and shook her fingers like little fans at her sides and blew out some air.

"Yeah. I'm okay." She sniffed her runny nose.

"All right. Then gather 'round, gather 'round."

They drew close to look at the page he'd turned to, but he covered it with a paw. Emily peeked over their shoulders from behind them.

"You asked about our names," said Sebastian. "Legend has it that I needed a couple of tranquilizer darts to take me down when the humans captured me. The person who named me said it reminded him of this."

He removed his paw from the book. There was a painting of a shirtless man tied to a tree. He looked to the sky with mournful eyes, and his body was pierced by many arrows.

"This is Saint Sebastian. Do you know what a martyr is?"

"Someone who dies for their beliefs," said Millicent.

"Yes. It wasn't until later that I learned how appropriate the name was. As nice as the research team was, I realized I'd rather die than be captured again. So, I do have sympathy for what my brother must have been feeling when he got captured; I just can't condone what he's doing now."

Chapter Six

"And Genesius?" asked Millicent. "Where did his name come from?"

"Ha. Saint Genesius was the patron saint of thieves, sinners, and actors. They thought my brother was a wily prankster."

John imagined the red bear at the edge of the path in the forest before he attacked him and his mother. He didn't *look* like a wily prankster.

"Then they renamed him Lucifur?"

"Yes," said Sebastian. "I thought it was because of his red fur but realized later that he'd changed."

There was a pause. Sebastian closed his thoughts and guarded his emotions again.

And Emily swirled the end of her trunk around. "Whew! This has been deep, I'll tell ya!"

"Yes, the detour is over. I shouldn't keep you any longer, though I'd love for you to stay."

He returned his book, and they left the library.

Emily excused herself again, saying she couldn't follow where Sebastian was about to take them, and she wanted to check on the food preparations. Fresh air hit them as they climbed higher within the Mesa. They came to a hallway that glowed at the far end. Once there, they squinted up into a vast, hollow tower. The sky was visible through giant, circular openings on three sides, and a stairway carved into the wall wound all the way to the top.

"This is inside the main tower!" said John, his voice echoing.

"I thought you'd like this," said Sebastian. "The view will take your breath away."

They climbed the stairs in single file, and even Miriam hugged the wall. Toward the top, a carving covered the wall across from them.

"I recognize that," said Millicent. "It's a diagram of Yellowstone like a — like a — " She snapped her fingers as she searched for the word.

Concerning the Habits of Animals

"It's a cross-section," said Sebastian helpfully. "That's the geographic caldera."

"Right!"

She wanted to study the artwork, but she needed to watch where she was climbing. The final flight of stairs led them onto the roof of the tower, and Sebastian was right; the view took their breath away. The sun dipped toward the horizon over the Central Plateau, and the forest spread to the surrounding mountain ranges like a dark, green carpet, full of hills and valleys and patches of tan. The crisp air turned the sky into pure, blue glass and blazed orange and yellow in the west. Below them sprawled the Mesa's lower roofs and towers, which glowed in the sunset and cast deep, blue shadows. Animals moved inside the openings, and alcoves flickered with the purple light of grelyxir.

Sebastian was quiet. He sat at the center of the roof near Miriam with his eyes narrowed in the wind. John approached with the white collar.

"As you can guess, I can't talk over the radio. Telepathy doesn't work that way. The scientists gave us voice commands when they sent us in. Later, they taught us Morse code, so we could tap responses."

"Is that how you'll talk to them?" asked John.

"No. No, you can talk to them directly."

He gulped. "Miriam should do it!"

She rolled her eyes. "All right. Give it here." She took the collar and knelt. "How does it work?"

Sebastian nosed a button, and the speaker crack-whistled to life next to two blinking lights.

"Press the gray button to talk."

She put her thumb on the talk-switch. John and Millicent looked at her eagerly. "What should I say?"

"Say hello! Ask if anyone's there. The microphone is behind that little hole."

She brought the collar to her mouth. "Hello? Is anybody there?"

Quiet static fizzled. They stared, waiting.

Chapter Six

"Try again."

"Hello, is anyone there, please?"

A man's voice came through a tiny speaker behind three little holes. "Channel check. Is someone on this frequency?" A click and a beep signaled that he was finished.

"Hello? Yes, I'm here!"

"This is a reserved frequency. Please switch to another channel. We thank you for your cooperation."

She looked to Sebastian and whispered, "What am I supposed to do?"

"Tell him you need help."

"Hello? I need help! I really need your help."

"Say again," said the voice. "Do you need assistance?"

"Tell him you're in Caldera," said Sebastian. "That should get his attention."

"Hello? I'm in Caldera! I'm trapped in Caldera! I'm where the animals can talk."

"Who is this?"

"My name is Miriam Laskow. I'm here with my brother and sister."

"Miriam! Are we glad to hear from you! We've been looking everywhere for you kids. Are you okay? Are any of you hurt?"

"No, sir. We're all fine!"

"That's *wonderful*! A lot of people are worried about you. When we heard that you went missing, some of us thought you might be there. How on Earth did you get in?"

She summarized, and the man was most concerned about how they'd escaped from Lucifur and asked several times if they were in a safe place and away from him. Then he turned his attention to Sebastian.

"Is he there with you now?"

Miriam paused, and Sebastian hesitated. He grumbled and gave a slight nod.

"Yes, he's with us."

Concerning the Habits of Animals

"Wow. Sebastian, if you can hear me, this is James. I — I hope you're doing well. We miss you. Everyone here does."

A spine of anxiety escaped Sebastian's hidden emotions. It was a feeling Millicent knew well, and she watched his eyes as they searched, as they looked for something to grab ahold of. Moved by a sudden compassion, she leaned forward to speak.

"He says he's doing fine. He's been happy here."

His eyes locked on her, which was terrifying, but he nodded and emitted a wave of appreciation. Her insides trembled with relief. She didn't want to upset him.

John fidgeted with the drawstrings of his hoodie. He cleared his throat and leaned in to talk, too.

"Sir, have you heard anything about our mom?"

"Yes! Your parents are fine! They've been looking for you nonstop. Look, we're going to get you out of there tonight, okay?"

Millicent's face tightened. "Are they there? Can we talk to them?"

"Oh, I'm sorry — they're not at this location. But they'll be waiting for you when you get back. It's going to be dark soon. Do you know where you are relative to the park?"

Sebastian nodded. "Tell him we're near Mary Lake."

"We're near Mary Lake," said Miriam. "Do you know where that is?"

"Yes, we do. Okay. This is going to sound complicated, but there's a special way we need to bring you home."

"We know about the tethers. Sebastian told us."

"Excellent. That makes this a lot easier. Plume geyser is closest to you. Let's see . . . It's about a two-hour hike from Mary Lake. Do you think you can reach it tonight?"

Sebastian nodded. "Tell him that I'll take you there."

"Yes, Sebastian will take us."

"Perfect. All right. Now, it's a good idea to turn off the collar in the meantime to save the battery. Take it with you and contact us anytime

Chapter Six

along the way if you need something. Turn it on when you get close to the geyser, and we'll give you instructions for the tethers."

"Okay."

"All right, Miriam. We'll see you soon. And, please, don't hesitate to contact us if something happens. Over and out."

"Over and out!"

The final pop and beep left them in silence but for the wind as his words, *if something happens*, echoed in their minds. Miriam rubbed her thumb over the three little speaker holes. A voice from home just came through them.

"Now what do we do?"

"You go home," said Sebastian.

They sat on the tower for a minute longer, until the sun touched the horizon. The past two days felt like a lifetime.

"We should go," said Sebastian. "We'll stop in the Amphitheater to get the food."

"Ugh," said Millicent. "We'll be hiking in the dark."

"Yes. But then, you'll see your parents and sleep in warm beds!"

He led them to the ground level and into the Amphitheater, the feasting hall of the Mesa. They stood at the top of a long ramp that descended to the middle of an enormous arena. Howls and screeches came from animals of every kind at curved tables that formed circles around the center and continued onto the domed ceiling as ledges and perches for the birds.

Strange, rhythmic music filled the space. Down at the center, a mink plucked a guitar that lay on the ground. A beaver slapped its tail against a rock or pail or metal tub, depending on which sound it wanted. And a pair of badgers tapped on glass bottles with metal spoons.

Emily stood with a pack of wolves at the center table. She heralded their arrival by waving her trunk and trumpeted for all to hear, and the stadium quieted in a rush as the animals turned to catch a glimpse of them.

Concerning the Habits of Animals

Something sharp poked John's leg. He looked down to see Benjamin jabbing him with a tiny walking stick.

"What's the big idea takin' off like that before havin' a proper breakfast? Was my mother that annoying?"

It was hard for John to believe that he left the marmot burrow just that morning. He knelt and said, "No! No. She was fine. I'm sorry, Benjamin. I never got to say thank you."

Benjamin planted his hiking stick on the ground and leaned close, his eyes narrow slits. "What did you say?"

"I — I said I was sorry — "

"No!" said Benjamin, tapping the stick on the ground. "What was that second part?"

John was confused. "I never said thank you?"

Benjamin leaned farther with his eyes wide and crazy. "Now, take off the 'I never said' part."

"Umm . . . thank you?"

He tossed the stick aside and threw his arms wide open. "There! Ya thanked me!"

They sat with Sebastian and Benjamin at a table with a family of otters and a Golden Retriever who panted and wagged his tail. Emily trumpeted another call to attention.

"Thank you. Thank you all for coming. Our new friends are leaving soon, so let's give them a proper goodbye. Let's wish them luck on tonight's journey!"

The hall erupted with animal sounds and the pounding of tables.

"Let's enjoy a wonderful meal with them!" With that, a storm of smaller animals entered and presented each table with platters loaded with vegetables or grains or meat.

John smiled at the Golden Retriever next to him. The dog wagged his tail again and said in an excited voice, "Hi there! I'm Samuel! How are you! I'm hungry — are you hungry? It's nice to meet you!"

"Yes. It's nice to meet you, too!"

Chapter Six

Samuel slowed his tail. "Aw, that hurts, doesn't it? Your tongue, I mean . . ."

John nodded suspiciously. How did this dog know about his tongue, of all things?

"I can heal it. That's what dogs do in Caldera. Can I heal you? I'm getting pretty good at it."

Miriam watched their conversation with growing interest. "Can you heal my sister's leg, please, Samuel?" Millicent shot her an evil look — she didn't like dogs. She didn't have an outright phobia of them, but she was always uneasy around them (and hated it when people assured her that their excited, jumping dogs were friendly).

"Yes! No problem!" he said. "Show me."

"Go on, Mill. Show him."

Feeling like the entire Amphitheater was focused on her, Millicent lifted a leg onto the bench and pulled up her pant leg to expose the cuts and scratches. Samuel sniffed and rubbed his head against her, licked, and he breathed his warm breath. His eyes glowed as he worked.

"I can help the other one, too."

Her leg hadn't changed, so she looked to Sebastian.

"Your wounds won't magically vanish. Give it some time, and you'll see. The wolves and dogs work miracles."

She grumbled and rolled up the other pant leg, and Samuel repeated the routine. She sucked on her bottom lip as she waited for results. "Hmm. Thank you, Samuel. Hopefully that helps."

Samuel looked at John and panted again.

"Okay. Go ahead," he said, and he clamped his lips shut.

Samuel sniffed and breathed on his face. He hummed, sounding more human than canine, and waved his snout around John's face like a security guard with a metal detector wand. Then he licked his mouth.

John sat disgusted — and unhealed — and wondered what the fuss was about.

Concerning the Habits of Animals

While they ate a quick meal, Miriam watched the animals in the ring of tables below them. Antelope sat at one table and grazed on their grasses while bears at the next table ate, among other things, antelope.

"Why are they okay with that?" she asked, nodding in their direction.

Sebastian chewed on a large salmon. "It looks strange to you, doesn't it?"

"What are those bears eating?"

"Normal antelopes from your world."

"That's what Sahra said. Huh." The arrangement bothered her, but she couldn't say why. "Where is she, anyway?"

"Cats don't like big crowds. She probably went back to Doyadu-khani."

"Doya do what now?"

"Doyadu-khani. It's where the cats live.'"

"Oh." Miriam thought it was an elaborate name for the little cave. Still, she scanned the crowd and verified that there were only a few cats. Her time with Sahra had been brief, but the big cat's bluntness was endearing.

"It's too bad. I would have liked to have said goodbye to her."

Emily loomed over them. She bounced her head to the music and waved her trunk. "Do you like the food?" she asked. "I know it ain't fancy!"

"Well, Mom always wanted us to eat more like this," said Miriam.

Emily continued her impressive shimmy. "Well, I'm glad I could throw a way-big party for you like this. Sometimes being the Honorary Mother has its perks!"

"You know," said Miriam, "since we already have a mother, maybe you could be our Honorary Sister instead."

Emily stopped dancing and stared, slack-jawed. Millicent was about to say this was the stupidest idea she'd ever heard when Emily blurted out, "That is the sweetest thing I've ever heard!" Millicent rolled her eyes and kept quiet. Miriam smiled and pet the end of Emily's trunk.

Chapter Six

They packed food into Millicent's backpack and stood to leave. The animals formed a receiving line to sniff, poke, and pat them as they walked up the ramp.

"Why are they making such a big deal out of us?" asked Millicent, cringing from the attention. "I don't know any of these animals."

"You must understand," said Sebastian. "Most of them have never seen a human being before."

As they reached the exit, John stopped and touched his lips. His tongue wasn't healed, but it no longer hurt, and the swelling had gone down considerably. He turned and waved a thank you to Samuel, who sat at the bottom of the ramp with a proud lift of his snout.

In the plaza outside the main entrance of the Mesa, in a ring of flickering purple torchlight, they met with four lynxes and the same three bears who accompanied them earlier. Two of the lynxes moved to the front, and two went to the rear.

"I thought I would beef up security with a little night vision," said Sebastian.

"Ha. That's pretty cool," said John.

One of the bears nodded. It was Dorami, the bear who carried Rodney back to the Mesa. His voice was gruff. "This full moon will be good. A stroke of luck!"

"Yes, thank you for agreeing to come."

"It's my pleasure. You've done so much for us. It's the least I can do."

John pulled up his hood, and the girls put on their knit caps. Miriam adjusted the radio collar clipped to her belt loop, and they embarked on their trek into the darkness.

"I was thinking," said Sebastian as they walked. "Anything is possible. It's too dangerous for you to be here until I deal with my brother, but maybe you can find a way back when you're older."

"But you said adults can't get in," said John.

"I know. Maybe it'll be different since you've already been here."

Concerning the Habits of Animals

"I wish Mom and Dad could see it," said Miriam. "They'd be fascinated by this place."

"Yes. And I wonder if they ever could," said Sebastian thoughtfully. "You three are great examples for your species. I hope I can convince Genesius of that someday."

Seven

What Happened at the Geyser

The long walk was almost over. They traversed rocky, forested terrain that descended to a vast plateau. The moon sat high in the sky and traveled along with them. As they left the forest, they could hear the distant, hissing churn of pressure beneath the geyser area, and the stench of sulfur stung their nostrils. In front of them lay a flat, alien landscape of bleached white mounds, rugged grasses, and wide patches of stone. Steam wisped through the crisp air past the blackness of shadows.

"It's creepy here," said Millicent. She held her fists under her nose to hold the top of her hoodie over her mouth and clamped her teeth on the zipper handle.

"There it is," said Sebastian.

In the middle of the basin was a jagged crack in the ground next to a river where the geyser would erupt. To their astonishment, several flashlights floated around, some carried by invisible people, while others hovered motionless a few feet above the ground, aimed at the geyser vent.

Millicent looked to Sebastian and pointed at the lights. "Is that them? That's them, isn't it? Somebody's carrying those flashlights!"

"Yes, that's them."

John's stomach dropped. "One of them could be Mom and Dad!"

Sebastian led them along the edge of the crater until the wind was at their backs, so they would be clear of the spray when the geyser erupted. The lynxes and bears stood vigil along the perimeter.

"Miriam, the radio," said Sebastian.

Chapter Seven

"Yes," she said, mesmerized by the lights. She unclipped the collar from her belt loop and turned it on.

Sebastian moved closer. "Okay, let's do this the same as before."

She lifted the collar to her mouth and pressed the talk button. "Hello? Are you there? We're here!"

The radio crackled to life, and a few of the flashlights whirled to scan the basin. Another one raced to where the stationary lights hung, and a bright rectangle of light appeared. It was a laptop screen opening. They saw a closeup of Miriam's face in a window on the screen. Surprised, she scrutinized the collar and, sure enough, she found a tiny camera lens.

Why didn't they mention that when we talked to them before?

"Hello, Miriam! You're here at the geyser?"

She smiled and pressed the button again. "Yes, hi! We're here! Are you here?"

"Yes, we are!" The flashlight by the laptop waved hello. "We're ready for you. Now, listen carefully. Stay clear of the geyser. It'll erupt soon. When it does, we'll send a dog through to your side. She'll be attached to our side by a tether, and she'll be carrying three rescue harnesses, one for each of you. After the geyser stops, you'll have time to put the harnesses on before it erupts again. Help each other and buckle them tight, okay? We'll pull you through from this side the next time it erupts after that. Do you understand?"

"Yes, we understand."

"Stand by. The dog will be coming through."

"Roger that!" She reattached the collar to her belt loop. Her hands went numb; she didn't know if it was from the cold or excitement.

"Well, I suppose that's that," said Sebastian. "We should say goodbye now. Things will move fast once the dog comes through."

He stooped to receive them, and John and Miriam hugged him tightly. Millicent teared up, frightened and confused by everything that was happening. She wanted to pet him at least, or hug him, but —

What Happened at the Geyser

The seething grew louder. The black hole coughed with a deep rumbling and belched the smell of rotten eggs. Sebastian pulled away and watched the steaming vent. Two lights hovered across the ground from the laptop area and paused beside the geyser.

That must be the dog! thought Millicent.

A few splashes of water lapped at the edge of the hole, and a tower of water and steam shot from the ground. A gust of air blew their hair back as the fountain arced past the moon and rained down on the other side of the basin. Their hearts beat wildly at the sight of it.

Blinding blue light flashed at the base of the geyser, forcing them to squint. A black, floppy-eared, Labrador Retriever leapt from the center of the light. Rigged onto the dog's vest were the two lights and the rescue harnesses among an assortment of gear.

The geyser stopped as suddenly as it began.

They approached the dog, who panted and waited for them but showed no signs of extra intelligence. Its tether pulled tight against its collar and rose to a spot in the air where it vanished. Millicent stared at the spot. Home began at the end of that line.

Miriam slipped into her harness, clicked the final buckle, and pulled the straps tight. "Milly? Come on," she said, moving to help. Out of the corner of her eye she noticed the four lynxes moving from their positions. As she watched to see where they were going, Lucifur's voice split the night. He chanted from across the basin.

"Brown bear, brown bear, what do I see? I see a tasty nest of bees."

Next to him stood a bear twice his size with a trunk-like neck of rolling jowls and an upturned lip, which exposed rotten, buckish teeth. The brown giant stomped the ground with his front paws, jostling his furry blubber.

"Rah! Look at those chews! Three little chews!"

Sebastian moved in front of the children. "Finish getting those harnesses on. Move close to the vent. Now!" He looked left and right to coordinate with the bears and lynxes as they spread out. "Lord Nagus. Genesius. What exactly is your goal here tonight, gentlemen?"

Chapter Seven

Lucifur scoffed. "The children cannot leave Caldera, not until I'm finished with them."

Lord Nagus stomped again and let out an ugly guffaw. "Ha! Idiots! Tasty, tasty! Cats chew chimps!"

Sebastian looked dumbfounded. "Has it come to this? My lord? My brother?"

The lynxes and bears continued to walk away on either side to surround Lucifur and Nagus, but they were leaving a large gap.

"Not so far!" said Sebastian. "Stay close to me!" Two of the bears whimpered and hesitated for him.

Lucifur marched, his eyes fierce. Sebastian stepped around the geyser rift to defend it, and the children huddled behind him. It terrified them to know scalding water would soon erupt, and they scarcely believed that some magical power would keep them safe. Miriam finished securing Millicent's harness and implored the geyser to erupt again.

Lucifur charged, and Sebastian braced for the impact. The lynxes and bears curved to surround him. They ran closer, picking up speed, ready to pounce. At the last second, Lucifur's eyes shone yellow. The four lynxes and two of the bears turned to join him. Their eyes glowed in unison, and the cats' gleamed like tiny daggers. Lucifur and the two traitorous bears collided with Sebastian and Dorami.

The lynxes phased across the remaining distance and leapt onto the children. Millicent shrieked as one of them gnawed with precision at her tether lines. John shouted and tried to jump backward, but the line that was attached to the dog held him in place. The cat tore at his hoodie, intent on biting the nylon straps. Miriam ripped the cat attacking her away from her sweatshirt and threw it aside. The fourth cat was already climbing her legs.

A cougar screeched across basin. Sahra paced at the edge of the moonlight with her eyes fierce and fangs gleaming. She screeched again,

What Happened at the Geyser

and the lynxes froze and looked from her to Lord Nagus. With their short tails tucked between their legs, they crept toward her.

Lucifur stopped grappling. "No! Sever the lines! Sever the lines!"

The lynxes sat next to Sahra and bowed their heads.

Lord Nagus roared and pounded the ground again. "Stupid cats! Stupid, stupid!"

Lucifur wrenched free and ran toward the children. Sebastian reared, relying on Dorami to hold back the other two, and slammed into Lucifur. The five bears growled, a tangle of dark fur and trembling muscles, as they locked and held each other. They groaned and thrashed. Hind claws scraped the ground. Fur fell around them in clumps.

The children flinched as the five bears fought in front of them. Lucifur howled and grabbed Sebastian by the throat. John waited for a crunch, a repeat of what had happened with Rodney, but Lucifur only held Sebastian in place. Two of the bears ducked beneath them. There was a loud, metallic snap, and then another.

A deep, rising gurgle issued from the ground, and the geyser eruption streaked past. The heat rose until a blaze of blue light engulfed them. Their harnesses yanked against their ribs from the homeworld.

Miriam noticed shackles around Sebastian's hind legs. As John, Millicent, and the black Retriever vanished in the light, she threw herself forward onto Sebastian. The shackles yanked and tripped him.

Lucifur released and stepped back. He bowed solemnly. "Enjoy your education, brother."

When John and Millicent disappeared, they fell to the ground with a thud as Miriam and the fighting bears vanished before their eyes. A moment later, Sebastian and Miriam burst into view.

They were home.

There was a loud clank, and floodlights lit the basin. A tranquilizer dart whistled through the air and struck Sebastian's backside as he pounced toward the geyser, but the lines pulled his feet out from under him again. With a resolute cough, the geyser eruption ended.

Chapter Seven

"Please, stay away from the bear," said a man. Silhouettes of people approached out of the shadows between the lamps that encircled the crater.

"Mom? Dad!" said John. He held his hand over his brow to shield his eyes.

"Step away from the bear, please!" the voice repeated. "We need to restrain it, and we don't want you to get hurt."

"He won't hurt us!" said Miriam. "He's our friend!"

"Please. Calm down."

Several adults dressed in blue hazmat suits approached. The man closest to them spoke in a gentle voice as he reached out a gloved hand.

"Relax. Everything's all right. You're home! You're safe."

Miriam unbuckled her harness. "Let go of him! You're hurting him!"

"Mom!" said John, searching the shadows beyond the people. He noticed Miriam without her harness and unbuckled his, too.

"Your parents aren't here," the man said calmly. His long, thin face and the sharp angles of his features made him ageless. He raised his hands to show he meant no harm, but he was coming too close.

Millicent counted ten adults. Two of them held rifles.

The man caught her staring. "Those are tranquilizers for the bear. Nobody's going to hurt you."

Sebastian strained against the shackles. "I can't believe it," he said strangely. "Stay away from them, Nidever!"

Nidever spread his arms in a friendly gesture. "Sebastian, welcome home!"

"Where are our parents?" asked John.

Nidever turned. "They're waiting for you at the ranger station."

"HE'S LYING!" said Sebastian.

"Sebastian, what — " Nidever began.

"No! Something's wrong! Don't let them take you!"

What Happened at the Geyser

They'd never heard such pain in his voice. His eyes flared yellow, and, for the first time, they felt his persuasion in their minds.

"Don't think! Just run!"

John and Miriam turned, but Millicent was still strapped into her harness. She crawled to Sebastian, crying.

"I can't! I can't!"

"Millicent, please! You've got to get away."

One of the adults approached and picked her up by her arms from behind.

Another man grabbed Miriam. His hands coiled around her skinny arms as she kicked and strained to break free. Her eyes glowed bright yellow, and, out of desperation, she launched her anger into his head. He dropped her and toppled onto his back.

A woman behind her screamed. "Varun!" She pulled a taser from her holster and fired.

Miriam flinched, but the electrodes didn't strike. She stopped them two feet in front of her with her mind, like an invisible hand was holding them in midair. She felt the cold metal, the latent electricity, and the bounce of the wires that led back to the gun. The woman stared in horror. With a shout, Miriam launched the electrodes back at her, and the woman collapsed and went rigid on the ground.

Now Millicent's eyes glowed. With an unexpected calmness, she looked up at the man holding her and spoke telepathically.

Let go of me, she said, and the man let her go.

She unbuckled her harness, keeping the eye contact. *Get away from me. Step back,* she said, and he stepped away.

Then, the children slipped past him into the forest. They stumbled down an embankment as the adults called in pursuit with their flashlight beams waving through the trees. John's eyes flashed. The dark network of trees created a jumble of open spaces in his mind, and nowhere looked like a safe place to run where they wouldn't be seen. One spot seemed darker than the rest. He rushed ahead to the bottom

Chapter Seven

of the hill and found a hollow beneath a crumbling ridge that was covered by the exposed roots of a conifer.

"Here!" he whispered as the twins caught up. His eyes pulsed brilliantly. "Wait here! Wait here!"

They pressed against the ridge as the search widened. Flashlight beams waved everywhere.

"Did you see what happened to Varun?" asked a man.

"No, just Sue," said another.

"The girl attacked him."

"Mentally?"

"I think so."

The light from their flashlights came close and swept the ground in front of the ridge. John was sure they'd be spotted.

"Did he get clearance?" asked the first voice. He was loud and close.

"For the children? He did, right?"

"I don't know. I don't think he has clearance on the parents yet."

"What?"

"Nope."

"He has to. We can't hold them otherwise."

"I know. And if it's true . . . "

"Great. Then we're all indictable. Great, great, great! This is a nightmare!"

One of the flashlight beams scanned of the area. It paused on a stump across from them and then went dark.

"Blast it," said one of the voices. "They could be anywhere, and I did *not* sign up for a kidnapping. You coming?"

"Yes."

The children slid to the ground and breathed again.

Millicent wrapped her arms around herself and shivered and shook. "How's it possible?"

"What?" asked John.

"We made it out, right? So, how are we doing these things?"

What Happened at the Geyser

"You're asking *me*? I don't know! Sebastian was still talking, too."

Millicent nodded. "Okay, you're right. He said the animals lose their intelligence over a couple of days, so . . . maybe it's the same for us?"

Miriam started nodding as they spoke, faster and faster to speed up their conversation. She couldn't believe Millicent was hung up on the details.

"Yeah, yeah, okay, okay," she said. "It's not important! Did you hear them? They have Mom and Dad! And Sebastian was scared to death! We have to follow them."

"What!" said Millicent. "Are you joking?"

Miriam poked her head over the ridge and crouched again. "No, I'm serious. We can't lose them!"

The urgency in her voice caught John off guard, because he hadn't formed an opinion. How was Miriam so quick to? He hummed and hawed.

"John!"

"I know!" He covered his face to calm down. "Millicent, do you know where we are in the park? How far is it to a campground or something?"

She thought for a moment on the verge of tears. She shook her head. "It'd take hours to get somewhere useful."

Miriam grabbed their hands. A charge of energy from her shocked them. "Then we follow them!"

Millicent yanked free. "No! We can walk overnight. We can find a ranger!"

"John, please!"

John covered his face again to think.

Millicent bit her bottom lip. The look in Miriam's eyes meant that she wouldn't give up.

John lowered his hands. "All right, Milly. How about this? If we go, we'll do exactly what you say."

Chapter Seven

This idea caught her off guard. John knew her too well, and she knew this. She was being played.

"You'll do what I say, huh?"

"Yes."

"Every step of the way?"

"Yes!"

"No matter what?"

"No matter what!"

"Promise me."

"We promise!"

He elbowed Miriam.

"Ow! Yes, we promise."

Millicent didn't trust the promises, but she knew that John's itentions were sincere. "We can go back that way. Toward the geyser. But slowly!"

"Okay. Slowly."

Miriam rubbed her back. "Thank you, thank you!"

"Big bullies."

They climbed the sloping landscape, but their confidence waned under the fear that someone would jump out at them as they approached the geyser basin. The area was deserted.

"What now?" asked John.

A flicker of yellow flame wisped from Millicent's eyes. She sensed colorful bodies of light farther up the hill. It was the people, and they were a safe distance away.

"Do you feel that?"

John and Miriam were still gasping at the fact that their sister had yellow light coming out of her eyes again. They joined hands, their eyes glowed in unison, and the vision flowed between them.

"I see them!" whispered Miriam.

"Me too!" said John.

What Happened at the Geyser

Millicent gave their hands a squeeze. "Now we can stay behind them. We can't get too close!"

They followed the scientists through the woods, careful not to overtake them. The people fanned out to broaden their search area. Twice their circles brought them back toward the geyser basin, but the children were able to avoid them easily, like playing hide-and-seek when the seeker's wearing a blindfold.

They proceeded up a steep grade and struggled to keep their breathing quiet. As the adults paused at the side of a road, they hid fifty feet away in the foliage. Six of the people followed the road. The other four continued searching and set out in opposite directions.

The kids reached the road. In front of them, on the other side, loomed the dome of the forested mountain they were on, and the night sky glowed from an unseen light source at the top.

"Okay, now I'm nervous," said Miriam. "They could circle behind us."

Millicent peeked around a bush to study the scene. "I bet this road goes to the top of the hill." She looked at her shaking hands. "I don't think we'll keep these abilities much longer."

Miriam brushed dirt from Millicent's face and tamed a few of her loose curls. "Okay. Then, let's go."

Eight
Hide and Seek

Following the road was risky, so they crept straight across it and into the foliage at the base of the hill. It was a steep hill. The climb made their foreheads sweaty and their lungs ache in the thin air, and John and Miriam struggled to pull Millicent along.

At the top of the hill were two white buildings connected by a sky bridge and surrounded by a trimmed lawn. Floodlights along the rooftops illuminated the grass and made the tree trunks of the surrounding forest look like a haphazard, ashen fence. Two stories each, the buildings were lined with long, black windows. Some offices and laboratories with cabinets and unidentifiable silhouettes of stuff were visible where the lights were on and glowed warmly in contrast to the stark exterior.

John knelt to study the buildings and listen for voices, but the buzz from the lights made it difficult. Just as he was about to ask how they should proceed, a pair of German shepherds walked around the corner of the nearest building. The dogs looked in their direction and froze with their ears at attention. They barked and sprinted across the lawn.

The children tumbled back into the woods. The dogs leapt at them, and Millicent tripped and screamed. One of them throttled her shoe. Its teeth pressed through her sole.

No, no, no! she yelled in its mind.

The dog stopped biting. "Speak?" he asked.

She propped herself up on her elbows. Struggling to control her breathing, she concentrated on the dog's eyes.

Yes, speak.

Chapter Eight

The shepherd hopped back and forth and wagged his tail. "Human speaks! Human speaks!"

Miriam focused and discovered that speaking with her mind felt natural. It was like the dog's skull had a small door on the front that she could pull open. It reminded her of a little coconut. All she had to do was focus on the door and think her words without speaking, though she mouthed what she was saying, anyway.

Do you know Sebastian?

The dog bowed his head twice and barked. "Sebastian, yes, Sebastian!"

Please don't bark so much! We're here to help him.

He stifled another woof. "Sorry. Hard. Help Sebastian?"

Yes! Do you know where he is?

"Yes! He came back!"

John strained to speak with his mind, but it didn't come as easily. A dense fog drifted between him and the dog.

Can show? Can't see us.

"Hide? You hide, yes."

Miriam resisted the urge to pet him, unsure of how he would react. *Yes, we need to stay hidden. Thank you! What are your names?*

"Gabriel. This is Sunshine." They wore tags engraved with a G and an S, respectively.

Thank you, Gabriel!

He jumped onto the lawn and trotted around the side of the building. Sunshine hesitated, but then barked and ran after him.

John ran his fingers through his hair. "Well, that's brilliant! We can't sneak around with two barking dogs. One of them can't even speak! What if he goes crazy when he realizes we're not supposed to be here?"

"Look!" said Millicent.

The dogs reappeared from around the corner and ran over to them. Millicent was wary. She expected the adults to follow.

"Okay, good," said Gabriel. "Okay to go!"

"I don't like this," said Millicent.

Hide and Seek

"Should we stay here?" asked John.

She did a double take at him, shocked that he was still trying to uphold his promise to listen to her. "No . . . No, we should follow them. I was just stating that I don't like this."

As John and Miriam left the trees to follow the dogs, Millicent checked behind them, sure that her scream would have alerted someone to their presence. Nobody came. She crept onto the lawn and searched the overhead lights, intent on spotting cameras. She didn't see any.

They walked along the wall through patches of shadow and swaths of light coming from the windows. They felt foolish, as though anyone could see them if they simply looked outside. The skywalk between the buildings spanned above them, and gravel crunched underfoot as they approached a featureless steel door.

John squinted and focused on speaking telepathically again by imagining Miriam's brain inside her skull. His synapses clanked and crashed. It gave him an instant, staggering headache, and all he managed to squeak out was, *How? No handle!*

Miriam winced. Receiving his words was almost as painful as it was for him to deliver them. *Try relaxing! Relax, relax.*

Gabriel stood in front of the door. "Sebastian is here. Up, up. Second floor."

The steel door opened, and light spilled into the courtyard. By good fortune, they were behind it, so whoever opened it couldn't see them, and they flattened against the wall. A man stepped out with his leg propping the door open. He petted the dogs with their tags jingling, brought them inside, and left the door to slam shut.

Before John could question Gabriel's motives, Miriam spoke into his mind. *It's okay! He had to go in! That guy would've known something was wrong otherwise.*

Several minutes passed, and John felt a thousand eyes on them. "We're stupid just standing here . . ."

Chapter Eight

A dog barked on the other side of the courtyard, beyond the sky walk. Miriam perked up and tiptoed toward the sound, tilting her head to listen. She tiptoed back to them, trying not to crunch in the gravel.

That's Gabriel! I know it!

How can you be sure? asked Millicent.

"Gabriel! Stop it!" said a man in the distance.

Miriam turned her palms up and raised her eyebrows. *Well?*

Millicent rubbed her hands over the top of her head to her pigtail buns and held them while she thought about what to do.

Okay. Go slow!

The barking continued, rising to a near-yelp.

"What?" said a woman. "You were so excited to come out here, and now you just wanna to go back in? Silly dog. I'll take him in with me."

The kids passed under the walkway and found the man and woman smoking cigarettes on a second-floor balcony up ahead. The woman put out her cigarette, held a key card against a security sensor, and went inside with Gabriel.

The man smoked another cigarette and played a game on his phone. They could hear beeps, crashes, and an occasional trumpet fanfare. Then they heard texting sounds.

Bling! Incoming message.

Bloop! Outgoing message.

Bling!

Bloop!

Bling! Bling! Bling!

He groaned and stretched.

Bloop!

As he slipped the phone into his pocket and turned to leave, Millicent felt compelled to step from the shadow. John and Miriam called her back, but she ignored them with a determined look on her face and clenched her fists at her sides.

The same calm she experienced at the geyser came over her again, and, as the man held his card near the sensor, she projected an idea:

Hide and Seek

Drop your card . . . drop your card, dropyourcard!

The white card fluttered behind him as he stepped inside. The door latched shut.

The silence was a chorus of buzzing lights. John and Miriam emerged from the shadow to join her.

"Wow," said John. "Is that how you escaped at the geyser?"

She nodded. Her calm disappeared.

Miriam walked around the balcony to size it up. Two, thin water pipes about shoulder-width apart ran beside it from the ground to the roof. She grabbed one in each hand like she was about to climb a ladder, flipped her feet to the wall, and walked halfway up by sliding her hands along the pipes as she went. Satisfied, she slid back to the ground and dusted off her palms.

"Millicent, do you think you can do that all the way up?"

Millicent screwed up her face. "Do what? I don't understand what you just did!"

"It's like climbing a ladder."

"Cha! A ladder with no rungs!"

"John can go first, and then I'll go after you. That way I'm under you if you slip."

I have no upper body strength.

It's easy. I promise.

This wasn't reassuring, but Millicent nodded.

John shared her skepticism but didn't want Miriam to call him a sissy, the kind too wimpy to hunt for bears, so he grabbed the pipes and climbed, expecting it to be difficult. To his relief, it wasn't, and he ascended quickly. It gave him a boost of confidence as he stepped over from the pipes to the balcony and wormed through the guard rails.

The key card lay on the floor in front of the door. He was almost afraid to touch it, like it might have an alarm sensor that would detect that he wasn't the owner. He dismissed the fear as baseless and picked it up anyway.

Chapter Eight

The door had two square windows set in a metal frame, and through the panes he could see a small foyer and a passing hall beyond it. It reminded him of a hospital, though it didn't have the convex mirror on the ceiling, which would have come in handy. He felt exposed. How dangerous would it be to try to scramble back down the pipes if someone else came out for a break? He looked over the side to watch Millicent begin her ascent.

She was also surprised by how easy it was to climb. It was almost easier than climbing a proper ladder. Unlike a ladder, though, she couldn't stop to rest on a step. She could brace her feet against the painted cinderblock and hold on, but it required constant effort. Her heart beat furiously. Surely the pipes will dislodge from the wall while she was climbing, she thought, and she imagined the sick feeling of tilting backward.

Miriam tapped her calf.

"What!"

"Nothin'. Just tappin' your calf. Keep moving!"

"Don't touch me!"

Once they were on the balcony, Millicent raised her eyebrows, scared and proud of herself. John presented the key card. She took it from him and said *wow* and tried to keep her hands from shaking as she touched it to the sensor.

Beep!

Click!

John pulled the door open, and they filed inside.

In the excitement, they hadn't noticed how cold it had gotten outside, so the heat in the dim foyer made them shiver as they warmed up. John and Miriam sneaked toward the hall. Millicent looked back at the door to see how it opened from the inside, studied the floor and walls and made a note of the fire extinguisher in its case in the corner — anything that would help them navigate later.

"I hope nobody else comes out for a break," said Miriam.

Hide and Seek

"I was thinking that, too," said John, looking both ways down the adjoining hallway. "Which way should we go?"

"I don't know."

John sniffed and then sniffed again. "Do you smell that? It smells like grelyxir."

Millicent sniffed and found that the scent triggered her nerves. Sahra's cave smelled like that. Most of the Mesa did, too. It was syrupy sweet, *the sweet smell of danger*, she thought.

You're not so sweet, grelyxir. I'm on to you.

The clicking and padding of dog's feet startled them. Millicent dashed to the door handle, turned it, and pushed it ajar, ready to escape, but Gabriel came around the corner with his tongue out and tail wagging. John glanced at the collar just to verify it was a G and put his hand over his heart.

"Jeeze, you scared me!"

"Sorry! You made it, good. Follow me!"

The foyer felt like the safest place in the world, and neither John nor Millicent could move their feet. Miriam took the first step into the hallway like she was testing the surface of a frozen lake.

Come one, you two.

Okay . . .

John and Millicent moved forward unsure of who was resisting and who was pulling. The three of them walked behind Gabriel down the hall, past several rooms full of lab equipment with lights on but no people inside. Millicent reached into each doorway and turned off the neglected lights as they went. It made her feel safer.

They turned a corner to a longer hall, which again felt riskier than the one they were leaving. Halfway down, Gabriel stopped and pawed at a door.

Go in here? asked Miriam.

"Yes."

They entered a dark laboratory, glad to leave the hallway. And John was right; the air was thick with the scent of grelyxir. The glowing,

Chapter Eight

purple liquid flowed through clear tubing along rows of cages and kennels. Mice burrowed and scratched in shredded newspaper. Rabbits looked alert, twitching their noses, and several dogs slept, all bathed in the eerie light.

Through a window into the next room, they could see James Nidever talking with another man wearing a lab coat. Frightened by how close they were, they ducked behind a table that was farthest from the window. Miriam recognized the other man as the one she knocked out at the geyser and was surprised to see him up and about.

Millicent swallowed hard but couldn't modulate her breathing. The loss of control made her angry, and the anger constricted her chest even more. Her anxiety always made her feel isolated, because nobody around her was aware of or understood what she was feeling. She hated this. She hated knowing that getting caught was inevitable.

"I can't hear what they're saying," whispered John. "Come on. Let's move up."

He and Gabriel crept closer to the window. Miriam pulled Millicent's arm to follow but then saw the state she was in. She rubbed her back and gave her a kiss on the shoulder.

It's okay. We can stay.

John and Gabriel maneuvered through the tables to rest against the wall below the window frame. He didn't dare to peek, but he could hear Nidever speaking. Gabriel quieted his panting and nestled up under his chin to wait, and John could smell the mix of dog scent and shampoo in his fur and was unsure of the sudden closeness.

"Tell him to schedule it for Wednesday," said Nidever. "It'll take twenty-four hours for the sedative to wear off, and then I'll want two days with him. Today, tomorrow . . . Yeah, I'll be finished by Wednesday. He'll be zeroed out by then."

"All right, I'll let him know," said Varum. "What's the word on Sue?"

"She's okay. I think she was more embarrassed than anything. What about you? How's your head?"

Hide and Seek

"It's killing me — but did you see? When she hit Sue?"

"Yeah," said Nidever. "I heard her yell your name and turned to look just in time. I saw her fire, and the electrodes just . . . *froze* in midair. The girl's eyes were glowing."

"Glowing!"

"Just like Lucifur said."

"James, this is huge."

"It's everything we've ever talked about. Ladd's work won't hold a candle to ours."

Varum chuckled. "And did you hear? He's reporting to the kid now."

"Hmm. That'll set them back even more."

"Yes. She's all talk, and man, does she like to talk. Anyway. What happened then with Sue?"

"The electrodes flew back and hit her right in the gut."

"So, true telekinesis."

"True telekinesis."

"I wish I could have seen it."

"You will. They can't have gone far."

"I hope so. If they get away — "

"We have no choice! We have to get them back."

"There's been talk. Do you have the go-ahead?"

"I'll get it."

Varum cleared his throat. "James — we're treading on some mighty thin ice here. Without clearance . . . "

The conversation between the two men was familiar and cordial, but a slam against metal and clatter of instruments frightened John. A spike of anger blasted into him through his empathic resonance.

"I'll get it!" said Nidever. "One brick at a time. We've built this one brick at a time. And now the potential is greater than the risk. So much greater! We're on the brink of one of the most important discoveries in human history!"

Chapter Eight

John felt a rush of fear from Varum. His emotions were as distinct as his voice.

"James, I —"

"Look," said Nidever. "This is something we have to do. It's unprecedented. It's history. Varum? We're making history."

"I know, boss. And if I wanted to be a traditionalist, I wouldn't have come. I'm with you all the way."

"I hope so."

There was a long pause.

"It's late. Try to get some sleep."

"If I can. Big day tomorrow."

"Big day."

A door closed. Nidever turned his back to the window between them and squatted out of sight, so John rose to watch him. Now he could see. Sebastian lay flat on his belly on a metal cart low to the floor. Nidever was stroking his head between his ears.

"Hello, old friend."

Sebastian growled.

"Hey, hey. What's gotten into you? There are a lot of people here who care about you."

"Care enough to . . . shoot first and . . . ask questions later?"

His voice was sluggish. John wondered whether it was from the tranquilizer or being away from Caldera.

"If you controlled your temper, you could have walked back with us freely."

"James. Everything you say . . . is a lie . . . and you know I can sense it."

"Ah. About that. Check this out."

Nidever turned a valve on a tank next to the cart. Clear tubes along the edge filled with grelyxir and glowed bright purple.

Sebastian strained to see what was happening. "What is this?"

Hide and Seek

"Grelyxir. We increased the harvest, so to speak, so we have a good supply. Fascinating, isn't it?" He lowered to speak through his teeth into Sebastian's ear. "Just try to read my emotions now — or control me."

Sebastian grunted. "I never used that power!"

"Oh, but your brother sure did."

"You did something to him — he's not himself anymore."

"Don't you dare blame us. Lucifur came with an agenda, Sebastian. He killed four people when he broke out. Did you know that? He killed four people I worked with and cared about. He controlled people. He controlled other animals, whatever it took to escape."

"No . . ."

"What, you don't believe me? Do you want me to bring the people in who can describe *exactly* what he did?"

"He was scared . . ."

Nidever's anger rose again. It was a volatile thing that made John flinch. How could somebody alternate between being so calm and so furious? He'd never felt anything like it.

"You don't get to make excuses for him! He knew what he was doing. It was like he planned to get caught all along."

Sebastian lifted his head, but his eyes drooped, and he had to rest again. "You need to make up your mind."

Nidever's anger bubbled. John felt it just below the surface and wished he knew how to turn it off.

"About what?"

"You insist that we're test subjects . . . animals . . . nothing more. Then you . . . expect us to behave like humans."

The rage hit John like a punch in the gut as Nidever grabbed Sebastian by the ears and pinned his head down. In a fit, he lifted and slammed it back down. John almost cried out but put his hand over his mouth. The yellow energy boiled up behind his eyes, so he clapped his other hand over them, too, and slid down the wall to stay out of sight.

Chapter Eight

"You're mine!" yelled Nidever. "Do you understand that? You've had two years of exposure. Two years! That's two years-worth of data, as far as we're concerned."

Sebastian's paws slid feebly on the metal surface. "You tortured him, didn't you!"

"We learned more from Lucifur in a day than we did in the past four years. I expect the same from you. Caldera is not your secret to keep!"

The pause was terrifying. John peeked at the hand over his eyes to see if the light was still shining from his them, but it was dark. His heart pounded. He turned to stand on his knees, so he could peek.

Nidever was still gripping Sebastian's ears but was hunched over. The image was disturbing. Nidever collected himself, pressed a button, and stepped back, but he looked shaken and unkempt with a bead of sweat over his upper lip. A whirring motor pulled the cart into a metal cabinet.

John was ready to duck again if he started to turn.

Nidever coughed and wiped his lip with a handkerchief. "You *are* just a test animal, no matter how clever you think you've become. And you'll be dissected in three days. How you spend the time is up to you."

He pressed another button, and a thick pane of glass slid to seal Sebastian inside the cabinet. The interior glowed purple with grelyxir. He started to turn, and John ducked. There were footsteps. A door opened and closed.

John waited, afraid to move, and clenched Gabriel's fur.

Miriam rubbed Millicent's back again. "Okay. He's gone."

Millicent nodded.

"Are you ready?"

Millicent shook her head but crept forward anyway. John opened the side door between the two labs, and she pushed past him and Gabriel to go in first. She hurried to the front of the strange cage to inspect the control panel because it gave her something to focus on. Her hand trembling, she pressed a button labeled Open/Close, and the glass

Hide and Seek

at the end of the cabinet slid aside with a soft hiss. The grelyxir went dark.

Sebastian gazed up at her with big, golden eyes and shook his head. "When I told you morons to run, I didn't mean for you to come *here*."

"There, press that one," said John, pointing to a white button. Millicent pressed it, and the cart rolled out of the cabinet.

"What are you doing here? What if you're caught?"

Every missed opportunity to touch or hug him crashed through Millicent. She fell onto him and wrapped her arms around his neck and sobbed.

John and Miriam whispered over each other. "We had to come!" "We couldn't leave you here!" "You have to get back to Caldera!"

Sebastian raised his brow. "Wow, you're a natural!"

"What do you mean?" asked John.

"Millicent, you're healing me!"

She pulled away, unnerved.

"You're doing it without even trying."

"Really?" asked Miriam. "Then we should try on purpose!"

The three of them hugged him and wondered how to heal properly. Then a warmth grew between them. They closed their glowing eyes and laid their heads on his back.

"Amazing," he said. "Here, let me stand."

They backed away, so he could push up on wobbly legs.

"Oh my . . . I'm still drugged."

"It might help to get off this cart," said Miriam, tapping the metal.

The hall door opened. The lights turned on. Varum strolled into the room and stopped short at the sight of them frozen around Sebastian. They looked up at him with wide eyes.

"What the hell!"

Gabriel growled.

Varum turned to run — they could see it in his face and in the twist of his torso and the way he left the door to start swinging shut. He was going to sound an alarm. Their urge to stop him reached out and yanked

Chapter Eight

him back into the room. He slid across the floor into the legs of a lab table. Sprawled on the linoleum, he opened his mouth to yell for help, and in their panic to keep him quiet, they launched a three-way attack on his mind. He passed out on the spot.

"Yikes!" said Sebastian.

"Woof!" said Gabriel.

Miriam panicked. "Ohmigosh, did we — ?"

Sebastian sniffed. "No, he's alive. But I've never seen anything like this. You're so powerful!"

Miriam watched Varum breathe to be sure he was okay. She pushed into his mind, which seemed like a bigger coconut than Gabriel's, and felt its pulse and vitality. Relieved, she pulled back and shook her head to clear her mind of him.

"He's okay. I think he's okay."

Gabriel licked Sebastian's nose. "Sebastian! Sebastian!"

"Gabriel," he said with relief. "It's been a long time." To the children he said, "Gabriel was just a puppy when I met him."

"Woof!"

"When was the last time they put you in?"

"Two days. I'm losing, huh?"

"You don't have long, no. Can you help us get out of here?"

"What about Mom and Dad?" asked John.

Miriam knelt to stroke Gabriel's fur and look him in the eye. "Have you seen our parents? A man and a woman? Somebody trapped in a cell or a room?"

Gabriel nodded. "Yes. Humans, yes."

"Really? Are they *here*?"

"Yes!"

"Ohmigosh! Can you lead us to them?"

"Yes!"

John moved with the same momentum as Miriam but paused to look at Millicent. "Are you okay?"

Hide and Seek

"No!" she said, losing herself. "We can't go blindly anymore! We need a plan!"

Miriam was on the balls of her feet and ready to sprint.

John rubbed his face. "Okay, Miri, hold on, would you?" He watched the light glint off the G on Gabriel's tag. Proposing that their odd group could sneak anywhere was ridiculous, but maybe . . .

"Okay. Gabriel? You go ahead of us. Let's say, when you get to a corner, you sit down if it's clear. But walk back to us if someone's there or something's wrong. Okay?"

Gabriel nodded.

"Millicent, does that sound good?"

She replayed his plan and nodded. "Yes . . . Yeah, that could work. But another thing: I think we're stronger when we're touching. We need to stay close to each other!"

"Yes. Totally."

"What about him?" asked Miriam, pointing at Varum. "He is not having a good night."

Sebastian wore a mischievous gleam in his eye. It took all of them to hoist Varum onto the metal cart. The glass panel slid shut, and he almost looked peaceful sleeping under the purple light.

Using John's idea, Gabriel led them from corner to corner. They were surprised by how large and confusing the floorplan was, because the building didn't seem as big from the outside.

At the end of one long hallway, Gabriel turned and trotted back to them. It took half a second for them to remember that this meant trouble, so they scrambled into an open doorway with Sebastian.

A woman called down the hall. "Hey, Gabriel!"

Gabriel stopped and turned to wag his tail to look peppy.

A man asked, "How can you tell it's him from here?"

"Gabriel has the big, black ears. Come here, boy! Come here, Gabriel! Well, all right. We'll see you later, buddy!"

A door closed, and Gabriel relaxed.

"They're gone. They're gone now."

Chapter Eight

Millicent teetered. Miriam steadied her and said, "Okay, you were right. It was good to have a plan."

"Yeah..."

Gabriel led them to the skyway between the buildings. They bent to stay below the long, black windows.

"Not far," he said.

"All right. Keep moving," said Sebastian. "We've been lucky."

They wound through hallways and past many closed doors, Gabriel stopped at one and nodded. "Your father here. Use the key!"

A digital placard next to the door read:

Subject 3-2638-27

Laskow, Barry Jacob

Intake: 3 Jun

Status: Indeterminant

John and Miriam looked to Millicent and her key card. She held it to the sensor pad, the door beeped and clicked, and John pushed it open.

In the doorway of a small, featureless room, their father brandished a metal bar like a baseball bat. He still wore his maroon sweatshirt and looked like he hadn't slept in weeks. Behind him on the floor was a disassembled cot where he acquired the metal. When he saw the children instead of his captors, his face melted from anger to shock, and he fell to his knees with a cry they'd never heard before. He spread his arms, and they fell onto him. The bar hit the floor with a clank.

"What is this? What is this?" He kissed their faces and squeezed them.

His emotions crashed into them and shocked them. They were the emotions a parent feels for their children, the limitless love and unbreakable care. Millicent smothered her face into his sweatshirt.

He pulled away to look at them, his eyes full of tears. "I don't understand! Why are you here?"

Hide and Seek

Miriam was in the middle of the huddle. She leaned back and planted her hands on his chest. "Dad, I know you're not gonna believe this, but I have to introduce you to someone, and I promise — *promise* — he's not going to hurt you."

"What are you talking about?"

She backed into the hall and beckoned Sebastian, who poked his massive head around the corner. Their father's body went rigid as he stood and pulled John and Millicent behind him.

Sebastian's eye contact was confident and warm, as if the golden flecks in his irises had the power to dissolve fear.

"Barry Laskow? It's an honor to meet you."

Gabriel slipped between Sebastian's forepaws and gave a woof.

"We're here to rescue you!" said Miriam.

"This is Gabriel," said John. "He helped us sneak in."

"Yes!" said Miriam, "And that was after Sebastian got us out of Caldera, but those people captured him, and then we had to come, Dad, we just had to!"

Their father shook his head. "All right, slow down. They don't even know you're here? Are you kidding me?" His eyes kept turning back to the giant, talking bear.

"Barry, let me answer," said Sebastian, "because I think you appreciate the situation. We've been lucky so far — probably because it's so late — but we have to keep moving. We can talk as we go."

Millicent panicked. "What about Mom!"

Gabriel whined and pawed at her foot. "Come this way! Your mother — this way!"

Their father gasped. "She's here?"

"Yes, come!"

Their father kept ahold of John's hand and put his arm tight around Millicent as they followed Gabriel out of the room.

"Are there security guards?"

"No," said John.

Chapter Eight

"The place is secure," said Sebastian, "but it doesn't have a standing guard, per se, only watchdogs like Gabriel — "

Harsh barking echoed from somewhere on their floor.

Sebastian tutted. "Well, I suppose I asked for that."

"Come on!" said Gabriel, and he dashed ahead. He stopped at a door near the end of the hall. "Here! She's here!"

Subject 3-2638-25

Laskow, Ana Marie

Intake: 2 Jun

Status: Indeterminant

"No — " said their father. "She's been right here this whole time?"

Gabriel woofed and then sprinted around the corner toward the barking. They crowded the door as Millicent used the key card and turned the handle.

"Mom?"

Their mother, wearing scrubs and slippers, was sitting on her cot and looked alert from the commotion. At the sight of Millicent at the door, she clasped her hands over her mouth. John and Miriam pushed the door open wider, and she took three long steps to meet them. Their father wrapped his arms around all of them, and she cried when she realized that it was him.

"Barry! Oh, God, Barry, what's happening?"

"I don't know yet. But we have to go."

As before, Sebastian poked his head in the doorway. "Barry, Ana! This way. We must keep quiet!"

And as with their father, their mother froze at the sight of him.

"I know," said their father. "It's all right; it's all right."

Bewildered, she stood and moved with them into the hallway. She couldn't take her eyes off the giant, talking bear, either.

Hide and Seek

The barking continued. It rose to the violent yelps and growls of fighting dogs. There was a moment of silence, and then two Doberman pinschers raced around the corner toward them.

Sebastian planted his forepaws wide and released a mighty roar. The dogs squealed and tripped over themselves to stop. Gabriel appeared behind them with blood on his fur. One of his pointed ears was broken and flopped onto his forehead. Sebastian charged and pushed the Dobermans back, past Gabriel, and around the corner.

Gabriel winced and whined at the ceiling. "There's an alarm!"

"I don't hear anything," said Miriam.

"High frequency — I hear!"

"What's the fastest way out of here?" asked John.

Gabriel's eyes shifted while he searched his memory. "This way. Follow me."

They caught up with Sebastian as he closed a door with his teeth. The Dobermans barked and cried inside the room.

John's emotions overwhelmed him. He threw his arms around his mother again. She kissed the top of his head over and over and breathed in the smell of his hair.

"Oh, I know. I know. I'm so glad you're okay."

Sebastian whimpered. "I hate to be insensitive . . . "

Their father put an arm around them. "No, you're right. Let's go."

Gabriel led them to the skywalk, but Sebastian hesitated and looked down the opposite hallway. The family huddled behind them. Millicent clung to her father, John held his mother's hand, and Miriam stood in front, ready to run. They looked in every direction at once — over their shoulders, down the adjacent hallway, and into the empty skywalk.

"Why are we going to the other building?" asked Sebastian.

"More people here — easier exit there."

He grumbled. "Okay. Cross quickly."

They were halfway across when security gates slid shut on both ends.

Gabriel barked and wailed. "No, I didn't think! I didn't mean!"

Chapter Eight

The research group arrived. Three people stood outside the gate ahead of them, and several more, most of them in sleepwear, crowded the gate behind them.

James Nidever joined the three up ahead. He glowed bright purple from tubes full of grelyxir that he'd wrapped over his shoulders and around his arms and legs. He pushed through them, wrapped his fingers around the metal lattice, and rested his forehead against the gate.

"Carefully. Tranquilize the bear."

A man aimed a rifle through one of the diamond-shaped openings in the gate.

Miriam lunged in front of Sebastian, her eyes ablaze with yellow fire, and thrust her hands toward the man. His rifle jerked upward out of his grip as he flew backward and landed on his back.

Their father grabbed her and pulled her close. "What do you want from us?"

Nidever gave the metal gate a single shake to produce a loud, frustrated rattle. "Mr. Laskow, we need to restrain this bear."

The man on the floor shook his head and pressed himself from the ground. He looked around, dumbfounded, and found his rifle in the corner next to the gate.

Miriam felt her mother's arm around her, and her voice yelled close to her ear. "You can't treat children like this! You're holding us against our will!"

Nidever fixed his eyes on her. He looked sinister in the purple light from his makeshift suit. He shook the gate again. "They were trespassing through a quarantined research zone. They need to be questioned and examined before we let you go."

"I do *not* give you permission to question them!"

He raised his voice, and there was that peak of anger again. "It's not your decision!"

He nodded at a woman next to him, and she turned a key to open the gate.

Hide and Seek

Miriam grabbed John's and Millicent's hands, so they looked like a row of paper dolls. Yellow light burst from their eyes. Miriam wound up her mind like a baseball pitcher, inhaling as she stretched, and she focused her anger and fear into a mental dagger. She yelled and hurled it at Nidever. The attack deflected off of him and struck the people on either side. Two of them dropped to the floor while the man with the rifle, radiating panic, ran away from the bridge.

The children recoiled as the blast backfired into their heads.

Nidever put his hands in front of him in a calming gesture, patting the air down. "That's enough. I understand. The three of you have been through a lot. Please. We need to make sure you're okay."

Sebastian charged. With the gate open and his people abandoning him, Nidever stumbled backward. Sebastian reared onto his hind legs and shoved his forepaws into the man's chest, sending him careening across the floor.

Sebastian lumbered over him and growled. Nidever curled into a ball and shielded his face behind his arm.

"Sebastian, no! Wait, wait, wait!"

He used his enormous paw to pull Nidever's arm down and reveal his face. "James? I'm not my brother. I'm not going to hurt you. But we're leaving."

The color was gone from Nidever's face, which looked ghastly in the purple glow. His desperation burst from him. "Is what he said true?"

"I have no idea, and I don't care." Sebastian looked over his shoulder. "Barry! Ana! Go!"

They didn't hesitate. They ran with Gabriel from the walkway, past Sebastian and Nidever, and into a stairwell. Their feet thundered down the metal stairs. Their father pushed the first-floor door open a crack to peek out.

"Hold on. There's a lot of commotion."

Sebastian bounded down the stairs to join them. "Why have you stopped?"

CHAPTER EIGHT

"It sounds like there are people everywhere," said their father.

"I'll get us through. Just be ready to run once we get outside."

Sebastian pushed the door open. There weren't as many people as it sounded like. Several of them stopped and cowered. He led the family toward an exit door.

"You can't take him!" said one of them, but, heedless, their mother rammed the metal latch bar.

A burst of cold air hit them. The grounds were empty and quiet except for the ever-present buzz of the security lights.

"Which way?" asked their father.

Millicent pointed. "We came up over there!"

They ran beneath the sky bridge and across the lawn and into the trees. They stumbled down the steep hillside, often sliding instead of running. Their mother suffered the worst as she stumbled in her slippers and shivered in the cold. They reached the road on the side of the hill and hurried across into the woods. Their father pulled off his sweatshirt and helped their mother into it. He looked trim in a gray t-shirt.

"We should split up!" said Miriam. "Sebastian and Gabriel can find a geyser!"

"No!" said Sebastian. "We stay together until we're all safe."

Their mother looked over her shoulder. "I have no idea where we are. Where can we go?"

Millicent's eyes flashed yellow as she searched the park in her memory, and seeing the strange energy made both of her parents gasp.

"Oh, baby," said her mother, pulling her head to her chest. "What did they do to you?"

"It wasn't them," said Miriam.

"It was Caldera," said John.

"It's real?" asked their father. "I mean, we see the proof right here, but I thought it was just a story they were using."

Millicent calmed herself enough to speak. Her arms hung around her mother's waist. "Mom, we're in the middle of nowhere."

Hide and Seek

"Barry, put Millicent on my back!" said Sebastian. "They're coming!"

Millicent clung terrified to Sebastian. Gabriel ran beside him, and the others held each other's hands as they ran. Bobbing lights and shouting voices followed and were catching up. No matter how they zigged or zagged through the forest, the pursuers stayed on them.

"All right," their father whispered loudly. "How are they tracking us?"

Gabriel whimpered.

"I'm an idiot!" said Sebastian. "It's Gabriel's collar. Take it off! Throw it in the woods!"

"Argh!" said their father. "There's a screw through the fastener — I can't — " He pulled and turned the collar and pulled again. "I can't get it off."

"Just . . . tug!" said Gabriel. He lowered his head and walked backward to help.

"Forget it; there's no time!" said Sebastian.

They left the forest at the top of a grassy hill overlooking a valley, where the Firehole river meandered across the low ground. At the side of the river, a mound of rocks shaped like a chair vented steam as water spilled from the seat of the chair into the river.

Millicent's eyes flashed as she recognized it. "That's Edgewater geyser."

Sebastian closed his eyes. "Kids, help me look for them!"

They rushed to him, ran their fingers into his fur, and closed their eyes, too. The jumbled presence of at least fifteen people approached.

"Oh no," said Millicent.

Their mother looked around nervously. "How close are they?"

"Close," said Sebastian. "They're anxious and angry."

Chapter Eight

The geyser spout bubbled and splashed. A sprig of water lobbed into the river. Then it roared like a locomotive and erupted in a giant plume that curved over the river to fill the basin with white mist.

A voice yelled from behind them.

"Nobody move!"

Nidever and his group arrived in a half-circle at the top of the hill. The family retreated with Sebastian toward the geyser as Gabriel barked and ran back and forth in front of them. Crossing the river was the only escape route.

"Sebastian!" said their father. "Do what you need to do."

"I won't leave you like this!"

They huddled against the wall of mist. Most of the geyser's downpour blew toward the river, but sheets of vapor often blocked their view when the wind swirled around them.

Nidever walked with his arms open. He still wore his glowing grelyxir tubes.

Their father raised his voice over the sound of the geyser. "We're sending this bear home, and then I want to talk to the police! If this is as real as you say it is, then you have nothing to hide."

Millicent grabbed John's arm. *Grab Miriam!*

"The bear belongs to us!" said Nidever with anger. He signaled to two people with dart rifles, who paused for a second and then aimed at Sebastian.

The yellow energy burst from the children's eyes, and a translucent sphere materialized around them. The image must have frightened the shooters, because the children could feel confusion and desperation when they fired. The darts bounced off the forcefield and whirled with trails of yellow sparks into the ground.

The impact hurt. The children rocked from the impact and strained to keep their shield intact. Millicent's hands went clammy.

Nidever's group inched forward. Their desire to apprehend battled with their fear. The shooters reloaded their dart rifles, cocked, and fired again. The shield was weaker this time. One dart ricocheted into the

Hide and Seek

forest. The second dart slipped through the membrane of energy and hit John in the neck.

Their mother screamed.

She cradled him and threw the dart aside. He panicked and clawed at her arm and her shirt and the back of her neck.

"All right, enough!" shouted their father over the roar of water. He raised his hands. "Please, don't hurt my children!"

Nidever stepped forward. "We were never going to hurt them!"

Millicent grabbed her mother's hand. *Come through with us!*

The parents exchanged looks. There was no time to debate. They held hands in a line and walked backward toward the geyser.

Nidever shouted and raced toward them. The people around him stared in shock.

Sebastian stole Gabriel by the scruff of his neck and flung him, twisting and yelping, into the geyser fountain. He disappeared in a burst of blue light. Then Sebastian leapt and vanished, too.

The family stepped into the geyser as Nidever jumped at them. They heard the beginning of his scream as blue energy exploded skyward from the vent. It illuminated the column of water like neon.

Their parents vanished from their grip.

John, Millicent, and Miriam tumbled to the ground. Sebastian was waiting for them and rushed to their side. The water eruption ended, but the blue light remained. It pulsed, climbed into the sky, and intensified to a blinding white. It flickered and thinned and sucked in the air around it, until, at the peak of compression, it exploded.

Sebastian shielded them from the blast with his body. The wind screamed past them like it would never end. When it finally died, the basin went dark and quiet except for the trickling of the river behind them.

Chapter Eight

Millicent slapped the rock, furious at herself for thinking their parents could come through with them. John slumped next to her and felt nauseous.

Miriam jumped to her feet. "But they're here! They're right here! Sebastian, we have to go back!" She kicked the side of the geyser vent. "Erupt! Erupt again!"

Gabriel climbed out of the river. He shook the water from his fur and hurried up the bank to John. His sniffed his neck and whimpered.

Sebastian sniffed, too. "We have to take care of him. If that dart was intended for a bear, he could die."

Millicent and Miriam didn't respond.

"Girls. Put him on my back."

Nine

Good Night

John opened his eyes. Purple light danced across the stone ceiling, and the air smelled sweet.

"The Mesa," he whispered.

"You're awake!" said Miriam. She and Millicent sat nearby on blankets on the floor. Millicent smiled with her big smile, an open-mouthed, unabashed smile she seemed to reserve for special occasions.

"How long have I been asleep?"

"About twelve hours by my watch," said Sebastian, plodding across the room to them. "Tranquilizer is dangerous stuff. Luckily for you, your sisters are great healers."

Miriam tugged his sleeve. "Guess what."

"What?"

"Mom and Dad are okay."

John sat up. "What! How do you know?"

"I was monitoring the radio," said Sebastian. "Your parents contacted us this morning. We'll talk to them as soon as you're ready."

"Oh, I'm ready now!" He grabbed his shoes and stuffed his feet into them. "How did they get away?"

"Mom said they saw the explosion of light from their side, too, said Miriam. "She said it knocked everyone out except for them, and they were able to sneak away. Can you believe that?"

"I think you protected them," said Sebastian. "Something about being in contact with you kept them safe."

"But they couldn't get through with us," said John, donning his hoodie with a frustrated tug.

"No. They couldn't get through."

Chapter Nine

"And? So? What did they do?"

"I wouldn't have thought of doing this myself," said Millicent, "but they walked straight back to the lab and called the police from there."

"Wow." He zipped up the hoodie and gestured toward the doorway. "Are we ready to go?"

"Wait," said Miriam with the sudden distress in her eyes. "Before we go . . . there's more. It's not good."

"What are you talking about?"

She looked to Millicent, to Sebastian, and then back to him. "All the geysers have stopped."

He stared as though his brain had turned to stone. There was no way he'd let this information in. Nope. It wasn't allowed. But his sister stared. Sebastian looked away. And panic slipped into his voice. "Does that mean we can never go home?"

Miriam shook her head. Millicent stayed silent.

"Hey," said Sebastian. "We can't jump to that conclusion. We don't know what it means. But we do have a more pressing matter. It's more than just the geysers stopping; the boundary has closed completely. So, the rodents can't forage, and . . . the carnivores can't hunt. It's already causing panic."

"Ohmigosh! What will they do? I mean, what *can* they do? Will they have to break the Code to eat?"

Sebastian raised his voice. "No one will break the Code!" He emitted a wave of regret and lowered his volume. "I'm sorry. Carnivores can go a long time between meals, and we'll figure something out. For now, we can eat . . . other things . . ."

John was afraid to ask what that meant. He wished someone would hit him with another tranquilizer dart. Things were much nicer when he was asleep.

Sebastian led them through somewhat familiar hallways, past bas-relief sculptures of animals and flaming tracts of grelyxir. It was surreal to walk there again after all they'd been through to get away from it.

Good Night

Millicent said that it felt like the prank their father pulled on them in Mexico the year before. They enjoyed a week at a family-friendly, all-inclusive resort south of Cancun, ate too much at the all-you-can-eat restaurants, played on the beach every day, and lost track of time. On what they thought was their last day — they'd even packed and went through the rounds of urgent nostalgia about leaving — he laughed and revealed that they still had one more night. That was his sense of humor, elaborately-constructed Dad Jokes. Their mother played along (reluctantly, so she said) and laughed the hardest when Millicent diagnosed them as being sadistic.

Who does this to a kid?

Think about it. You've got a whole 'nother day you didn't know about!

Yeah, but now we have to say goodbye all over again!

Walking the halls of the Mesa felt the same. Only this time, the extended stay could run far longer than *a whole 'nother day*, and they weren't in a paradise like Cancun. They could be trapped forever in Caldera, and though none of them wanted to bring it up again, the prospect haunted every thought.

The top of the main tower was bathed under a warm, evening sun. Benjamin the marmot waited next to the radio collar and opened his arms wide.

"John, my boy! I didn't think we'd be seein' ya again so soon!"

Miriam picked up the collar and handed it to John, who stared at it like she was offering a snake.

"Me?"

"Yes, you. We already talked to them."

"Okay . . . " He searched for the talk switch and brought the microphone close to his mouth. "Hello?"

"John!" said their father.

He smiled and gripped the collar harder. "Dad! Yes! It's me!"

"John!" said their mother. "Are you okay?"

Chapter Nine

"Mom! Yes! I still feel a little woozy, but I'm all right. I'm glad to be talking to you! Where are you? Are you okay?"

"We're okay. We're still at the lab. The people here were eager to cooperate once we called the police. Federal agents arrived this morning."

John gaped at the collar and then at Millicent and Miriam. They were as shocked as he was.

"Federal agents? Like the CIA?"

"Like the FBI," said their father. "This mess is a lot more complicated than we thought, but at least now we have some help on our side. We're just trying to put all the pieces together."

Miriam leaned closer to the collar with her hands clasped together under her chin. "What happened to Nidever, Dad?"

He paused for a second. "He was injured pretty badly, buddy. They life-flighted him from the geyser to a hospital. I'm — we don't know more than that."

Miriam's brow furrowed. "Injured . . . Do you mean scalded?"

"I'm afraid so. He'll have to answer for everything he did, but they need to take care of him first."

The children nodded. Nidever was unstable. John felt it in his emotions and heard it in his voice. He was a horrible man, despicable, even, but he wouldn't wish getting hurt by a geyser on anybody.

Sapphire sheets of energy blended with the warm colors of the sunset. They ended up talking until the stars came out. They knew they risked draining the battery, but they couldn't say goodbye.

"I know you need to get inside," said their father, "but one more thing. What the three of you did was so, so dangerous. I can't believe how brave you were sneaking in there to get us. If it weren't for you . . . your mom and I would still be there. And Sebastian, too."

"Yes. You saved us," said their mother. "I can't believe what you did. I was scared then, but I'm so proud of you now."

Good Night

"Whew," said their father. "All right. All right. It's time for you to get inside and keep safe for the night." His hesitancy and anguish were clear. "Sebastian, thank you for taking care of them."

Sebastian nodded. "Tell him that it's my pleasure."

John smiled and repeated him.

"Hey, look at the sky," said their mother. "Can you find the Summer Triangle?"

"Yes," said Millicent immediately. She pointed out Deneb, Altair, and Vega. Her finger lingered on Vega because it was her favorite. She knew it was twenty-two light years away, and sometimes she fantasized about visiting there someday, though there wouldn't be much to do once she got there.

"We're looking at it right now, too." They heard a crimp of pain at the end of their mother's sentence, as though the word *too* was the one that sneaked up on her and made her cry. "See? We're right next to you."

"It's hard to say goodnight," said Miriam, wiping away her tears.

"I know. But you'll be home soon. I know you will. We love you."

"Try to sleep well," said their father. "We'll talk to you first thing in the morning."

"Promise?" asked John.

"We promise."

John turned off the radio. He wiped his face with the back of his sleeve and handed the collar back to Miriam. Millicent continued to stare at Vega, bright and blue in the clear sky.

"Sebastian?"

"Hmm?"

"Do you think there's life out there? You know, like us?"

Sebastian leaned close until she looked at him and noticed the twinkle in his eye. "Do you believe a bear can talk?"

They bathed in a natural pool in a lower chamber of the Mesa and scrubbed off days of dirt. Sebastian told them to enjoy the warm water

Chapter Nine

while it lasted because, with the geothermic activity gone in Caldera, it would soon turn cold.

But they bathed in silence. Now that they weren't talking to their parents, the truth of the situation kept swinging back into them like a door that wouldn't stay closed.

"Hey," said Sebastian. "The water? I said to enjoy it!" He swiped his paw across the surface to drench them.

Millicent was not pleased, but John and Miriam screamed and ducked and splashed back at him. Miriam was the quickest to retaliate and the best splasher. John, not to be outdone, climbed out so he could run across the slippery rock and douse Sebastian with a cannonball. Not to be outdone by John's not being undone, Miriam climbed out, circled behind Sebastian, and shoved his posterior with all of her might. He caved under her momentum and plunged into the pool.

Once again, she had the best idea, but John was delighted. Even Millicent smiled. They were swimming with a grizzly bear.

After they dried off, Millicent released her pigtails, so her hair expanded to a mass of curls twice the size of her head. They changed into long pajamas that they found in the Den, and Sebastian showed them to their room, which was across the hall from Emily's. The mammoth was so happy to see them again that they talked in the hallway for twenty minutes until Sebastian said it was time to sleep.

"I know my Dad already said this," said Miriam as John and Millicent got situated, "but thank you again for taking care of us." She kissed his big, black nose.

"Well. Thank you for rescuing me from the clutches of the evil scientists," he said.

John hadn't thought about it in those terms and straightened his posture. "Wow, that is what we did, isn't it?"

"There's really no other way to put it. If you need anything, my room at the top of those stairs. I'll see you in the morning."

After he left, they looked around the simple room. A row of blankets, pillows, and sleeping bags lined the wall and a basin of

Good Night

grelyxir burned purple in the center. Millicent approached it and waved her hand over the heatless flames.

"So . . . that suit Nidever was wearing . . . "

"Yeah," said John. "He knew it would block us."

"Yes, and painfully," said Miriam. "I still have a headache. How do you feel?"

"Good. Strange."

"Yeah, me too. I can feel your feelings, and they feel the same as my feelings, so it feels kinda weird."

John laughed. "That's a lot of feelings."

They talked until yawns replaced questions, but they couldn't seem to fall asleep. A shadow of worry tapped their shoulders every time they came close. They gathered armfuls of pillows and blankets and tiptoed up the steps.

Sebastian stirred. "Is everything okay?" Flaming grelyxir fell in narrow waterfalls in each corner of the room.

"We don't wanna sleep there," said Miriam.

"Ah. Well? Come on in. There's plenty of room."

John threw his pile to the floor and jumped onto Sebastian's back. It was his turn at last, and it felt as amazing as he thought it would. The girls laid their blankets alongside his belly.

"Well, this works, too," he said.

John and Miriam fell fast asleep, and Millicent watched Sebastian watching them. He seemed deep in thought, like he was looking through them.

"What are you thinking about?"

"My brother," he said.

She nodded and wondered what he thought might lay ahead of them but decided not to ask. She was often guilty of asking too many questions, but, in her defense, she always knew that they were good ones, unlike John, who never used his brain long enough to put things together from context. He asked about what was in front of him. Millicent liked to think that she asked about things yet to be considered.

Chapter Nine

Mm-yes, she thought to herself, and she stroked an imaginary beard. *I am quite wise. Quite wise. Mm-yes, mm-yes.*

She chuckled and whispered in a deep, movie-trailer voice, "In a wor-rld where she found very little entertainment entertaining, who better to entertain herself than herself?"

Sebastian laid his head on his forearm and closed his eyes.

She was surprised that he hadn't asked what the heck she was talking about. People were always asking her what the heck she was talking about.

Wow. Tough crowd.

Still, she liked being alone, and now that they were all asleep, it was agreeable to be safe in their company while having a moment to herself. She watched the silver and lavender flow of grelyxir and wondered where it came from, and what is was, exactly. Nidever used it to prevent the animals from using their special abilities, so bears couldn't control him, and human children couldn't stab him with mental daggers. Her questions were endless. How did they find out about its properties? Did they do a chemical analysis? What could that have shown them?

She hoped to find out one day.

A flash of warmth radiated through her body. Yellow light lit her hand from her eyes. The image of her puzzle toy came to mind like a hunger, and she found herself teetering on the floor, screwing up the courage to walk out of the room. She tiptoed barefoot down the cold steps to her hoodie to fish it out. Overcome by creepiness, she dashed back to Sebastian's room with her bare feet making little pitter-patter sounds on the stone floor and ducked back into their nest of blankets.

"Okay," she said, turning the rods and beads. She watched how they moved. The light from her eyes lit up her hands, the grelyxir in the room flared, and she solved the puzzle in five, precise steps. It seemed impossible the day before. She lay her head on her arm with the toy on the floor in front of her.

She dreamt about solving it.

Good Night

five easy steps

slink . . . turn . . . slide . . . click . . . clack!

[record player skip] — slide . . . click . . . clack!

. . . click-clack!

. . . click-clack!

The puzzle faded into darkness. Her peripheral vision lightened as though she were staring down a tunnel with a bright light behind her. But she couldn't turn around.

A voice whispered from the dark.

"Help me."

Click-clack!

PART II
Where Nature's Temper Reaches

Ten

Contraption

John was in his room making a flipbook animation of a bird swooping and crashing. His sisters giggled each time he flipped the pages, and they asked to see it again until he lost his patience and gave it to them, so they could watch it as often as they liked. His room dimmed. His eyes were closed, after all.

He woke up in Sebastian's room. Violet flames slid down the walls, ethereal tips glided by in whispers, and the light flickered along the carved stone. He sat upright in the pile of pillows and blankets with his sisters asleep next to him. Sebastian nosed through a stack of books and papers across the room.

"Good morning, sleepy," he said. "Did I wake you?"

John shivered and yawned. "No. I was just dreaming and woke up."

"How's your neck doing?"

"Oh." He'd forgotten about that, which he decided was a good thing. He touched the spot where the dart struck him and winced. "It still hurts to the touch, but it's a lot better."

"That's good. I think people would stop using those things if they knew how much they hurt."

"Yeah." He stepped over Millicent to look at Sebastian's collection. The largest document was a tattered map of Yellowstone. "Are these yours?"

"No, they're from the library. I've been awake for a while. Talked to a few friends. We're deciding what to do next."

John knelt over the map and studied it with more interest than he ever had before. They could be trapped for a long time, and he wanted to know as much about the area as possible. He found the Norris Geyser

Chapter Ten

Basin, where his family's campsite was — he wondered if their stuff was still there — and Grizzly Lake, where he and his mother hiked. He traced the green ink of the forest on the paper and the lazy black line of the trail.

Lucifur attacked us on that line.

"Where's the Mesa?" he asked. "I mean, I know it's not on here, but where are we compared to the real world?"

Sebastian chuckled. "This is my real world, you know."

There was the bear's sense of humor again. No matter how nervous or scared John was, Sebastian had an uncanny way of putting him at ease.

"The Mesa's right here," he said, and he tapped one black claw on the map. "Mary Lake is out back. Awesome fishing."

John traced the route from the Mesa to Benjamin's burrow and south to where he and Rodney encountered Lucifur by Arnica Creek.

Wow, I walked far! he thought.

"You sure did."

John startled. "Huh?"

"You sure did walk far."

"I was thinking that, but I didn't say anything."

"Ah. You see, there's a difference between private thinking and projecting your thoughts. You were projecting."

"Let me get this straight. I can talk out loud, I can think so you can hear me, or I can think to myself?"

"Yep."

"Huh! That's complicated. So . . . have you figured anything out?"

"No. We need answers, and I think Sahra might have some. The carnivores are going to go hungry soon — "

"But she was there!" said Millicent from the blankets. "She was a part of the trap!" Her mass of curls spiraled about her head and sprang to life as she sat up.

"Good morning, Millicent."

Contraption

Unsettled by the dark dream in her restless night, she ignored his pleasantry. "The lynxes went right to her! She didn't help you fight at all! She just sat there."

Sebastian sighed. "You may be right, but we need to be sure."

"What if she talks to Lucifur?" She stood in the center of the room in her pajamas and looked both harmless and ferocious.

"I have to take that chance," said Sebastian. "Remember, she's a friend of mine. I think she did all she could by calling the lynxes away, so you could go home."

Miriam appeared next to Millicent. She looked far too kempt for someone straight out of bed. "I trust her."

Millicent tutted. "How? Why? We only spent one night with her."

"It's just how I feel. She couldn't take on all those bears. We got home, didn't we?"

"Yeah, I'm sure she just wanted to get rid of us, so don't go telling me she's a hero."

"All right, look." said Sebastian. "We're not going to solve this now. Since I'm staying with you, I've asked some friends to form a search party."

Millicent looked sideways at Miriam. John couldn't decide which sister he agreed with, so they dropped the subject.

Before talking to their parents, they stopped to grab food in the Amphitheater. It was empty aside from two warblers who fluttered around the ceiling and a family of coyotes who gnawed on a pile of bones.

While they waited for the food, Millicent performed the monumental task of taming her curls back into mini buns. She froze with her hands on her head as three mountain lions entered across the Amphitheater from them. The tawny cats strode along the curved row toward their table, and the largest of the three approached Sebastian while the other two hopped to the benches above and below them.

Miriam thought they behaved like a pack of bullies on a playground, so her fists were ready.

Chapter Ten

"Lord Copernicus!" said Sebastian. "I was coming to look for you."

The big cat spread his front paws and touched his nose to the floor. "Please, no titles, Sebastian Grizzly Bear," he said. "We apologize, we apologize, we apologize! We cannot prostrate enough for Sahra's betrayal. We are ashamed!"

The other cats bowed, too. They looked like odd lawn statues.

"Please," said Sebastian. "This isn't necessary."

Copernicus tilted his head, his yellow eyes wide. "Oh, but it is! We can't have you thinking poorly of the cats."

"I don't think poorly of you."

"Sahra chose to ally herself with your brother. I'm here to pledge our allegiance to you." He lowered his head again.

Sebastian's emotions swirled in the children's stomachs like a flu, a combination of worry, anger, and embarrassment.

"Stop it!" he said, and the cats looked fearful. "This kind of thinking is what got us here. Genesius hates the humans, so he takes on this crusade and turns me over to them to teach me a lesson. Well, guess what. His plan didn't work. What I learned is that there's good and bad in every species. My heart is still breaking for it. But there are no sides! This is a private matter between me and my brother, and I won't have you rallying behind me like it's some kind of war."

Copernicus sat upright. "You're wrong, grizzly. It will be war. It may have begun as a disagreement between brothers, but it escalates."

"What?"

"Sebastian. There is no food. The animals are scared. We have a Code that says we live in harmony, and Lucifur broke that code by killing and manipulating. You heard the Honorary Mother. Rumor has it he's recruiting more animals to his cause.

"Sahra broke the Code by helping him. So, you see, it affects my species now, too, and it proves to everyone that the Code *can* be broken. What are the consequences? Are there any? What happens when the wolves get hungry? The bears? *My cats?* What keeps them from hunting when they're starving?"

Contraption

"You wanna help?" asked Sebastian.

"Yes."

"Then withhold judgment till we talk to her. Agreed?"

Copernicus glanced around. "Agreed."

"I'm meeting with a few of the animals in the plaza at midday."

"At midday." He bowed again, and he and the two other cats slinked away.

John realized he'd been holding his breath and breathed again. "Wow, that was intense!"

Millicent nodded, looking quite pale.

"I'm sorry," said Miriam, watching him leave. "I don't trust him."

"Cats are feisty, Miriam," said Sebastian. "Feisty and finicky."

A badger and an otter entered the Amphitheater with leaves, nuts, and berries, and Sebastian lightened his tone. "Here comes the food. Let's take it outside and talk to your parents."

He led them up a winding stairway and out onto a broad terrace. Since they'd already been on top of the main tower twice, he suggested trying the new spot for a change of scenery (and because it was easier to get to). The floor of the terrace was inset with a shallow dome of blue glass that he strolled onto with clicks from his claws.

"Hey, I remember seeing this circle from up there," said Millicent, pointing to the tower. "I wondered what it was."

Miriam ran across to Sebastian and slid the last few feet to bump into him. John raced after her but was never as good at sliding on things like ice and slippery floors as she was, so he skidded and stopped in an exaggerated way to make it seem like he'd done something more impressive.

Millicent crept onto it. Her stomach turned when she saw levels below them through the glass. "Holy . . ."

"Don't worry. It's quite safe," said Sebastian.

Miriam unclipped the radio collar from her belt loop, turned it on, and spoke into it while she was still standing.

"Hello, Mom? Dad?"

Chapter Ten

"Miriam!" said their mother.

"Good morning!" said their father. "How did you sleep?"

"We slept well! We ended up sleeping in Sebastian's room."

"Are you still at the lab?" asked Millicent.

"Yes," said their father. "They've been evacuating the park because of the explosions last night, but we're staying."

"They couldn't make us leave if they tried," said their mother, which made them smile. "People reported seeing the light storm from as far away as Colorado and Oregon!"

"Wow!" said John. "And they're closing the whole entire park?"

"The whole thing. All the campers are leaving and most of the park employees. People from nearby towns are in the middle of evacuations, too. It's a pretty big deal!"

"Do people know about us?" asked Millicent.

"No," said their father. "The agents are keeping our story private, but I get the feeling they don't believe you're in another dimension — or whatever it is. The agent staring at me right now thinks you're hiding somewhere with a radio and pulling a prank."

"Ha! That would be a good prank!" said Miriam.

"That what, Miri? You cut out — " The speaker crackled and went dead.

"Dad?" asked John. He lifted and shook the collar. "Dad, can you hear me?"

Millicent panicked. "Did the battery die?"

"Quick! Turn it off and back on again!" said Miriam.

John clicked twice, and static burst from the speaker. Their father returned mid-sentence.

" — came of it, though. Now we have proof that Caldera exists — "

"Hello? Hello?" John called. He turned the radio off and on again. "Hello? Hello?"

"Ooh!" said Miriam. "Take the batteries out and put them back in! That works with toys sometimes."

Contraption

John inspected it and groaned. "Aw, it's screwed shut! First Gabriel's collar and now this. We need one of those tiny screwdrivers."

Sebastian stood. "All right. Let's run down and grab the rest of the collars. We'll be back here no time."

He was nimble for his size. They sprinted to keep up with him through the hallways, skidded into the Den of Antiquities, and raced each other along the shelves to where the radio collars were kept. Miriam slapped her hand on bare stone.

The collars were gone. The normal radios were gone, too. Anything capable of transmitting a signal was missing. Sebastian made hurt, grumbling sounds as he sniffed the empty spaces.

A voice echoed from elsewhere in the Den, cold and monotone.

"Must, must, must!"

"Must, must, must!"

They ran to find it, but the voice was gone.

Defeated, Sebastian took them to Emily's room and knocked on the doorway.

"What's all the racket?" she asked from inside. She arrived rubbing her eye with her trunk and looked like she woke up a moment before. This morning she wore an enormous cotton muumuu. "Well, aren't *you* the saddest-looking bunch I've ever seen? Come on in!"

They shuffled inside where three little marmots greeted them. The room was splendid. Sheer curtains divided the space into a living area, dressing room, and a bedroom. Red and gold fabric draped across the walls and from the ceiling to form a canopy with lengths of ribbon hanging everywhere. Lights on the ceiling looked like stars peeking through gauze. Piles of Emily's handmade clothing littered the floor with mounds of unused fabric. And the smell of grelyxir mingled with the scent of fresh cut flowers.

"Welcome to my abode," said Emily. "So, what's with all the gloom?"

Chapter Ten

"The battery in our radio collar died, and someone stole all the other ones," said John. When she didn't react, he clarified with, "That means we can't talk to our parents, and we have no way to let them know."

"Oh? Oh my! Oh, that's terrible!" Her trunk twisted in a knot. "Please, make yourselves at home. Can I get you anything? I wish I had hot cocoa or something."

Miriam managed to smile and craned her neck to look at Emily's big brown eyes and long eyelashes. "We didn't have much of a breakfast . . ."

"Oh! We can remedy that! Ladies, would you be so kind?"

The three marmots cheered and bounced and scampered away.

Millicent lingered next to the doorway, watched the marmots as they passed, and leaned against the stone threshold. Sebastian approached her cautiously.

"How are you holding up?"

She shrugged.

"Please don't be mad at me," he said. "I wish I could tell you what happened."

She shook her head. *I'm not mad at you. I'm just scared.*

"We'll figure something out."

I hope so. Her anxiety eased, and, touched by his concern, she gave a little smile.

"You know," he said, "you have a beautiful smile. You don't show it very often, but when you do, it lights up the room."

That made her smile more. She was warming to this bear, all right. He always seemed to know the right thing to say.

There came a scratch at Emily's doorway, and Gabriel poked his head into the room. Freshly bathed, his broken ear flopped onto his forehead. They forgot their sorrow and leapt to greet him.

"Gabriel!"

"How are you?"

"How are you feeling?"

Contraption

"Good, fine!" said Gabriel. "I'm so happy to see you!" His tail wagged in agreement.

Sebastian nuzzled his snout. "Hello, my friend. Your collar's gone!"

"Rats."

"Oh, is that a bad thing?"

"No. I mean rats gnawed it off for me."

"Ha! I see. Kids, Gabriel has agreed to stay with you and Emily. You'll be covered high and low. How does that sound?"

"It's perfect," said Miriam, petting Gabriel. "Thank you."

"All right. I'm due to meet with the scouting party to get them on their way. I brought you here to lay low until we can figure how to contact your parents again. They have to be worried sick, so I need you keep your chins up, okay? Do it for them."

"Okay," said Miriam.

"For now, get some rest. And stay in this room."

Sebastian walked away, and John looked after him until he was out of sight. "It's funny."

"What?" asked Miriam.

"He's like a big brother one second and a babysitter the next."

Millicent chuckled. "More like a *little* brother, you mean."

"Definitely," said Miriam. "He's just trying to figure everything out. What was he like, Emily? Before we came along?"

Emily was busy putting a few throw pillows on a makeshift couch made of sheets thrown over some boxes. She re-tucked the corners under and arranged the pillows to look nice. She stepped back to appraise her work.

"He's been a great friend to me," she said. "I think he appreciates my title more than some of the others, and we *really* bonded over poetry. I think if everything was happy and rosy, all he'd want to do is spend time with you and goof around. But that ain't the case. I think he's scared to death of something bad happening to you, so he gets a little overprotective."

The marmots returned with three little baskets of food.

Chapter Ten

One of them pointed at John and cooed. "Look at him!"

"He's even cuter than Sheba said!" said another.

John's face contorted. "Huh?"

"Wow," said Miriam. "Why do they like you so much, John? What did you do to them?"

"I've never met them before in my life!"

"Don't mind him, girls," said Miriam. "He gets nervous around his fans." She sat next to Millicent on a rug at the center of the room and helped with the baskets. "Thank you for the food!"

Millicent waved a raspberry for John to see. "You're gonna have to join us if you wanna eat." She bit into it and smiled with gruesome, red teeth.

Gabriel slipped between the girls, grabbed one of the baskets, and carried it to Emily's makeshift couch.

"Hey!" said Millicent.

"You traitor!" said Miriam.

John hopped on the couch and ruffled Gabriel's fur. "Ha! Good boy! Thank you!"

Miriam shrugged. "See, ladies, he's kind of a jerk, definitely not worth your time."

Emily lowered her massive body to rest on her hairy knees next to the girls with her own clutch of leaves to eat. In a sing-song voice she acted like they were at a gala. "Why, hello, ladies. How do you do? Welcome to the pah-tay."

Gabriel reclined on the couch next to John and panted happily. "You have new girlfriends?"

John blushed. "Ah, no. I don't date marmots. But I have a girlfriend back home."

"Oh, no you don't," said Miriam. "You haven't even asked her. You hafta ask her, or it's not official."

"Ugh. She's way too dark and moody for him, anyway," said Millicent as she ate. "Especially for a seventh grader. What's she trying to prove?"

Contraption

John pointed both hands at her. "What are you talking about? You're the *queen* of dark and moody!"

Emily smiled beneath her trunk. "I love this. I always like sitting around with company, but the other animals don't stop by much, mostly just my family and Sebastian. It's awesome to hear you talk about normal things."

"Yeah. We're pretty much like this at home, I guess," said Millicent. "We pick on John, John and Miri pick on me, and nobody picks on Miri."

Miriam grabbed a wide-brimmed straw hat from a pile of clothes, scooped it onto her head, and slurped a huckleberry. With a Texas accent she said, "Yep. Tha'sright. Ain't nobody messin' with me."

"That's because you fight dirty," said John.

"You give up too easy."

"I do not! I stop before you leave teeth marks!"

"She bites?" asked Gabriel. "That's my kind of kid."

Millicent repositioned to lie against Emily's folded leg. "I'll explain. John's been mad at Miri because she stood up for him."

"They were bullying him!" said Miriam. "I couldn't just *sit there*."

John groaned into a throw pillow. "I told you! No boy wants to be defended by his little sister. It's not cool, Miri. They're gonna pick on me twice as bad next year."

She pulled the hat over her eyes. "Hey. A girl's gotta do what a girl's gotta to do. Like I said, you need to learn how to defend yourself."

Those words would have set him off, just short of saying he was *too wimpy to hunt for bears*, but he felt no rush of adrenaline. His blood didn't boil. The bullies at school felt paltry compared to facing down giant bears, stepping through magical geysers, and escaping unscrupulous scientists. Miriam seemed older to him now, sitting with her big hat and her knees up around her ears as she leaned over the baskets of food. Even the way Millicent composed herself surprised him.

Confused by these new thoughts, he decided to let the argument die. The tranquility that followed was almost deafening. He touched the sore spot on his neck again.

Chapter Ten

"Hey, do you know what's missing?" asked Emily. "Marmots, come help me change!" She lurched upward and went to the bedroom area with the marmots. Music blared from behind the curtain. Emily reemerged. With her trunk she held a CD player that played a hip-hop song they didn't recognize, and she'd changed into a mammoth-sized "I ♥ NY" t-shirt and blue jeans. She bobbed to the beat, waved her trunk, and wagged her behind. The marmot girls danced with her.

"Come on, kids! This will cheer you up. It's a dance party!"

Miriam didn't hesitate. She leapt into boogying.

Millicent's mouth hung open. "Okay. The Unreachable Trees were weird, but this is officially the strangest thing I have ever seen in my entire life."

John's inclination was to throw his head back and bury his face into the throw pillow, but his attention shifted to the CD player. He stood, tossed the pillow aside, and watched the player as it floated around the room at the end of Emily's trunk.

"Wait a minute!"

Miriam stopped dancing and jumped backward to avoid one of Emily's legs. "Emily! Hold up a second!"

Emily stopped, disappointed that the dance party was ending so soon. She pressed the pause button with the fingerlike tip of her trunk. "Wassap?"

"Can we have those batteries?" asked John.

She tried to hide the player to the side. "Umm . . . will I get them back? We don't exactly have a battery store around here."

"At least, let us get a message to our parents about the collars. Please?"

"Oh! Of course, you can!"

Millicent was impressed by his thinking. She opened the back of the player to inspect the batteries. "These are normal ones. The collar uses a lithium battery. Hmm . . . All we have to do is hook the plus and minus sides to the right leads with the right amount of power and current!"

Contraption

"Ri-ight," said Miriam. "Just tell us what to do."

Millicent drummed her fingers over her lips. She gave the marmots a list of objects to look for in the Den of Antiquities. They returned dragging a plastic storage tote full of miscellaneous junk like circuit boards, twine, and duct tape.

She evaluated the collection and nodded. She handed John a small screwdriver. "See if you can open the collar."

He opened the casing and pulled out the dead battery, which was sealed in plastic.

"Can you read the voltage?"

"There's no printing."

"Hmm. Take this cover off."

He broke the plastic with the end of the screwdriver and read the voltage to Millicent.

"Okay," she said. "It'll take all four of Emily's batteries, but it needs a resistor, so we don't fry the collar."

They converged over the project like three surgeons around an operating table. Their hands glided. They twisted wire and pulled twine. They leaned until their heads were touching, and the yellow glow from their eyes lit their workspace.

They stepped back to behold their creation. Miriam shook her head like she needed to get water out of her ears. Millicent rolled the tiny screwdriver between her thumb and forefinger. Inside the plastic box, wires connected the collar to the four batteries, with a resistor attached to the return wire. Everything was tied in place, bracketed by pieces of metal. A test of the power button created a beautiful burst of static. Millicent was giddy.

Proud of themselves, they placed the radio box in the center of the room to present it to Sebastian. To pass the time, John and Miriam played with Gabriel, while Millicent continue to adjust the radio components.

But time stretched into a blur, and there was no clock to tell them what time it was or how long they'd waited.

Chapter Ten

"Where is he?" asked John at last, tossing a paper airplane he'd folded.

"He said he was going to meet the search party and come right back, right?" asked Miriam.

Millicent turned from the radio. "Why don't we look for him?"

"Where would we start?" asked John. "This place is huge!"

She held her hands out like a psychic inviting people to a séance. "No, I mean like this."

"Oh? Sure!"

They joined hands and found it was easier to focus with their eyes closed. They saw Emily, Gabriel, and the marmots, and then a few animals in the immediate vicinity, and experienced the emotional state of each creature as they passed. Their progress turned sluggish. The grelyxir in the walls acted as a barrier.

"Come on, we can do it!" said Miriam, but the impenetrable purple membrane stopped them.

"Um, kids?" said Emily.

"Push harder!" said Miriam.

Emily raised her voice. "I really think you should stop now!"

Pain shot into their minds, and a zap of energy forced their hands apart. They opened their eyes to discover Emily's room engulfed in a vortex of purple fire. Millicent was about to scream when the fire snuffed, and the room went back to normal.

Emily trumpeted. "What-da-heck was *that*?"

John collapsed onto the couch pressed his palms to his forehead. "I don't know, but it hurt!"

"Did you see Sebastian?" asked Gabriel.

"No," said Miriam. "We didn't get far."

"Okay. Let me look. I can run fast, ask around."

The exhilaration from rigging the radio vanished. They waited again while Gabriel searched the Mesa, which gave Millicent time to dwell on how each accomplishment seemed to be tarnished by some

Contraption

new setback. Miriam tried to stay optimistic, but then Gabriel returned, panting from his patrol.

"I couldn't find him. Nobody knows where he is!"

Miriam comforted Millicent while muttering about how she hadn't trusted Copernicus and how he must have had something to do with Sebastian's disappearance.

Millicent let out a swear word.

John slumped, lost on what to do.

Regardless of Sebastian's whereabouts, they were anxious to contact their parents. They couldn't wait any longer. Emily led them outside to a terrace that overlooked the lake side of the Mesa. And, if the radio worked, they decided to not tell their parents that Sebastian was missing. Not yet.

John set their contraption on the floor and turned it on.

"Hello? Mom and Dad, are you there?"

"There you are!" said their mother, and they melted into a heap of relief. "What happened? Did your battery die?"

"Yes!" said John. "And we couldn't tell you the battery died because the battery died!"

That made her laugh. "Oh, it's so good to hear your voices! We were so worried! We've been listening all morning in case you came back on."

"Hey, what have I missed?" asked their father, out of breath. They cheered, "Dad!" with another round of hellos.

They'd also decided to not tell them about the missing radios. John wanted to, but Miriam was afraid it would scare them too much.

But these batteries are going die, too! Then what do we do?

We'll figure something out.

Their mother read the news from her phone, an article entitled *Old Faithful Unfaithful?* that didn't reveal much except for one major development.

"There's a sidebar. *Three Children Missing in Yellowstone.* So, you're in the news now. I don't know how the story got out, but there we are."

Chapter Ten

"Did they interview you?" asked Miriam.

"No, that's the crazy part. Nobody knows we're here, as far as we know, and they're not letting anyone near this place."

Gabriel became alert. His good ear pivoted. "Listen!"

A scratching sound came from the side of the terrace. A large raccoon leapt from beyond the edge and sprinted across the platform to the radio and started tearing it apart.

"Must, must, must!" it chanted.

"Where are they coming from?" yelled John.

Gabriel grabbed the raccoon by the scruff, and it thrashed to scratch him. Miriam shoved her hands forward with a telekinetic burst to throw the raccoon from Gabriel's mouth.

Emily trumpeted. She slammed her feet around the radio, and John rushed to protect it with her. The raccoon climbed his body, intent on getting past him, and scratched his face.

"Must, MUST!" it cried.

Shouting, Miriam pried it off him, but it turned on her. It bit and scratched her arms.

A porcupine bounded onto the terrace from the entryway.

"Must, must, must!"

Gabriel tried to intercept the spiky animal but yelped and recoiled with his snout covered in quills. The porcupine dragged the box toward the edge.

"Must, must, must!"

Miriam ran and dove but missed as it jumped off the roof. She crawled to the edge and hoped it was still within reach. On another roof thirty feet below, the porcupine lay motionless next to the shattered box. Another rodent scurried out, grabbed the box, and made off with it.

"No!" cried Miriam. She rolled onto her back and pounded her fist on the ground next to her, looking at the sky. "Why is this happening?"

John ran to the edge. He scowled at the lower rooftop, at the dead porcupine, and held his hand to his face to stop the bleeding from where the raccoon had scratched him.

Contraption

Miriam looked at her arm and gasped at several nasty wounds oozing blood. Dark trails of it ran over her wrist and hand.

The raccoon sat terrified between them.

Gabriel approached and growled. "Who are you?"

"T–Tipper," said the raccoon, his voice shaking. "W–what's happening?"

"You don't know? You attacked with a porcupine and destroyed our radio! We're going to the hospital, and you're coming with us. No arguing! Lady Ze'eva needs to know about this."

Emily stood at the edge and whispered something to pay her respects to the porcupine. She pulled away and swung her trunk around Millicent's shoulders. "Let's go."

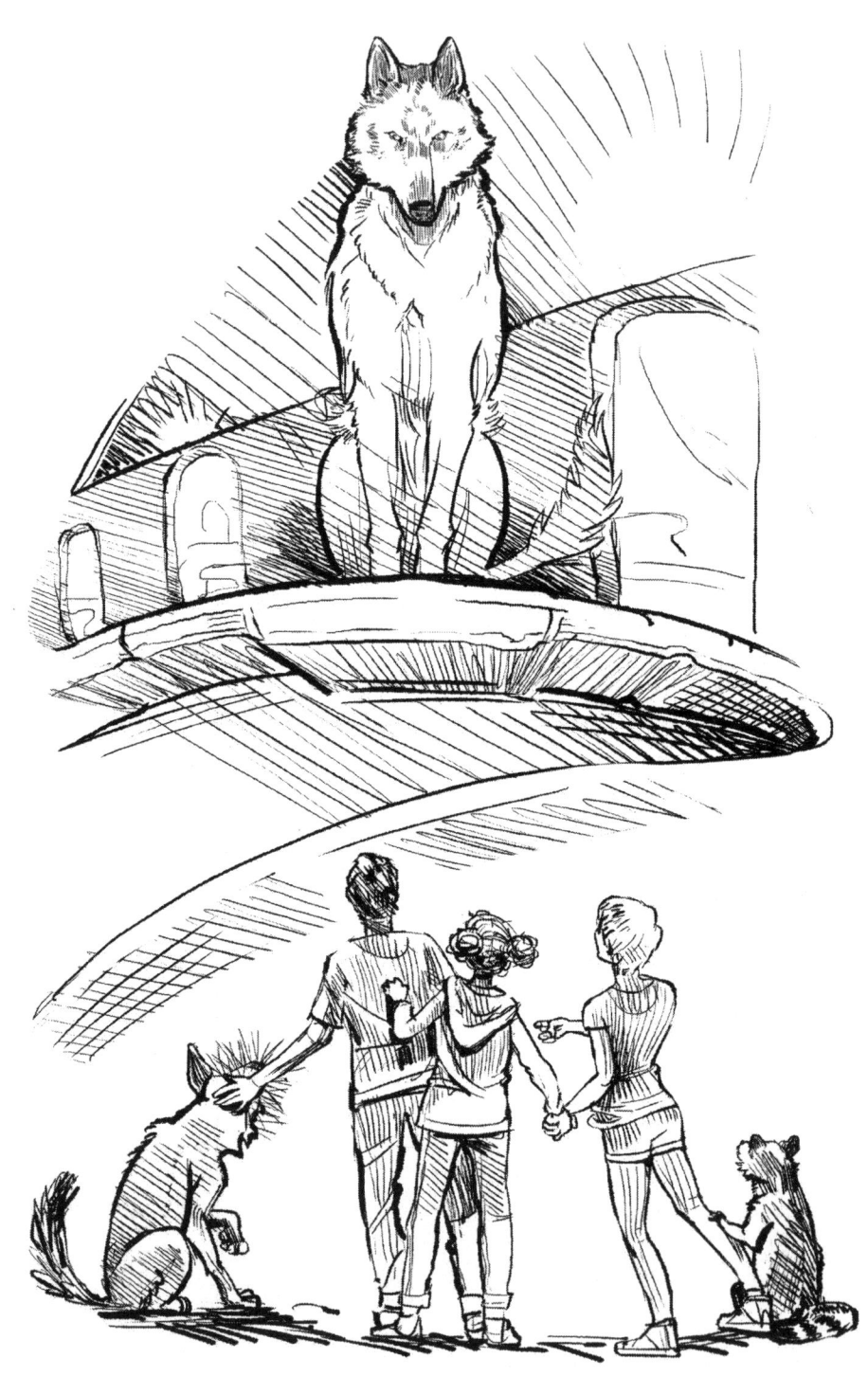

Eleven

Ze'eva

Full of quills, Gabriel's head looked like a cactus. He led them without a complaint through the Mesa to the hospital. It was a cone-shaped chamber with spiral ramps that crisscrossed to the top, high above them. Several wolves moved along the ramps or lingered in the doorways of countless rooms. Incense in stone burners filled the chamber with frankincense, which mingled with the sweet smell of grelyxir.

"Humans," said a female voice into their minds. A great, silver wolf sat several levels above them. She stood much taller than the wolves around her, and the children would have mistaken her for a statue if not for her brilliant blue eyes. They seemed to glow in the dimness. "I didn't think I'd be meeting you," she said. "What's happened?"

"Lady Ze'eva," said Emily, bowing her head. "A porcupine and this raccoon attacked us. They destroyed our radio, and the porcupine — he jumped — "

"Did he die?"

Emily couldn't seem to continue, so Miriam cleared her throat with a nervous hum to find her voice. "We think so, ma'am. He fell a long way."

"Where is his body?"

Gabriel bowed and showed no sign of the pain he was in. "He's on a roof near the base of the southwest terrace."

Two wolves sprinted to retrieve the body. Ze'eva leapt twenty feet from the ramp onto a circle of moss in front of them. Up close she was enormous, taller and leaner than Sebastian. Her fur was bristly but

Chapter Eleven

moved like silk, like it would hurt and tickle to touch it, and the silvery coat rippled white one way and black the other.

"Come here, Tipper," she said to the raccoon.

"I don't know what happened!" he blurted out. "I was at the creek with Chum — we were — we were just drinking an– an– an– and talking — and then all of a sudden, I was on that terrace!"

"You remember nothing?"

"No, ma'am!"

"This is puzzling. I ask you to stay with us, so we can examine you. The rest of you, please let my wolves attend to your injuries."

A mouse escorted Gabriel to a private room while wolves and coyotes cared for John and Miriam on the spot. The canine nurses hummed near their wounds and winced and trembled. Their eyes glowed yellow as they worked. To their astonishment, the pain faded. Two mice dressed Miriam's arm with gauze and taped a bandage over John's cheek.

Stupefied by the process, Miriam waved her arm around to assess the pain. It disappeared as she moved it.

Ze'eva stood. "Once our siphons wear off, your wounds will be tender but should heal faster. Now, if you'll follow me — I believe a friend of yours is here."

They climbed one of the spiral ramps. Miriam walked faster to get closer to the wolf.

"Excuse me, ma'am?"

"What is your name, girl with the golden hair?"

"It's Miriam, ma'am."

"Yes, Miriam?"

"I wanted to say thank you. This feels amazing!" She waved her arm again.

"You're welcome. This is our honored purpose."

"I was just curious. Do they *feel* the pain when they siphon it? That's what it looked like."

"You have good instincts. Yes, we do, but it's dispersed throughout our bodies."

"Wow," said Miriam, humbled by the concept. "What if somebody's hurt really badly?"

"We accept a greater amount of suffering to comfort the patient," said Ze'eva as a matter of fact. She stopped at a doorway and lowered her voice to a whisper. "Children, I'd like to speak with you privately. Will you meet with me?" Her eyes were so intense they seemed able to compel anyone to do anything.

Unsure, though, they looked to Emily for guidance.

"Yes, they will, Lady Ze'eva."

"Thank you, Emily. Bring them to my garden after you're finished here." Like a phantom, she leapt from the ramp and out of sight.

"Rodney!" yelled John.

On a bed of straw in a small room sat Rodney the bighorn sheep. His neck was swollen from Lucifur's bite, and claw marks raked scars down his face. And he was missing an eye.

"Greetings, young Laskows!"

When he saw the dark, empty eye socket, John stepped backward and almost fell off the ramp. Rodney stood and approached him.

"Now, now, John. Our injuries today serve to strengthen us for tomorrow, yes?"

"But you — I — "

"Look at me, John Laskow. Lucifur did this to me, not you. Not you! It was Lucifur who attacked you and your mother and stole your sisters, and it was Lucifur who attacked us in Hayden Valley."

John was speechless. Numb.

Rodney stepped closer. "It may seem impossible for you to find comfort, but please consider this: You and your sisters have survived, and, cheers to you, your parents are safe! You have much to celebrate."

John stayed quiet, consumed by guilt. He knew it was his fault, no matter how Rodney tried to comfort him with words of wisdom.

Emily hugged the ram with her trunk. "It's good to see you, you old rascal. This day has been much different than I was expecting when I

CHAPTER ELEVEN

woke up this morning, that's for sure!"

"Oh?" he asked. "Interesting! And you two must be Millicent and Miriam?"

"Yes sir!" said Miriam.

"It's a pleasure to meet you at last."

"Um, hello," said Millicent.

Emily looked back and forth and then whispered, "Hey. Ze'eva wants to talk to the kids in her garden. Are you well enough to come along?"

"Oh, she does, does she? Then, indeed, I'm well enough. This sheep wants to know what the wolf is up to."

Emily led them to the Atrium. By far the largest chamber they'd seen in the Mesa, it was a vista of plant life. The air was thick and warm like in a greenhouse. Lush gardens populated the main floor, while trees, plants, and flowers filled long, curved terraces above, with matching windows that let in the sunlight. They heard insects and a thousand singing birds. A lazy stream flowed end to end, fed by waterfalls that cascaded down the walls. At the center of the valley stood a grand, stone roundtable, dusty and overgrown with ivy.

"Hey," said Millicent. She pointed at a giant circle of blue glass in the ceiling, which was vibrant from sunlight. "That's where the battery died. We were on top of that." Nobody responded, but she was content with connecting a new piece in her imaginary map. She loved the way the light looked coming through the glass and much preferred being on this side of it.

Gabriel led them along a path past an immense line of sunflowers and over a bridge that crossed the steam. Miriam ran her fingers along the edge of the stone table and wiped the dust on her jeans.

They climbed a broad stairway set into a hillside. It was so immense, they could have been outside. Rodney clattered up the stairs with a spring in his step like he was in his natural habitat, while John watched, on the lookout for any sign of other permanent injuries.

Ze'eva

The stairs led to a grassy courtyard at the top of the hill. Miriam turned to see the view and grabbed John's arm.

"Look!"

The climb hadn't seemed exceptionally steep, but once they could see how high they were, with a commanding view of the Atrium, it looked incredibly steep indeed.

"Keep movin'!" said Emily, and she jogged to the back of the courtyard and stood breathless against the wall.

Ze'eva's voice flew around them. "You have grown powerful, young humans." Her tall ears and long snout appeared at the top of the steps. "But you have yet to reach your full potential."

Her icy blue eyes paused on each of them. She leapt from the stairs like a streak of silver. She nipped John's heel, Miriam's elbow, and the back of Millicent's neck with lightning speed. Millicent squealed and hunched her shoulders. They flinched in case she attacked again, but when they looked for her, she was already sitting next to Emily at the back of the hilltop. They formed an awkward huddle and held the places she'd bitten.

"Thank you for coming," she said. "We're away from prying ears here." A curtain of water fell from the ceiling to surround the courtyard, giving them complete privacy. The sheet of water obscured the view with a shimmering, translucent film. Ze'eva seemed to smile. "Please relax. There is method to my madness. Did my teeth hurt you, Millicent?"

Millicent's stomach convulsed as she nodded. Her private thoughts were a tirade, and she didn't care if they slipped out. *Did your teeth hurt? Yes, your teeth hurt, you crazy wolf! Please relax? Please relax! Gourd almighty, I hate this place!*

"You would be dead if I were an enemy, your neck snapped. And John, what about you?"

"Yes. It hurt," he said. He touched the spot and looked at his hand. He expected to see blood, but she hadn't broken his skin.

"You would be crippled, hobbled at the ankle. But not you, Miriam.

CHAPTER ELEVEN

Oh, you're the quick one, aren't you?"

Everyone's eyes shifted to Miriam. Her face flushed. "I thought you must have missed me, ma'am."

"Never," said the wolf.

She tried to remember. Ze'eva appeared. She ran, and then . . . "I guess I sort of blocked you."

"Yes!" said Ze'eva. "But how? Tell them how!"

"I don't know — "

"You're the hardest hitter, the highest jumper, and the fastest runner. So, you know how, whether you realize it or not."

Miriam gulped. It was like a teacher had asked her a question when she wasn't been paying attention. "I'm sorry, but I — "

Ze'eva sprang, her eyes fierce, and her teeth closed around Miriam's forearm. Miriam screamed, toppled backward, and hid her face.

"Mir, look!" said John.

She peeked. Ze'eva's jaw opened and closed like she was gnawing on rawhide, but little bursts of yellow light blocked her teeth from touching the skin. She pulled away and sat next to Emily again.

"Egads," said Rodney. His face slackened so his bottom teeth protruded.

"It's simple," said Ze'eva. "You need; therefore, you do. I wasn't using my full strength, but, in the same way, the raccoon should have caused grave damage, yet you managed to block most of his attack. You must share this skill with your siblings."

Miriam didn't know how she would do such a thing, but she nodded anyway.

"Learning to defend yourselves is wise, but I believe the time will come when you need to fight."

"Let's take one thing at a time, Lady Wolf," said Rodney. "I think it's wiser that they learn to avoid conflict all together."

"Can you disagree, Domcorn, the possibility of danger exists no matter how careful they are?"

Rodney's fuzzy chin rocked back and forth as he ground his teeth and broadcast two emotions: *Agitation. Uncertainty.*

"You cannot disagree."

He shook his head. "It isn't right."

"No, Domcorn. Robbing them of every advantage isn't right. The children must learn to be ruthless, for they will be treated ruthlessly!"

"Let me understand this urgency, please."

"The boundary is closed. The carnivores are depleting their food stores and will have nothing left to eat. They can endure on carrion for a while, but desperation will set in, and they — we — will be forced to decide between adhering to the Code or breaking it to survive. The time is ripe for Lucifur to offer them hope. He's becoming a champion to them, a dangerous leader."

Rodney lowered his head and projected sadness. "I see — I had no idea. Yes, then I agree they should practice, but I caution you, children, you must do so privately."

"Okay, we will," said John. "But why privately?"

"We now know that Lucifur has agents among us. While he cannot walk boldly into the Mesa, no one thought twice about the stride of an incoming raccoon and porcupine. We mustn't let the other animals see what you can do — nor what you may learn to do — lest they report back to him. Personally, I wish to continue protecting you while at the same time protecting the citizens of Caldera. Seeing what you can do would be unsettling to them."

"Well spoken," said Ze'eva. "From now on, we'll all be watching over to keep you safe."

Rodney shifted his weight between hooves and flicked his tail. "Lady, I mean no impudence, but may I ask why you have this sudden interest in the children?"

"I tried to ignore the fact that they were here," said Ze'eva. "I stayed in the shadows when Emily welcomed them and during their farewell banquet. Sebastian told me his plan, and I deemed it a good one."

She looked at the children with her icy blue eyes. As cold as they were in appearance, there was incredible warmth there, too. "And I was

Chapter Eleven

relieved when you returned to you homeworld. I thought your time here was done. Fate, it seems, has something else in store for you.

"So, Domcorn, I can no longer ignore what's happening. If Lucifur continues to break the Code and means to harm these children, then it's my duty to protect them. And if he's building an army, then it's my duty to protect Caldera."

"I misjudged you, Lady Wolf," said Rodney. "I have pledged to protect them, as well, and it will be an honor to work beside you."

Millicent decided she would never get used to seeing a wolf and a sheep engaged in a conversation.

John reeled as their words jumbled in his head. Danger? Ruthlessness? *Armies*? He felt like he was being thrown aboard a departing train without knowing the destination or why.

"Excuse me, ma'am?"

"Yes, John?"

"It's just that — I don't know. I still don't understand what's happening or how we'll get home again. And nobody seems to be worried about Sebastian!" His throat tightened as he spoke "He disappeared, and nobody cares that he's missing!"

He glanced at Rodney's missing eye. A horrible feeling surfaced that had been building up since they returned.

"Is all this our fault?"

"No!" said Ze'eva. "No, John, the answer is no. You mustn't burden yourself that way."

"It's like Rodney said," said Miriam. "It's all Lucifur's fault."

"Yes, Miriam," said Ze'eva. "But it's critical to ask *why* Lucifur behaves this way. Gabriel knows the answer."

"It was Nidever," said Gabriel. "He changed everything. I know. I saw how he treated the animals."

"Yes," said Ze'eva. "Lucifur was tricked by the humans. They were cruel to him, so he believes humans to be cruel. He believes that if people find a way into Caldera they will exploit it and destroy everything we hold dear, so — whether this is true or not — he's telling the animals that human beings are a threat."

"Oh," said John, his face pale. "That's not good."

"No, it isn't, especially for the three of you. Does this answer help?"

"Yes, ma'am," he said, but he hesitated with the same questions. "But what about Sebastian? And getting home?"

The wolf clapped one of her enormous paws on his shoulder. "I wish I were as powerful as you think I am, but I don't have those answers, not until we understand what's happened to the boundary. Please know that I'm as worried about Sebastian as you are, and his disappearance *has* created a panic among the animals."

John nodded. The tone in her voice was comforting, though her words were not.

"This is Pandora's box, my boy; you've opened it and seen the evils of the world. Now close it quickly and hold onto your hope!"

The curtain of water fell open. She sniffed the cool breeze that swept through the Atrium.

"It's going to be a fine evening. I'll be on patrol while you sleep. And you keep resting, Domcorn."

She ran from the hillside.

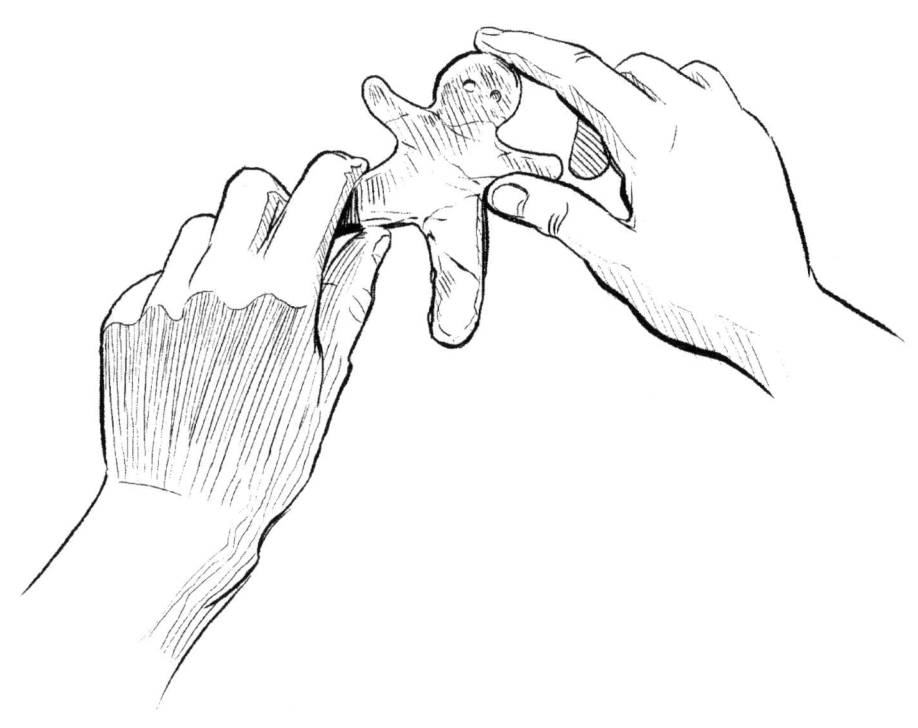

Twelve
Curious Minds, Curious Caves

"You've been quiet, Emily," said Miriam as they walked back to the mammoth's room.

"Yeah. I know. With all this talk of war, I'm worried that I won't be able to protect you. I couldn't live with myself if anything happened to you!"

"Are you kidding? You're our biggest, strongest defender!"

Emily smiled. "Thanks. I had nothing to contribute to that conversation, though. The whole time, all I kept thinking was, 'Wow, she's a big wolf!'"

Miriam gave a halfhearted laugh. "Yeah, me too."

Once they were back in the room, they felt more trapped and directionless than ever. But then Rodney asked, "Do you know anything about physics?"

"Huh?" asked John.

"Physics! What do you know about it?"

"Not much. A little, I guess. We probably should know more since our dad is a physics professor."

"Well," said Millicent, "I've done some experiments. Messed around with circuit kits and old computers."

"Can you tell me the definition?" asked Rodney.

"Of what, *physics*? Uh . . ."

She bit her bottom lip and thought about it. Her parents' voices swirled in her head. One conversation with her father when she was five years old was about gravity keeping them on the ground. Another conversation with her mother when she was six was about how a construction crane used a counterweight to carry big things.

CHAPTER TWELVE

"Your eyes are glowing!" said Miriam.

"Physics is how the universe works," said Millicent, "and we use the rules when we create everything, like pulleys or space shuttles."

"Delightfully described!" said Rodney. "Now, I believe — strongly — that you should practice your mental skills as much as the physical manifestations of your abilities."

"I like that idea!"

"That sounds like *school* to me," said John, crossing his arms.

Rodney's eyes narrowed, looking coy. "Is that so? Sounds like school? Well, how would you like a School for Telepaths?"

John nodded with a bemused, you've-got-my-attention face.

"Excellent. Let's see how well you can transfer information to each other. Think again about physics! What have you learned?"

They held hands. At first, they weren't sure how to proceed, but then their eyes started to glow, and images started to appear in their minds. There were flashes of textbook pages. Their father's voice. Their mother. Bill Nye. Carl Sagan. John's seventh grade teacher. Millicent's internet searches.

More of Millicent's internet searches.

"Good gravy!" said John. "Mill knows a lot more about physics than I do."

"Yeah, a whole lot more!" said Miriam.

"All right!" said Rodney. "So, tell me: what is the first law of thermodynamics?"

They searched the swirling images. John and Miriam discovered that Millicent knew the word but not its meaning. They peeked at each other and shrugged.

"We don't know," said Millicent.

"Hmm. Let's try an easier one. Gravity causes two bodies of *what* to be brought toward each other?"

"Mass," said Millicent.

John and Miriam gave her wry looks. "You can't just answer if you know," said Miriam. "Try to give it to us."

"Oh. Sorry. I thought . . . everybody knew that. Okay. Give us another one, Rodney."

The ram thought for a moment. "How far is Jupiter from the Sun?"

Light flashed in their eyes, and they answered together. "480 million miles!"

"Yep. Millicent knew that one," said John.

Miriam wore a goofy grin. "Ha! I had no idea, but then I did!"

"Excellent!" said Rodney. "Let's see . . . Who published Astronomia nova?"

"No clue," said Millicent without even trying.

John gave her an overdramatic, puzzled look. "Um, Milly, do you not fully understand how this game is supposed to be played?"

She tutted and lifted her chin. "As if you would know that."

"Let's stay on task here," said Rodney. "What is Einstein's famous equation?"

"$E=mc^2$," they said together.

"And what does this equation mean?"

They stumbled. Their eyes glowed brighter as they pieced it together.

"It's . . ."

"He said it meant . . ."

"Something about nuclear bombs . . ."

"The E is energy . . ."

"Right."

" . . . and energy equals . . ."

"Mass!"

"Mass times the speed of light squared!"

"So, a little bit of matter — "

" — can release an enormous amount of energy!"

"BOOM!"

Chapter Twelve

Rodney looked dizzy from following their train of thought. "Quite right! It's conclusive! You can't recall something if you haven't learned it, but you *can* share knowledge if at least one of you knows it."

John chuckled. "You mean if Millicent knows it."

Miriam rubbed her temples. "This is making me dizzy."

"Yes. It's been a long day. We can pause here. That was just something I was curious about." *I'll let Emily watch them for now. I must tell the council that the situation is worse than we feared.*

"Why is it worse?" asked Millicent with a trace of light behind her eyes.

Rodney did a double take. "What did you say?"

"You said you were gonna talk to the council while Emily watches us, and the situation is worse than you thought."

How horrible! They're reading minds outright! Dangerous! Horrible! The others will hate them!

Millicent's eyes glowed brighter. "I'm sorry! I can't help it! Who will hate us?"

"No! Stop!" said Rodney, and he sprung across the room and shook his head.

She looked at the floor. She felt like a monster.

"You must control this intrusion! You have no right to read the private mind of another animal!"

Emily startled them with a loud trumpet blat. "Give 'em a break, Rodney!" *You pompous oaf! I'll squash you like a grape!*

Those were Emily's private thoughts, and while they were humorous, the words felt ugly, like they'd read her diary without permission.

Rodney stomped. "If the animals learn that their deepest thoughts aren't safe, them they will sympathize with Lucifur."

"What's the big deal?" asked Gabriel. "We all have special abilities. Wolves heal. Cats phase. Bears read emotions — control minds."

Rodney closed his one eye. "And if the children read your deepest thoughts?"

"Let them! I have nothing to hide."

"Neither do I," said Emily.

They wondered if she would say the same if she knew they'd overheard her thoughts. Miriam stepped forward and put her hand over her heart. "We'll work on controlling it. We'll control it and keep it a secret. No one will know."

"If you'll excuse me," said Rodney, "I must retire. Stay in this room until I return."

At first, the kids didn't know how to react, despite Emily and Gabriel's reassurances. As the hours wore on, their insecurity and fear gave way to anger and impatience.

Miriam paced and fumed.

"It isn't fair, him treating us like that! He was the one who wanted to us to practice! How were we supposed to know? Now there's this invisible line we're not allowed to cross, but we don't know where it is!"

John sat on the couch and petted Gabriel. He gave the dog a squeeze. "Hey, do you trust us?"

"With my life."

He believed him; his swollen face and broken ear made him look like a prize fighter. Gabriel kept his poise the way only dogs can after they've been hurt, He carried on as though nothing was wrong.

"Can we try it with you?" asked John. "Like, you think of something private, and we'll try to see what it is. That way, we can find the line, you know? Would that be okay?"

"Sure. I have no problem with that."

They surrounded him but decided not to hold hands since they weren't holding hands when Millicent read Rodney's mind. Their eyes started to glow, which made Gabriel look back and forth between them with some apprehension.

"Gulp! All right, let me think of something."

He slipped from his telepathic voice to his private thoughts. To their surprise, they followed him with ease and glided through his mind as

Chapter Twelve

he searched for a moment that they wouldn't see. His memories floated like bubbles along strands of seaweed in a blue ocean. He settled on a time when the scientists trained him in Nidever's lab and then focused on a beef treat they gave him whenever he did something correctly.

"Okay, I'm thinking of something."

"Beef treat!" said Millicent louder than she intended.

"Wow! That was fast!"

"Fast," she said, self-conscious, "and incredibly easy." She twisted the drawstrings on her hoodie.

"The important thing is — did you find the line you were looking for?"

Miriam nodded and pantomimed. "Yeah, it was like we were cruising along like this and then — shloop! — we went into your mind and could see everything."

"Okay, that *is* a little scary," said Emily. "I can see why Rodney made the fuss, but I still think he overreacted."

John agreed with her. This was scary. His brain tipped toward hers and then Gabriel's as though everything was made of magnetic jelly. He could slide into either of their minds if he wanted to, so he straightened his posture to resist.

They retreated to opposite sides of the living room. Emily's chamber had become a place of solace, even though their first time there was just that morning. That's the way Caldera seemed to work. It presented a thousand strange and scary moments, so the least strange and the least scary felt the most comfortable.

It struck John again that everything they learned about Caldera was, ultimately, so they could leave it again.

He adjusted the throw pillows on the couch and lifted the sheet and comforter thrown over it to see exactly what it was comprised of. It was an assortment of milk crates, a mini-steamer trunk, and stacks of folded cardboard. Lifting the drape released a pungent scent of musty paper, so he let it drop back down. It reminded him of visiting a friend's house. Everyone has a friend whose house is just a little messier, whose sounds and smells become familiar and endearing even though they were questionable at first.

He petted Gabriel's head and then rested his chin on him to feel the warmth of his fur and to remind himself of when Gabriel nuzzled up to him in Nidever's lab. He loved this dog.

Yes, this was a comfortable place. But Rodney's concerns about them still filled him with dread.

"Emily?"

"Yeah?"

"Rodney said the other animals would hate us if they found out. Um . . . are we still safe here?"

Ze'eva's voice brushed into the room. Everyone looked to find her standing in the doorway. "Yes, you are safe. Don't let a friend's momentary lapse of judgment worry you. I've had a good chat with him."

She stepped in with a graceful tip toe and sat next to Emily. The clip-clop of hooves approached. Rodney arrived with mounds of blankets draped over his back.

"I should very much like to camp here with you, if you would be so kind to permit me."

The group met him with silence. Millicent didn't trust him. Miriam waited to hear more. And John stopped petting Gabriel and stared again at Rodney's missing eye.

Rodney dropped the blankets and stood tall. "Children, I owe you an apology. I invited you to push your capabilities, and then I responded terribly. The truth is, I have come to care for you dearly, and I should not have left you in that way. I am sorry."

John approached him. "It's okay, Rodney. Our wounds today serve to strengthen us for tomorrow, right?"

Rodney leaned his head back. "Good show, young man. Good show."

The group arranged their sleeping spaces, and the long day came to an end.

Chapter Twelve

In the middle of the night, Millicent's dream about her puzzle toy returned.

Click-clack!

This time, the puzzle dissolved sooner to leave her facing the dark tunnel. Pain hung in the air like humidity and clung to her. It slipped into her belly button, filled her stomach, and rose up into her throat until she could taste it. It was copper on her tongue like a dirty penny. An invisible force pulled her into the blackness, and the sensation reminded her of how her body moved under Lucifur's command. He was nearby. She knew that his eyes would appear in the dark, and the farther she went, the sharper the fear became until —

Her eyes shot open. She and Miriam were snuggled up to Emily, who snored with her long, knobby limbs spilled across the ground. Ze'eva was gone, and Gabriel sat near John as he slept on the couch.

"Good morning," he whispered.

She furrowed her brow momentarily. She had to separate the bad feeling from the dream from the bad feeling she always had when confronted by a dog. Gabriel quirked his head, though, and his broken ear reminded her of who he was and all he'd done for them. She took a deep breath.

Good morning.

"Nightmare? You moaned in your sleep."

Yeah. It wasn't too bad. She quickly scanned the room and saw that Ze'eva was missing. Suddenly missing her was surprising. Out of all the animals they'd met, the giant wolf should have been the most terrifying, yet Millicent had been inexplicably comforted by her presence and wished she were still there. *Where's Ze'eva?*

"Checking in at the hospital. Said she would ask around about Sebastian. No new news."

She hadn't held much hope that they would hear something, yet her heart still sank. She decided that she should have been more cynical. Skepticism always helped her avoid disappointment.

Though Gabriel wasn't the largest animal she'd encountered, he was still a good-sized German shepherd. She patted the top of his head (because that's what people do with dogs, right?) and was careful to avoid his broken ear and the swollen flesh with tiny dots of dried blood from the porcupine quills.

Boy. You look like a pin cushion.

"Is it that bad?"

His emotions hit her. He was pure love, pure attention, pure poise and action and patient impatience. But mostly he was pure love. Why did this dog care so much for them? From the moment they met him, he seemed willing to risk his life to help them, and his humility was overwhelming. It was against her nature, but she kissed his forehead and was surprised to enjoy the soft, warm fuzz against her lips.

No, it's not too bad.

She sat on the ground next to him and surveyed her companions. Rodney slept with his head rolled to the side, and his horns looked like someone discarded a Medieval helmet. John slumbered with his mouth open and his legs draped over the sides of the couch. Miriam, on her side next to Emily, always looked serene while she slept.

Sickening, thought Millicent. *No unflattering poses, no snoring, no wide-open mouth. My sister is a friggin' Disney princess.*

And Emily — how on Earth did they get to be friends with a Columbian mammoth, and such a quirky one at that? She admired Emily's room. It had the false-Bohemian style older girls seemed to like, and she realized that she didn't know how old Emily was. She acted like a teenager sometimes.

The Motherly Mammoth of the Mesa, she thought, and she was proud of her alliteration.

With one hand on Gabriel's head, she rubbed the lumpy stone ground with her other hand. The irregular texture felt like a petrified carpet. Her fingers found a crack and traced it along a curve.

A defined edge in the crack made her look. It hadn't come from wear or the ground shifting; it was carved and intricate and traversed the floor like a winding river. She moved onto her hands and knees and

Chapter Twelve

followed it to the center of the room where it continued under the carpet. Curious, she folded the rug back to reveal a smooth patch in the floor in the shape of a stingray.

Her eyes flashed yellow.

Mary Lake.

The stingray looked just like Mary Lake, which she recognized from pouring over maps of Yellowstone. And then it dawned on her: the crack *was* a river, and the bumpy texture was the forest.

Gabriel trotted along with his tail wagging as she explored the rest of the room. She stepped over the sleeping bodies and peeked under Emily's piles of clothing and fabric.

Holy custard! This whole floor is a map!

She pulled aside a banner of gold fabric on the wall. The assemblage dislodged from whatever was holding it up and fell over her. The wall was covered in a bas-relief sculpture of a mountain vista. Her eyes flashed in recognition again.

The Gallatin Range. This is facing west.

She tiptoed along the wall and realized that it was curved. She hadn't noticed the curvature before because the partitions and drapery blocked the view. The horizon scene continued all the way around.

This isn't just a map. This whole room is a panorama!

She returned to Mary Lake. *This is where we are,* she thought, and she put her hands where the Mesa would be. The carpet of forest rippled as though wind was blowing across the treetops. She gasped as three human handprints sunk into the floor, like someone had pressed their hands into wet cement. They were left hands, arranged in a circle so the fingers pointed inward. She put her hand in one, which was adult-sized, and it engulfed her tiny fingers. After a moment, the forest puffed up like rising bread under her hand and erased the prints.

"What was that?" asked Gabriel.

I — I don't know! She activated the handprints a few times, just to be sure she wasn't hallucinating. Each time, they appeared, remained for a moment, and then disappeared again. Her thoughts went crazy.

Curious Minds, Curious Caves

Handprints? Human handprints? Is it because I'm a human? Why are they here? Why are there three of them? How is the rock moving like this? What the HECK is going on here?

She shook John and Miriam awake and showed them the map but resisted showing them the handprints.

"This is cool, Milly!" said Miriam. She kept her voice down so as not to wake the others. "I can't believe you noticed it. Well, yes I can, but you know what I mean!"

Millicent nodded. She wanted to let them process the room, but they didn't seem to be as impressed by it as she was. She sighed and brought them to the center.

"This lake is behind the Mesa. I put my hand here, where the Mesa would be." She gestured over the spot without touching it. "Check it out."

"Huh?" said John.

"Put your hands here."

"Mm-kay?"

John placed his palms where she indicated, and the three handprints sank into the rock again. He and Miriam gasped. Miriam dropped to all fours to trace the edges with him. They yanked their hands away when the indentations rose.

"Holy cow!" said Miriam. "What is this?"

"I don't know," said Millicent. "I don't know what it means."

"Here," said John, scooting over on his knees. "Everyone put their hand in one."

They knelt in a circle, and they each placed a hand in one of the prints. A flash of yellow light sent a jolt through their arms. The walls rumbled around them, and they turned to see tiny, carved animals stampede across the floor like windup toys. Gabriel barked. Rodney and Emily startled awake from the noise.

A stone wolf ran to the center of the room next to the lake, and the tiny animals surrounded it in neat rows. The wolf threw its head back and howled into their minds. Gabriel whimpered.

Chapter Twelve

"Is that coming from the rock?" asked Miriam.

The wolf panted, and they could hear the breath. They were afraid to go near it, even though it was only an inch tall. It howled again.

Ze'eva rushed into the room and froze at the sight of the animated rock. She threw her head back, too, and howled in unison.

"What is this? What did you do?"

"Three handprints appeared, and we touched them," said Millicent.

"Handprints?"

"Yes," said Miriam. "Like . . . human handprints!"

"What are they doing?" asked Emily, waving her trunk over the scene. The stone animals looked around as though they were waiting for something to happen.

Ze'eva studied the wolf. It would have been enormous compared to the animals around it, even larger than she was. It bayed again, and her pupils contracted to tiny dots as she howled along with it.

"I remember this call! Though I've never heard it before, I know it by heart!"

"What does it mean?" asked John.

"It's a cry of calling, a great beckoning."

"A great beckoning," whispered Millicent.

The stone wolf bayed, and Ze'eva joined again. "Curse it!" she said, sounding flabbergasted. "I can't resist when he does that!"

"He?" asked Rodney, who'd been watching quietly. "You can sense that it's a male wolf?"

Ze'eva paused. "Apparently so." She stepped to the center, careful not to step on any of the little animals and sniffed the wolf. "I wonder who he is."

Millicent explained how the room was a map of the area and that the place she touched was where the Mesa would be.

Rodney looked around and clucked his tongue. "Good gracious! I wouldn't have seen it, but you're right! This is our plateau!"

The stone wolf howled, but this time Ze'eva struggled to compose herself. She winced, cocked her head, and opened one eye. She looked at the children when the howling stopped.

"That wolf," she said, "is calling for a human."

She declared that they should clear the room. After promising Emily they would put everything back where they found it, they disassembled and carried all her belongings, partitions, and draperies into the hallway.

Millicent was right. The empty chamber presented a sweeping, three-dimensional panorama of the Central Plateau. Every object was in motion. A hole in the wall opened to let light stream in and was meant to represent the sun as it rose and moved along its path across the sky.

They sat in a circle outside the assembly of stone animals. The big wolf at the center howled and waited.

"What do you think it wants, calling for a human?" asked Miriam, but nobody had an answer. She wrapped her fingers around a miniature bison. To her surprise, it lifted from the floor and squirmed like a living thing. She let it hop down to rejoin its herd.

"How is this possible? I mean — how can stone move like this?"

Millicent held her palm to the floor next to her. The stone was hard and cold, yet the treetops swayed against her skin like feathers. The floor sucked the warmth from her hand. In response, she rubbed back and forth to create heat through friction. Yellow light flashed from her eyes, and when she looked, some of the rock had rolled into an oblong tube, like putty.

"Um, guys? Come and look at this."

They gathered around her and murmured, but she ignored them and put both hands on the floor. Energy flowed from her and grew warmer as the ground squished like clay until it was as soft as dough. An idea struck her.

"The wolf is calling for a human?"

Her eyes glowing, she lifted a bit of the rock and molded it into the shape of a person. It looked like a tiny, grey gingerbread man, less than an inch tall. She set it on the floor as the light in her eyes faded.

Chapter Twelve

To their astonishment, the figurine came to life. It shook its head and looked at its crude shape in wonder. The rounded ends of its arms split into fingers. Stone molded to look like cloth to cover its body, which was becoming male, and details rippled into his face, hair and clothing until he matched the level of artistry of the scene around him.

He sprinted down an aisle between two rows of animals to the wolf at the center. He dropped to his knees, and the wolf bowed in return, their foreheads touching. He ruffled the wolf's fur. All the animals bowed.

Miriam was covering her mouth in shock. "Milly . . . How did you do that?"

She shook her head. "I don't know. I just did it."

There was a quiet moment. The man and the wolf looked outward. Hundreds of human figures appeared at the edges of Emily's room, arriving from the miniature forest.

The children yelled, Emily trumpeted, and Gabriel yelped as they moved aside to let the tiny humans pass to the center. There were men, women, and children, all dressed in the same, simple attire and all an inch tall.

The stone wolf rubbed against the man and then ran out to the edge of the assembled animals, all of whom turned to face outward. The humans at the center fell on their hands and knees and rubbed the ground in circles in unison. The ground swelled beneath them.

While they worked, some of the people collected food and water. Older children helped the adults while the younger ones played under the care of the wolves and sheep.

It occurred to Millicent what they might be doing in that spot, the very spot where she was standing in real life, and her mouth fell open.

"Are they creating the Mesa?"

They watched, stunned.

Ze'eva nodded. "The creation of the Mesa! Etched right here in its living rock!"

Curious Minds, Curious Caves

The amazement cooled as they watched, and watched, and watched. Questions replaced wonder, questions about who these people were, why they were doing what they were doing, and how long this animation would last.

As the day wore on, Rodney and Ze'eva took turns leaving to tend their duties. Gabriel patrolled the hallway several times but preferred staying in the room. The marmot girls brought them food for lunch and then a late dinner as the hours passed into nighttime.

The Mesa scene continued to play. More miniature humans entered the scene and helped to raise new sections of the ground around the base and widen the structure's footprint.

The kids rearranged their bedding, which was supplemented by even more blankets and pillows that the marmots brought from the Den after John mentioned how hard the couch was the night before. Despite Miriam's warning about him being kind of a jerk, they still hovered around him wherever he went in the room and giggled a lot when he wasn't looking. He relaxed and played nice with them, though, because he was good with small children and knew their crush on him was harmless. And once they were able to play a hand-clapping game with him, they seemed to relax, too.

They changed into comfy clothes. Millicent sat with her legs folded and watched the Mesa scene play. The weight of the day left her exhausted. Now that it was bedtime, all she could think about was how much she missed her parents. They'd outgrown being tucked into bed, but she missed their nighttime routine, the asking to stay up later to watch another episode of something on Netflix, dragging her feet toward brushing her teeth, and the great hugs that ended each day.

I miss them, too, said Miriam, reading her mind and emotions. *I miss them so much.*

Sad gobble. Squelch . . . feels, said John.

The girls nodded at first, as though this was a normal thing to say.

Wait. What? asked Miriam.

Grr! How talk good?

Chapter Twelve

John? asked Millicent. *Was that supposed to be in English?*

Grumble.

Miriam shook her head in disbelief.

Millicent giggled. "Did you just say, 'sad-gobble-squelch-feels'? What does *that* mean?"

"Argh! I can't do it like you two!"

Miriam couldn't keep a straight face. "Sad gobble? Tee hee."

And Millicent fell over laughing. "Squelch feels! Doctor, I've got a case of the squelch feels!"

John wanted to be angry, but his belly convulsed. It was pretty darn funny, and he suddenly couldn't breathe through the laughter. "Imagine . . . imagine trying to explain that to somebody!"

Miriam's face turned red, and her eyes watered. "Sad-gobble-squelch-feels? Oh, that's just — that's just how my brother talks!"

Millicent's gut hurt. "Stop! Stop! I can't! I can't! No more!"

The fit of laughter was a perfect release after days of seriousness. They settled back into missing their parents, worrying about Sebastian, and wondering how they were ever going to get home, but the cathartic mirth helped to ease them to sleep.

The Mesa continued to rise.

"He's tireless," said Ze'eva.

Miriam woke a moment before and lay with her eyes closed. *How did she know I was awake?* The melodic sound of Ze'eva's voice was lovely to wake up to, though. She missed Sahra's voice, too. It was terser, more clipped, while Ze'eva's was warmer, almost motherly. She wondered what the cat was up to and if she'd ever see her again.

She propped on her elbows to find the big wolf sitting outside the circle of stone animals. The miniature Mesa was three feet tall and beginning to resemble its current silhouette.

She stood next to Ze'eva and watched. Even seated, Ze'eva was a head taller than her.

"Who are you talking about?"

Curious Minds, Curious Caves

"Him," said Ze'eva, nodding toward the giant wolf. He ran around the perimeter and paused to speak with an eagle. "He's gone around ten times in the past hour, yet he doesn't seem tired at all." Her eyes sparkled, and warmth radiated from her. "He's leading, offering morale to the animals so they keep their strength. He's ensuring that they have food and water. His lieutenants are the smaller wolves, and each is assigned to an animal group. See? There's one by the beavers. There's another with the bison. They're all protecting the humans while they work."

Miriam watched with a sudden sense of dread. "Protecting them from what?"

"Good question.'

While they ate breakfast, Miriam told John and Millicent what Ze'eva had told her. "Don't you think it's a strange coincidence that both she and Copernicus talked about war, and then we find this scene the next day?"

"There are a lot of strange coincidences," said John, "but yes, I do."

"What do you mean?" asked Millicent.

"Follow me."

He led them to Sebastian's room at the top of the stairs, where the bear's borrowed materials were still in a pile on the floor. He unfolded the tattered map of Yellowstone and invited them to kneel around it with him.

"Okay, look. Lucifur attacked me and Mom here by Grizzly Lake. You and Dad went from our campsite here at Norris all the way across the park to the Lake Clinic. Lucifur took you from there, right? Isn't that strange? That means he walked all this way in one day to get to you when he could have grabbed any two kids along the way."

Millicent became alert and leaned close to the map. "I never thought about it like that. He walked over twenty miles to get to us!"

Miriam shivered and crossed her arms. "He came for us on purpose? Like, specifically us?"

Chapter Twelve

"Yes," said John. "And here's another thing: he didn't use me to get back here. All he did was force me in and then went after you."

Miriam shivered again. "That's creepy. Like the fact that there are three handprints and there are three of us. I mean, if it were only two of us, we couldn't have activated Emily's room."

John and Millicent looked at each other and then jostled Miriam's arm. "You're a genius!" said Millicent.

"Sebastian said Lucifur was obsessed with learning about Caldera," said John. "But if only humans can do certain things . . . "

Miriam caught up with their thinking and looked horrified. "What do you think he wants us to do?"

They sat in silence and watched the little stone humans work and wondered if they were right, and if they were right, what it could mean.

The Mesa was complete with one, glaring omission: the main tower wasn't built yet. Millicent guessed it must have been a later addition. The miniature people and animals dispersed. Most of them entered their new home while some returned to the forest. The structure melted into the floor, and the room returned to its original state of stillness.

"It's a history book," said Millicent, sure of herself.

"That's my hypothesis, as well," said Rodney. "And if all of the artwork throughout the Mesa is connected, then this is but one chapter in a very large book."

They stood lost in thought. John asked the question that was haunting everyone.

"What happened to all those people?"

Thirteen

Dust Is the Only Secret

Ze'eva demanded they take a break to rest their minds and bodies and fears. "You need baths," she said, "and the lot of you should have your wounds redressed — you're like magnets for mishap."

As Sebastian warned, because the geothermal activity stopped, the water in the bathing pool had long turned cold. Miriam bristled with goosebumps and bellowed like a warrior to prove that she could take it. Millicent turned blue and shivered uncontrollably. "I'd r-rather b-be d-dirty, d-darn it!"

The scratches on her legs healed, and she had no other injuries aside from a bruised tailbone from falling on her bottom so often. Ze'eva's mice wrapped Miriam's arm and gave John a new bandage for his face. The swelling in Gabriel's face subsided. Ze'eva lifted his broken ear to its proper, pointed position and sighed as she let it flip down again.

"I'm afraid you're stuck with this, little brother."

"Well, I can't see it, so what does it matter?"

"Ha. Good point."

On their way back to Emily's room, they paused in one of the main hallways. Surrounded by bas-relief carvings and intrigued by Rodney's notion that the artwork might be connected, they decided to investigate.

The scenes in the hallway were arranged in panels and depicted animals in various settings. Sheep grazed near a pond. Bobcats lounged on a bluff. And Millicent's stomach filled with butterflies. She was daunted by the endless artwork.

"I guess we could start here, right?"

Miriam ran her hand along the bumps and grooves of a forest tableau. Her eyes flashed, and the surface of the wall rippled under her

Chapter Thirteen

fingertips. Grass in the scene swayed. Boughs waved, and squirrels jumped between the branches.

"Oh, wow!" she said. "Everyone, look!"

"You already did it?" asked John. "We just got here!"

"All I did was touch it!"

He leaned close to the wall to watch the rock move. "I can't believe this is *rock*, you know?" He touched a tree that undulated and tickled his fingers. Then he rapped on it with his knuckles. He reached over to touch the center of a lake in the next panel, which caused the water to ripple to life. "Wow!"

They were filled with an overwhelming desire to see more, so it became a contest of who could activate the most scenes. They shared every animal they discovered.

Millicent leaned to study the detail on a pair of mallard ducks in a scene she'd activated. The hallway disappeared. The scene she'd been looking at became real, as though she was standing there in person. The wind blew on her face with the smell of pine and marsh and sulfur. Panicked, she shrieked and toppled. She landed on her bottom with a thud in the hallway.

Miriam ran to her. "Milly! Are you okay? What happened?"

"It came to life."

"What did?"

"That wall! It came to life! Like I was there!"

"Huh?"

"Just . . . touch it yourself!"

With John beside her, Miriam activated the panel. Millicent dusted herself off and urged them into it.

With a sickening whoosh, they were teleported to the edge of the marsh, out in the open air and surrounded by ducks. Miriam spun to see that the scene extended in every direction. John couldn't believe they weren't still in the hallway and reached to touch the wall in front of him. His vision fluttered between the hall and the reeds of the marsh.

They pulled themselves out and gasped.

Dust Is the Only Secret

Miriam spun again in the hallway to ensure that she was really there. "What the heckfire was *that*?"

"I have no idea," said Millicent. She looked down the wall at the remaining artwork.

John leaned against the wall to catch his breath and caught Millicent's gaze. "Oh, no. Are you thinking they're all like that?"

Millicent and Miriam eyed each other. Without a word, they sprinted in opposite directions to activate separate panels. It was a race to see who could find out first. It was a tie.

Millicent stood at the top of a cliff with a group of bears. They were taking turns sliding down a natural rock slide into a lake, just for fun. When her turn came, she screamed and ran to the edge and jumped with an urgent tug in her guts. The water was freezing. She hated doing things like this in real life, and it was no different here, but she had no control over it.

Miriam was at the top of an enormous tower. The view of the forest and surrounding mountains was stunning. A grizzly bear nearly the size of Emily sat at the center of the deck. Gray and regal, he looked at her and nodded.

From John's point of view, the girls stood motionless with their hands on the walls while the scenes played in the animated rock. They both gasped and cried out.

Then they stepped away. Miriam stumbled against the wall to catch herself. "Yep! I think they all work like that!"

Millicent shook from the anxiety of being forced to go down the slide. "Ohmigosh. Never again."

Ze'eva said she was curious about the larger murals and led the group to the widest hallway in the Mesa. It looked like the promenade gallery of an art museum with its massive panels of artwork.

Millicent stopped at the first one. "This is Dragon's Mouth Spring. I'm not touching it."

"Let me try," said John. He felt around but couldn't find the right

Chapter Thirteen

spot to touch. Just when he was about to give up, a shock seized his arm. With it came a terrible sound, a rueful mix of trumpet and rasp, like someone was dragging a rake across a chalkboard. A dark emotional current swept from the wall. It forced them to their knees, and they clapped their hands over their ears, but this did nothing to block the assault.

Ze'eva and Gabriel growled savagely and bared their teeth. Emily cowered against the opposite wall with Rodney.

It was quiet. The children felt cold wind on their faces and opened their eyes. They stood on a mound of earth that overlooked a shallow pond. The pond led into a rocky cave, and steam billowed out of the opening like its namesake: a giant dragon's mouth.

The terrible sound came again, and a massive creature arrived from the forest. The center of its forehead shone with a brilliant yellow light. Its pointed ears faced forward, and it towered over them as it marched with percussive footsteps to the seething knoll. It had the musculature of a bear, the tail of a cougar, and the snout and ears of a wolf. Its bristly fur was a mixture of all three. Extra limbs hung from its deformed skeleton. Its torso was as broad as a wine cask.

Carnivores of every type surrounded the pond. The creature climbed to the top of the hill above the cave with harsh breathing and grunts. It unhinged its maw full of terrible fangs and bellowed like a woeful foghorn.

Droves of humans marched from the forest. They stood emotionless behind the creature until it blurted a string of retches that compelled them to drop to their hands and knees. The carnivores, with glowing eyes, barked in unison. The humans rubbed their hands on the ground in mindless circles. The rhythm of the barking intensified, and the humans swerved faster. And the earth moved.

"Stop it!" screamed Millicent.

Ze'eva and Gabriel yanked them from the spell of the wall, and their vision returned to the hallway. The mural continued its animation, a flat, stone version of what they'd witnessed in person.

Dust Is the Only Secret

"What are they making?" asked John.

"It's the spire. Süütakkan," said Ze'eva. "It's a white tower shaped like a blade. This is disturbing, children. I don't know how this creature existed. I'm ashamed that wolves could ever behave this way. And, most unsettling, we've learned that Lucifur has taken up residence in Süütakkan."

"He's there?" asked Millicent. "At Dragon's Mouth?"

"Yes," said Ze'eva. "It's crudely poetic. The bear named after the devil is resting in the very place they say Hell bubbles up."

"I can't watch anymore," said Miriam. "Those people . . . "

Ze'eva sniffed the wall. "Yes. John, you wondered what happened to the humans? Well, I can predict what happens to these people once they finish raising the spire, and I don't want you to see it. We should leave this hall."

John, Miriam, Emily, and Rodney followed Ze'eva and Gabriel, but Millicent glared at the creation of Süütakkan. She couldn't take her eyes off the horrible creature as it commanded the humans and animals alike.

If Lucifur knows about this . . .

"No!" she cried. She rushed to the next large mural and activated it, and then the one after that, bringing them both to life.

"Millicent, please!" said Ze'eva.

She didn't respond. With tears in her eyes, she stepped back and watched the two scenes play without entering them. "We have to see! We have to see what this is!" They huddled around her and watched.

In one scene, the massive creature leapt atop a marmot burrow and roared fiercely. The marmots spilled from their home under his command. Giant brown eagles swooped in and dive-bombed the creature. He growled and bellowed and swatted at them. He phased and caught one of the eagles in his jaws and swallowed it whole as the others clawed at his back. One by one the eagles fell. The remaining birds gave up their attack and scooped up what marmots they could. The rodents paddled their tiny feet as though they were still walking on

Chapter Thirteen

the ground as the eagles flew away with them. The creature barked a final command, and the rest of the marmots filed into a line to follow him out of the picture.

The other scene showed a herd of elk lined up along a riverbank across from the creature. They were intent on stopping his progress. With the mindless throng of marmots still behind him, he summoned a dark cloud of hornets from the forest to attack the herd. He barked and retched as he traversed the river, and the elk either fled or joined him as new followers.

The final mural in the hallway was enormous. Millicent activated it and stepped back into Miriam's arms, and John put his arm around both of them. They tried to resist being drawn into the scene, but it pulled them in anyway.

Whoosh.

They stood at the edge of Mary Lake with the Mesa behind them. The air was crisp at daybreak. They heard frogs in the marshy shore.

The creature arrived and scowled at the Mesa. He bellowed at the sky.

Humans with spears and an army of animals waited for him near the lakeshore. They threw their weapons and launched rocks with their minds, but the Great Enemy, the Asaquatzi they called him, deflected the attack with flashes of yellow from the bright spot on his forehead.

Their defense became desperate. A woman rode a giant wolf and splashed in the water's edge as she hurled a spear into the Asaquatzi's chest. The beast gripped the staff with one of his extra claws and yanked it free. A beam of light escaped the wound until the hole sealed itself clean.

The humans threw another volley of spears, but this time the creature caught them in midair and hurled the weapons back. The people scattered and cried in panic, stricken by the spears. The creature barked a signal, and his army of carnivores and possessed animals stormed from both sides of the lake.

Dust Is the Only Secret

The battle was vicious. The children huddled in the middle of it, unable to block the empathic resonance that flowed around them.

Pain. Rage. Terror.

They heard a bump, and then another, which jarred their minds back to the hallway. Emily was throwing herself against the wall.

"Stop! Stop! Stop!" she cried.

Chunks of rock and pieces of the figurines broke from the mural and squirmed on the floor, but the scene played on.

The Asaquatzi's army fought until there was no one left to fight. The battle ended. The grounds surrounding the Mesa were littered with the bodies of humans and animals. The surviving humans followed the Asaquatzi into the Mesa.

They returned to Emily's room, shaken and quiet.

"No one can know what we've seen," she said.

"I'm sorry you witnessed that tragedy at all," said Rodney.

"I don't understand," said Emily. "What *was* that thing?"

"They called it the Great Enemy or evil. The Asaquatzi," said John. "That whole hallway was devoted to him. It felt so real!"

"I'm not going to be able to sleep tonight," said Millicent.

"No," said Ze'eva, "none of us will. Children, this has cracked the foundation of all that I know. This place has been my home for a century. Knowing what happened here and that these stories have surrounded us lying in wait all this time — I can't accept it, but I must!"

"The way it took a spear to the chest!" said Miriam. "It pulled it out like it was nothing."

"We have to keep looking," said Millicent.

"No, child!" said Rodney.

John touched the ram's forehead to calm him. "Rodney, after Lucifur attacked you, he told Sebastian he knew the secret of Caldera. That's why he brought us here — we're sure of it — but we need to know what that means."

"But at what cost? My dear boy — "

Chapter Thirteen

"Ruthless, for they shall be treated ruthlessly," said Ze'eva. "I agree; we must continue, but, as Rodney would say, cautiously."

Millicent sat next to the miniature of Mary Lake at the center of the floor and traced its shoreline with her fingers. "This is where it happened, the battle we saw." The fear she felt in the hallway returned. Her stomach twisted into knots. "As soon as I saw that thing, I imagined Lucifur seeing it, too."

Then a question hit her so hard that it made her shout. "But how could he know? How could he know about *any* of this? There's no way he could, not without a human — three humans in some places — to activate them!"

Miriam hummed. "What about the Fisherman?"

The room went deathly quiet. Millicent hopped to her feet with her hand over her mouth. "He's the only other human here — it had to have been him!"

"Lady Ze'eva," said Emily, "when was the last time he was here? I've never met the guy, and I've lived here my whole life."

"Emily, he hasn't been here since before I was born."

"But — " said John.

"Yes, John. It was over a hundred years ago when he was here. With his two siblings."

As night fell, they made themselves as comfortable as they could, given the situation. Rodney stared at the mountainous northern horizon on the wall. Emily stood by herself against the south wall and seemed shy about making eye contact with anyone.

Ze'eva paced like a caged animal. "My father told me that the Hume children used to live here in the Mesa, but he never said anything about the walls or this history. It makes sense though; my instinct was to keep it a secret, too."

"Hume was their last name?" asked John. "And there were three of them?"

"Yes, there were three boys, according to my father, though no one alive can verify this. I never gave it much thought — like Emily, I haven't met him."

"Three again," said John to himself. "That's crazy."

Millicent scanned the false horizon on the walls. She still wanted to explore the rest of the Mesa but was too terrified to suggest it. She decided that she'd traded her small puzzle toy for something much larger, a puzzle more impossible to solve than the toy ever was.

"We have to ask him if he told Lucifur about this," she said. "How can we talk to him?"

"He's made Abatakai impenetrable," said Rodney.

"Abatakai?" asked John.

"Remember?" asked Millicent. "The giant fish tower in Yellowstone Lake? Crazy bird man?"

John nodded in an exaggerated way. He remembered the story but would have never remembered the name. "Ri-ight. The fish tower. How could I have forgotten?"

"I'll send scouts tonight," said Ze'eva, "to see if they can communicate with him. For now, let's get some rest."

That night, Millicent's dream returned for the third night in a row. This time, her puzzle toy was gone, and it began as she peered down the dark tunnel.

Click clack!

Something scraped, and she looked down to find that she was dragging her fingernails down a rocky wall. It was rough against her flesh and filled dirt under her nails, so the tips became dark crescents. Both hands scraped together. She wanted to stop. Her skin was raw, and her nails were filing down.

"Help me," she said to no one. The pain became unbearable, but she couldn't stop scratching the rock. The pain flowed into the shadows, and beneath her pain came sadness. Under that was seething, bitter rage. She ground her teeth. Her fingernails were coming off.

She screamed.

Chapter Thirteen

She woke and sat upright in Emily's room. "It's here! It's here in the Mesa!" She started crying and rubbed her healthy fingertips in disbelief. Everyone jumped awake.

"Milly, what's wrong?" asked Miriam.

"I keep having this stupid nightmare! It's getting worse and worse every night!"

"After everything we've seen? Yes, you're going to have nightmares!"

"But . . . I don't think it was a dream anymore! It was underground. In a place I've never seen before. I think it's here in the Mesa!"

"Show us," said John. "Show us like we did before."

She nodded. With a pained look, her eyes burst with light, and the light spread through each of them, even into the animals, as she shared the memory of her dream. They felt her pain and anger. They all winced and gasped and yelled.

"Ohmigosh!" said Miriam. "We have to go to it!"

"What?" cried Millicent. "That was the most horrible thing I've ever felt in my life! I'm sorry, but I don't exactly want to run straight toward it!"

"I think," said John, "I think I feel the same way, I think," said John.

"Think, think, think!" said Miriam. "That's all you do is think!"

"Miriam," said Ze'eva curtly. "It's plain to me. Where they feel only pain, you, the caretaker, feel this call for help so powerfully that it demands your action. We wolves are driven by inescapable purpose, too. Perhaps we've awakened something in these walls that has long been sleeping. If it's another terrible scene, for example, then we'll investigate and move on. But if someone is truly in distress, then I *must* go — that's *my* inescapable purpose."

Emily tooted her trunk. "Are you heading into the passageways?"

"Yes, I think we'll start at the well. I know that precludes you from joining us."

"Yeah."

Ze'eva turned to Millicent, towering over her in her nest of blankets.

Dust Is the Only Secret

There was a brilliant, icy flash of blue that warmed her from her head to her toes.

"Millicent. You can stay here with Emily, or you can come with us. The choice yours. If you come with us, you can ride on my back. You would feel safe there, yes?"

Millicent stood. She could feel that Rodney's fear of going was almost as strong as hers. Emily was wishing that she would stay with her. And John, oh John, was ever on the fence. But her sister! Miriam stood out like a beacon in the mental landscape. Millicent couldn't help but imagine a gradient scale from black to white with little stickers of their faces placed on the appropriate values. That was just the way she thought of things. She was scared and shaking but set her jaw and fixed her pigtail buns. Why did Miriam always get her way?

"I'll go."

Ze'eva lowered herself, and Millicent gulped and grabbed her fur to climb onto her back. The hair was just as sharp and soft as it appeared — silky when she petted it with the grade but pokey when she touched it straight-on. It was thick and warm and seemed full of downy layers underneath. Some textures were a source of comfort to her and helped to ease or distract from her anxiety, and this was a great one. She squeezed chunky fistfuls.

John handed her bookbag to her and realized that he should ready himself, too. Why did Millicent get to ride the giant wolf? Why was Miriam the one who felt compelled to action by the dream? He wasn't even sure if he was scared of what they saw or just didn't understand it. He paused as he slipped on a new hoodie.

That probably means you don't understand it, he said to himself.

He yanked on his backpack.

There came a single clop of a hoof. The group turned to see Rodney at the center of the room. It was clear that he wasn't joining them.

With Millicent on her back, Ze'eva led them with Gabriel to the Atrium. It looked like a holiday wonderland at night, brilliant with

Chapter Thirteen

grelyxir, fireflies, and bioluminescent plants. At the far end of the massive chamber, down the hillside past the stone roundtable, was an ancient-looking well with spiral stairs descending into darkness.

Ze'eva suggested they each take a grelyxir lamp, which were planted along the path. It took effort to loosen them, but they plucked them from the ground and carried them like torches. Miriam handed one up to Millicent.

They climbed down the winding stairway. John turned to see how Ze'eva would navigate, and she flowed around the center column of the stairs with deft, silent steps.

The deep sections of the Mesa were cold and damp, and every crevice glowed violet. They passed abandoned rooms full of cobwebs and dripping sounds. John said it reminded him of a Medieval dungeon, which frightened Millicent, who clung to Ze'eva's fur and half hid her face between the wolf's shoulder blades.

It became utterly dark aside from their torchlight. Ze'eva navigated through several corridors until they were sure she'd taken them in circles. When they reached a dead end, a decrepit alcove thick with moss, she stopped and sniffed the dank air.

"This is the lowest point I know of. Something is foul."

"Is this it?" asked Miriam "I think we're close."

"We can double back," said Ze'eva. "There might be — "

Millicent slipped from her back. She approached the dead-end wall and stripped the moss to reveal crude brickwork beneath it. She froze with a clump of the gritty flora hanging from her fingers.

"These are the only bricks I've ever seen in the Mesa." Then, as her companions began to puzzle over what she was implying, she added, "I think there's something on the other side of this wall."

"Huh," said Miriam, joining her. "You don't say?"

They removed as much of the moss as they could and then pushed to see if any of the bricks were loose. John found one he could wiggle in place, so he rocked it back and forth until it dislodged and fell through to the other side. Millicent was right; there was darkness beyond.

Dust Is the Only Secret

"Stand back," said Miriam, and she laced her fingers and grimaced to release a telekinetic burst that sent dust and debris flying from the bricks.

"Ohmigosh!" said John.

"You can do it, too. I know you can."

"Okay. Let me try." Copying her technique, he laced his fingers. *How did she . . .* It started as a coin between his palms. That's what it felt like, a coin that warmed his skin. The metal grew warmer, first as if it'd been lying in the sun, then hotter, as if it were touching a stove. He knew that he was creating this energy, and it scared him. It would burn through his hands. He couldn't keep them together. Rather than wimp out in front of Miriam, he shouted and released the energy.

His blast sent another brick into the void.

Miriam was competitive, but she was also genuine in her excitement for other people when they succeeded. She clapped John on the back like a soccer teammate. "You knocked one straight through!"

He seldom won against her, but, when he did, she never seemed concerned about losing. That took the fun out of winning. Not that blowing bricks from the wall was a contest —

She blasted again. He concentrated, felt the warmth, and let it fly. No, this wasn't a competition, but he was determined to match her blow-for-blow and brick-for-brick. They took turns blasting, faster and faster, until they synchronized. The wall gave way with a hole large enough for Ze'eva to step through.

Ze'eva panted. "I had no idea you were capable of this!"

Millicent clutched her fur. "Cheeses. Neither did I."

"I just had this feeling," said Miriam. "We're supposed to be practicing, right?"

She gave a blink of a pained smile as their purpose returned. *Caldera, you are full of momentary joys,* she thought, *surrounded by terror.*

The coldness seeped in from the blackness ahead of them.

Absolute terror.

She dipped her torch through the hole and paused to let her eyes

Chapter Thirteen

adjust, but it was too dark. She stepped through. Her foot crunched into loose rock, like gravel, and a lazy plume of dust rose from under her feet. The others climbed in and held their torches high in front of them to look around. The tunnel was hewn through the rock and riddled with divots and gouges. Millicent climbed onto Ze'eva's back again and hugged her.

"Ugh! It smells awful," said John.

Gabriel trotted ahead of them to the edge of the torchlight. "I'll go first. Okay?"

"Yeah, okay."

They found a carved scene of Dragon's Mouth. It looked like someone had cut through the rock to get to it, like a paleontologist would expose dinosaur bones.

"Should we activate it?" asked John.

"No!" said Millicent. "Please don't."

"But isn't this what we — "

"No," said Miriam. "Whatever-it-is is close. Up ahead."

John rubbed his thumb and forefinger inches from the wall, and then decided to put his hand in his pocket.

Gabriel whimpered. He nosed ahead and waited for them to bring their torches. "Hold on."

"What is it?" asked Miriam.

He dug with his forepaws to expose a small rodent. "Dead mole."

She knelt next to him to look, brushed away more debris, and lifted the tiny body from the stones by one of its paws. "Aw, the poor thing." She set it on the rocks. "Maybe it got trapped in here or something."

Ze'eva stepped closer to get a better look. "It's barely decomposed; it must have died recently."

Millicent dug her heals into her sides.

"Well, it couldn't have gotten in the way we came," said John.

"Maybe there's another way, up ahead," said Gabriel.

Miriam scooped gravel to create a simple grave.

"No," said Ze'eva. "Touch your torch to its body."

Dust Is the Only Secret

"Okay?" Puzzled and nervous, Miriam lowered her torch. The grelyxir flame engulfed the mole in a flash of light. Only sparse ashes remained on the stones.

"This is how we tend to our dead," said Ze'eva.

Ahead were two more scenes carved into the walls. One was of the great fish of Abatakai, standing on its tail on an island in Yellowstone Lake, just as Sebastian had described it, and the other depicted a tower shaped like a tall, skinny hourglass, which they didn't recognize. Both were in niches where someone dug through the rock to reveal them.

"That's Abatakai, right?" asked Millicent.

"Yes," said Ze'eva. "The Great Fish."

"And that other one?"

"Tihuzaveh, the Time Tree. It's southwest of here. It's where the bears live."

"Ti-HOO-zuh-vay? Boy, where do all the names come from?"

"I don't know, Millicent. These were the names even my grandmother knew, and that goes back a long time."

Gabriel barked. "Another one."

They extended their torches toward him and expected to see another carving. Instead, he was sniffing near a dead squirrel. It lay on its back with its legs sticking up.

John held his torch far in front of him, so he could peer deeper into the tunnel and saw two more dead animals. "There's a raccoon and a marmot, I think."

Millicent gripped Ze'eva. "I don't want to go any farther, Ze'eva. I don't want to."

"We're stopped. We're stopped."

Gabriel sniffed the raccoon and whimpered. "Look at the paws. Nails are gone. Dried blood."

John grabbed Miriam's arm. "We should go back."

"No," she said. "I mean — so far it's only a few dead animals, right?"

"Right! And whatever happened to them could happen to us."

"We don't know what happened to them!"

Chapter Thirteen

"Exactly!"

A faint voice whispered ahead of them in the pitch-blackness. "Help me."

John and Miriam held their breaths. Millicent bit hard the inside of her mouth. She could feel Ze'eva's heart pounding through her ribcage. If this giant wolf was scared . . . All she could think was, *It's a trick. It's a trick. It's a trick.* If they continued, they'd get hurt.

But then, a glimmer of warmth whispered into her mind.

"Please help me," said the voice, and she trusted it.

She slipped again from Ze'eva's back and walked past John and Miriam. Gabriel whined for her to stop. The pain and disgust intensified with each step — *pain, disgust, disgust, DISGUST* — until she was absolutely scowling with empathy. Images flashed into her mind. She saw Lucifur. She saw claws scraping against rock. She saw animals slumping dead near a small, round chamber. She saw a broad face with stripes that streaked from its nose and wide, terrified eyes.

HELP ME!

She screamed and thrust her torch over her head, and the grelyxir blazed and illuminated the entire tunnel. It widened in front of them and ended at the entrance of the chamber she'd seen, which now glowed with its own grelyxir. A thousand dead animals coated the ground, piled deeper near the end. They were squirrels, otters, raccoons, marmots, badgers, and beavers.

She tiptoed between the bodies to where a badger lay flat on the ground near the wall. She fell to her knees beside it and cried.

Miriam raced along the path, fell onto her knees, and wrapped her arms around her. John stood behind them and looked at the dead animals with a terrible grimace. The smell was unbearable. He covered his nose and mouth with the crook of his elbow.

The badger growled. It was near death and angry. They knew it would hurt them if it had the strength, not because it hated them, but because it knew hatred and could only feel hatred. A terrible image of Lucifur blurred into their minds.

"What happened here?" asked Millicent.

The badger grunted. It found some reserve of strength and turned to snap at her. It wanted to claw her eyes out.

"We're here to help you. You asked for help!"

The badger swiped at her. Its paw was blunt and bloodied and missing its claws. "No more!" he said.

Millicent's mouth tightened, and tears dripped down her face. "No more," she said. "No more digging." She dared to lay her hand in his broad back. He jerked to bite at her, so she ran her palm down his spine to stay away from his mouth. "No more," she said. "No more digging. You're all done. No more."

She mustered her will to relax as much as she could into healing him. As Ze'eva described, his pain poured into her and permeated her entire body. With her hand on him, she buried her face into Miriam's chest and shook. Miriam stroked her hair. The badger never stopped growling.

"Did Lucifur do this to you?" asked John. The badger snarled. John braced himself and slipped into its mind. It wasn't a blue ocean of memories like Gabriel's but a swirling morass of red. He saw fragments of the badger's life, a normal life of digging and hunting and rearing young, but they were scattered by the anger of recent memories.

"Lucifur gathered these animals. He never told them why," he said, and he clenched his teeth. "He forced them to tunnel through the rock. Right through the rock! He wouldn't — he wouldn't let them stop until they reached this place. Oh no! No! Please don't!" He saw himself lying there as the badger. His hands were on fire from digging and his body too weak to move, and the light from the exit dimmed, brick by brick, until there was nothing but blackness and hunger. He broke the connection and gasped, catching himself with his hands on his knees.

The badger slackened. Its pain drained from Millicent's body through her hand and back into him.

"No!" she whispered. "No . . . " She rested her head on his back and felt the warmth leave him.

Chapter Thirteen

Now they were surrounded by complete death.

"Children," said Ze'eva. "You should never see such things. Let's find out what this is leading to and leave this wretched place. But first, Millicent, please dip your torch, if you could be so merciful."

Millicent touched the purple flame to the badger's body. It spread in all directions and was so bright that they were forced to shield their eyes. The tunnel was clear but for fine ash that floated to the ground.

The round chamber at the end of the hall was empty except for a hexagonal pedestal that reminded them of a standing birdbath.

"What was he looking for in here?" asked Millicent. She imagined Lucifur sniffing around and shuddered.

"I don't know — I don't understand," said John.

Miriam inspected the pedestal. "This is the only interesting thing in here."

"Then the three of us should touch it," said Millicent.

As soon as they placed their hands on it, the entrance sealed shut and the wall bubbled to life. An image of the Mesa formed. From it flowed a stream that wound its way around the chamber to a larger river. "That's Alum Creek," said Millicent, "flowing into the Yellowstone River."

The river became a waterfall and curved along a lazy course before plunging over an even taller waterfall. "Those are the Upper and Lower Falls."

A woman entered the scene near the base of the Lower Falls. She was levitating a flat, hexagonal stone that could fit in her palm. She touched a spot on the cliff face, a matching receptacle appeared, and she maneuvered the keystone into place. A passageway opened, and the woman went inside.

With that, the animation ended.

Millicent looked at the depression in the top of the pedestal. "That key she used . . . must have been kept here."

"And now it's gone," said Miriam.

Dust Is the Only Secret

"Because Lucifur took it, I'll bet," said John.

"We came all this way for nothing."

"No," said Millicent. "We know that a key opens something by the falls. And we know Lucifur killed a lot of animals to get it."

Fourteen

If I Could Bribe

The rest of the day was somber. Back in Emily's room, the children didn't eat or speak. Ze'eva hummed for them to ease their grief and coaxed them to sleep before she left to attend to the hospital.

The next morning, John woke first. Miriam snored beside him (and she never snored), and Millicent was curled against Emily, who was still wearing her mammoth-sized New York t-shirt. Gabriel sat next to him and looked alert as usual.

"We have company," he said, and he nodded across John's shoulder.

John turned. In the center of the room stood a mountainous bison, still and staring at them. He towered over them with his humped back and dark, wooly mane, and one of his horns was missing, cracked off at the base. He breathed like a grim, wet ventilator.

"You are not welcome here," he said in a deep, monotone, and mumbling slur that vibrated the inside of John's skull. "You endanger every animal in the Mesa by being here."

John sat upright and gripped the back of Gabriel's neck.

Gabriel woofed. "He's our guest, Bozhe."

"An uninvited guest, by our estimation. The Honorary Mother throws a banquet, and we must acquiesce? I don't accept this. We don't accept this."

"But Lady Ze'eva —"

"Has been overruled," he said with a reverberating hum. "She has been overruled. The bison, elk, pronghorn, and sheep have decided: the wolves cannot be trusted."

John shook his head to jettison the sleepiness and focus on what the

Chapter Fourteen

bison was saying. This wasn't another history wall. This was actually happening.

Gabriel stepped forward. "Have you gone crazy? You trust the wolves plenty when you need their hospital!"

"That was before. Wake the humans and come with me."

"What happens if we refuse?"

Bozhe remained still and emitted a grumble that blurted into a moan, one long note, louder and louder, until the air reverberated harshly.

The girls, Rodney, and Emily woke up. Millicent grimaced and cupped her ears. Miriam looked to John and read the worry in his eyes. They couldn't speak through the bison's dirge.

The moan tapered off. "Come with me, humans."

"Bozhe!" said Rodney. "What on Earth are you doing, Good Sir?"

"The humans must leave the Mesa."

Gabriel gave a single, harsh bark. "He says the council has decided. *Your* council."

"My council — " said Rodney. He released waves of anxiety and anger. "No . . ."

Emily rolled to stand. "You say what now? Nobody bothered checking with me!"

"You are not a member of the council," said Bozhe.

"As Honorary Mother, I —"

"Have been overruled. You have been overruled."

"I beg your pardon!"

Gabriel growled. "He keeps saying that. Be careful. He might start moaning again."

"Disrespectful dog," said Bozhe. "It will interest you to know that Copernicus lies bleeding in our quarter. It will also interest you to know that he knows what happened to Sebastian."

Miriam hopped to her feet to confront him. She looked tiny in front of the brown giant.

"Do you know what happened? Can you tell us?"

If I Could Bribe

"Follow me, and Copernicus will tell you."

"Fine! Lead the way."

John clenched the air in front of him. "Grr! Miriam, can you press pause for one second, please?"

"*You* press pause! If Copernicus is here, then we should talk to him, right? What's the problem?"

Millicent stood and wrapped her arm around Emily's trunk to hide behind it. "I agree with her, but I'll only go if everyone comes with us."

Gabriel woofed. "Everyone will."

Bozhe led them to the east wing of the Mesa, past walls covered with the overwhelming, unread history. They entered a long, broad chamber that looked like the nave of a cathedral. At the far end, in the apse, stood a colossal statue of a bison poised to charge. On the ground at the foot of the statue lay Copernicus, surrounded by members of the council — a pronghorn, a moose cow, and an elk.

Miriam's instinct was to barge down the aisle, but seeing him on the ground and being inside the church-like chamber quieted her steps.

"Lord Copernicus!" said Rodney. "You're positively soaked to the bone, dear cat!"

Copernicus lifted his head. "Please, I need your help."

"Where's Sebastian?" asked Miriam. "He was leaving to talk to you when he disappeared."

"He was captured! It was the wolves! They surrounded us — attacked us." He rolled to reveal claw marks and lacerations down one side of his body that looked fresh and painful. "They didn't care about the cats at all. They took him and left us for dead."

"Have sense, man!" said Rodney. "Get to the hospital!"

"No! That's what I'm telling you; it was her wolves that attacked us!"

Miriam had heard enough. With a flash of yellow in her yes, she clenched her fists and pressed into Copernicus's mind. She saw a massive, white blade of rock in the distance, the Spire of Süütakkan. A

Chapter Fourteen

wolf leapt at her from the thicket. She fell backward in the aisle with her arm raised to defend herself as the imaginary wolf clamped onto her and thrashed. Its claws raked down her side.

Behind them in the forest lay Sebastian, bound by rope.

John cradled her as the images faded. He caught glimpses of what she'd seen and gasped. "Ze'eva's wolves have him!"

Rodney stomped a hoof. "What's happening? I demand to know at once!"

"I read his mind," said Miriam. "He's telling the truth!"

Rodney's ears flicked in disbelief. "You — What did I tell you?"

"Give it a rest, old man," said Emily. "We're not playing the Polite Game here. It was another pack, though, right? Maybe Lucifur has his own wolves?"

"I'm sorry," said Copernicus. "I wish you were right."

Gabriel woofed. "If they have Sebastian, we have to help him!"

"You do what you must, shepherd," said Rodney, "but the children are staying here."

"No!" said Bozhe, but the group ignored him.

"Will you, Gabriel?" asked Copernicus. "Help me?"

"Yes."

"We're coming, too," said Miriam.

John looked to Millicent. *Are you still agreeing with her?*

No.

"Wonderful. Then it's decided," said Bozhe, "and we all get what we want."

The moose cow sniffed. "Yes. This is agreeable."

The pronghorn nodded.

"And once the humans are gone," said the elk, "we'll continue to shore up our defenses."

"*Humans?*" said Rodney. "You refer to them as though they carry their entire species on their shoulders. Look at them! They're children!"

"Why would the wolves take Sebastian?" whispered Millicent.

"What did you say, human?" asked Bozhe. "Speak up."

If I Could Bribe

She trusted Ze'eva, which meant a lot because she was stingy with trust. But what if the wolf was harboring other intentions? If she was after the same power that Lucifur wanted . . . No. Ze'eva's care was genuine. Millicent needed to believe that.

"I asked why the wolves would take Sebastian."

"My only guess," said Copernicus, "is that it's a play against Lucifur. Holding Sebastian would raise his ire."

This tactic hadn't occurred to Millicent, so she retreated into being quiet again.

John sensed that Miriam was at her last wits, and he was close behind. "If we're not wanted here — "

"I want you here!" said Emily.

Bozhe hummed. "The council has spoken, mammoth. We will not apologize if you don't agree with our decision."

Rodney gave a low bleat and bared his teeth. "I brought it to you as the leader of my species. Why did you convene without me? Doesn't my voice — "

"Overruled. Your voice has been overruled."

Gabriel growled. "Bison, if you say that one more time, I'm gonna bite your leg off."

"Savage!" said the elk.

"See here?" said the moose cow. "This is why we don't allow dogs on the council."

John raised his voice over them. "Excuse me! What I was going to say is if we're not wanted here, then we'll go. We'll help you find Sebastian."

We? asked Millicent.

Rodney stomped a hoof. "John, it's too dangerous outside the Mesa!"

"You'll be with us! You can help us!"

The hall went quiet. Rodney stepped backward and glared at him. "Yes. By all means, John Laskow. Lead the way. I didn't realize that you were so anxious to watch me lose the other eye."

Chapter Fourteen

"Oh, Rodney . . . " said Emily.

He turned on her. "Yes? Yes? What words of wisdom do you offer, oh astute majesty? What's that? We should saunter forth and see how many carnivores it takes to fell a Columbian mammoth? Oh, you can be such a needless mountain of flash and worry!"

Emily lifted her chin. "Pompous oaf! It's your fault for running off to gossip with these nimrods. You're the one who told the kids to keep it a secret!"

Bozhe tilted his massive head. "Eh? What's this? Keeping secrets?"

"Shaddup! I wasn't talkin' to you! What does Lady Ze'eva say about all this?"

"She has been detained," said Bozhe, "until we determine who we can trust. We are allowing her wolves to remain with the standing guard, but no more. They are being watched."

Millicent grabbed Miriam's arm. *They detained Ze'eva? This is crazy!*

Copernicus stood and stumbled. "I'll watch over them, Domcorn."

Rodney scoffed. "Do you really want to play custodian in the state you're in? So be it. I relinquish my custody and fare thee well with the ungrateful."

He turned and marched down the nave toward the exit. John watched him leave and was about to call after him, but a sudden anger made him stop. This was the second time Rodney seemed eager to abandon them, and this time he couldn't make amends simply by walking back into the room.

"We'll go with you," John said to Copernicus.

Millicent transmitted a pang of fear.

It keeps going from bad to worse. It will again when we leave here.

In the Den of Antiquities, they found two more backpacks and stuffed them with extra clothes and whatever provisions they could find. John dusted off a decent-looking canteen, sniffed inside be sure it wasn't foul, and shook it upside-down to empty it of a few, random pebbles.

If I Could Bribe

Emily changed into a flannel top and wore two saddle bags that they filled with food. The marmot girls climbed her side to heft a comforter onto her back. One of them begged her to stay. Another asked if they could come. Emily caressed them with her trunk and explained how she needed to go, and they needed to stay. She turned to face the children and looked rather impressive all decked out with everything they might need.

"You've got miles to go, and I've got legs for walking. *Overruled?* Feh! They can overrule my big, hairy butt as it walks out the door!"

Copernicus nodded. "Very good. Thank you. We'll move faster with you with us."

Millicent was nervous about riding Emily; the top of her back looked quite far from the ground. She was about to inquire how they'd get up there when Emily scooped up Copernicus with her trunk and draped him over her back. He looked like a fresh kill.

Millicent deflated. *Oh. Great. So, I guess this means we're walking?*

Miriam put her arm around her shoulder. *We'll be okay. Just stay by me.*

After days of being cooped up, they breathed the fresh air outside the main entrance at the top of the stairs that led down to the grand plaza. Wolves, cats, and bears were stationed around the perimeter, where the gardens began, and their grim and stoic posture was a stark contrast to the jubilant crowd that welcomed them a few days before.

John and Miriam exchanged worried looks and wondered how everything had changed so quickly. She offered him a little smile and gestured with her eyes toward Millicent. He couldn't muster a smile in return, but he understood what she was thinking and nodded back. The two of them would need to stay close to her to keep her from crumbling.

Four cougars came out of the Mesa and reported to Copernicus. The same four lynxes who betrayed them at the geyser also arrived, which made Miriam clench her fists.

"I know what you're thinking," said Copernicus. "These cats report to me and me alone."

Chapter Fourteen

His directness surprised her. She didn't want to question his judgement in front of everyone, but her fists stayed tight at her sides.

"Humans. Look at me, please. My lynxes were under Lord Nagus's control when they attacked you. We are all susceptible to that persuasion — you know this from experience! If we're attacked, if Lucifur's bears try to control us, then we *must* work together to resist their commands. Do you understand?"

Miriam studied the lynxes. They stared with round, earnest eyes, as though their shame bulged within them and needed to come out. She let her hands relax.

"So, it is possible?" she asked. "To resist them?"

"Yes. We've learned that some animals are more susceptible than others, like the rodents, but it's harder for the bears to control the cats and especially the wolves. I'm hoping your newfound abilities will help your resistance."

Miriam decided this was welcome news. She wanted to go back in time and try harder to resist Lucifur when he kidnapped them from the Lake Clinic. But how could she have known?

Copernicus led them west across the front of the Mesa, along the edge of the plaza. Gabriel was thrilled to be outside again. He alternated between trotting beside John and stopping to sniff every other stone or tuft of grass. They passed many doorways, some of which were so massive that they could have been mistaken for the main entrance. Towers with bulbous outcroppings and a myriad of windows loomed above them, and passageways wound out of sight between the towers. The alleys reminded Millicent of photos she'd seen of the streets of Cairo, so narrow that they were always in shade.

The miniature version of the Mesa popped into her mind and left her feeling dumbstruck.

"We watched this be built," she said half to herself.

"Wow, yeah," said John, craning his neck to look up at it. He'd almost forgotten that the giant structure was the same thing. Knowing how the ancient humans raised it from the ground with their bare hands

If I Could Bribe

made it even more incredible. It was impossibly huge.

They climbed a broad stairway to an outdoor theater that formed the Mesa's southwest corner. Everything made more sense. The animals didn't use these things, not in the way they were intended, because it was a human dwelling first, made by humans *for* humans. The strange, rounded, and organic shapes that made up every section and detail, like the bulbous protrusions on the towers, seemed to have been crafted out of artistic whimsy, like the entire city was a stone doodle that the builders made up as they went along.

Mary Lake came into view behind the Mesa, and the horrible moments from the great battle, when the Asaquatzi attacked with his hoard of carnivores and possessed rodents, flashed into Millicent's mind as though they were her own memories.

Her eyes glowed yellow as she transmitted the fear and desperation from the battle scene into John and Miriam's minds. Miriam shuddered and looked around as though something tapped her shoulder. John ducked because he could have sworn a giant eagle swooped past his head.

"Cripes, Mill!" he said, shaking off the feeling.

"It feels like we were just out here in the middle of all the fighting," said Miriam.

"All those bodies," said Millicent. She pictured them on the empty ground. This was much different than reading about some old battle in a textbook and then visiting the battlefield. Echoes of the past pulsed just below the surface of all things.

Emily trumpeted and waved her trunk to beckon them forward. "Can we keep moving, please? I'd rather not hear about that stuff again!"

They walked away from the Mesa and into the forest next to the lake. John stooped to pick up a walking stick. It was shorter than he liked, so he kept an eye out for a replacement.

"Copernicus?" he asked.

"Yes, boy?"

Chapter Fourteen

"You haven't told us — where exactly are we going?"

"Ah. That would be nice to know, wouldn't it? We're heading northwest to Doyadu-khani."

"Oh. What's that?"

"Our home, the cougar temple. We'll meet with my glarings, and then they'll help us find Sebastian."

What's a glaring? John asked Millicent.

She glanced at him and wondered why he hadn't asked for himself. Then it was obvious: he didn't want to sound stupid for not knowing.

"What's a glaring?" she asked with a swell of apprehension as she glanced up. She didn't want to be talking to a mountain lion, not even a half-dead one. She could only see his feet hanging over the side of Emily's back and was thankful for that.

"A glaring is a clan of cats, like a family. Twenty glarings form the Doyadu-khani Clowder."

What's a clowder? asked John.

Millicent scoffed. *Cheese-and-crackers, John, use the context to figure it out!*

Huh?

A glaring is a small group. Twenty glarings make up the clowder. So, a clowder must be a . . . ?

Larger group?

Bingo, Geronimo.

She had several more questions of her own, but she couldn't seem to open her mouth. When she tried to, the bubble of anxiety caught in her throat. A couple of her steps turned into frustrated stomps — not so hard that the others would notice but hard enough to vent, make tiny clouds of dust, and feel a rock shoot sideways from under her shoe. The urge to stop walking was overwhelming. She would let the group go on without her. She would walk back to the Mesa and find a little room of her own and wait for it all to be over.

I won't be a bother, I promise.

But she knew she couldn't do that. She lagged behind Miriam and

If I Could Bribe

concentrated on the rhythm of her sister's sneakers along the path.

Okay, she thought. *Just one more question.*

"If you please, sir, where is Doyadu-khani?"

"It's in the far northwest quarter of Caldera. You call the area Mammoth Hot Springs."

Her mouth dropped open. It would take them days to walk there. At least two. She wasn't ready for this. She turned to watch the trees obscure the last bit of the Mesa that she could see and ached to go back. This was her last chance.

But then she saw it. A silver blur slinked through the shadows between the plants at the edge of the garden. She felt a rush of happiness, though she couldn't understand why. She'd met Ze'eva just three days ago — the wolf was still a stranger, and a frightening one. Necessity forced hasty alliances in Caldera, she supposed. She looked to see if anyone else had noticed that they were being followed, but her companions were facing forward.

Nobody could detain that wolf, she thought. She pushed the good feeling down and reminded herself to stay cynical.

They huffed in the thin air, and even Miriam admitted that she was winded as their path tipped upward. The grade was relentless. Before long, each step felt like they were wading through molasses, and it made the front of their legs burn with fatigue.

"Whew! Is it going to be uphill the whole way?" asked Miriam.

"No," said Copernicus. "Just initially. We're crossing over Mary Mountain. The way will be easier past the dome. In the meantime, just take one step at a time and drink your water."

It was a long and horrible climb. As he foretold, the ground turned level thirty minutes later, and their steps eased. Millicent demanded they take a break. They rested and passed the canteen.

John choked on a drink of water.

Cough-cough!

He stared at the canteen, and remembering the moment with his

239

Chapter Fourteen

mother, the moment before all this began, squeezed his throat. He teared up and couldn't breathe.

What's wrong? asked Miriam.

Why are we doing this?

Because we have to.

I know, but . . . Copernicus doesn't care about us getting home. Gabriel likes to help, but he doesn't know anything about getting us home. And Emily is too ... goofy. Sebastian and Ze'eva were the only ones who could help. And Ze'eva's been detained? I mean, what the hell?

Whoa. John. I know. I know all of that. I meant we literally have no other choice. We have to find Sebastian. Then we look for a way home. We find him, free him — again — and he can help us.

He nodded. He wasn't certain that they were in total agreement about what they were doing and why, but hearing her confidence was comforting. His little sister, the one with the sunshine in her hair, was still looking out for him.

They continued walking until the shadows stretched and blanketed the forest. Copernicus called for them to set up camp while they it was still twilight. He lay at their feet as Emily lowered herself behind them. Gabriel looked exhausted, but he was stubborn and insisted on patrolling while they slept. The bears, cougars, and lynxes formed a circle around them.

Miriam lingered next to Copernicus. She glanced at him out of the corner of her eye as she arranged a sleeping bag and rolled a blanket to use as a pillow. He was larger than Sahra, with muscular shoulders and limbs. His emotions that she could read hovered between anxiety and pain.

"Copernicus?"

"Yes? Marian, is it?"

"Miriam, sir."

"Miriam. My apologies."

"If you like, we can heal you. Sebastian said we're getting pretty good at it."

"You would do this? Accept my pain?"

"Yes, sure we will!"

Millicent wanted to kick her. *Can we take a vote before you offer our services?*

He's in pain, and we can help him. Period. Don't bother if you don't want to.

She laid her hands on him. Feeling around with her mind, she found the channel of energy that would connect them. Her eyes blazed yellow, and she felt his injuries in succession: a stinging pain from the lacerations across his side, gnawing barbs where two claws were ripped out, and a throbbing ache from a blow to his head. John hurried to join her. Millicent grumbled and put her hands next to John's. The aches and pains dispersed and equalized, but Miriam pressed harder to take the brunt of them. Millicent slacked off and let her.

When they released him, he sniffed his wounds to assess their work. "Ah, he was right — you *are* skilled! Your siphon was strong! Thank you. Thank you so much."

The air was quiet, and Miriam knew she would be able to fall asleep now that he wasn't in pain. Millicent emitted a pulse of resentment, but it made Miriam smile. This was nothing new.

John begged Gabriel to take a break, and the shepherd collapsed next to him and fell fast asleep, though his paws twitched from patrolling in his dreams. One by one they fell asleep until only Copernicus and Millicent were left awake.

This did not please her.

"She's cunning," he said softly.

"Huh?" asked Millicent. She assumed he was talking about Miriam.

"I know you don't trust me, but I don't think it's wise to put your faith in someone so ruthless. Her allegiance is to her wolves."

What? He knows that Ze'eva is following us? No, keep quiet. Maybe it's just a coincidence.

She shrugged and pretended to not know what he was talking

241

Chapter Fourteen

about.

He stared at her. "Well. We'll see. Good night, kitten."

Yep. He knows.

And she was tired of being called kitten.

The next morning after breakfast, they resumed hiking and came to a sharp decline where a gap in the trees gave an astonishing view of a valley full of rolling hills to the east and a barren, bleached plain to the west. After twenty minutes of arduous, downhill walking, the cracked plateau blinded them in the noon sun.

Millicent announced when they reached the Norris Geyser Basin.

"Our campsite was over that way somewhere," she said.

This news filled them with a dreadful nostalgia, a longing to search for the campground and to see their site again, but they knew that it would only be an empty, grassy field in Caldera.

"Stay to the right. We'll follow the tree line," said Copernicus. "That crust is thin with scalding water below the surface. You wouldn't want to break through."

The midday sun beat down on them, so Miriam unfolded a blue sun hat from her backpack. The soft, straw weave was crinkled and lopsided, but it protected her head. Millicent complained about forgetting to bring a hat and fashioned a headscarf out of a pink t-shirt. To be funny, John used a belt to cinch the waist of a pair of shorts around his head, so the legs flopped behind him like khaki bunny ears.

"Ha!" said Emily. "That's a great look, John. The three of you are quite a sight, that's for sure!"

Proud of his invention, he smiled and made his sisters and Emily laugh by wagging the ears.

"All right, that's about enough," said Copernicus.

Millicent glanced at him on Emily's back, puzzled by the tone of his voice. He stretched like a housecat rising from a nap and flexed his paws. His claws splayed grotesquely.

"Yow!" said Emily. "Whatcha doin' up there?"

If I Could Bribe

Copernicus stared down at Millicent with malice, and her face slackened.

Oh, no no no no!

The big cat reset his claws into Emily's hide. She reared and swung her trunk to slap him, but he held on.

"Stop! That hurts!"

Millicent screamed. "Let go of her! Let go of her!"

The other cougars leapt at the two bears, and the four lynxes piled on top.

Gabriel growled and barked at the forest. "John, Miriam!"

They whirled to look. An army of mountain lions phased toward them through the trees like wraiths with yellow, glowing eyes that trailed streaks of light.

Copernicus bit into Emily's hide. She trumpeted and bucked. Millicent tried to blast him off, but he resisted until he lost his grip and was flung from her back. Emily screamed and swung her trunk like a giant baseball bat to swat him away. In her backswing, she snaked under Millicent's arms and yanked her from the ground.

Millicent recoiled from the bloody claw marks in the comforter, but she needed to hold onto something as Emily shot forward.

The cougars sprang from the forest. Gabriel sprinted and rolled and ran from the brush to get closer to Emily. Emily threw John and Miriam onto her back with Millicent and gaited along the edge of the forest next to the bleached plateau.

"Hold on to me!"

Miriam looked over her shoulder. Gabriel was keeping up with them, but the cougars phased along the edge of the barren rock and were about to pounce on him. She wrapped her forearm around John's waist and thrusted her free hand at the cats with a burst of energy. The cats nosed into the ground and tumbled head over heels. She felt their fur and the mass of their bodies — and their pain from the impact and a couple of broken bones. Horrified, she withdrew, but she'd kept them down long enough to keep Gabriel safe.

Chapter Fourteen

Three grizzly bears leapt from the forest. Emily shrieked and swung her tusks, jabbing one of them, and barreled through the other two.

Ten more bears arrived, their eyes glowing yellow. They shouted "Fall!" in unison, and Emily stumbled and landed chin-first on the ground. The kids lurched over her shoulders and landed in a pile next to her head. Her trunk flopped like a fire hose up the base of a natural tower of sandstone that looked like an eroded staircase.

Dozens of bears arrived, and Lord Nagus lumbered behind them. The kids joined hands as the animals surrounded them — the cougars from the south and the bears from the north. The steaming landscape blocked their escape to the west.

"You've put up a good fight, kittens," said Copernicus, "far better than I was expecting, but it's time to stop."

Miriam spat dust and saliva. "What do you want from us?"

"It's simple. The three of you are the key to some great power, and we intend to know what it is."

"Where's Sebastian?" asked John. "You've been lying this whole time!"

Miriam took a step forward, but John grabbed her arm. She yanked free and stood defiantly. "You said you were attacked by wolves! I saw your thoughts!"

"Will you come willingly?"

"Where is he? Tell us!" yelled John.

Copernicus approached with his cougars following. The children retreated from Emily to the base of the rock formation and began climbing hand over hand. Two of the cats walked around the rock to get beneath them, but they flinched and stopped shy of the blistering ground. The ground hissed, and they hissed back.

Miriam reached the top. The cracked earth sizzled ten feet below her, and she shoved against Millicent to get her to stop climbing. John, stopped behind Millicent and folded his legs to his body. The denim of his jeans felt like tissue paper.

Lord Nagus walked to the fore of his bears. "Gaw! Come down on

If I Could Bribe

your own, chimps, or we'll persuade you."

Copernicus nodded to his cats. "Bring them down."

Three of the cougars climbed the base, and John inched into Millicent, who in turn pressed against Miriam. Pieces of loose rock crumbled from her perch.

"Wait! Stop pushing me!"

John pressed against the cougars with his mind. They flattened and raked gouges in the sandstone to hold their positions. The one closest to him lashed out. Its claws pierced through his jeans into the meat of his calf.

He screamed and exploded with energy. The cougars hurtled away, spinning through the air to land in the crowd of bears.

Miriam slipped from the edge. She screamed and landed hard on her feet. Her left foot broke through the surface like a finger through a pie crust and plunged into boiling water. Her shriek of pain sounded inhuman. She fell onto her back and yanked her foot from the hole with steam, debris, and boiling grelyxir trailing from her shoe. The purple oil clung to it.

Millicent looked over the edge in horror.

John turned to see, saw that Miriam was missing, and felt like he'd been stabbed through the gut.

Ze'eva howled from the south. She ran along the tree line with her pack, fifty wolves strong. They arrived behind Copernicus's glaring of cats, and the bears jeered from the other side of the rock. The pack crashed into the glaring, and the cats, being cowardly, fell back until they merged with the army of bears. The bears reared and roared and joined the fight.

All eyes sparked into glowing as though a bolt of lightning ran through them. The cats phased to dodge and phased to attack. The bears persuaded in devious ways. They stopped wolves from attacking, convinced cats to attack for them, and forced wolves to attack each other. With a display of great power, the wolves hummed and growled in unison and blocked the effects of the other two species.

Chapter Fourteen

John pressed this back against Millicent's legs and watched the battle. Millicent was hooked to the edge of the rock to stare at Miriam on the ground below them. She wanted to race down to help her but was too terrified to move.

Lying where she fell, Miriam could only see the bright, red insides of her eyelids. The pain from her foot engulfed her, and tears streamed along the sides of her face and into her hair. The ground sizzled against her back. She was afraid that any movement would cause her to break through. The thick scent of the grelyxir boiling beneath the surface was sickening and sweet.

The cats and bears outnumbered the wolves, and the wolves were losing. Lord Nagus swatted one of them aside as though the battle was mere annoyance. With his eyes fierce and shining, he reared in an impressive display of girth.

"STOP!" he bellowed, and his bears stopped fighting. Several of the wolves saw this as a window of opportunity and bit, throttled, and snarled at the bears. "I said STOP!" he roared again, and the wolves settled down. He moved to stand beside Copernicus.

"Baw, the Big Bad Wolf is here! Think you're so scary? Whatchoo want?"

"The children must return with me to the Mesa," said Ze'eva.

"Ha! The little chews are staying with us, especially the crispy one."

Ze'eva looked confused. Then she spotted Miriam and stopped short. "No! I call for a truce! Let me save the girl!"

Copernicus raised his head high. "You're brave, calling for a truce when you're half-beaten."

Ze'eva snarled. "You know my wolves are holding back. I don't know how you fabricated those memories, but we're happy to provide you with real ones."

All of her wolves glowered and snarled. Copernicus's eyes narrowed.

In the quiet moment between them, John could feel his heartbeat in his ears and was terrified that the animals would erupt into fighting

If I Could Bribe

again. But then he felt a peculiar trace of relief from Copernicus, an emotion that the cat struggled to keep hidden. He doubted that the bears would notice this in their oblivious, bloodthirsty bliss.

"All right, a truce then," said Copernicus. "Go get her."

"I will get her," said Sahra.

The arrival of her voice made every head turn, and John searched for her in the crowd. She hung upside-down from a spit that was suspended between two of the bears. Her tail flopped backward to the ground, and she strained to keep her head up.

"Untie me, and I will get her," said Sahra.

"Nagus?" asked Copernicus.

Nagus gave a throaty cackle. "Ha! If the queen wants to walk the boil, then let her! It will be fun to watch. Eh, fellows? Walk the boil? Walk the boil! Walk the boil!"

The bears laughed and taunted as the two who held Sahra lowered her to the ground and untied her. She walked around John and Millicent and paused at the edge of the scorched earth.

A wad of phlegm dripped from the corner of Nagus's mouth. "Whatsamatter? Is the human-girl not worth the trouble? Come on! Walk the boil! Walk the boil!"

His bears joined and cheered and stomped.

"Walk the boil! Walk the boil!"

Millicent's eyes watered as Sahra sighed and stepped onto the tenuous plain. She sneaked around the formation, and her padded paws buoyed her up.

"I'm here, Miriam."

Miriam nodded, her mouth trembling.

Sahra flicked her weight from paw to paw, never keeping them in one place. Her tail waved to maintain her balance and flow.

"You know what position you're in. Don't put pressure on the ground. Roll onto your belly."

Miriam cried out. She didn't want to move.

"You must do this."

Chapter Fourteen

Miriam sucked in air and let it quaver back out of her. The hot ground burned against her arm as she rolled.

"That's good. Now, rise to your knees and forearms. Gently — lightly — like a cat!"

She whimpered as she pressed up. Her whole body shook. Hot water mixed with grelyxir flooded around her knees, and she screamed as Sahra ducked beneath her to lift her from the ground.

John and Millicent climbed down the rock formation and waited for Sahra as she treaded back to them. She lay Miriam at their feet and then limped a few feet away to sit with one paw curled to her body.

"Ooh-he-he!" said Lord Nagus. "Get your paw there, did you?"

Ze'eva rushed to Miriam and moaned and groveled from the pain as she began to siphon. Millicent yanked off her pink t-shirt headscarf, dropped to her knees, and pressed her cheek against Miriam's. She whispered to her and stroked her hair. John knelt beside them and held Miriam's hand. They began healing, too, but the pain was excruciating, even with Ze'eva absorbing most of it. They took turns but couldn't bear it for more than a few seconds.

John's face hurt from scowling.

After a few minutes, Ze'eva turned her head away sharply. Miriam was listless and stared at the sky in a daze. Millicent collapsed and sobbed into her t-shirt.

John continued to hold her hand. The pain was gone. He stared at her soiled left shoe and wondered how serious her injury was. He looked back and forth to watch the bears as they circled closer, and something brushed his shoulders that spooked him — it was the legs of the shorts that he was still wearing as a hat.

The commotion around them died down as all eyes watched Sahra limp to Copernicus. She paused for a second and then swatted him squarely on the snout. Her face knitted with rage, and she swatted him again, harder.

"Lucifur tried to tell me. I didn't want to believe him."

"My love. Please know that what I do I do for our house."

If I Could Bribe

The bears completed a circle around the kids. They seemed to admire their rotund and ill-mannered leader and didn't act at all like Sebastian. The worse Lord Nagus carried on, the more they behaved like a barbarian hoard.

Emily struggled to stand. A dozen grizzlies escorted her into the forest. They teased and swatted at her legs as she walked. She didn't make a sound.

John realized in a panic that he hadn't seen Gabriel since they were being chased. He scanned the crowd. He winced. Four puncture wounds burned in his calf where the cougar clawed him, and four circles of blood soaked through his jeans. He squeezed Miriam's hand. Now that she was safe, he had no idea what was going to happen.

In Miriam's stupor, she rolled her head around and moaned. *We were home. We were home. We were home!*

John scowled because she was right. Their plan to go through the geyser worked. They had hugged their parents. They had found them and hugged them. They could have hopped in their van and gone home, and none of this would have happened.

Ze'eva growled. "Copernicus, this girl needs to be in the hospital. Let my wolves return to the Mesa with her. You have my word there will be no deception."

Copernicus tutted. "Your word is the only one left in Caldera, isn't it? The wolves can go, but you and the girl must stay."

Lord Nagus belched. "Wha! If we let them go, won't the pups compete for food? Why don't we eat them?"

"I agree, Lord," said Copernicus, "but not today. We're going to need healers before this war is over."

"Beh! You mean *they* will!" He laughed and jiggled his rolls of furry blubber. "Go on! Send the mutts crawling back."

Ze'eva hesitated. With a stiff wave of her snout, she commanded her pack to leave. They hesitated, as well, but then turned and ran into the woods.

Sahra limped to Ze'eva. She looked small next to the giant wolf, like

249

Chapter Fourteen

a tawny little sister, sleek with rounded ears and a low profile compared to Ze'eva's sharp angles and pointy tufts. She snarled at Miriam's foot.

"How bad is it?"

"Bad. Beyond my ability to heal. It's something about the grelyxir. I'm not sure. We've made her comfortable for now."

"This is unforgivable. I'm truly sorry this has happened."

"Thank you for getting her. I wouldn't have expected that from you."

"I'm lighter on my feet."

"Ah. Of course. I can see to that paw now."

"No. Never mind me. Save your strength."

Millicent's body shook as she rocked and fretted over Miriam. She wanted to take off the steaming shoe for her but knew it was a bad idea until they reached shelter — if they reached shelter.

"Come, she-wolf!" said Lord Nagus. "I have a good use for you! You're so keen on sending your pups home to play doctor?" He motioned to two of his lieutenants. "Take the Lady to our wounded and persuade her to siphon their pain. Every bite and bruise! Every broken bone! All of it!" His eyes flashed bright yellow.

Ze'eva shared a look with John and Millicent. By contrast, her eyes had lost their brilliance, and she offered no emotions for them to read. She lowered her head and followed the cougars.

Now John gulped. The fact that Lucifur wanted them alive was the only thing that kept him from panicking, but he didn't know if Copernicus and Lord Nagus felt the same way.

Copernicus scoffed. "You're projecting your thoughts, human-boy. We're not here on his behalf."

"Well, now that you have them," said Sahra, "what is your plan, oh king?"

He raised his voice as three of his cougars approached. "John and Millicent will go to Abatakai, and they will find out what the Fisherman knows. These cats will escort you to the lake."

Miriam stirred at the sound of his voice. Copernicus phased over to

If I Could Bribe

her and kept her pinned to the ground with a paw on her chest and placed a claw against her throat.

"I'm glad you're awake. I was about to explain to your siblings how they can save your life. They will walk due east until they meet the Yellowstone River. They will follow it south and be wary of Dragon's Mouth — are you listening?"

John nodded. He hoped Millicent was listening.

I'm listening, she said, but she couldn't take her eyes off the claw that tugged at Miriam's skin.

"The area surrounding Süütakkan is teeming with Lucifur's animals, so you must veer to the eastern foothills. Follow the river south to the lake. Find the boathouse. A ferry will take you to Abatakai."

John listened but was distracted by Millicent's pained expression. Would she remember? He predicted that she would be useless without Miriam, and everything would be left to him, and he wasn't *good* at remembering directions like this. He attempted to replay them: East. River. Avoid . . . something. Foothills? Lake . . . ferry . . . something.

Friggin' muck.

They would make it. He wasn't sure how, but they would make it.

"What do we do once we get there?"

"Make your way into his sanctuary and find out what he knows."

Sahra rolled her eyes. "Why don't you ask him yourself?"

"He refuses to speak to anyone, and he's made that tower impenetrable to us, my love. But to humans? I'm betting the Fisherman will let them in."

"Bawd!" said Lord Nagus. "And Red Bear won't tell me. He speaks of power but won't tell me! I am his lord, and he won't tell me!" He stomped like a child throwing a tantrum.

"Yes," said Copernicus. "He's been speaking in half-truths. He claims that his purpose is protect Caldera from a human invasion. But I know that he'll keep this power, and, once he has it, he will bend us to his will. For the protection of our species, we must know!"

A yelp startled them. A grizzly bear plodded though the trees

Chapter Fourteen

dragging Gabriel by a hind leg. The bear dropped him to the ground and held him in place with a paw.

"Goodness," said Copernicus. "Now there's even more at stake. Save your sister. Save your dog."

Ignoring the growling bears, John ran to Gabriel and hovered his hands over him, afraid to touch him because he looked so tattered and dirty. Gabriel looked up and let his tongue droop out once he saw it was John. The bear holding Gabriel pushed John back with a mighty paw.

Copernicus stared until John met his gaze. "Come back the way you came, and my cats will lead you to Doyadu-khani."

John searched for a way to protest, but he couldn't see a way. There were far too many of them to fight, and even if they could somehow get Miriam away, she wouldn't be able to walk. If Ze'eva's wolves were no match for them . . .

Millicent wasn't crying anymore, which surprised him. He helped her to stand, put his arm around her, and followed the three cougars into the forest.

Miriam's voice whispered after them.

Please. Be careful.

Fifteen

Two Journeys

Miriam strained to feel John and Millicent as long as she could before they left the range of her senses.

Then she was alone.

Okay. Okay. Nothing wrong here. Nope. This is all perfectly normal.

She strained to lift her head from the ground to look at her foot. Her right shoe still looked new with a white body, blue stripes, and silver laces, but her left shoe was dark gray and ragged. Holding her head up took too much effort. She closed her eyes and tried to wiggle her toes, but she felt nothing. It was as though her left leg was gone below the knee.

Good gravy, what did Ze'eva do to me?

This was a bad one, she could tell. She'd sustained plenty of injuries from soccer and just playing around, and she always measured her wounds on an imaginary version of the chart that doctors use, the kind with a green smiley face on one end and a red, angry face on the other. Her foot may have been numb, but this would be the red, angry one to end all red, angry ones. No, this one was worse than that, and she knew it. She'd never seen a chart with the face necessary to describe the pain she'd felt. It would be demonic and black and horrible.

She kept her eyes closed from exhaustion and because she didn't want to make eye contact with her captors. Her head swam. She swallowed hard to fight waves of nausea. She fell in and out of consciousness.

The bears chomped and slurped and celebrated with boisterous voices, awakening her. She wondered how much time had passed.

"Lord Nagus is still hungry!" said one of the bears.

Chapter Fifteen

"He's chewed his way through the carrion on the bluff," said another. "Yet he hungers!"

"We're surrounded by forest," said a cougar. "Tell him to keep looking. We're not doing it for him."

Miriam was puzzled by how she could distinguish the bears from the cougars with her eyes closed. They were as distinct as the timbres of a viola and a cello.

Copernicus was nearer than she thought he was, and his voice made her flinch. "Tell the Lord to find his temper. He'll soon be feasting in Doyadu-khani!"

The bears cheered.

"How dare you!" said Sahra, and, hearing her voice, Miriam ached to be close to her. "You have no right to take them there."

Copernicus purred. "I have every right, love. The Rule of Carnivores will soon be in effect throughout Caldera, isn't that right, fellows?"

The bears laughed and taunted.

Ze'eva spoke next, and the weakness in her voice scared Miriam. She sounded near death. "You are a proud little monster, aren't you? Does our Code mean nothing to you?"

"Well, Lady, I had an epiphany. I can't ask my species to adhere to something when I myself don't know where it came from. Who wrote that code? Even you don't know. But guess what. The Fisherman knows. And Lucifur learned about a much older code from him. Once we're finished, the Carnivores will rule as we should have all along."

"For someone named Copernicus . . . you have a terrible model of the universe."

He chuckled. "That was sly, wolf."

His whiskers brushed against Miriam's cheek. "You can open your eyes, kitten. It's obvious to us when someone is awake." Then he called to the group, "It's time to move. Bring the mammoth."

Miriam opened her eyes at the mention of Emily, but she could only see Lord Nagus. He rocked back and forth as he plodded down from the bluff, and the closer he came, the larger he appeared, until he loomed above her. He coughed and belched and sat his enormous posterior on the ground, which made him look as wide as he was tall. He smelled like bad cheese.

"What's this noise?" he asked. "No food till we reach the cat house?"

His voice was wet and sloppy in Miriam's brain, and she yearned for a cotton swab to scoop it out.

"Lord Nagus, I beg your patience," said Copernicus. "Your appetite will be fulfilled, I promise. We have plenty of food stores in the temple."

Nagus squinted at him. He shook his massive head. His furry jowls swayed beneath his haggard snout and froth-lined mouth, which hung open at the corners. "Bah! I'll find something along the way. Oh, how I could make a meal out of that mammoth, though!" He choked with laughter. "Ooh, I would suck on those big bones for days! I'm loving this new code!"

The other bears hooted and howled.

"Isn't it divine, my copious friend? It opens an endless field of prey."

"Endless field of prey! Oh, I like the way you think, coog."

Miriam winced as a needle of spite pierced her mind. Copernicus didn't like that word, *coog*. He didn't like it at all.

"Yes, Lord," he said.

Ze'eva grunted at them. "Braggarts! You threaten everything."

Nagus cocked his head and stared dumbfounded. "Every-what-thing?"

"You want for nothing yet look at you! Are you such a glutton that you'll let your appetite dictate your morals?"

Nagus buried his head into his shoulders as though he'd tasted something sour. "You're so smart? Shut up! Shut up!" His eyes flared yellow, and Ze'eva slumped to the ground. Miriam wondered what they'd done to her, how much pain they forced her to siphon from the wounded on top of what she'd already taken from her foot.

Chapter Fifteen

Nagus opened his eyes coolly. He almost looked studious. "Seriously, though. I would like to dine on the mammoth right about now."

"Like tar you will!" said Emily. Miriam turned to find her surrounded by bears in a nearby grove.

Nagus rolled onto his back, laughing, and exposed the bloated expanse of his soiled underside. "Ooh! She'll put up such a good fight!"

"You bet I will, you jackal!

Without a further word, he rolled onto his feet and charged at her. He collided with her and wrapped his arms around her trunk and held onto it with his mouth.

She screamed. "Get off of me!"

Miriam couldn't stand it anymore. She sat up on her elbows with a shout and attacked Nagus's brain. He released Emily and bellowed as he countered, so Miriam had to push harder.

Stay down! Stay down! STAY DOWN!

Another bear rammed into her and blocked her assault with a loud "Stop!" and a yellow flash in his eyes. This time, she could feel the bear's command like fingers kneading into her brain. She felt that she could've forced them out if she wanted to. It gave her a vindictive streak of confidence.

Nagus bellowed again. He righted himself and roared.

Copernicus slinked between them. "Before you do anything, Lord, we need her! We need her alive. Kill her now, and we'll never learn the secret."

"Secret! What secret? Bah! Secrets and powers! That's all I hear, but what! When we finish — learn all this stuff — she's mine. Do you hear me, little pink? You're mine!" He stomped away, coughing and retching.

But buried in his brain was the slightest glimmer of fear. Its presence gave Miriam goosebumps. She delighted in it and longed to attack him again, to hit him with his back turned and strike him senseless, but Copernicus glared at her.

Two Journeys

"One swipe of a paw. That's all it would take from him to kill you. So, mind yourself! I might not be there next time."

She glowered and turned away from him. That's when she saw Gabriel tethered to a tree with a crude muzzle over his snout. He was attentive, as always, as though he'd been waiting the whole time for her to see him.

"I'm here," he said. "I'm here."

She nodded and fought back her tears.

Nope. Nothing wrong here. This is all perfectly normal.

Another wave of queasiness hit her, but this time it was from a feeling of hollowness, because they'd won, because they escaped Caldera and needed only to walk away but ruined the chance by going to the lab. She cringed at her bravado, her single-minded confidence that they would be successful. She wanted to go back to that moment and throttle herself.

The hollowness turned into despair. A sudden attack of homesickness made her whole body constrict. She thought, even if her mom and dad could appear, they wouldn't be able to help her. And she'd be scared for their lives.

She knew that they were out there, somewhere, scared for hers.

Thank goodness you can't see me.

I wish you could see me.

Several miles away, John and Millicent walked east with two cougars behind them and one who led the way. Birds chirped and sang overhead, and John could hear them whispering beneath the birdsong. They moved from tree to tree. A variety of birds joined, all being sneaky, but it was impossible for the gathering to remain inconspicuous.

Millicent was silent and paid no attention to the growing flock. She walked like a robot.

The cougars hissed. After another mile of the birds' incessant chatter, their noise became deafening. Larger birds like falcons and eagles arrived. John tugged Millicent's arm for her to stop as the cats

Chapter Fifteen

spread out and screeched at the air.

The birdsong reached a crescendo, and as a single, fluid mass, the flock divebombed from the trees. John and Millicent stumbled to the ground to shield themselves, and the cougars cried and scrambled to escape. Some of the birds were enormous up close and terrifying with their giant wingspans and sharp talons. The cats fled, and most of the birds chased after them.

And just like that, it was quiet again.

"Heading, captain?" asked a tiny French voice.

"Who's there?" asked John, unable to find the source.

"Sir! I'm on your trouser-hat!"

"My —" John began, looking up. An enormous, brown, furry spider peeked with eight beady eyes over the edge of his makeshift hat. He screamed and doubled over and threw it off his head.

"Yee!" said the spider as it flew.

Above them in the branches, the remaining birds scattered and regrouped and pretended they weren't there. The spider scurried from beneath the shorts. With a better look at him, it was clear that he was a tarantula.

"That was a great throw, Captain! Shall we play again?" He waved his front legs and said, "Yee!"

John hated spiders. Miriam always teased him with them in their sandbox and laughed when he "screamed like a girl." Millicent wasn't fond of them, either, but Miriam knew better than to terrorize her.

The tarantula grabbed the edge of John's shorts with his mandibles and dragged them across the rocky soil. "Here, Captain! Your trouser-hat!"

John shook his head. *I am not befriending that thing.*

The tarantula stopped and grumbled.

Wait, said Millicent in private as a test. *Can he hear us?*

"Loud and clear, Lieutenant," said the tarantula. "I get it. I do. Humans hate us. So, I shall take my leave of you." He disappeared into the foliage.

Two Journeys

John picked up his shorts with a thumb and forefinger and turned them to check for other stowaways. "The ants I met were a little loony, too."

"It's because their brains are so tiny," said Millicent with a deadpan rasp.

"I heard that!" said the tarantula from the forest.

John stuffed the shorts into his backpack and scanned their surroundings. He wondered how far the birds would chase the cougars and whether or not the cats would double back to intercept them.

"Where do you think those birds came from?"

"I have no idea."

The more detached Millicent became, the more her voice sounded like a dry, little carburetor. He couldn't blame her after what happened to Miriam, but he knew that the secret to keeping her up was to let her choose what they did next.

"So. What do you think we should do?"

She stared at nothing, rocked her jaw, and breathed through her nose like a bull.

"Milly — "

She yelled. "We're stuck! I don't know! What do you want me to say?"

"I know we're stuck. That's why I'm asking you."

"I hate this! We're never going home!"

He wanted to sound optimistic, but he couldn't lie to her. She would see right through him. "We don't know that," was all he could come up with.

"Nobody knows! Not even Ze'eva. I just don't understand how everything changed as soon as we came back, and — boom! — we're in the middle of some crazy animal war. Ugh, I hate even calling it that. It's ridiculous!"

The clarity in her anger surprised him, but she was right about everything. Even though Ze'eva had explained how Lucifur rallied animals to his side by inciting a fear of humans, John still didn't

Chapter Fifteen

understand why. They could activate scenes in the Mesa, but what did that have to do with Lucifur? Lucifur moved to Dragon's Mouth — Süütakkan, the Spire, whatever they wanted to call it — but what did that have to do with . . . anything?

This was a puzzle, all right, and he knew that Millicent was the best at solving puzzles.

"What's the next piece?" he asked.

She was deep in thought and muttering to herself. He heard a few swear words.

"Milly!"

"Huh!"

"What's the next piece in the puzzle? We know humans lived here. We know the Asaquatzi killed them. We know Lucifur needs us. It all fits together somehow, but we're still missing something."

Millicent looked at him with fiery disappointment. "I don't care about any of that — I can't stop thinking about Miri!"

"Are you saying I'm not? It's my fault she fell!"

They were quiet for a moment. The late morning was warming up with the sunshine speckling through the fir trees. It would have been the perfect time to hear birdsong if all the birds weren't sneaking around the branches for some odd reason.

Millicent spoke again, but this time in a clear and normal voice. "All we're missing is the answer to the biggest question: What does Lucifur want?" She shrugged and cupped her palms upward and looked a little loony as she repeated the phrase with different inflections. She sounded like a row of confused people. "What does Lucifur want? I dunno, what does he want? What does he *want*? I dunno, what *does* he want?"

"Stop. I get it. You're scaring me. What do you *think* he wants?"

She paused for a second and then stated a suspicion she'd carried since they watched the creation of Süütakkan. "I think he wants to become like the Asaquatzi."

John stared. He knew she was clever, but this idea shocked him. "Do you mean, like, turn into it?"

Two Journeys

"Yeah." She rolled her hands outward in a big wave. "An-n-nd we come to yet another mystery. Where did the Asaquatzi come from? The only clues are whatever the keystone opens and whatever the Fisherman knows. Lucifur has the keystone, so we're kinda stuck doing what Copernicus wants."

She bounced her fingers on her lips, and John could feel her frustration melt into nervous curiosity, like somebody was changing the radio station in her head.

"So." She sucked in a lungful of air. "We need to talk to the Fisherman and hope he can tell us something useful."

This was the last thing he expected her to say. And though he started with no opinion about what to do next, his gut told him that they should probably meet the only other human in Caldera.

"Are you sure?" he asked.

She raised her eyebrows, wrinkled up her forehead, and let her mouth hang open. She wasn't *sure* about anything.

"Okay, okay," said John. "We'll go, meet this guy, and get back here."

"Ha."

"Ha what?"

"You have no idea how far away it is, do you?"

"No, Mill, I don't. How far away is it?"

She hated when he used her name for emphasis. "Well, you see, *John*. It's twenty miles away. Twenty miles through a Yellowstone with no real paths. It'll take us a couple of days to walk there, then a couple to walk back, and then a couple — "

"I get it." He ran his fingers through his hair. He checked on the hundred-or-so remaining birds, who were still trying to stay hidden above them. They fluttered between branches, and he wondered what they were waiting for.

"At least we'll have company."

The birds looked at each other and argued over whose fault it was that they'd been detected.

Chapter Fifteen

The forest was an endless maze of trees, like someone planted crusty telephone poles one after another after another. John found a better walking stick at last and offered his old one to Millicent. She shrugged at first, but it was the perfect size for her, and he caught the corner of her mouth give the slightest smile. The sticks came in handy as the land rose and took their breath away. It curved over a dome, a broad, blunt, forested peak. Hiking down the other side was a relief from climbing, but it grew wearisome after a few minutes, too.

John wheezed in the heat and wiped his forehead with the sleeve of his t-shirt. Millicent panted next to him. Her face was red and blotchy.

"We have all these amazing powers, but we can't even go for a walk without dying."

Keep her going, he thought. *Don't let her stop.* "Well, what do you know about the foothills Copernicus talked about?"

"Here, I'll show you."

She grabbed his hand. They were both disgustingly sweaty. A map of Yellowstone suddenly floated in front of him like a hologram in his mind's eye. The amount of detail stored in her brain was astounding.

"That's Dragon's Mouth," she said. "Copernicus wants us to go around it like this." She drew a line that traveled due east from where they were standing to the Yellowstone River. Then it turned southward with a large curve to the east again to avoid a spot that she marked with a big, red X. *AVOID.*

John spied a shorter, straighter route that ran southeast instead of going all the way to the river and down. "Can't we cut across here?"

"No. See this? Avoid. That means this whole area between us and them." She saw the skeptical look on his face. "I know he lied about a lot of things, but I don't think he lied about this. He was too anxious."

He got distracted by the map and the fact that she could do this. "Huh? Anxious?"

"Yeah. He was calm about everything else, but he got all fired up when he started talking about Lucifur. I think he needs us to get this information, so he gave us very specific instructions. He wants us to get there."

"Okay," he said. "We'll go that way. It just seems like an awful long way around."

She nodded.

Out of the blue, John clamped his hand over his belly and shouted.

Millicent shouted with him. "Aah! What's wrong?"

"We didn't bring any food! Of all the stupid things! Emily had a ton of food with her, too!"

She punched his arm. "Crimminy Jickets! You scared me! I thought your appendix had burst or something!"

"Ow!"

"I have some food in my bag, dummy." She slung it around and produced two brown-paper packages, one filled with nuts and the other soaking through with raspberry juice. "The berries are a little squished."

He frowned at the sad offerings but knew they couldn't be choosy. "It's better than nothing. We can ration it."

"Captain!" called the spider from behind them. "There are good nuts all around!"

John sighed. "It's the tarantula, isn't it?"

Millicent looked over his shoulder and found it approaching with a long pinecone. "Yep. There's a big, hairy spider crawling up behind you. Um. He's carrying a pinecone."

"Sensational."

The tarantula dropped the pinecone and ran away.

Millicent gasped. "Oh, my goodness! Oh, my goodness!"

"What?"

She stammered and rolled her hand in the air to summon her words. "I read about this! Pine nuts! Bears eat them! Only, they can't find them as much because the region's whitebark pine trees surrendered to an invasive pine beetle on a scale of death and devastation the world has never seen!"

"Whoa! What?"

"I read it in a magazine on the way here. It was about global

Chapter Fifteen

warming and its effects on the bears. But here isn't here, you know? We're *here!*"

He grabbed her by the shoulders. "Speak a cohesive sentence, Millicent!"

She laughed. "Ha! I remembered all that by rote!" She grabbed the pinecone from the ground, cracked it in half, and peeled its hard, wooden petals. The crumbly debris yielded a few, pitiful, black seeds. "Hmm. These don't look like pine nuts . . . "

"Maybe we can eat them in a pinch?"

She licked the seeds from her palm and wiped her hands on her overalls. "Whoopsies. I teased Miriam because she wanted to eat one. Let's keep this our little secret, okay?"

John ate a few of the squished berries and peered after the spider. "I wonder where he went. He sure did follow us a long way."

"Yeah. I don't like spiders, but I think he just wants to be helpful."

"You ready to keep going?"

She sighed. "Yes."

She adjusted her pack and readied her walking stick. John was proud. He knew the slightest provocation would send her back to worry and tears, but she seemed to have found some confidence.

Miriam sat upright next to Gabriel on Emily's back. Commotion ahead brought the caravan to a halt.

"What's happening, Emily?"

"I'm not sure, but it sounds like Copernicus is angry."

Miriam projected her thoughts forward. She hopped from bear to bear until she could hear the argument.

Copernicus was livid. "Birds! The three of you ran away because of *birds*? Tell me there were a thousand of them!"

"Yes, my king! Thousands and thousands!"

Lord Nagus guffawed. "Birds! Bwahaha! The plan's not going so good, eh, coog?"

Copernicus ignored him and walked back to Emily. "Miriam, free that dog of yours. He'll track your siblings and assist them."

Gabriel whined. His ear flopped over, his face bore scars from the porcupine, and his fur was stained with blood and filth from the cougar and bear attack. He looked at Miriam with sad, brown eyes.

"I wanna stay with you! You're hurt!"

She removed the muzzle. "I know, but I would feel better if you were with them. They need you more. Tell them that I'm okay."

"It's settled," said Copernicus. "Off you go, pooch."

Gabriel climbed down Emily's bent arm. He paused and whimpered. "Take care of her, Emily. Please."

"You know I will," said the mammoth.

As the line of cougars and bears marched through midday, the pain in Miriam's foot returned. She took deep breaths and looked around and fidgeted to push it away, but the stinging worsened in sickening waves. She lay on her back and covered her eyes with her arm.

Oh, it hurts!

"You poor kid," said Emily. "Hey, pumas! Bring Lady Ze'eva. Miriam needs her!"

Copernicus called to the bears. "Bring the wolf!"

Nagus shook his jowls with a hardy grumble. "What's that for? Why bother with that about?"

"The child is in pain," said Copernicus.

"Like I care so much? Your head! It'll be your head if the wolf gets away. I'll crunch it like toast!"

"So be it."

Nagus cackled. "You're so silly, cat! Let the wolf slobber the brat. I don't care."

Ze'eva was at the back of the line surrounded by bears who secured her with ropes. They released her, and she caught up to Emily.

"Lift me up, please, Emily."

Emily struggled to lift the giant wolf onto her back. Once there, Ze'eva began siphoning.

Miriam pushed her snout away. "No! You've done enough!"

Chapter Fifteen

Ze'eva pushed back. "Child, if I stop, the pain will rush back into you. Remember. This is my privilege."

Miriam relented. As Ze'eva growled and furrowed her brow, she placed her palms flat on the wolf's head to absorb some of the pain in return.

"You have such a sweet heart. We call this mutuality, and it helps me greatly. But don't take on too much — it defeats the purpose."

All her pain was gone when they finished. Ze'eva mustered some warmth in her eyes, but the brilliant blue that seemed to glow in the dimness of the hospital when they first met was gone, replaced by a smoky gray. Her upswept tufts and points of hair were deflated and lumpy. She looked sickly.

"Remember, this is temporary, and your injury will take a long time to heal. Don't go running around on it."

"I won't."

"I'm so sorry this happened to you."

"I was out of it, but I overheard you and Sahra talking." She cleared her throat with a sarcastic chuckle. "What, ah, exactly does 'beyond your ability to heal' mean?"

Ze'eva paused for a second. "It means there's cellular damage that I can't reach. We can't magically repair an injury that wouldn't have healed on its own. We can only quicken the natural process and alleviate pain."

"Wait — wouldn't have healed on its own?"

"Miriam. This is a lasting injury. Were you at home, you'd be in the hospital for a long time. There would be skin grafts and endless cotton wrappings and a lot of pain."

Miriam nodded. She did ask, after all. It wasn't Ze'eva's fault that the prognosis was awful.

"Thanks for being honest with me."

"It's important for you to know." Ze'eva leaned close and whispered, "I know you'll be okay."

Miriam smiled and turned around and put her feet on either side of

Two Journeys

Emily's neck. The scenery looked much the same, but the air was thicker with moisture. She watched the bears and cougars as they loped ahead in their tireless gait. Her foot was pain-free. It was bliss.

"The wolf!" bellowed Lord Nagus. "Where is the wolf?"

Miriam spun around. Ze'eva was gone.

Oh no! He's gonna be so angry!

"We're losing daylight," said John. He pushed the ground past him with his walking stick like he was a gondolier. "We should find a place to sleep."

The birds still followed them. Their numbers dwindled, and those who remained looked bored. "There goes another one," said Millicent as a yellow warbler flew away.

A female nuthatch, a small bird with a pointy, black beak and a bright, white belly and face under a slate-blue hood that wrapped down her wings, landed on a branch in front of them. Her voice sounded like that of a young child.

"Okay. We give up! Where are you guys going?"

"Who are you? Why are you following us?" asked Millicent.

"Don't be rude," said John. "Thank you for scaring the cougars away. Why'd you do that?"

The little bird cocked her head one way and the other and hopped to a lower branch. She never stopped moving. "She is not rude! Not at all! I would ask the very same thing. Yes, I would! We were just curious is why I'm asking."

"Do you know Lucifur?" asked Millicent.

The nuthatch looked back and forth nervously. "Some of us do!" she whispered in an amplified way that negated the purpose of whispering.

Millicent raised her hands. "See? Now he knows we're here for sure!"

"Mill, shush," said John. He stepped closer to the bird. "I'm sorry, but what do you mean *some* of you know him?"

She chirped. "I have never met him, but some of my friends were

Chapter Fifteen

there the day he tried to recruit, yes they were."

"Recruit?"

The bird hopped to the trunk of the tree and hung sideways with her spindly toes gripping the bark. "He controlled many, many animals, and he tried to control us, yes he did, but we fly free, we birds, and he proved it that day!"

Millicent drummed fingers on her lips. "So, Lucifur can't control birds..."

The nuthatch hopped to the branch again. "We swooped and chattered and dropped rocks on the rodents to shoo them away, but they wouldn't listen to us. He led them right into a Mesa cave, never to be seen again."

They processed her story and shared a guess that these were the rodents he used to dig through the keystone tunnel. They felt sad for her, because they knew that she didn't know the rest of the story.

"If you please," said John. "What we want to know is, whose side are you on?"

"Whose side!" She hopped up a few branches. "We see most everything, flying free, and we do not like this bear, not the way he treats other animals, nope, nope!"

"Okay, so, who are you and why are you following us?" asked Millicent. "My original two questions, by the way," she said parenthetically.

"I am Jiya! We saw you with the cougars and bears. We watched you leave with those naughty cats, and we wondered where you were going. Lady Ze'eva sent a request for us to shoo them away. Shoo, shoo, shoo!"

"Ze'eva sent you!" said Millicent. With that, she decided it was safe to tell her. "We're going to Abatakai. Copernicus wants us to talk to the Fisherman."

Jiya chattered and flew to the other side of the tree.

"What's wrong?" asked John, following her around the trunk.

Jiya shook her head. "Copernicus is a wise cat and a friend to us birds, but this is folly. To put you into peril? Why would he want to put you into peril? Such peril!"

The blood drained from Millicent's face. "Sweet mother of peaches, that was three perils in a row. What are you talking about, Jiya? Why do you keep using the word peril?"

"Because of the lake. We stay away from the lake! Animals go in, but they don't come out. The water-bears, they will snap, snap, snap! And the mosquitoes like to bite, bite, bite! Ooh, oh, and the birds are so big, they can bite your arm off like a little carrot!"

Millicent backed away as panic crept into her voice. "This is a trap. John, this whole . . . 'mission' is a trap!"

"I know it sounds like that, but why would he send us clear across the park just to kill us? You said it yourself, right? He wants us to get there? What happened to that?"

Millicent slapped her hands to her sides. "Fine. So, we can't go forward, and we can't go back. But we have to go forward if we wanna go back!"

"Jiya, do you know this area?" asked John.

"No, because this is not my forest. You should ask Arthur!"

"Okay," he said, scanning the birds above them. "Which one is he?"

Jiya craned her head to see where he was looking. "I do not think he crawled up there . . . "

"Hello?" he called, and the birds ruffled their feathers and looked at each other.

Jiya laughed. "Oh, silly, silly! A tarantula is not a bird!"

John slumped. *Of course!* He glanced at Millicent, who rolled her eyes. "Is Arthur the tarantula?"

"Yes. But sadly, you rejected him."

John rubbed his eyelids. He wanted to be more trusting and confident with the animals, yet here was another example of —

It was a tarantula! Millicent yelped, breaking into his thoughts. *It was perfectly acceptable for us to be afraid of it!*

"I know. I know."

Chapter Fifteen

And we trusted Copernicus and look how that turned out!

Arthur's voice charmed into their heads. "Fear not, Captain! Come with me, *s'il vous plaît**, and I shall guide you to shelter!" The little tarantula was sitting on a rock and waving his two front legs again. "It's not far, if we hurry."

Apparently content, the rest of the birds flew away. Jiya landed on the tip of John's walking stick. "Do you want me to come with you?"

Trust the little bird, John, he said to himself. *Start small. You can do it.* "Yes, please. If you'd like to, I mean. Yes."

"Come on! Come on!" said Arthur, and they followed him, they hoped, to shelter.

Lord Nagus was as angry as Miriam feared. He swatted a bear across the face, stormed up and down the line, and demanded to know who was responsible for letting Ze'eva go. The bears murmured about not knowing anything, which made him angrier. He sniffed the wind with a throaty snort, and, not catching her scent, he roared and stomped.

"You!" he said to Emily. "Your hairy hide must have felt her leave! When did she leave?"

Emily stood still. Nagus swiped his paw across her trunk and sent it whirling. She tucked her chin into her chest to protect it. He held his claws up again.

"I don't know!"

"You don't know! And you, little pink, you're so quiet up there!" He rammed his shoulder against Emily's shaggy side, and Miriam lurched and clung to her. "Come down! Come down and talk!"

Copernicus approached. "They didn't know about the wolf. I sensed their surprise when you brought it to our attention."

Nagus turned on the cat, towered over him, and bared his yellowed fangs under his curled-up lip. "You were right there! Right there! Your orange kitty nose didn't smell? Those lousy kitty eyes didn't see? Some hunter you are!" He wound his arm back to strike.

Copernicus didn't blink. "Stay your paw, or you lose this

   272   *See *Arthur's Phrasebook* on page 455.

partnership. And if we lose that, we lose everything. It's your choice."

Nagus's face twisted. "Bah! Send your kitties into the forest to find the nurse-dog!" He turned to walk toward the front of the line.

Miriam felt him bury another flicker of fear, and she clenched her jaw.

Yeah. You better run.

Several cats approached Copernicus, but he shook his head. "I'm fine, thank you, and you don't have to go anywhere. Nobody can track Ze'eva, and you couldn't outrun her if you did, even in her condition." The cougars shifted their eyes to Nagus. "I know. Go on ahead and look after Sahra. Don't allow the bears to mistreat her."

Four bears arrived to summon Emily. She gave a long sigh. "Save it, bears. I'm movin'. I'm movin'."

Copernicus walked beside her. He was irritated, but Miriam felt an underlying anxiousness. He glanced up at her.

"Are you okay?"

She was dumbfounded because he sounded sincere. At the same time, she was holding on to the exposed, bloodstained fluff of the comforter where he'd scratched Emily's back.

"I'm fine."

"I know you're in strung-out shape but stay frosty and alert with that bear around." He slowed to walk behind them.

Dusk gave way to starlight, but the animals didn't slow. Miriam scooted forward her head rested on Emily's head behind her shaggy, bony crest. She held on to it like it was a life preserver.

Emily?

"Yes?"

Is your trunk okay?

"It hurts. A lot. Don't even think about siphoning it."

Miriam closed her eyes and hoped the night would pass swiftly, but thunder in the west made her heart sink. She turned her head to watch the lightning on the horizon.

Chapter Fifteen

The cold wind grew stronger across the edge of Hayden Valley as dark clouds rolled in to block the stars. Arthur skittered along an animal trail down the face of a steep, forested hill, and John and Millicent hurried to keep up with him in the dark. Jiya flew from branch to branch.

"Here!" said Arthur. "I'm sorry about the nightfall, Captain."

He led them around an outcropping of rock on the hillside, and they scrambled into a shallow cave beneath it.

"Wow, this is like a natural lean-to!" said John. "Great job, Arthur! I'm — I'm sorry for how I treated you."

"It's understandable." He waved his front four legs in circles. "I'm cree-eepy!"

A downpour hit the roof. The ground sloped away from the entrance, so the cave stayed remarkably dry. Jiya perched near the opening and drank from the pooling rainwater.

"I'll stand guard while you to sleep, Captain," said Arthur, and he rotated to face outward.

"Can I ask . . . why do you call me Captain?"

"Yeah! And why am I a *lieutenant*?" asked Millicent.

He rotated to face them again. "He is your leader, no?"

"Ha!"

"No, I'm not the leader," said John. "We're just brother and sister."

"You're not the captain?"

John was sure that this was the strangest conversation he'd ever had. "No, I'm not the captain."

"Suit yourself," said Arthur, and he turned to face out again, looking vigilant.

Millicent released her hair from her pigtails and untangled her curls. It was tedious work. She laid her head on a rolled-up sweatshirt and felt numb. She closed her eyes in a futile attempt to feel Miriam across the void. Again, she thought of their nighttime routine at home, her mother's voice, her father's jokes, and how Miriam slept in the next bed when they were younger. But their new house was big enough for

Two Journeys

each of them to have their own bedroom. While it was wonderful to have a space of her own, all she wanted now was to be back in their old bedroom with her sister sleeping across from her.

"I hope Miri's okay."

"Me too," said John. He pulled off his shoes and lay next to her.

"It's not your fault, you know. Her foot?"

John did a double take. *How does she know what I'm thinking? Oh. That's right. We can read minds.*

I wasn't reading your mind.

You now!

She blinked a few times and tried to understand what he meant. *Boy, you really need more practice at this.*

He sighed. "It wasn't my fault about her foot just like it wasn't my fault that Rodney lost an eye. Be careful around me. You'll end up disfigured."

"Ouch. Don't say that."

"It's just what happens here."

"We should reach Dragon's Mouth tomorrow afternoon."

He nodded and propped himself up to see if the little nuthatch was still at the edge of the cave. She was a tiny little ball of feathers next to Arthur, with her head turned backward to rest on her wings.

"Hey, Jiya?"

Her head popped up. "Yes?"

"What do you know about the Fisherman?"

"Oh, no, not too much. Only that he has been here for a long time. A long, long time! Grandbirds tell us he used to walk the banks and lived in a cabin, but that's long gone now. He has moved to the Great Fish and does not come out, nope. Lots of eagles and hawks fly there. Some thought he was dead until Lucifur talked to him."

Her words sent a chill through them; this was the first inkling that they were right about where Lucifur received his information. John wondered what Abatakai would look like in person, standing on its tail in the middle of the lake. He wondered what Lucifur's spire looked like,

Chapter Fifteen

too, and whether they would see it from the foothills. He wondered about Miriam's foot and Rodney's missing eye, and about Sebastian. He realized, as of that moment, that he and Sebastian had been apart longer than they were ever together. And he realized, with everything that was happening, he hadn't thought of the bear in a long time.

And then, with a horrible gush of pain up his throat, he realized that he hadn't wondered about his parents in a long time, too. They somehow kept stepping farther away from home the harder they tried to reach it.

. . . and — boom! — we're in the middle of some crazy animal war. Ugh, I hate even calling it that. It's ridiculous!

He shook his head. He was about to ask Millicent more about the war because he still didn't understand it, but she was already snoring.

Yes. It's ridiculous, he thought to himself.

Miriam woke to raucous hoots and howls. The bears bumped into each other and wrestled as they walked.

Are we there?

"Yes," said Emily. "There's Doyadu-khani."

They arrived at the top of a magnificent field that descended to Mammoth Hot Springs. A colossal stone bridge wound down the countryside and then over the steaming, alien landscape to Doyadu-khani, "the cat house," as Sebastian had explained, a black and yellow trapezoid that reminded Miriam of a Mayan temple.

"Feast!" bellowed Lord Nagus, goading the bears, and they chanted with him, "Feast, feast, feast!"

The pyramid towered over them as they travelled the walkway that gave smooth passage over the travertine terraces, natural platforms of bleached and yellow rock that looked like somebody melted candlewax all over them. Doyadu-khani, by contrast, was made of sharply-cut slabs of rock. It wasn't as large as the Mesa, but it was still impressive. Tall shanks of obsidian bracketed walls of shiny ochre. Cougars lounged on window ledges, and they slipped out of sight once they noticed their guests were arriving.

Nagus gurgled and coughed as they made their way across a beautiful plaza in front of the temple. Tendrils of saliva trailed from the corners of his mouth.

"There'll be some good eats here, I can tell! Oh, ho-ho! No bear has ever walked in this cat-place!"

A giant, obsidian panel at the end of the walkway slid open, and the cougars ran out to form ranks on either side of the bridge. They faced inward like two rows of lawn statues.

"Welcome to Doyadu-khani," said Copernicus. "On to the feasting hall!"

"Yes, yes!" said Nagus.

Copernicus slid next to Emily. "Ahem. You may be Queen Mother in the Mesa, but your title means nothing here. Let the bears go first and have their fill."

Emily sighed. The bears funneled into the entrance, cheering and licking their chops as they passed the cougars, lynxes, and bobcats who lived there. They filed into the next chamber, and a thick, black door slid shut.

All the cats relaxed.

"There," said Copernicus. "Our guests are situated."

Muffled yells and thumps came through the wall. Miriam sat upright. Nagus bellowed over the rest of them about how they were captives instead of guests.

The bears had been tricked.

John and Millicent woke to a generous breakfast of salmon, nuts, and berries. Arthur presented it to them and danced an odd, little jig.

"Ahoy and enjoy!"

"This makes for a nice birthday breakfast," said Millicent.

John stopped chewing and counted the days since their arrival. "Oh, wow, you're right!"

"Happy Birthday," she said, and she toasted him with an almond.

Chapter Fifteen

"Happy Birthday, Captain! I hope you don't mind me calling you that. I'm partial to it."

"Wow. Thank you. I would've forgotten all about it." He shook his head as he ate, as he tried to absorb the fact that this surreal place was the setting for his thirteenth birthday and that a tarantula had arranged his breakfast.

Millicent trapped her curls into new mini-buns. They finished eating, packed their belongings, and followed Arthur toward the sunrise. Jiya glided from a tree and reported that several birds would be watching from above.

They reached the Yellowstone River by noon. As the water rushed past, it occurred to Millicent that getting east of Dragon's Mouth meant they needed to cross it, and she had no idea how to ford such an aggressive river.

"How do we get past this sucker?"

"You must cross, yes?" asked Arthur.

"Yes. Do you know a way?"

"I will show you."

He dipped one leg into the water. His eight, tiny, round eyes glowed yellow, and a patch of calmness extended from his clawed foot to the opposite bank. He crawled onto it and beckoned them to follow.

"Voila! I present to you a bridge!"

Millicent was dumbstruck. "Are you floating?"

"Nope!" He drummed his feet without creating ripples. "I am standing. Come, please."

John stood by the edge and poked the solid water with his stick. "How are you doing this?"

"It's a gift, I'm told."

"For all spiders?"

"Yes! Water masters are we."

A hiccup stuck in John's throat. "Okay. I don't know about this." He expected to plunge into the water when he stepped, but the surface bowed under his weight and held him up. The overall sensation was like walking on a trampoline. "Oh my gosh! Mill! Check this out!"

"Oh dear."

She plugged her nose as she stepped and gave a surprised shout when she landed on the invisible membrane. She tapped the surface with her foot and exchanged incredulous looks with John. Arthur waited for them to hurry across and hop onto the opposite bank before he released his hold and let the current rush past.

"That . . . was amazing!" said John.

"Aye, Captain."

Millicent shook her head in disbelief. "Wait. So, all spiders can do that?"

"Mm-hmm, all the good ones!"

"Crazy."

Now that they were across, she had a keen sense of where Dragon's Mouth would be, but she wasn't sure how far into the hills they needed to hike to be safe. The way ahead would be uphill and then uphill again beyond that, and then the foothills would fold into the eastern mountains with peaks like Pelican Cone – which she assumed was Unreachable.

"Arthur, do you know this area?" she asked.

"Hayden Valley, yes. But in these hills? No."

"Hey Jiya," said John. "Can you ask the other birds how far Lucifur's animals come up on this side of the river? Please?"

"Sure. I'll be right back!"

They continued through the woods up the steep incline. By the time they reached the top of the first rise, their wheezy breaths reminded them how thin the air was. Their hair stuck to their sweaty foreheads and their cheeks were flushed again. The view of the valley back the way they came was beautiful, but the climb ahead was steep if they needed to go farther east.

Jiya flew through the trees and crash landed in the tall grass. She tumbled beak over tail until she came to rest at John's feet. He scooped her up gently.

Chapter Fifteen

"Are you okay? What happened?"

The little bird panted. "I'm okay. I'm okay. Let me catch my breath!"

Millicent assumed that her frantic arrival was an indication of bad things to come, so she waited for something awful.

Jiya slowed her breathing. "Okay. I ran into a couple of vultures — big creepy things — and they started asking lots of questions about where I'm going, what I'm looking for, and who I'm with. Oh my, I didn't trust them, so I flew away, yes, I did! They flew after me, so I zipped and zagged and zigged!"

Millicent looked into the woods. "Are they still following you?"

"Yes!"

They took off running. John huffed and puffed in front of Millicent. "Are we sure . . . they're actually following us?"

"I'll check!" said Jiya, and she swooped into a graceful arc to fly back down the hill.

Something that looked like a thick, black snake lunged from behind a tree and swallowed her whole. Millicent screamed. John ran with his walking stick down the slope, with both skill and a lot of luck to jump from knoll to fallen tree to rock without slipping.

The snake turned out to be the head and neck of a turkey vulture, and the bird rose from its hiding place and spread its wings six feet from tip to tip. Its bald head was a deep, reddish-purple, and its ivory, hooked beak looked sharp and terrible as it hissed. There was an odd passage through its nostrils that was unsettling to look at.

John stumbled to a halt. Another bird, smaller with a black, fleshy mask on its naked head, appeared from behind another tree. The two birds took turns hissing.

John swung his walking stick. "Stay back!"

The vultures waddled closer with their humped shoulders swiveling, their beady eyes staring, and their open beaks clicking and hissing. Terrified, John reached with his mind and lifted a fallen branch from the ground behind them and levitated it against the back of their heads. They stooped and hollered as he stared at the branch. This was what Miriam did with the electrodes at the geyser, but he hadn't expected to feel it as though he had an invisible hand. He felt the full weight and the crumbling bark. The sensation unnerved him, so he dropped the branch between the vultures with a thump.

Jiya flew from the forest and chattered.

Millicent stumbled down the hill. "Jiya! You're alive!"

The tiny bird panted. "He didn't get me! It was close, but he didn't get me!"

"Why are you chasing us? What do you want?" asked John.

"Ooh, 'e's a strong little man-chick, isn't 'e!" said the turkey vulture.

"Yes, yes!" said the black vulture. He snapped his beak. "Chick, chick, chick!"

"Escape the tawncats, did you?"

"Sneakin' 'round the Red Bear, are you?"

"Headin' to the mountains?"

"Goin' through the trees?"

"Stop it!" said Millicent. "He asked what you want!"

"Ooh! Another chick!" said the turkey vulture. He brought his razor-sharp beak within an inch from her face. She flinched, and he snapped and sliced her skin.

"*Scélérat!*" said Arthur.

John grabbed both vultures with his mind and lifted them from the ground. His imaginary fingers tightened around their gangly, brown necks.

"No! Mustn't!"

"Don't kill us!"

The word "kill" surprised him, and he loosened his grip.

"I'm not — I don't wanna hurt you!"

He checked Millicent's face. An inch-long slice across the apple of her cheek was bleeding profusely. He brought the birds closer to her, but not *too* close.

"Look what you did!"

"Aah! So sorry!"

Chapter Fifteen

"It was a mistake!"

"Shouldn't have —"

"'e's clumsy that way!"

John let go, and the vultures collapsed in a heap of feathers. He wanted to wipe his mental hands on something to get rid of the icky feeling of their scaly skin and feathers.

Jiya flew to his shoulder. "You two are awful folks! Stupid buzzards!"

Millicent held her hand against her cheek to stop the bleeding. The wound stung, and she wondered if vultures carried anything like rabies. She focused on their beady eyes. "We're going to let you go, and you are not going to follow us." Her eyes flashed yellow. "You won't tell anyone about us. Got it?"

They broke into obnoxious laughter.

"What's so funny?"

The turkey vulture threw his head back with a cackle. "She's just like the Red Bear!"

The black vulture fell sideways into him, laughing. "Remember when 'e tried to talk to us like that?"

"Got so-o serious an' sure of 'imself!"

"Like we'd do whatever 'e wanted!"

"Ooh, 'e was so mad!"

John relaxed. The vultures didn't seem dangerous, just foolish and exuberant.

"You're not here for Lucifur?" he asked.

"What? No!"

"Ha! Side with the Red Bear? Nevah!"

Millicent growled. "Then why did you bite me?"

"I'm terribly sorry! Please believe me!"

Arthur climbed onto Millicent's shoe, and she was surprised to find how reassuring it was to have a tarantula on her shoe. He pointed a leg at them. "You need to control your snapper!"

"I was jus' messin'! And you jumped, and I jumped, and it was all an accident! I swear on rocks!"

John opened his backpack and rifled through for a towel and something they could craft into a bandage. He pointed at Millicent. "We need water to clean her face, but we can't hike back to the river. Are there any streams nearby?"

The vultures looked around, unaware that he was talking to them.

"Hey! You! Where's the nearest stream?"

"Us?" asked the turkey vulture. "You're askin' us?" He looked around sheepishly. "Well, there's one straight up there, up the way you were headin'."

John slung his pack over his shoulder and gave the towel to Millicent. "Here. Use this to stop the bleeding until we get to the stream. What are your names?"

The turkey vulture looked at his partner and back at John. "I'm Mort."

"I'm Druck."

"All right, since you've managed to stay away from Lucifur's animals, do you think you could guide us? We have to get to the lake but avoid Dragon's Mouth. Understand?"

The vultures nodded.

"Is that a yes?"

"Oh. Uh, yes," said Mort.

"Okay," said John. He gestured ahead with his walking stick. "Lead the way."

They hesitated at first but then ambled past him. "Right this way, man-chick."

John shook his head. *Man-chick?* "You can call me John."

"Ah. Follow us, John!"

He expected Millicent to object to keeping their company, so he let them walk ahead several paces. On cue, she yanked his arm and seethed into his ear.

"What are you doing?"

He paused to watch the vultures lumber ahead and listened to them

Chapter Fifteen

talk.

"'is name is John! Did you hear that?"

"'e called us goydes!"

"Oy've always wanted to be a goyde."

"Yeah, so 'ave Oy!"

"You snipped that little chick's face . . . "

"Oy didn't mean to. Oy'm such a buzzard!"

"Oh, don't say that about yourself!"

Then John looked at Millicent. "We need all the help we can get."

She pulled the towel away from her face. "What about this!"

"I know, I know. I think it was an accident. You flinched, and he bit you; it's as simple as that. I'm not blaming you — "

"Oh, you're not?" She glared at him for a beat and then stormed ahead.

They continued the climb in the midday heat, footstep after footstep, until Millicent plopped her head onto her arm against a tree. She heard rushing water. Mort and Druck were already drinking from the stream.

After John wiped her wound with a wet towel, it didn't look as bad. "Facial wounds are funny that way," he explained, but she wasn't having it. Although, watching the gangly creatures skulk along the river, she had the sinking feeling that the bite had been an accident after all.

John ripped a t-shirt for cloth to cover the bite and strips of medical tape to secure the cloth. It wasn't a pretty dressing, but it worked. He asked Millicent how the scratches on his face from the raccoon were. She oohed at how well they were healing.

"Thank you for leading us here," he said to the vultures. "You're excellent guides!"

His compliment had the effect he hoped for. Mort perked up and ruffled his chest feathers. "Oh, well, thank you! We just, ah — I dunno! We just sort of walked here, ya know? I guess we did do a pretty good job!"

Two Journeys

"How much farther do we need to climb?"

"This is good. His animals don't come up here,"

Druck nodded. "Yeah, and there's a lookout a few miles that way where we like to watch for carrion. You'll be able to see Süütakkan from there."

John swallowed a mouthful of water. "That's perfect. Thank you."

"I am sorry I called you buzzards," said Jiya.

"Oy, it's all right. We're used to it."

Emily walked into the grand throne room of Doyadu-khani. The impressive chamber was the hollowed-out interior of the entire temple, which revealed how much of the structure was open space. Sunlight poured through window slits all around and cast long streaks of light across hundreds of balconies. At the center, four giant, obsidian obelisks stood like black pincers reaching to grasp a blue circle in the ceiling. And between the obelisks stood a twenty-foot-tall step pyramid.

"Wow, this place is perfect for cats," said Emily. "It's all windows and high places and sunbeams."

Miriam winced. All she could think about was finding a saw to cut off her foot. A million needles pierced her skin.

Emily curled her trunk back over her head to sniff around. "Aw, you're really hurting up there, aren't you?"

Miriam nodded, not that Emily could see it.

Sahra beckoned them with a paw. "Here, Emily. I'll take her up. I'm sorry we don't have any healers, Miriam. The fool king sent away the only dog we had left. But we can offer food, water, and a place to rest."

Emily lowered Miriam onto Sahra's back, and Sahra climbed the pyramid steps. At the top was a dais covered with blankets, urns, and incense burners. An array of dangling baubles hung from the circle of blue glass in the ceiling high above them. Sahra crouched so Miriam could roll off and sink into the bed of blankets.

Miriam could barely speak through the pain. "Thank you . . . Is this your spot?"

Chapter Fifteen

Sahra pawed at one of the baubles. "Yes. I thought I might never see it again." And she gazed up at the four black monuments surrounding them. "Before the boundary closed, spring water poured from the top of these obelisks. It was wonderful. All you could drink. Now we have to transport it from the river."

Miriam nodded. She wished she could appreciate the tour, but she couldn't pretend anymore.

Sahra seemed to catch herself being off topic and paused. "Forgive me. Oh, dear kitten, I know. I know. It's time."

She fetched a copper tub the size of a bread basket that was filled with water and placed it next to Miriam's foot.

"This is for you to soak in. The water is tepid. But we must get that shoe off first."

Miriam sat up, and the edges of her vision dimmed. The queasiness hit. Swallowing to push through it, she started with her right shoe, the unharmed and safe one. It felt good to pull off the sock and feel the open air on her toes. Lint clung to her clammy skin like blue ants.

She looked at her dirty left shoe and whimpered.

The laces were soggy and dingy and covered with a grimy residue of grelyxir that she had to peel away like semi-dried Elmer's glue. She pulled the ends apart, thankful that it wasn't double-knotted. The pressure already hurt. With a little pop, the knot came undone.

Okay. It's untied. Okay.

Sahra slinked behind her for support and looked over her shoulder. "I'm here. Lean into me, if you must. Bite, kick, scream into my fur. You need to get that shoe off."

Miriam nodded. Her heart thumped. She took three, quick breaths and pulled as steadily as she could, and the pain stabbed and wouldn't let up, and she panted through her teeth and buried her face into Sahra's chest and squeezed and shouted long and hard until the shoe was off.

"There!" said Sahra. "All right. Lift your chin! Lift your chin, you brave little kitten!"

Miriam dragged her face across Sahra's fur, smearing snot and

Two Journeys

tears, and lifted her chin as instructed. It allowed her to gulp mouthfuls of air. She thought she'd already felt the worst of the pain, but this was nonstop agony. She stared up at the blue glass circle and bellowed.

"AAAAAAH! This *SUCKS!*"

Sahra nodded.

They looked at her sock. Formerly white, it was gray and damp with ugly blotches of black and brown. Red, blistered skin extended above the sock-line.

"One part down," said Sahra. "One more to go."

Miriam tried to reason with herself that shoe removal was a more physically violent affair than sock removal, but she held no hope that this next part would be any easier. At least the socks were no-shows, she thought, so there was less sock to deal with.

She worked around the edges to peel it down, but her damaged skin stuck to the cotton. She worried that removing it could do more harm than good. But the sock was awful-looking, and she knew that burns were highly susceptible to infection.

"Do you want me to bite your shoulder?" asked Sahra.

The surreality of the request sent Miriam into an out-of-body stupor for a second. She saw herself sitting in this alternate dimension inside a Mayan-looking temple with a Columbian mammoth watching from below while a mountain lion was asking whether she could bite her shoulder while she took her dirty sock off her scalded foot.

It made perfect sense.

"Yes. Yes, do it."

Sahra put her teeth around Miriam's right shoulder. "Ready?"

"Do it . . ."

Sahra clenched her jaw with enough pressure to hurt but not break the skin, and in the shock of the bite, Miriam shouted and pulled off her sock. Then she shouted again. She wrapped her arms around Sahra's neck and sobbed.

"You did it. It's done. Hush, hush, hush. It's done."

She dared to look down. Her foot was angry red, as though she'd

Chapter Fifteen

dipped it in red dye up to her ankle, and large, yellow blisters bulged all over, with several already broken and exposing raw flesh. Dead, loose skin hung like strips of linen.

There was no way she could dip it in the water. It would hurt even more. Sahra seemed to understand this and remained silent. She simply sat and allowed Miriam to hold onto her.

"You okay, Miri?" called Emily from below.

"She will be," said Sahra, and she nuzzled against Miriam's head. "She will be now, won't she?"

Miriam nodded and hugged her tight.

John and Millicent, with Jiya, Arthur, Mort, and Druck, had hiked four miles across the foothills of Stonetop Mountain before dusk set in. With the darkness came the drop in temperature. They layered on extra clothes and pulled up their hoods.

Millicent rubbed her fingers. "Gloves would be nice." She stuffed one hand into her hoodie pouch. She debated discarding her walking stick but decided to keep it.

They saw Süütakkan ahead through the trees. It loomed larger and larger as they hurried along, and they wanted to get a clearer vantage point. After another quarter-mile, Druck proudly presented the lookout.

The tower was right in front of them — a thousand feet away and much closer than they thought it would be. They crept up the slope of an outcropping of rock that jutted toward Süütakkan like a thumb from the hillside.

Directly below them, the Yellowstone River meandered around an oxbow curve, and in the middle of the land encircled by the river stood the massive, white tower. It rose like a bleached cuttlebone, silhouetted by the sunset, with graceful, sweeping lines that converged at its pointed top. Fire and grelyxir light glimmered gold and purple from countless tiny windows.

Thousands of animals covered the grounds surrounding the base of the tower. They filled all the way to the water's edge across the river.

Two Journeys

The chatter and shuffle were raucous. Bears, cougars, and rodents outfitted with torches in leather holsters created an immense field of light.

Millicent scanned the scene as fast as she could to take a mental picture and then laid on her belly. She pursed her lips to keep from hyperventilating and tapped John's arm.

How did we get so close?! We're supposed to be avoiding this place!

John kept his head low but continued to peek and duck. He squeezed her forearm.

They can't see us — I think we're downwind — Ohmigosh, there's so many of them! Druck, we're too close!

Druck was embarrassed. "But, you said this would be perfect. Oy told ya you'd be able to see Süütakkan from here!"

I didn't think we'd be right on top of it!"

"My apologies. Whew! We're definitely downwind. Smell that stink!"

Mort hunkered against the slope next to John. "Oy've never seen anything like it, so many animals in one place!"

They waited, though they weren't sure what exactly they were waiting for. Blind luck had allowed them to get close, but now it felt like they couldn't move without being spotted.

"What is it?" asked Arthur. "I can only see a few feet away."

"It's an army!" said Jiya. "This is what they call an army, right?"

We think — , said John, struggling to transmit the words. He frowned and concentrated harder. *We think so, yes.*

We need to get away from here! said Millicent.

The crowd roared. It was angry, obnoxious, and impatient, and the power of the voices made them cringe.

What's happening? she asked.

He shifted to his hands and knees, so he could raise his head just enough to see. All the animals — the grizzlies and black bears, the mountain lions and wildcats, the throngs of rodents and small mammals — turned to face Süütakkan. Lucifur emerged from the

Chapter Fifteen

entrance, which faced east, and the cheers and roars grew louder.

Lucifur reared to stand tall on his hind legs. The animals fell silent as he slowly surveyed the crowd. An army of bears marched out of the tower behind him, and it split into two lines to fill the terrace that overlooked the crowd.

Lucifur dropped to all fours and walked to the top of a magnificent stairway. His voice was loud and strong.

"Citizens of Caldera. Beings of light. The energy within. It has flowed from a spark at the dawn of time through every living thing, and now it flows through us. But we are temporary conduits, inconsequential in our scale and in our worth, but unique in our time and in our purpose.

"Today, the energy within continues its journey.

"Today, we are a part of that journey.

"And today, the light is threatened at every quarter, coveted by every living thing. The Wolves of the Mesa covet it."

The crowd of animals roared and booed.

"The Cougars of Doyadu-khani covet it."

Another round of roars came louder.

"Even some of my own — they covet it, too."

This time, the crowd murmured out of respect.

"The Fisherman. The Fisherman! Oh, that Fisherman, locked up in his Great Fish, wiling away the hours as he waits for an opportunity to strike? Surely he covets it!"

As soon as they heard the word "Fisherman," the crowd started jeering and growling until, once he finished, they roared again. He waited for them to quiet down.

And in the waiting, John realized that he was gripping the rock so hard that his fingers hurt. Millicent lay with her hands clasped and pressed the hard points of her knuckles against her lips.

"But it is the humans of the Otherworld who covet it the most. They hunger for it. Their compulsion is relentless. And Caldera is angry! The human children offended her by breaking through her boundary. Mere days later, even more humans attempted to break through, but she stopped them. She would not allow it! And now, because of their arrogance, we face starvation. The foragers cannot forage. The predators cannot hunt.

"Their attacks will continue. They *will* breach the boundary, and they *will* take all that is ours. I have seen this in a vision played out across time. It is not a question but a certainty.

"Our choice is clear: we must survive, or we will perish. In my vision, I saw a world of prosperity, one in which the animals hold the greater power, and the Rule of Carnivores prevails so that all creatures might flourish!"

The crowd erupted with cheers and mayhem. John had never witnessed such fervor first hand, only in historical footage of political rallies. Lucifur was an amazing public speaker — there was no denying that — but his lies seemed transparent. Why were the animals responding this way? Why did the rodents and other prey animals cheer for an idea that would enslave them? It didn't make any sense.

"Dear citizens," said Lucifur, "I have a confession. I have underestimated the children of the Otherworld, and, because of my carelessness, they were given the chance to become powerful. And they have taken it! Hear me now: they can read minds!"

The crowd shrieked and cried.

"Hear me now: they can move the very earth with their hands!"

They shouted louder.

"And hear me now: these are mere children! Do you want to know what the humans are truly capable of? Behold!"

He reared and swept an arm behind him.

"Animals did not create this tower. Humans did!"

The crowd roared with anger. It was clear to John that Lucifur had already told them this, perhaps many times. This was a boisterous song and dance designed to stoke them like a pep rally before a big game.

"Doyadu-khani. Si'aka. Süütakkan. Abatakai. These are Shoshoni words brought here four centuries ago. The Hourglass. The Mesa. These

Chapter Fifteen

names are more recent. You see, humans always find a way in."

"Our duty is clear. The children must be stopped, we must prepare for the human invasion, and we must eradicate the histories and these dwellings and the weapons of their species from the face of Caldera forever, and we must start now, we must start here, we must start tonight!"

The crowd lost their minds. They began cheering at "the children must be stopped" and rose to pandemonium by the time he said the word "tonight."

The children must be stopped tonight was all Millicent heard.

John stopped watching. He slumped onto his back beside her, held her hand, and felt her head against his shoulder. This was everything Ze'eva had warned them about, but seeing it in person made what she told them in the Atrium seem quaint. They'd ignored it for too long, and now it was too late to do anything about it.

He peeked over again. Lucifur was waiting for silence.

"The reason for my new haste. The purpose of my urgency. I'm sure you'd like to know?"

They responded with a single, rowdy cheer.

"Our dear friend Copernicus, the King of Doyadu-khani, the leader of the cats, has betrayed us. Under the false pretenses of partnership, he has taken a league of our bears as prisoners — including our own Lord Nagus and my dear brother, Sebastian!"

From the crash of emotions and wails, it was clear that this report was news to them, and it came as a terrible shock.

"He has made his move, and it will cost him dearly. We march tonight!"

His eyes blazed yellow. The bears surrounding him on the terrace swooned and raised their chins and joined him to form a row of light, one bear after the next. And once they all were glowing, the light pulsed brighter. Like paper on fire, it caught outward into the crowd as a ripple through the eyes of every animal present until the field that was already aglow with torchlight and grelyxir blasted the nighttime away.

Two Journeys

John ducked but could feel the pull of the energy. He clutched at his sweatshirt as though he aimed to pull his heart. Anything to avoid the sway. Millicent buried her face into her folded arms. The lure to stand and obey was powerful.

Mort hopped onto John's legs, so his talons dug into his flesh through his jeans. He knocked against his skull like a woodpecker, and when John raised his arms to shield his face, he pecked at his arms.

At first, John thought the vulture had turned on him, but then he realized that he was pecking the sense back into him.

Millicent was horrified at first, too, but then she understood. She shook her head at Druck, who stood ready to do the same thing to her. Watching Mort attack John was quite enough.

Lucifur's voice rose again, this time reverberating with the power of the bears of Caldera. "Tonight, you march to Doyadu-khani! You will free the bears! You will bring me the Obsidians! Bring me the keystone! Bring me the children! And when you are finished, you will tear the temple down to the travertine terraces stone by stone and kill every cat who dares to oppose you!"

John and Millicent looked at each other in panic.

Miriam!

The crowd cheered and began to split into three large groups. Their torchlight left gaps of darkness between them, so it was easy to see their forming ranks. The bears began to chant, "Hrah, rah, RAH! Hrah, rah, RAH!" and the glow of thousands of eyes brightened when they yelled their final syllable, "RAH!"

The shift from chaos to order was swift and terrifying.

"Look around you!" called Lucifur. "Our numbers are strong! One battalion marches north! One stays here! One marches south! While your brothers and sisters attack the temple in the north, you will also topple the Great Fish in the south. And you will bring me the Fisherman! Tomorrow we attack simultaneously so that our enemy may know our might and cower.

"Then we will march together on the Mesa, and you will never

Chapter Fifteen

know hunger or fear again."

After a final, riotous cheer from the crowd, he sat at the top of the stairs and appraised his command. The ranks of animals bound for Doyadu-khani and Abatakai began their march in opposite directions.

John and Millicent couldn't speak. Their pulses raced, and they were afraid that their emotions would attract the attention of the animals below. Then Millicent felt it, the reason why they hadn't been detected, and she grabbed Druck and hugged him.

Bears can't control birds! Bears can't control birds! Why? Because birds deflect them! You're keeping us safe without even knowing it!

Again, her insight amazed John. He felt his tears welling, though he didn't know why. Maybe it was relief. Maybe it was gratitude for their dumb luck. He grabbed Mort and hugged him, too.

"Oy! Help! Oy've never been hugged!"

John laughed and choked.

"*Sacré bleu!*" said Arthur. "It is no wonder he has so many followers! I don't like this fellow, and even I was enraptured by this hideous spell."

Millicent scooted down the slanted slab of rock until her feet met the level ground. She covered her face with her hands.

What do we do? What do we do?

John slid down to be next to her and whispered. "We have to warn them! All three of them! Argh, again with the threes!"

"Three places to tell?" asked Jiya. "One, two, three birds who can fly! I'll go to Doyadu-khani!"

Mort puffed up his chest and held up his head. "If a lil' nuthatch is willin' to go, then so am I. Oy'll fly to the Mesa."

"Can Oy still be your guide?" asked Druck desperately. "Oy can lead you! Show you the rest of the way to the lake!"

Jiya chirped sharply. "But, but . . . three of us, three places to go and tell! You must fly there now!"

"No," said Druck, "those greater birds won't listen to a buzzard like me!"

Two Journeys

"Druck, you have to try!" said Millicent.

"What do you mean, 'greater birds'?" asked Arthur.

Mort clicked his beak. "Time's a wastin', Druck, my friend. Tell 'em it's an emergency."

John cupped his hand behind the black vulture's wrinkly head. "Please? Can you try? We'll catch up to you as soon as we can."

Druck's eyes looked like two onyx pearls with tiny, black pupils. He was nervous, John could tell, even though he felt no emotions coming from him. Druck turned his head to press against John's palm and put his beak around one of his fingers. Then he pulled away.

"All right. Oy'll go."

"Oh good oh good!" said Jiya. "Please wish us luck. Please!"

"Yes. Good luck," said John.

Mort crouched, unfurled his wings, and launched into the air to fly southwest. Jiya darted off to the northwest.

"Velocity, humans," said Druck as he took off going south, the direction they would be walking, and disappeared into the darkness.

John suddenly panicked. They should have moved farther away from Süütakkan before the birds left. If Millicent was right, then it meant their emotions were no longer shielded. Naturally, this dawned on her, too. She scooped up Arthur and ran from the lookout.

Don't panic, don't panic, don't panic — ugh, this is impossible! I'm panicking about not panicking!

Just it ring! said John, trying to speak with his mind and failing.

What?!

He grumbled and resorted to whispering. "Just keep moving! How far is it to the lake?"

Six miles! But John! What about Miri? They're heading straight for her!

He wanted to yell but restrained himself to a hoarse whisper. "What can we do? We just walked I-don't-know-how-far to get to here, and now there's a thousand animals between us and her, and they've just been told to destroy everything human!"

There has to be something more we can do! Friggin' muck, I just wanna go

Chapter Fifteen

HOME.

The presence of an animal appeared at the edge of their senses. They stopped, grabbed hands, and held their breaths to listen.

Something's hunting up the hill! said Millicent.

I know!

Gabriel leapt through the foliage and plowed into John.

"I found you!" he said.

"Gabriel!"

The German shepherd lavished attention on him and dug in with his claws the way dogs always do when they're excited.

"Okay, okay! Down! It's good to see you, too!"

Millicent stared at him in disbelief. *You got away!*

"No. I didn't, actually. Copernicus sent me here after his cougars returned. Something about birds?"

"What? That's crazy," said John. "Man, I just don't understand him. Did you hear he trapped the bears in Doyadu-khani?"

"What? No! Wait . . . *what?*"

Millicent was teary-eyed. "How was Miriam?"

"She's hanging in here. I wanted to stay with her, but she made me come. She said you needed me more than she did . . . so, here I am."

John scratched him behind his ears but couldn't speak. That was his little sister looking out for them again.

"Ahem," said Arthur from Millicent's hand. "*Comment ça va,* puppy dog?"

"I'm well. Most of the time," said Gabriel.

Millicent lowered Arthur to Gabriel's eye level and said, "This is Arthur."

"Ahoy!"

"Hello, little spider."

Arthur held up one of his front legs, and Gabriel tapped with a paw.

"*C'est bon!* I've just met you, and I'm already liking you!"

"Likewise."

Millicent took a deep breath. "Okay. Gabriel, listen. Lucifur's army

Two Journeys

is splitting up. They're going to attack Doyadu-khani and Abatakai at the same time tomorrow. We can't —" A sudden urge to cry caught in her throat. "We can't do anything about Doyadu-khani. It's too far away, and by the time we got there..."

Gabriel nuzzled against her hand. His cold, wet nose against her skin filled her with the urge to touch his fur and feel his warmth. She crouched, wrapped her arm around him, and lay her head against his neck.

"I'm so glad you came," she said.

"Hey, hey, hey. Miriam's going to be fine. All the cats need to do is seal that temple, and then there's no way the animals can get in, no matter what Lucifur said."

"Really?"

"Yes. That place is a fortress. Are you still heading to Abatakai?"

She looked to John, who squatted and rested a hand on each of them. He nodded. "Yes."

"It's the only thing left that makes any sense," said Millicent.

"But we have to get there before Lucifur's animals do," said John.

"All right," said Gabriel. "I'm glad I got here in time. I hear there are many perils near the lake."

Millicent covered her face with her hands again. "Oh, I wish people would stop using that word."

Part III
War Is Oblique

Sixteen

Abatakai

John and Millicent, carrying Arthur and joined by Gabriel, hiked through their exhaustion and through the night, fueled by the fear that they would arrive at the lake too late. They could hear Lucifur's army in the darkness on the other side of the river, so they veered farther east. As they did with the research group on the way to Nidever's lab, they kept their senses trained on the army to ensure that they didn't stray too close.

They moved ahead of the animals. Millicent guessed that they were marching slowly on purpose. "Lucifur wants the attacks to happen at the same time, and Doyadu-khani is a lot farther away."

She whispered to herself as she walked. She repeated as much of his speech as she could to commit it to memory. One thing he said near the end stuck out to her:

Tonight, you march to Doyadu-khani! You will free the bears! You will bring me the Obsidians! Bring me the keystone! Bring me the children!

"So, he thinks we're still together. But *bring me the keystone*? Doesn't he already have the keystone?"

John shrugged. Sometimes being with her felt like he still had access to the internet with her never-ending store of knowledge. She was on a roll, so he stayed quiet.

"Do you mean to tell me that after everything he did to get through that tunnel . . . he never even got it? I don't even want to think that could be true!"

She paused for a second. She muttered in a low, Lucifur-like voice, "*And you will bring me the Obsidians.* What the heck are Obsidians? We haven't seen anything about any Obsidians."

Chapter Sixteen

"One piece at a time, Mill."

"Yeah? Well, we don't have time for one piece at a time."

There came a cry from the sky that startled them. Druck swooped down to land in front of them and groveled and grieved.

"Oy tried! Oy tried and oy tried, but they wouldn't listen to me! Cast me out they did, like jesters pretendin' to be kings!"

John dropped to one knee to comfort him. "Are you okay? Are you *kidding* me? They didn't listen to you?"

"Jus' told me to go 'way. Said oy was in league with Lucifur, said oy was nothin' but a worthless, old buzzard! An' they're right!"

Gabriel sniffed him. "Are you hurt?"

Druck sniveled and sniffed.

"You're in a lot of pain."

"Oy tried and oy tried, oy did!"

Gabriel started to siphon and whimpered. "Ouch, I think they pecked the heck out of him."

John set about helping and found that Gabriel was right. He felt every poke, jab, and bruise. And this time, Millicent was there. She dropped to her knees to help and reeled from Druck's pain. They equalized and pulled it away.

Millicent hugged him. "I'm so sorry! You tried to tell us, and we forced you to go anyway."

Druck looked down at himself. "You took my pain? Oy feel, well, this is brilliant!"

John pet the back of his feathered neck below his naked head. "I know it's asking a lot, but will you still come with us? This time we'll be with you."

"Yes, mate. Let's do this."

Day broke. The final hill rolled down toward Yellowstone Lake, and Arthur commented on the beautiful weather. "We're in for a calm boat ride, methinks."

As with Süütakkan, they started to catch glimpses of Abatakai in the distance through the trees and ached to get an unobstructed view.

Abatakai

Druck beckoned them to a clearing and extended a wing.

"Oy present Abatakai, the Great Fish, home of the awful ones."

Abatakai stood in the distance, a four-hundred-foot-tall tower in the shape of a fish with its mouth open to the sky. It stood on its tail anchored to Frank Island at the center of the lake, and the fish's eye that they could see shone like a sapphire in the sunlight.

"Wow," said John. "That's enormous!" He scanned the lakeshore. "Now we just need to find this boathouse."

"'oo told you there was a boathouse?" asked Druck.

The tone of his question made Millicent sigh, because she could predict what he was going to say. "Copernicus."

"Oy think that boathouse burned down a long time ago! Fisherman did it 'imself."

"Well, that's just fa-ascinating — ouch!"

She slapped her neck and displayed a giant, squished mosquito in her hand. Its legs drooped over both sides of her palm, and it still sawed the air with its inch-long, jagged proboscis.

"Holy moly! Look at the size of this thing!"

"Holy moly is right!" said John. "Thank goodness it's not getting dark out."

"Ahem," said Arthur. "I believe I may be of assistance with the water."

"Oh yeah? You can't possibly make a bridge that long . . . "

"This is accurate. I cannot. Have you ever ridden on a waterleaf?"

"A water — ouch!" John slapped a bite on his shoulder and then another on side of his neck. Both mosquitos screamed melodramatically as they fell to the ground.

Gabriel sniffed the dead insects and grumbled. "Folks, I think we should keep moving."

But tiny voices joined an upwelling of awareness around them.

"Blood?"

"Blood!"

"Smell that?"

Chapter Sixteen

"Want that!"

"Get that!"

"BLOOD!"

Thousands of the oversized insects arose from the foliage and drew near them, accompanied by their distinctive buzz, but a loud and abrasive version of it because of their size. The stabbing feeders felt like sharpened sewing needles. Millicent screamed and beat herself about the face and neck while John waved his arms to shoo them away. One stabbed him between his shoulder blades, another on the back of his neck, and another on his thigh through his jeans.

Druck flapped his wings to keep them at bay with bursts of air. "Scram, mates! Oy can fly, but you need to run!"

"Blood, blood, blood!" said the mosquitoes.

"Follow me!" said Arthur, and they sprinted after him toward the water. He jumped from the shore and landed on a platform of solid water as he created it beneath him. John didn't hesitate. He leapt onto it and turned to catch Millicent and Gabriel. Arthur stretched the edges of the platform upward to create walls that curled around them to form a protective bubble.

The mosquitoes cascaded against it and bounced into the water.

"Blood . . ."

"Blood . . ."

A few of them lingered before they gave up. The horrible buzzing was gone.

"Oh, thank you, Arthur," said John as he caught his breath. "Thank you so much."

"Aye, Captain. I've never seen the like! Please, sit back and enjoy your ride on this, my waterleaf." He stood gallantly on the bow, which jutted forward like the stem of a leaf. He gazed ahead and propelled them across the lake toward the island.

Millicent lay gasping on the floor. John helped her to sit, and they seemed to look at each other for the first time in a long time. They were a mess — sweaty, dirty, full of cuts and bruises, and now with welts everywhere they'd been bitten by the mosquitoes. Millicent let out a long shout. She was sleep deprived and felt crazed. She wasn't sure whether she wanted to laugh or cry. John hugged her and shouted, too. In the absurdity of the moment, their bodies chose laughter. They gripped each other and convulsed with it.

"Why are we laughing?" he asked.

"I don't know!"

He wiped back her stray curls. "You okay?"

"Yeah. You?"

"Well, I don't want to go back that way, that's for sure!"

"Ha! No siree!"

"'No, thank you, ma'am. I already donated this year!'"

Millicent laughed until her sides hurt.

Druck swooped down to glide beside them. "Everyone okay in there?"

"Yes," said John. "I think so. How do things look up there?"

"Great. No sign of Lucifur's animals. Oy don't think they've reached the lake yet."

"Okay, thank goodness. Thanks, Druck!"

They composed themselves and appreciated the incredible boat they'd found themselves in. Millicent looked between her crossed legs through the bottom to the blue-green murk below them, and her stomach lurched. The membrane of water was clearer than glass, and it looked like nothing was preventing her from plunging through.

"Wow. Look at that."

She ran her hands along the surface, amazed by how she wasn't getting wet.

Gabriel licked John's cheek. "You did good, finding this spider."

"Oh, he definitely found us." He raised his voice, so Arthur could hear. "I don't know what we'd do without you, Arthur!"

"Ah, Captain. I have no lips, yet I am smiling!"

John watched Druck circle to stay above them. *Yes*, he thought, *I did good*.

Chapter Sixteen

A mile ahead of them, Abatakai was waiting. It appeared much larger now that they were speeding toward it, and its reflection on the lake made it look twice as tall. Its pale surface was blue in the haze, and there appeared to be few windows and no light shining from within. Even from this distance they could see flocks of black dots circling the tower.

And somewhere inside was a man, the only other human in Caldera, supposedly over a hundred years old and living in a giant fish surrounded by birds. Not knowing anything about him other than these bizarre traits was unsettling.

A school of trout played along the bottom of the waterleaf. Slender and brown, they swam through the water with their fins fanned out like little wings. Millicent watched them through the floor and wondered how deep the lake could be. The trout scattered in a flurry of ripples.

"Aw, that was cool. I wonder where they went?"

She looked over her shoulder to the forested lakeshore that was already half a mile away. All was nondescript and quiet, a benign and endless covering of trees. She wondered how much of a lead they had on the animals and what the giant mosquitos would do with such a feast — and how the army would deal with them.

She looked down again. Now that she was getting used to the waterleaf, peering into the lake was soothing in the way the sunlight streamed like a tunnel through the water. Ghostly white forms emerged from the gloom. She squinted to see what they were, and they came into focus as bloated, segmented creatures with eight stubby legs and round, doughy heads. And as they approached, they loomed larger and larger.

She wanted to back away, but there was nowhere to go.

"John!"

He looked down and jumped. "Aah! What the heck are those things?"

"Jiya said 'water-bears,' but I didn't understand what she could mean. Those are tardigrades! They're supposed to be microscopic!"

"Are you nuts? They're the size of manatees!"

Abatakai

The creatures converged beneath them and tracked along like the trout had, undulating their bulbous bodies to propel themselves through the water. They swam closer and probed curiously. One of them butted against the bottom. It opened its circular mouth ringed with pointy teeth and chomped in the open water.

Snap!

The others joined and formed a tangle of mouth holes opening and closing beneath them.

Snap! Snap! Snap!

One, then another, and another attached to the bottom of the waterleaf. Millicent screamed and pulled her feet away as water leaked in.

Arthur struggled to hold the form as he pushed them faster across the surface. The lumbering animals dragged along with them.

"Yah! They're heavy! Heavy beasts! *Envoyez-les loin!*"

Gabriel barked and bit at one of the snapping mouths. It let go, but the hole it left behind let even more water gush in.

"Hoy!" said Arthur. "I can't — !"

Millicent's eyes glowed. Coldness rushed into her fingers, and just as she felt the warmth from the rock in the Mesa when she created her little gingerbread man, she felt a connection with the waterleaf. She found the holes with her mind and strained to close them while Arthur worked to maintain the hull.

"John! Help!"

Her eyes flared like two flashbulbs as she transmitted what she was doing into this mind. His eyes flashed in return, and he slapped his palms flat against the bottom to help her.

Arthur grunted. "Captain! Lieutenant! Just a wee bits more!"

The water-bears attached and reattached faster than John and Millicent could keep up. Water filled the bottom and cascaded hard against the front where the boat ploughed its wake.

The waterleaf disintegrated.

They tumbled across the surface of the lake like wiped-out water-

307

Chapter Sixteen

skiers and slid into silted ground. They scrambled onto the shore. The water-bears flopped on their bellies like walruses in the dirty foam. They moaned horribly. John and Millicent scooted backward as Gabriel barked sprinted back and forth in front of them. With disappointed grumbles, the tardigrades sloshed back into the water.

Millicent backed into the legs of an enormous golden eagle and screamed again.

"They're over here," said the eagle with a female voice comprised of four notes that produced sweeping, ringing chords like a barbershop quartet. She looked down at Millicent and rotated her head 180° to face her correctly.

John turned to look and did a double take; they were near the tail of Abatakai where it rose from the ground, and from this angle the giant fish was an oblong, gray wall that reached to the sky, unrecognizable as a fish.

A ten-foot-tall bald eagle stepped into his view. He also spoke in harmony — low, rich, and precise. His eyes were the size of John's fists, and his orange beak was as long as John's arm. His markings were crisp with a head of white feathers and a chocolaty-brown body.

"Do you come to usurp the Fisherman?"

John shook his head no, terrified. This eagle could snap his head off with a flick of his beak.

The eagle's leg struck out. He wrapped his thick, scaly toes around John's chest and swept him off of his feet, so he hung like a ragdoll.

"You're a small one, human. Are you to a man as a hatchling is to an eagle?"

"Yes, sir. I'm twelve — er, thirteen!"

The eagle turned John. "And you've come to Abatakai looking for?"

"We're here to warn to the Fisherman." He hung facing the ground and tried to remain calm. "Copernicus sent us."

The eagle turned him again, so they were facing eye-to-eye. "I have not met this 'Copernicus.' Why did he send you?"

"If you please, sir, he's holding our sister hostage. But we have to warn you about Lucifur's army. It's on its way here!"

The mighty claw squeezed John's ribcage. "*Lucifur*? You are in league with Lucifur? You are the heralds, then, for this army, come to tell us we are undone?"

John winced. "No! We want to stop him!"

Millicent blurted out, "We think the Fisherman told Lucifur about a power that can control all of Caldera!"

The golden eagle looked to the bald eagle. "Quan, surely they want this power for themselves!"

"No!" said Millicent. "We don't even know what it is! Aren't you listening? Thousands of animals are coming here now! They're going to attack the tower!"

"They're telling the truth!" said Gabriel, hurrying to John's side. "They're my friends, and I trust them. Please, let them go."

"A brave canine is allied with humans?" asked Quan. "The Fisherman once kept dogs as companions, but he cast them out. He trusts only the birds now!" He set John on his feet. "I assume the buzzard is your ally?"

"Yes. He's our guide. Our friend!"

"Then I say to you what I said to him. You must leave this island and never return."

"What!" said Millicent. "What about the army that's on its way *right now*?"

"It does not concern us. Leave and leave the Fisherman in peace!"

Her chest caved in. *John, what do we do?*

John was so angry that his words flashed red in her mind. *We just got here! We can't go back!*

Normal-sized falcons and ospreys landed atop the rocks and glared at them, but John hooked his arm around Millicent's and planted his feet. "You can't make us leave! We're staying until we see him!"

"No," said Quan. He clicked his deadly beak. "You will leave."

A door opened at the base of the tower.

Quan looked to the top of the tower. The birds looked at each other.

Chapter Sixteen

John and Millicent held their breaths.

He stepped back and bowed. "Please, forgive us. We must protect him, you see. He's our only ally." He spread his wings twenty feet wide and took off with a blast of wind.

Druck flew from the other side of the tower to meet them near the entrance.

"Oy'm sorry, really oy am. The greater birds wouldn't want to see me comin' back."

Arthur scoffed. "Greatness comes from within, no? I will ride on your back, *s'il vous plaît*, and we shall find this greatness for you."

"If you say so."

John was still fuming. He had half a mind to leave and let the attacking army teach the birds and the Fisherman a lesson.

The faster we get up there, said Millicent, *the faster we get this over with.*

He glared at her.

No, I'm not reading your mind. You're projecting again. Clear as a bell. You're better at it than speaking.

Ha. Funny. Let's go.

It was dark inside Abatakai's vaulted foyer, windowless and uninviting. The only light came from recessed tracts of grelyxir. Moisture from the lake hung in the air and dripped from stone columns. John ran his fingertips along the wall, and the deteriorating rock deposited damp grit that he rubbed between his fingers.

"This thing is crumbly; it feels like a strong wind could knock it down."

"You hush," said Millicent.

"Yes, hush," said Gabriel.

"There are old spiders here," said Arthur from Druck's back. "Not a bad place to live, no?"

"Not bad at all, mate," said Druck.

They climbed a broad, spiral stairway through several dark floors. Grelyxir offered the only light, and they hoped it wasn't this gloomy all the way to the top. For all its dungeon-like appearance, it didn't have a matching odor. It smelled lush but not foul.

They reached a level where immense, pale vines splayed from the center of the ceiling and grew, tapering, out to the walls. It looked like the root system of something massive above them, and sunlight beckoned from across the room. They hurried to the next set of stairs.

A mighty oak tree stood at the center of a vast space where the entire circumference of the tower was visible around it. The tree's canopy was an impressive sphere that reached to soak up the light streaming in through the windows, and its leaves glowed brilliant green. Hawks circled the tree and crisscrossed each other on the updrafts.

That's beautiful, said Millicent. *I wish I was in the mood to enjoy it.*

There was nothing to climb — there were no stairs, and the lowest branch was twenty feet up. The only exit seemed to be a hole in the center of the ceiling fifty feet beyond the top of the tree.

"Huh," said John. "How do you suppose we get up there?"

"I'll fly and see," said Druck. He flew around the tree, which irritated the hawks, and slipped through the hole. A second later, he dropped back out and glided down to them.

"What happened?" asked John.

"Pitch black up there, it is. Nowhere to go once you're through. Bonked right into the ceiling."

"It was exhilarating!" said Arthur.

They walked around the base of the tree. John stepped on something hard and stooped to pick up an acorn. He tossed it up and caught it in midair with his mind.

"We can't climb this trunk. We can't climb the walls . . . "

Casually, while he was looking around, he levitated two more acorns from the ground and spun them around the first one like moons orbiting a planet.

Intrigued by how he was showing off his abilities, Millicent aimed her palm at the floor to levitate several acorns, too. They were light and pleasant to manipulate. She guided them through the air like a train.

"Wow, these are super easy to move!"

CHAPTER SIXTEEN

John studied the branches. "We could, um . . . we could . . . What could we do?"

Gabriel sniffed around. Arthur suggested asking the hawks for help. Druck said that they would reject him, so Arthur convinced him to go by assuring him that he'd do the talking. The hawks sneered and laughed at them.

"*Fermez vos gueules!*" yelled Arthur at the hawks. "You are lucky that I cannot spit, for I would spit at you!"

"Told you, mate," said Mort.

"*Oui.* Your greatness must lie elsewhere."

Millicent led her train of acorns to wherever she was looking. When she paused to scrutinize something, they bunched up. They knocked into each other with tinkering sounds. Then they stretched out again when she led them to the next spot. They tugged at her mind when she led them beneath the windows, and she noticed a line of holes in the wall that went all the way around. She maneuvered an acorn to slip into one of the holes point-first, and it fit with a soft *shlipt!* Its cap acted like a stopper.

"John, look!" She filled the next four holes with the rest of her acorns. *Shlipt, shlipt, shlipt, shlipt!* "You try it!"

"All right." He sent his acorns to the opposite wall. *Shlipt, shlipt, shlipt!* "Did you feel that, too? It sucked them right in!"

Millicent was the least competitive person in the world, but she gave him a devilish smile. They ran around the trunk of the massive tree, lifted acorns from the ground, and sent them zipping into the holes.

As soon as the last hole was plugged, the ground at the base of the tree buckled. A staircase erupted from the floor and wrapped around the trunk. It weaved between the branches and then rose above the canopy and fit neatly through the hole in the ceiling.

"Oh no . . . " said Millicent. "I can't climb that!"

John tapped the back of her head. "I'm not going alone, and I'm not leaving you here by yourself."

She scowled and slapped the side of his head harder than he

deserved.

He ignored her. He walked with Gabriel to the base of the stairs, smoothed down the hair she'd messed up, and reached a hand toward her.

"Come on. Miriam is waiting for us."

She thought it was a jerk move to invoke their sister's name. Still, she smirked. Miriam would have raced up the stairs before they even finished rising. Maybe she could make it, too, if she took her time and didn't look down. Then again, she was a clumsy girl, and —

"Millicent! Let's go."

Gabriel went up the stairs ahead of them. The first laps weren't scary because Millicent could keep her hand on the trunk, but after a few turns, as the horizon dipped through the windows and the breeze picked up, she suffered a terrible bout of vertigo. Druck flew around the tree with Arthur on his back.

They reached the spot where the staircase continued beyond the top of the tree. She climbed on all fours and clung to the middle without looking beyond the edges. Her heart thumped. She was afraid that the whole staircase would break free and tip over. It would dislodge while she was on it, and there would be a long, sickening whoosh as it toppled over as she climbed and climbed.

They climbed through the ceiling, and the stairway continued tightly through solid rock. Light above urged them forward. Millicent's legs felt like sponges, like they weren't part of her body anymore. She'd never walked so far, ran so much, or climbed so high. She calculated that they'd been awake for nearly thirty hours and had no idea how she was still moving.

They arrived in the sweeping apse that made up the inside of the fish's head. The dome was bracketed by two huge, partially broken, blue-glass circles — the fish's eyes — and an enormous opening with rounded corners that was its mouth. The marble floor was inset with mosaic tiles covered by debris and pieces of the blue glass. A bas-relief sculpture covered the curved wall beneath the fish's eyes.

Chapter Sixteen

The place seemed deserted.

"Where is he?" asked Gabriel.

"All zis way for nothing?" asked Arthur.

John stepped to the center of a flower mosaic on the floor and searched the room. "Hello? We're here! We didn't turn back!"

The noise, said the Fisherman with disdain. He stepped from a ledge outside the fish's mouth onto a platform above them. He was a tall, lean, African-American man. Though his face was shadowed by a wide-brimmed fedora, he looked well into his eighties. He wore a linen vest over a cotton tunic, and through holes in the cloth they saw his emaciated ribs. His hands were large and boney, and despite his cadaverous appearance, they looked sinewy and strong.

The noise is awful, he said.

I'm sorry, sir, said John. He focused on every word to get them out right. *Do you prefer . . . we speak like this?*

He stood silently. He was motionless except for the wind rippling across his clothes.

Yes.

If you please, sir, said Millicent, *we've come a long way to see you. Lucifur's army is on its way here.*

He took a step and rubbed his thumbs against his fingers like an Old West gunman about to draw his pistols. *Come up here,* he said, and he turned to face the opening.

Millicent shook her head. The platform had no railing. *He could shove us off . . .*

John searched for the man's emotions. He found a storm of sadness and confusion, of irritation and curiosity, and of longing and regret. He channeled some of it to Millicent, which forced her to catch her breath.

He's not going to hurt us, Mill.

Their muscles trembled from exhaustion as they climbed the stairs that led to the platform, and they paused several feet from him. Out through the fish's mouth they could see the horizon, the Gallatin Range, and the endless forest that met the western shore of the lake.

Abatakai

The man's profile jutted from beneath his hat with a square, stubbly chin. It was obvious from the wrinkled pucker of his lips and hollow under his cheekbones that he was toothless. His eyebrows were thick, gray, and unruly. And his eyes, shining in the afternoon sun, welled with tears. They were deep brown, and the whites were stained pink and yellow.

So, he has his army now? he asked.

Yes, said Millicent. *They're planning to attack here and Doyadu-khani at the same time.*

His voice affected the air of poetry. *Sin of knowledge, ambition undone, here watch Icarus too close to the sun.*

Millicent knew the story of Icarus but didn't know whether he was referring to himself or to Lucifur.

I heard . . . there are three of you? he asked.

Yes, sir, said Millicent.

A brother and two sisters?

Yes, twin sisters, sir.

He looked directly at them for the first time. His mouth formed a toothless, black circle, and his emotions fluttered.

Twins?

Yes, said Millicent. She hadn't meant to upset him. *Are you okay?*

I had a twin once . . .

Oh. What happened to him? Or her?

He died a long time ago.

After the initial awkwardness, John was glad she found the man's conversation.

Sir? he asked.

Don't call me that.

That's what I was going to ask. Animals call you Fisherman. Or Bob. That your name?

A smile etched into his face and formed crags, dimples, and crow's feet. *You're friends with Sebastian,* he said.

Yes!

315

Chapter Sixteen

My name is Robert Hume. The animals call me the Fisherman. Only Sebastian calls me Bob. You can call me any of those; it makes no matter to me.

How long have you been here, Mr. Hume? In Caldera? asked Millicent. She glanced out of the fish's mouth to see if anything was happening. The fish faced west, so north, where the army would approach the lake, was over her shoulder to the right. She didn't want to be rude, but she was desperate to scan the shoreline.

Robert looked down and covered his face with his hands. His body shook as he sobbed with the sound muffled in his palms.

So long, he said. *I've been here for so long!*

He lifted his chin and composed himself, wiping his tears with the back of his wrists. He looked at them with shocking youthfulness in his eyes despite the wrinkles.

I was trapped here when I was twelve years old . . . in 1872.

Millicent reeled. *You're 160 years old?*

Lost in thought, Robert's mind transmitted a swirl of confused notions. The only thing they could discern was the repeating date. *1872 . . . 1872 . . . I don't know how. Must be this place.*

Caldera? asked Millicent.

He gave her a look of surprise, perhaps because she'd plucked out that one, important thought. *Yes. Caldera.*

Something twinkled in his eyes. His smile was a quaint, toothless thing that made him look like an elf. *Oh!* he said. He grabbed their hands and lifted their arms over their heads, which was a precarious thing to do near the four-hundred-foot drop-off. *I haven't spoken with another human being in such a long time — I'd forgotten how rich a thing it is! How long have you been here?*

Twelve days, said Millicent.

Not long at all . . . Come. I need to talk with you. There's so much you need to know!

They followed him (gladly) from the platform to the main floor where Gabriel, Druck, and Arthur were waiting. He stood at the center of the flower mosaic with his fingers posed like a conjuring magician,

Abatakai

and three of the petals raised from the floor to become chairs. He pulled obsidian goblets from a dusty shelf and filled them with water from a basin along the wall. He even filled bowls for Druck and Gabriel. They thanked him and drank hardily.

He smiled again and gestured for John and Millicent to sit. He took a sip from his goblet. *I saw some of your memories as you arrived, but please tell me, in your own way, how you came to be here. In Caldera.*

Millicent was flabbergasted. Did he not hear her about the approaching army? Why was everyone on this island so set on ignoring it?

I understand your anxiety, he said, but, *we're quite safe here. I ask because your story will help me to frame what I need to tell you.*

Okay, thought Millicent to herself. *That I can understand.* She knew that no animal except for the birds could penetrate the tower — and it dawned on her why he had such affection for the birds. Abatakai was swarming with them. They were his defense against mental attacks.

She and John recounted their story. They hurried to explain Copernicus's demands and how he was holding Miriam until they returned with answers about Lucifur. They described the scene at Süütakkan and how they now had two armies between them and their sister. John was thankful that Millicent remembered the details of Lucifur's speech.

Robert sat in contemplation. Then he looked at them with a solemn sincerity in his eyes and spoke aloud for the first time. His parched voice rattled. "I will show you what the cougar wants to know, but you must never tell him."

"What do you mean? What about Miriam?" asked Millicent.

"You'll solve that . . . in time. I'm sure you will." He cleared his throat and coughed. His voice came a little stronger this time. "For now, let an old fisherman show you his tale. Come with me."

He led them to the curved wall of sculpture beneath the fish-eye windows and waved his hand in an all-encompassing way. "This here is mine. I know you haven't figured it out yet. The walls you saw in the

Chapter Sixteen

Mesa aren't just a history book. They're memories! The people who lived here left their memories in the rock!"

Millicent stared at him slack-jawed. Everything made sense: the vividness, the dreamlike trance, the feeling of teleportation and time travel, and the way the scenes stayed in her mind as though they were her own memories.

"You see, they're long gone, but their thoughts still surround us."

"It's like a download!" said Millicent. "I mean, a transfer. When you experience the memories, it's like they become your own."

"Yes! Yes. So, yeah . . . " He tapped his fingertips on the carved wall. "This here is mine. I made this."

John reviewed the length of artwork. There were countless animals. He recognized the Mesa and spotted three tiny kids who looked about his age. It made his stomach flip. "These are *your* memories?"

"Yes! You know how to jump into them, right?"

"Yes . . . "

"Then you go ahead now. Jump on in."

Again, his apparent lack of concern about the approaching army confounded them.

"I know. Trust me," he said. "Please."

They touched the wall.

Whoosh.

They were transported to the town of Mooresville in southern Indiana, as the Civil War began, as slavery inched toward its long end. This time and setting hit them first. They looked through Robert's eyes and heard his thoughts in their head in his young voice.

The air burns my throat with cold and coal dust.

I am nine years old. It's wintertime, and, being from the South, it's the coldest cold I've ever experienced. The fume of my breath mingles with the steam from the train. I'm standing on a station platform. Long, wooden planks. A stationhouse. A ringing bell. My brothers are next to me: Will is my twin, and Sam, who's a head taller, is two years older than us.

We are children of a freed slave, our mother. Our father is gone. We think he's dead? Our mother and grandmother brought us here to meet a man named Jack Hume, and we like him right away. He's an intellectual, and he's kind to us. This is our new home.

He weds our mother in secret. Her eyes sparkle as she tells us. Her face isn't as thin as it used to be. I always traced her cheekbones when she kissed me goodnight. Now I trace the curve of her cheek and know what it's like to have food in my belly. Will and I look to Sam for his response to all this. He tells us that he's happy because she's happy, so that makes us happy, too.

Over the next year, Mr. Hume treats us like little lords and teaches us how to read and the importance of speaking eloquently. He's a hard worker, a good man. He owns the apothecary downtown. We know our mother's stories of her life and how hard it was, and she tells us to cherish ours. We do.

I'm ten years old. It's warm outside. I run errands and deliveries from Papa Jack's apothecary. The store's floorboards creak under my second pair of shoes (ever!). White people watch us as we go by, but their attitude is congenial. It feels nicer here than it did in the South.

Still, they don't accept a marriage between a white man and a black woman. Papa Jack is convinced we'll find an even better life out west. He's aware of how arduous the journey we're about to take is, but we are swept up in his excitement. Scarcely packed with necessities, we leave Indiana in our wagon to walk — essentially — to walk across the country to the Pacific Ocean.

As a present for our departure, my father — that's how I think of him now — gives me a book by Alexis de Tocqueville titled *Democracy in America* (which was translated just three years ago!). I devour it. I dog-

Chapter Sixteen

ear a page with this passage, which I read over and over:

> "It is odd to watch with what feverish ardor Americans pursue prosperity. Ever tormented by the shadowy suspicion that they may not have chosen the shortest route to get it. They cleave to the things of this world as if assured that they will never die, and yet rush to snatch any that comes within their reach as if they expected to stop living before they had relished them. Death steps in, in the end, and stops them before they have grown tired of this futile pursuit of that complete felicity which always escapes them."

John pulled Millicent away from the wall, frightened by the passage of time. The memories were strung in a series of vignettes, and they filled his mind with thousands of details. He remembered the weight of the mud caked on his boots. He remembered the smell of the oxen and wood and linen of their wagon. And though he'd never read *Democracy in America*, he was sure he could give an A+ book report on it.

"How long have we been standing here?" he asked.

"Less than ten minutes," said Robert. "With practice, you can read them even faster."

Millicent thought this was impossible. She looked out through the fish's mouth, and though the sky was the same as the last time she looked, she would have believed it if he told her a month or even years had passed. She worried about getting lost in his lifetime and leaving Miriam all alone.

His life was vastly different from hers. It was harsh and scary compared to the comfort and safety she knew, yet his memories were full of love and excitement and hope.

"This is why I need you to trust me," he said. "You can learn a great deal like this instead of listening to me talk. It's much faster."

Skeptical about how long it was taking, they returned to his story.

Abatakai

From Mooresville we reach Independence, Missouri, one of the great jumping-off points. Our grandmother is with us. We play with our baby sister. We're heading to Spokane Falls, just founded, where Jack plans to open a new apothecary. The new railroads there mean prosperity, and Jack's cousin is already making a living as a prospector. It's like a dream. Here we go!

We step off into the Great Plains, and it seems like the whole world is spread out before us to that endless horizon. Our drover coaxes the oxen over a well-worn route.

By the time we reach North Platte in Nebraska, the trip has proven too much for our grandmother. She passes away in her sleep, and we bury her near the bank of the South Platte River.

When we reach Fort Laramie, father says we left Indiana early enough to stay for a couple of weeks to give our mother time to mourn.

He bursts into our room with exciting news: President Grant signed a law to create the country's first National Park. Yellowstone. The area is wild, he says, with rough roads and few services, but it will be a once-in-a-lifetime experience for us. Our mother and sister will go on with friends, and we'll meet them in Montpelier.

Remorse flowed through John and Millicent from the wall. They could tell that Robert had recorded this memory with profound sadness. It was the last time he saw his mother and sister.

The four of us — my father, my brothers and I — travel four-hundred miles into the Rockies. There is the Sleeping Giant Mountain! There is Lake Yellowstone. We fish for enough meat to last for a few days. We marvel at Old Faithful.

My father is an adventurer, and we often go off the established paths and double-team the oxen up steep, forested hills, just to see the

Chapter Sixteen

view. We're foolhardy. We seek thrills and wander boldly through the Norris Basin. What a volatile place it is!

We yell into the steam of a geyser. We are the gods of creation!

Crack!

The wheel sinks into the ground

down to the hub.

Father falls from the wagon bench.

The oxen cry and are frantic

escape the boiling gumbo of bleached earth

Father holds his leg below the knee

yells at us to save the stock

or they'll buck and destroy the riggings.

We pull the trace lines that connect them to the tongue

the tension is too strong

Blinding flash of blue light

clings to us like a thousand bees.

We hack through the girth with our pocketknives, and it takes all three of us to heave off the yoke. The oxen bolt.

The wagon is gone.

My father is gone.

The trace lines hang in midair!

We yank on them, and they yank back. We're terrified of getting too close to where they vanish, so we let go of them. We watch them disappear as some invisible person pulls them into some invisible place.

Silence.

With no sign of our father, we debate what to do. Our mother is south, so we'll go that way as far as we can, even though we know we'll die without help.

We drink water and get sick.

Starving, we find the Unreachable Trees.

Have we gone mad?

Abatakai

The animals have been watching. The first to talk is a bison named Parsolomon, and, exhausted and sick with dysentery, we welcome his help.

Yes, we must be mad.

He takes us to Pentigoi, and Sam says that it looks like a big mesa, so we call it that instead. We wonder if we've discovered something that Washburn and Hayden missed during their expeditions.

The Mesa is an amazing place! While we recover, we learn how to activate the walls and experience the memories here. We watch the creation of this place and of the Spire (they call it Süütakkan) and the battle between the humans and the Asaquatzi. It's terrifying. I thought monsters like that only existed in stories!

We can read minds!

We can move things just by thinking about it!

We've been here for three days. Our missing oxen arrived at the Mesa this morning. They can speak now. Seeing them again jars us back to what we need to do now that we're well — to find our mother.

We explain to Parsolomon that she's waiting for us in Montpelier, and we draw a map to show him where we need to go. But it's beyond his comprehension. He seeks counsel with Ze'evarmon, the Silver Wolf King, but he doesn't understand, either. As far as they know, their land, Caldera, has a boundary past which they know nothing about. We set out to discover the true nature of things.

Robert shouted. He yanked John and Millicent back to the present as his goblet tumbled and spilled water across the ground. He panted and hunched as though he expected something to strike him.

"What's wrong?" asked John, afraid to touch him.

"Give me your hands!" he said, grabbing them. An incredible jolt of telepathy shot through them and proved how powerful he was.

"Don't be slow! Look! Look around!"

Chapter Sixteen

His mental projection leapt. Their minds soared through the roof to gain a startling, vertiginous view of the lake below them. He searched in every direction.

"What are you looking for?" asked Millicent, pleading.

"Something attacked me!" bellowed Robert. "Show yourself!"

John and Millicent looked for anything out of the ordinary but could only see the lake and forest. Then their minds dropped back to their bodies. As they reentered, there came a flash of black and two, glowing, yellow eyes.

Millicent had a terrible premonition. "Did you — did you show this to Lucifur?"

Robert stared at her for a long moment. "Yes."

"You were about to learn the true nature of things."

"Yes, my brothers and I went — "

He winced and yelled again, louder this time, and fell to his knees. He swayed and jerked with gnarled fists over his eyes.

"It was him! It was that bear! He — "

His anger caught in Millicent's throat. She didn't like this, not at all.

The Fisherman stumbled to his feet and knocked his hat off to run his fingers through his ashen, wavy hair. He swiped at the air like he was shooing a wasp. He collapsed against his memory wall, and pieces of it crumbled to dust where he touched it.

To try to help him, Millicent grabbed John's hand and jumped into Robert's mind. It was violent, scalding, and orange. They saw him floating in the center of the orange sea but could see calm, blue memories outside it. They swam to his withered form, caught him under his arms, and tried to pull him toward the cool light, but it was too painful. They had to back away.

"I promise," he said with urgent submission. "I won't tell! I won't. I'm away from it. See?" He slid down the wall and cried into his palms.

Millicent's eyes darted side to side. The presence overshadowing Robert's thoughts was familiar. She turned to John. "Lucifur blocked him! He can't go near that memory!"

John stared at the crumbling pieces of artwork. "How can we avoid asking about something if we don't know what it is?"

"Imagine how he feels!"

"He tricked me!" said Robert. "He came often to visit and talk — feigned friendship. He was much different than his brother — yes, I knew the difference — but he was charismatic, got me talking about my past. I'd tell him something, he'd go away, and he'd be back with new questions. Until — "

He stopped and pressed his palm against his brow.

Millicent hugged him, and Millicent never hugged people outside the family. But he needed comfort. He needed contact with another human being, and she felt this longing like never before. His physique shocked her, as he had no meat, and his bones stuck hard and knobby through his clothes.

"You know something about this power he's after," she said. "He found out and then locked it inside you — did something to your wall?"

Robert nodded and hugged her. His hands were enormous around her tiny shoulders.

A wisp of feathers sounded from the window. Quan, the giant bald eagle, landed on the lip of the fish's mouth, saw Robert on the ground, and then swooped down to shove them aside.

"What have you done?"

Robert pulled the eagle's beak to him. "You were right, old bird."

"What?"

"You told me not to trust the bear." The eagle bowed his head, so his feathers nestled Robert's face. "What — what news do you bring?"

"An army of animals has arrived from the north. They're crowding the shore and forcing spiders to ferry them across the lake."

John and Millicent stared at each other. This was it.

Robert stood and straightened. "I'm afraid I can't assist you further, other than to say that — " He paused to select his words, with glimmers of pain trembling across his face. "You were on the right path. Continue in my footsteps."

Chapter Sixteen

"Okay," said Millicent confidently. "We will."

John never equated much confidence with Millicent, though, and wondered what had gotten into her since meeting Robert.

Robert touched their shoulders and then pointed a long, bony finger at the shadow beneath the observation platform. A crude, wooden chest sat there.

"Take — " he said, his hand trembling.

John and Millicent ducked under the platform and pulled open the lid. Purple light bathed them from below. Inside lay a hammer and two staves. The staves were four feet long with a sharp, tined crescent on one end. The hammer had a cross pein on both sides of its head and a long, slender handle. All three were made of a shiny, black material marbled with glowing veins of purple ore. A hum of energy surrounded them.

Millicent gasped and looked over her shoulder at Robert. "Are these the Obsidians?"

He nodded.

"And Lucifur thinks they're in Doyadu-khani?"

Robert paused for a second and then nodded again.

John couldn't take his eyes off them, but he turned to clarify. "And you want us to take these?"

Yes.

His heart skipped a beat as he reached for the hammer. The handle sent a charge up his arm that took his breath away. It was heavy at first but moved like part of his arm once he picked it up. He swung it in a slow figure eight.

"Wow . . . did you make these?"

Robert placed his finger over his mouth and shook his head.

"He can't talk about them," said Millicent. She picked up a staff, and the same energy surged into her. Her hand shook. Her skin buzzed. As she reached for the other staff, she noticed a thin, hexagonal stone the size of a hockey puck next to it. She grabbed it and clutched it to her chest.

Abatakai

Tumo Nataquinde, Robert whispered. *The Written Story.*

Millicent looked to him and wagged the piece in front of her. *The keystone?*

He nodded and averted his eyes.

Everything Lucifur did to get that slice of rock made it heavier, sacred, and impossible to hold. She squeezed it tighter.

Robert climbed the steps to look out of Abatakai's mouth. "It's time for you to go. I fear my lonely citadel faces a bigger threat than I gave him credit for. The eagles will take you as far across the shore as they can."

They ran up the stairs to look out with him and saw an armada of waterleaves sliding across the lake toward the island. Each one carried several animals, but the height was too great to make out any details.

"Yes," he said, "You should go while you still can."

"Wait!" said Millicent. "What about you?"

"Don't worry about me. I have friends." He nodded toward the opening. The sky filled with birds of every size.

A ruckus of screeches and roars echoed from four-hundred feet below. There came a *crack!* and then another. The hits grew into a chorus of percussion, like an army of lumberjacks was attacking.

John and Millicent exchanged looks. They knew they needed to leave, but how were the eagles going to —

"John," said Quan, "tighten your backpack."

He choked. "What? You're really gonna carry me?"

"Yes."

John yanked the straps of his backpack. Robert helped by sliding the handle of the hammer through a nylon loop to secure it. He tightened Millicent's straps for her and slipped the keystone into one of the pockets. She was rigid and pale and held a staff in each hand with the tines pointing up, so she looked like the effigy of a little saint.

"Here, give them to me," he said, and he lashed the staves together and bound them to her backpack.

"All right, Quan! Go!"

Chapter Sixteen

Quan leapt into the air. "Turn around, John! Face the opening!"

John turned. His heart beat violently. All he could see was sky and forest. The eagle grabbed around his shoulders with his massive, scaly talons and hoisted him from the ledge. He gripped them like they were a safety harness and yelled. A long, relentless lurch pulled at his guts as they plummeted along the face of the tower. He saw lines of bears with logs fastened between them as battering rams. Birds of prey dive bombed them. Something was on fire, but Quan pulled up to glide out over the lake before he could see what it was. His eyes watered from the air ripping past and sent streaks of tears back into his hair.

The golden eagle swooped into Robert's sanctuary and circled. Millicent screamed as she snatched her from behind, and she wrapped her arms around the bird's talons as John did and closed her eyes for the drop, which lasted forever, and she was sure it would end with them crashing into the ground. With a sickening tug, the eagle pulled out of the dive and glided over the lake.

The eagles didn't flap their wings, and John felt like he was hang-gliding with a mythological creature as his aircraft. Quan caught an updraft and soared high above the water until they cleared the lake.

Past the tardigrades. Past the mosquitoes. Past the peril!

They glided much farther than John thought they would go. Süütakkan stood in the distance ahead of them, and John strained to look back at Abatakai. Millicent's eagle soared behind them. He adjusted his grip as the treetops lurched closer.

Please don't drop me. Please don't drop me.

Quan tilted his wings as he descended between the towering pines and, in an elegant landing, set John on his feet. Millicent's eagle arrived, followed by Druck, who managed to carry Gabriel.

"Bravo!" said Arthur from Druck's back. "Ah, if only spiders could fly!"

"Well flown, vulture," said Quan, and he bowed his white head. "You serve these humans well."

Arthur tapped Druck's neck and whispered, "You see? Greatness."

Abatakai

Millicent stood looking quite white and unable to move. John readjusted his backpack and stared up at Quan in awe.

"I'm sorry we can't carry you farther," said the great eagle, "but you're too heavy for us to lift from the ground. We must return to him in haste!"

"We understand," said John. "You need to get back to him!"

"We're a mile north of Süütakkan. Wherever you travel, small humans, be watchful — you're in a dangerous position."

Quan leapt into the air and pushed his wings three times to clear the trees. The golden eagle flew after him.

"Mates, come this way!" said Druck. He led them to a rocky clearing at the edge of a hillside where they could see Abatakai in the crux of the forest on the horizon. Hazy and distant, it was tiny, like the view of Chicago from the suburbs.

"Ohmigosh, did you see what they were doing?" asked Millicent.

Gabriel nuzzled her hand. "It's okay. He'll be okay."

They watched and wished they could see better but were thankful for the distance. Smoke drifted from the top of the tower.

"What is that?" asked John. "It's made of rock! What could be burning?"

"The tree could . . . " said Millicent.

Smoke obscured the tower. They stared for a long while, and their hearts pounded, desperate to know what was happening. The tower shifted. The great fish turned its back on them and slipped downward. A series of muffled cracks rolled across the forest to them.

Abatakai was gone.

John shook. He wrapped his arm around Millicent, and she crumbled against him. His voice was dry and hollow.

"Arthur? Druck?"

"Aye, Captain. A place to hide. A place to sleep."

"Follow me, mates," said Druck, and they stumbled into the darkening forest.

Seventeen
The Battle of Doyadu-khani

Miriam ran fast and free across a field near her house in Naperville in the best stride she'd ever found. A twinge of pain shot up her leg from her left foot, but she didn't care. Runners adjust and push through small pains like that, and she was a runner. She looked forward to joining the middle school cross-country team next year and then trying out for track and cross-country in high school. She would break records and be the envy of her teammates. The pain returned with each step. *What is this?* she wondered. She angled her toe strike to avoid it, but it worsened to the point where she couldn't ignore it. A smart runner would stop before causing damage, so she slowed to a frustrated walk. It wasn't enough, so she stopped and sat in the grass. She was surprised to see bare skin above the rims of her shoes instead of socks. *Did I forget to put socks on?* She pulled off her runner and gasped. Her bare foot was as black as a burnt hotdog, with cracked, papery skin. She slid her fingers down her calf to touch the border between healthy skin and brittle damage, and when she dared to touch the blackness, her foot turned to ash and crumbled from the end of her leg. She grabbed at the pieces as they disintegrated in her hands.

She woke drenched in sweat and in her delirium clasped her foot to prove it was there, which gave her a shock of pain. It was wrapped in a thick, clean bandage.

Oh, wow. That was a vivid, vivid dream.

The acute pain tapered away, but what remained was still a constant, gnawing agony that came with waves of needles. Her nausea was subdued, but remembering it made her queasy again.

"How are you feeling?" asked Sahra. She was sitting at the edge of

Chapter Seventeen

the dais. Jiya was beside her and pecked at a pile of seeds. The little nuthatch looked up. She tilted her head, chirped, and tilted it the other way.

"Hello, Other-Millicent!"

"What?" asked Miriam.

Jiya hopped toward her and giggled. "It is so funny that you have the very same face, but she is so curly, and you are not!"

Miriam sat upright. "You know Millicent?"

"This is Jiya," said Sahra. "She arrived not long ago on an errand. Sent by your siblings, in fact."

"Oh my gosh! Where are they? How are they?"

Miriam noticed a pulse of activity. Cats ran to-and-fro on the main floor and across the balconies. Emily was placing large stones around the doorway to narrow the entrance to the throne room. Whatever was happening felt serious.

Sahra approached with a limp. "Thank you, Jiya. I'll explain from here."

They shared a moment of eye contact, and then Sahra butted her head against Miriam's cheek like a housecat.

"I've been worried about you, little kitten, you and your foot."

Miriam wrapped her arms around the cougar's neck. She held tight and didn't want the conversation to proceed. For a moment, she wanted only to find comfort in Sahra's warmth and think of nothing else.

Sahra shifted to keep the weight off her scalded paw.

Miriam loosened her grip. "Oh! How's your paw?"

"What paw?"

She was baffled for a second but then realized that Sahra was dismissing the injury. That was her way of not drawing attention, and Miriam recognized it because she normally did the same thing. She kissed the fur on the side of the cougar's neck.

"Ah, you poor thing," said Sahra. "You're all sweaty. I brought dry clothes from Emily's pack."

"Oh-thank-goodness. I've been wearing the same dang underwear

The Battle of Doyadu-khani

for like four days."

She watched Emily heft another stone into place by the entrance.

"So . . . what's going on?"

Sahra pulled away. "All right. Here's what we know. Jiya was traveling with John and Millicent and left them near Süütakkan last night. They should have reached Abatakai by now. Reports there have gone dark.

"But she flew with grave news. Lucifur has assembled a much larger army than we anticipated — large enough to form battalions. One such battalion is marching here. Now. As we speak. We'll be under attack by midday, maybe evening."

Miriam felt her color drain. Sahra didn't dance around, and while she appreciated that about her, the news was abrupt. There was no punchline coming.

"Why would they attack here? Is it because of me?"

"Frankly, I'm still ascertaining the motives. And there seem to be plenty. When Jiya told me they were coming, I assumed it was Lucifur's response to Copernicus for imprisoning the bears. But it's far worse. She, with your brother and sister, watched Lucifur deliver a speech to his troops. He's gone beyond stirring the animals with talk of a human invasion; now he's calling on them to destroy everything human-made! That includes this temple."

"What?" Miriam scanned the massive obelisks and thick, stone walls. "How on Earth could they do any damage to this place?"

"I can't believe that they can, but we're battening the hatches regardless. But hold on. There's more. Jiya also said that there are objects here that Lucifur wants. A keystone and something called Obsidians, both of which I am unfamiliar with."

"I know what the keystone is!"

"Oh?"

"I didn't see it in person, but we watched a woman use it in one of the history walls. It opens a door beneath the falls. That's all I know about it. But we — I thought Lucifur already had it. Oh, Sahra, it was

333

Chapter Seventeen

awful. He killed hundreds of rodents to get to the room where it was kept."

"I know. A discovery like that doesn't stay secret for long. What do you know about the Obsidians?"

Miriam frowned. "I've never heard of them."

"It's irritating! I'd much prefer to fight when I understand what we're fighting for! But so be it." She paused and raised her brow. "And, yes, he wants his army to retrieve you and your siblings. That part remains the same."

Miriam's heart sank.

"There may be a silver lining."

She thought for a moment but couldn't think of a positive side to any of this. "What is it?"

"Think. If he's asked his army to capture the three of you here, then it stands to reason that he doesn't know John and Millicent are right under his nose."

"Oh, you're right!"

"It's a guess, no more. But I hope it's correct."

Miriam looked at her bandaged foot and cursed the injury. She felt hollow. Helpless.

"How do we keep them out once they get here?"

Sahra released a painful tang of gratitude. "Look at you. You think of everyone ahead of yourself, don't you? Using the word *we* without hesitation. Don't worry. They won't get in. I won't allow it!"

Her eyes narrowed as she surveyed the room for a moment, and her white whiskers seemed to spread to capture more information. Miriam felt a bit of fear coming from her, but it wasn't overwhelming. She was consumed by irritation and an intense attention to detail, if there was ever a word for that emotion. She turned back to Miriam.

"Now that you're awake, I have a present for you."

She unfolded a nearby blanket to reveal a pair of beautifully-carved pinewood crutches.

"I asked a beaver to craft these for you while you were sleeping. I

The Battle of Doyadu-khani

think they're exquisite."

"Oh, wow. Wow, thank you!"

Miriam hopped up on her good foot and grabbed the crutches. The wood was handsome and polished smooth. The blood rushed to her foot from standing and the fresh wave of pain forced her to rock in place. The tightly-wrapped bandage helped to contain it.

The crutches were the perfect size. She tucked the curved rests under her arms and maneuvered around the top of the pyramid to watch the cats as they bustled about the throne room. Emily had finished with the entryway and was helping to secure the lower windows.

Miriam inhaled through her teeth. She had a lot of pretending to do to ignore the pain in her foot. She gasped as a dreadful idea came to her.

"Are there rodents in his army?"

"Jiya said so, yes."

"Sahra, if the bears are controlling them, they could force them to tunnel through the walls!"

Sahra hissed, and a bobcat appeared out of nowhere. "Ensure that a cat is stationed at all points. Tell them to watch the rodents when they arrive and keep them from digging!"

"Yes, Lady," said the small cat, and she sprinted away.

Miriam fidgeted with the wood. "So, are you . . . *ahem* . . . the leader here?"

"I am queen."

Miriam rocked backward.

How could I know someone for two weeks and not know they're a queen? "I had no idea! Ohmigosh! How should I be addressing you?"

"There are no titles between us, Miriam. I am simply Sahra."

Miriam gave a slight nod. "Um, I overheard something else. About Copernicus? But it might be too personal to ask."

"Yes. He's my husband."

"Wow. I thought so. So, does that make him the king?"

Sahra sighed. "He likes to think so."

CHAPTER SEVENTEEN

"Did he set you free once we got here? I'm confused."

"I was never truly a captive, once I realized what he was doing. But he played me the fool by not letting me in on his schemes. He's trying to bring honor and glory to our house, and he thought this warmongering would impress me. He was incorrect."

"Where is he?"

"The eager prince is parading around outside, readying his troops for the grand melee."

"I'm sorry, but I don't understand whose side he's on."

"It is a complicated mess, dear kitten. Let's just say he's on his own side."

"And that's . . . not necessarily your side?"

Sahra smiled with her eyes. "I do so admire your pluck, Miriam. Yes, he and I disagree on many things, especially this quest he created for John and Millicent. It was much too dangerous. I'm not one for sentimentality. I don't have time for it. But I've been worried about them. Jiya's report granted me some — "

Miriam quirked an eyebrow and waited for her to finish. Over the years, her mother had coached her not to finish other people's sentences, because it was rude, and she had a bad habit of doing it. It took willpower to keep quiet.

"Forgive me," said Sahra. "I wish not to wax on."

"It's okay. I think I understand."

Two cougars climbed the steps to ask Sahra about the shutters. One of the windows was being stubborn. She told them to ask Emily to help if she could reach it.

"You don't need to stay with me," said Miriam.

There came a spike of three, strong emotions. Embarrassment. Irritation. Affection. The affection was the strongest.

"I'm where I need to be," Sahra said simply.

Miriam rubbed her thumbs along the smooth handles on the crutches. She thought the animals seemed to see Sahra as a bit of a mystery. She was guarded and particular. *She likes things the way she likes*

The Battle of Doyadu-khani

things, her father often said about Miriam's curmudgeon of a grandmother. Sahra was the same way. She was scary at first, being a mountain lion, but the moment when her head popped up at the top of the cliff became the lasting impression of her.

And Sahra was right. Now wasn't the time to wax on.

"Why did Copernicus trap the bears? What did he think would happen?"

"Ah. That," said Sahra. "He thinks he's playing a game of chess with Lucifur. Trapping them was a dangerous move."

"Okay. Seriously, what can I do to help?"

Sahra's eyes narrowed. "I'm curious. Get changed. There's something I want to show you."

Miriam swung deftly on her crutches. She had a lot of practice from a tibia fracture (when she fell from a tree) and a twisted ankle (from a soccer match) and liked showing off on them in normal circumstances. She was more careful in the temple as she followed Sahra up endless flights of stairs connected by a maze of passageways. She'd gotten good at going up the stairs at school, when she insisted on getting the exercise instead of taking the elevator, but this was excessive.

Every cat they passed bowed to Sahra, and then Miriam could feel their eyes search the two of them with a nervous curiosity.

They arrived in a round chamber situated high above the throneroom. A granite sphere took up most of the room. The ball was enormous, ten feet in diameter, and it rested on the dome of blue-green glass that she'd seen from below. She looked down through the dome and saw the throne room. The tops of the four, black obelisks extended toward them in dizzying perspective.

She screwed up her face as she scrutinized the giant sphere.

"What is it?"

"Nobody knows. Judging by what I've heard, though, I wonder what would happen if you were to touch it."

"Huh. Well, let's find out!"

337

CHAPTER SEVENTEEN

Miriam pressed her palms flat on the stone. It was polished smooth but lined with lumpy, shallow grooves. A low, unearthly vibration filled the air. Something popped, and she could rotate it on its base as if it floated on oil.

A jolt of energy shot up her arms. Images from throughout the temple bombarded her mind. She yanked her hands away.

"What happened?" asked Sahra.

"I — It was like — I saw this whole place all at once!"

"I don't understand."

Miriam thought for a moment and then reported. "Most of the windows are closed. The bobcats are working on the last few, but that one shutter is still stuck open, and Emily can't reach it. They are eager to please you and a little frightened of you. The cougars outside are brave. They're talking to each other to stay calm, but they're scared, too. They don't wanna fight the other cougars — the ones in Lucifur's army. And . . . I didn't realize how many little cats were here! So many cubs!"

She took a deep breath to recoup her oxygen after the run of words.

Sahra stared in disbelief. "You saw all that? But you only touched it for a second!"

Miriam nodded. She stepped away from the sphere to lean against the curved wall and reassemble her thoughts. A shock of recognition hit her. Among the myriad of images that teemed through her brain, she saw Sebastian sealed in a dark cell deep below them. She screamed.

"Sahra! Sebastian's here!" She projected the image into Sahra's mind. "There! He's there!"

Sahra's eyes flared. "What! How is this possible? How could this be kept from me?" She paused. "Stay here! Do not leave this room!"

She sprinted out the doorway.

Miriam replayed the image of Sebastian in her head. She fixated on the ridges etched around the sphere and hoped that it was true. The rest of the images of the cats and Emily were live and real, but she feared this could be a trick, another lie, something to lead them astray. Her heart thumped in her chest.

The Battle of Doyadu-khani

Sebastian bounded into the room. His fur was disheveled, and he looked enormous in the small space between the sphere and the wall. His voice choked.

"Miriam!"

She bellowed with a mix of confusion and anger as she tossed her crutches aside and pounced on him. She squeezed his neck. Her tears soaked into his fur. She beat the side of his shoulder with her fist.

"You left us! You left us! You left us!"

She wrapped her arms around him and wept. She was close to ripping out fistfuls of his fur, she was gripping so hard.

He took it all. He pressed against her and took all that she had to give.

"Oh, Miri! I've thought of nothing but getting back to you. What happened to your foot? Where are John and Millicent?"

She pulled away. "*I* ask the questions! Copernicus lied! He said you were attacked by wolves! I saw you getting captured! What happened to you? Where did you go?"

"What! No! It was all him. His cats trapped me. Dragged me here. I didn't want to go!"

Sahra sat in the doorway, watching. Her face was bitter. "I didn't know . . ."

"I know, Sahra. I know you didn't. He slipped me in here and locked me up as quick as he could before anyone could ask questions."

"I'll have his head. If this battle doesn't kill him, I'll kill him myself!"

"Battle?"

"Yes. Much has happened. Miriam, share your memories with him. Quickly."

A flood of confusion poured from him. "What are you talking about?"

Miriam sniffled and clenched her jaw. "*So* much has happened since you left. I'm going to show you."

"You can do that?"

She hopped on one foot to reposition and stand in front of him, put

339

CHAPTER SEVENTEEN

her hands on either side of his head under his ears, and pressed her forehead against his.

"Yes."

She closed her eyes as they started to glow.

She thought back to the last time she saw him, when he dropped them off in Emily's room and said he'd be right back, before everything went bad. Their minds snapped together like a plug into a socket, and the story of the past few days began to trickle from her brain into his.

We're in Emily's room. We're talking about normal things.
. . .
. . .
. . .

Emily puts on an I ♥NY t-shirt.
She has music? What? She wants a dance party!
John and Milly hate this. I love to dance.
. . .
. . .

John wants Emily's batteries for the collar.
Milly sends the marmots to the Den of Antiquities to get stuff.
. . .
She knows how to make a working radio?! Of course, she does.
. . .
Where the heck is Sebastian?
Milly suggests we look. Flaming grelyxir MADNESS!
Gabriel searches. Nobody knows.
Rooftop, talk to Mom and Dad.
RACCOON! Radio smashed, porcupine dead
Poor Gabriel! Cactus head.
Hospital, Ze'eva, Rodney
Atrium — WOLF BITE
talk-about-war-and-lucifur

The Battle of Doyadu-khani

rodney mindreading creation of the mesa
hallway-walls-enter-scenes-experience-for-real
ASAQUATZI!
battleatthemesaterrifying
*millicentsdreamtunnel**MASSACRE**badgergrelyxirkeystonewaterfallsboz hecopernicuscouncilm**abushSCALDEDMYFOOT**jonandmillicentgonelordn aguswalkingtodoyadukhani.*

The glut of information came faster and faster and made his knees buckle.

Sahra slinked alongside to support him.

He moaned and stumbled into her, and he opened his mouth to cry out, and he opened his mouth again to roar. It was deafening in the tight chamber.

Miriam leaned against the outer wall. She wiped her face of tears. "That's what we've been doing. No contact with our parents. No talk of going home. Just this stupid war."

Sebastian plopped onto his rear and looked dazed. He gasped for air and looked back and forth between her and Sahra.

"I'm so sorry. I never meant for any of this to happen. To either of you. My brother —"

His voice pinched in agony. He turned and walked to find privacy on the other side of the sphere.

Sahra sat before Miriam and lifted her chin. "Show me. I want to see all that you have seen, so I can see it for myself. too"

Miriam stared at the sphere as though she could see Sebastian through it. "I don't want to hurt you," she said blankly.

"You won't. I already know the highlights. Please."

Without a word, Miriam assumed the same position and held Sahra's head below her ears with their foreheads pressed together. Her eyes rolled under her lids like she was in REM sleep as she replayed the memories again, only this time with better control.

Still, Sahra tripped backward and looked around as though the

Chapter Seventeen

room was closing in on her.

"So much! You've been through so much! The emotions! I've never dreamt! I — " She lowered her head. "The pain you've felt and the decisions you've had to make — " She looked Miriam in the eye again. "The fighting would end if every animal could experience this."

Sebastian returned, but Miriam could feel that he was still shaking. His eyes were sullen.

"Genesius is dead. He's gone. Until now, I thought he was redeemable. What he's done — what you saw in the keystone tunnel is unforgivable. Our past means nothing now."

Miriam walked her hands along the outer wall and took two hops forward so she could embrace him again.

Another cougar entered the room.

"Lady Sahra. Scouts have returned. Lucifur's animals are approaching the South Pass."

"They've passed the Gardner River?"

"Yes, Lady."

"Then it's time. Thank you. Spread the word. Send someone outside to tell Copernicus." She turned to Miriam and Sebastian. "I'll deal with him afterward. For now, I must see about my cats. The two of you will be safe here."

"Yes," said Sebastian. "We'll have much bigger problems if someone manages to make it all the way up here."

"Yes. We will."

Sahra bolted from the room.

Miriam slid to the floor and winced.

"I need to elevate my foot. It hurts."

Sebastian lay beside her so she could prop her leg on his hip.

"I don't understand how you're still functioning," he said.

"Barely. Barely is how I'm still functioning!"

"I'm never leaving your side again."

She nodded. But she wondered how it was possible to keep such a

The Battle of Doyadu-khani

promise during a time like this.

He stared up at the giant sphere. "Your memory of this thing is so new, but everything you saw in it transferred to me just like all the rest."

"It was scary," she said. "The things we saw in the Mesa were like watching a show. Touching this was way too much."

"Yeah. Don't touch it again. How's your foot? Better?"

"This helps, yeah. But it still hurts."

"We'll get you back to the hospital as soon as we can."

Her stomach caved in.

"How are we going to get out of here?" she asked plaintively.

"We're going to be okay. Okay?"

"I don't know."

"Look. Some people believe everything happens for a reason, but too many bad things happen for that to be true. Right? I believe we take what happens to us and *give* it meaning. That's what makes us strong. That's what makes us powerful. It's awful, what happened to your foot, but it forced you to slow down when all you want to do is go, go, go, right?"

"That's one way to look at it. You know how much I hate this, right?"

"John and Millicent going to Abatakai — I hope they're safe. But they saw the army leave Süütakkan, which made it possible for Jiya to warn us about the attack. And think about it. Sahra just happened to bring you to this room? Which led you to finding me in that cell? Come on. That's crazy. All these little things give me hope."

"Copernicus tricked you, didn't he?"

"Yes."

"Because he doesn't trust Lucifur?"

"That's part of it. Lucifur started this crusade because he learned something — we're assuming from Robert. Copernicus is copying him, but he doesn't know what he's chasing! He just doesn't want my brother to have it. So, it's a combination of him not trusting and wanting it for himself.

343

CHAPTER SEVENTEEN

"Nagus is just as lost and power-hungry as he is. He forced wolves to attack him, and Copernicus let them do it. Right in front of me. I couldn't understand why until now. It was all to lure you out of the Mesa with the false memories."

"Oh my gosh."

"That Asaquatzi creature," said Sebastian. "I think Lucifur was the only one who knew about it, and, if you think about it, he's been acting just like it."

There came a punch of sadness and regret from him that made Miriam's gut clench.

"I'm sorry," he said. "I've been missing him for the better part of a year . . . as we've drifted apart."

His eyes watered. His claws dug into the floor. And he moaned. Miriam ached with him and wanted to understand, so she imagined the most horrible thing she could think of: what if it were her brother? What if she learned that John had killed people, kidnapped children, and commanded armies to destroy cities? It was impossible. It was unthinkable. For Sebastian, it was real.

She hugged him. "What happens to the love you feel for him because he's your brother?"

The afternoon passed with no sign of Lucifur's army. Miriam stretched and walked the circumference of the room on her crutches. She stopped to examine the sphere again. It was a bold design choice, to be sure — hard to ignore the thing. It was opaque, but the surface was translucent, like it was coated with glass. She kept wanting to touch it but was afraid of its power. So, she sat down next to Sebastian again and tucked her crutches against the outside wall.

The wait was agonizing.

Her face was tense. The longer they waited, the more frustrated she became. "So, all of this, what's about to happen, is because two animals want the same thing, and one of them doesn't even know what that thing is?"

The Battle of Doyadu-khani

"Yes."

Her heart beat harshly, and the pressure was uncomfortable in her chest and throat and ears. How was it possible that an army of animals was heading straight toward the one place in Caldera where she happened to be?

She tugged on Sebastian's ear and focused on the fact that she was playing with a real grizzly bear. She folded it and let it pop back up.

He put his paw over her hand.

She put her other hand over his paw.

And on they went.

They lay together with her head on his ribcage. She closed her eyes and listened to his heart and breathing.

"I don't want to die," she said.

"I'm not going to let that happen."

She gestured at her foot. "Up until *this*, I never thought it was possible. You know? I figured we'd be safe or always find a way out of trouble. But now — "

"Miriam, look at me." She scooted to face him. "Your story doesn't end here. It won't end here."

The urge to cry pressed against her throat, so she looked at the ceiling above the sphere and choked back tears. She wanted to leave the temple and see John and Millicent again and rescue them. They weren't helpless, but they were clumsy. How on Earth were they surviving without her? She wanted to grab them and run toward the Unreachable Trees until Caldera had no choice but to let them go.

Then she remembered that she couldn't run.

"I can't just sit here. I mean, I have to, but there has to be something we can do with this . . . *thing*."

From her spot on the floor, she hovered her fingers over the surface of the sphere. Sebastian stood and stepped back to give her room.

"Hey, hey, hey. Don't hurt yourself."

"No pain, no gain, right? What do we have to lose?"

"Um . . . your mind?"

CHAPTER SEVENTEEN

"I'll be careful."

"All right, but if you get into trouble, I'm yanking you out of here."

It was like she was about to touch a live electrical wire on purpose. A rush of adrenaline hit her — like when she climbed too high in the tree or saw the opening between two center-backs before the good kick — and she slapped her hands flat on the surface.

The images from all over Doyadu-khani shot into her brain. Cats. Stone. Rows of windows. The bridge. Bears. Little baby cats. It hurt. The pain built like the most intense brain freeze, and just when she couldn't stand it, she shouted and pressed harder. The surface of the sphere cracked like an eggshell. She tumbled inside, submerged in a dark, purple liquid. Relief washed over her senses as the images stopped and her vision dimmed.

"Something's happening," she said breathlessly.

It was her mind in that place, and her body was still sitting on the floor with her hands on the outside. Her mind swam through a purple void in a graceful arc and floated at the center. She pushed to widen her view and saw the room they were in. She saw herself next to Sebastian and waved like she always would when she'd see herself on the security monitor at the grocery store. Curious, she pushed farther and saw the surrounding area, and farther. She detected hundreds of cats and cubs as she went, until she could see the entire temple.

This was what they'd tried to do in the Mesa when they searched for Sebastian. Without a vessel like this, the grelyxir blocked them. Here her mind glided like a boat through a system of canals.

"Hey," said Sebastian. "Part of the wall is going crazy!"

"Really? Hold on." She concentrated and zoomed in on a lynx in a windowsill. "What are you seeing?"

"It's unbelievable! I think I'm seeing what you're seeing. Did you just focus on a lynx? Take a look!"

Oh. Hopefully I can get out of this . . .

She pulled away, her mind slipped back into her body, and her vision returned to normal. Something flashed as she left. A panel on the

The Battle of Doyadu-khani

wall depicted the same lynx animated in the rock.

"I've got it!" she said. "I just saw, like, a signature or something. They called this the Palacemind, and there used to be mindspheres like it all over Caldera. So, imagine a bunch of people standing around it in a circle. They could project whatever they saw onto the walls. It's like a control room!"

"Okay. I take it back; maybe things do happen for a reason. You know, you could be a lookout when Lucifur's army gets here. Do you think you could do that?"

She smiled and nodded.

Reentering the Palacemind wasn't as frightening now that she knew what to expect. She took quick, deep breaths like she was about to go under water, placed her hands, and barged through the jumbled, scary part to get to the purple calmness in the middle.

She took her time and scanned Doyadu-khani. She studied its layout and caressed every cat's mind as she floated past. They responded with surprise when they felt her presence, but she must have exuded goodwill, because they relaxed and found comfort in her touch. All the cubs had been taken to a secure room where some played and others cried and mewed their scratchy cougar mews. Several doula cats, the wet-nurses who cared for them, stood outside the door and patrolled the hall.

She found Lord Nagus in the sealed chamber with the rest of the prisoners. She stopped short and watched him for a moment. His calmness seemed odd, because she expected him to be railing against the walls or at least barking at the other bears. She pulled away from the sphere again and watched the panel that depicted him.

"Look."

"I see," said Sebastian. He sniffed and scrutinized the image. "Why is he so calm? That's not like him."

"What's wrong with him, anyway, if I can ask? He's awful."

"I know. Believe it or not, I looked up to him when I first got here.

347

CHAPTER SEVENTEEN

He was larger than life. Jovial like Bacchus. But that didn't mean he was a good leader. Genesius stepped in and knew how to butter him up. I think he was a bad influence, catering to the ego and self-righteousness. Then Nagus lost his . . . "

"Manners? Morals? Respect for life?"

Whoops. Finished his sentence.

Sebastian winced. "Yes. All of those things."

"I'm sorry. He ticks me off. You saw how he was on the way here in my memories, right?"

"Yes. It was disgusting. You handled yourself well, and I'm glad Copernicus was there to regulate him. Hey, can you do me a favor?"

"Sure."

"Can you find Copernicus?"

"Do I have to?"

"I'd like to see how he's doing."

She grumbled, put her hands back on the Palacemind, and searched until she found the big cat outside, surrounded by a glaring of cats at the center of the mountain bridge that led to the entrance. She felt a streak of desire for vengeance up her spine.

"There he is."

Copernicus looked over his shoulder. "Hello? Who is this?"

In that moment, she realized that she could not only see and feel through the Palacemind, but she could speak through it as well. It was as natural as talking aloud now that she was plugged into it.

Marian, remember?

"Ah yes, Marian."

MIRIAM! My name is Miriam! Miriam is the little girl you dragged back here after you SCALDED HER FOOT!

He cowered and searched the air around him. "What is this witchcraft?"

For me to know, she said, her temper short, *and you to keep guessing, big jerk.*

"Miri," said Sebastian.

The Battle of Doyadu-khani

"Well, you wanted to see him. There he is."

"I understand your anger toward him but remind yourself that we're on the same side, and that he's leading our first line of defense. Ask him if he needs anything."

She tilted her head and cocked her jaw. *Your Majesty, is there anything you require to make your battle more agreeable?*

Sebastian bopped the back of her head. "Miriam."

Copernicus observed the panting cats around him. "Water. We need some water out here. Please."

His plain request gave her a dose of sympathy. The cats around him were ready to die for something they didn't understand, and they needed to drink.

Water. Yes, of course. I'll see what I can do.

"And," said Copernicus. He paused for a long while, looking at the stone surface of the bridge between his paws. "Tell my wife I'm sorry I brought this on us."

Jiya flew into the Palacemind room and landed on Sebastian's nose. Her sweet little voice cracked with worry. "We do not understand what is happening! They should have arrived by now, but they have not."

"Hmm. Miriam, how far do you think you can see with this thing?"

"I dunno. Where do you want me to go?"

"Farther south, back along that bridge."

She traveled to the perimeter, past the cougar guards, and across the brightly-colored travertine. Her movement turned sluggish in the surrounding forest and slowed to a stop at the top of the hot spring terraces — only, there were no hot springs.

"What happened to the water?"

"Everything stopped, remember?"

"Oh, right. I can't get past the mountains, but the woods are clear as far as I can see."

Sebastian hummed to himself. "They should be there."

"I don't see any animals at all. Did they go back?"

349

Chapter Seventeen

"It doesn't make any sense."

Something sharp scraped down Miriam's back. She reeled, her hands fixed to the sphere. Sebastian wedged in with enough force to free her, and she tumbled to the ground.

"Miri! Miri, are you okay?"

She was sure something had ripped open her back. She reached around to touch the intact skin but couldn't believe she was unharmed.

She gained a moment of clarity.

"They're inside! I wasn't focused there, but now can I see! A bobcat was — I can't remember where! Something attacked him from behind! And he — " Her eyes filled with tears.

"Miriam, you're all right!"

She replayed the scene in her head and caught the surroundings in a flash from the bobcat's mind.

"There's a low ceiling . . . They call it the subterrain . . . It's the lowest level — and it's normally filled with water!"

"Jiya!" said Sebastian. "Fly to Sahra, as fast as you can! Tell her they've breached the temple. Tell her where!"

Jiya was gone in a gray streak.

Miriam was shaking. She'd experienced the bobcat's death mentally, and it was like something inside her had died with him. She scowled and shoved her hands back onto the sphere. She raced through the temple to find the spot where the bobcat died. Only a few of Sahra's cats remained in the subterrain. Countless animals from Lucifur's army were sneaking up behind them through ancient sluiceways. Panicked, she flew into the mind of one of the unsuspecting cougars.

Behind you! Tell your friends! They're coming up the tunnel!

The cougar ducked just in time. A brown bear charged and leapt over her head. She rolled and righted herself and screeched at him and bared her fangs, and her long tail swished behind her.

Get out of there! There are too many of them!

The cougars hesitated. Miriam could feel their shock and disbelief.

Please!

The Battle of Doyadu-khani

But it was too late. An endless line of bears and mountain lions charged through the tunnel.

The bears relied on mind control. They forced the defending cats to attack each other or stand still while they struck. The cats shifted around like wraiths in the tight space to avoid the bears. But the attacking cougars dashed around and thwarted them. Two guards remained to block the main stairway. The bears tore through them.

"They're through!" said Miriam.

"I see!" said Sebastian. "Can you make an announcement?"

She widened her view and caught herself — she didn't want the invaders to hear the warning. With the utmost concentration, she whispered into the deep, purple void only to Sahra's cats.

Lucifur's army has breached the subterrain! Through the old tunnels! Bears and cats are heading to the south stairs!

Surprise erupted throughout the temple. She found Sahra and focused on her to filter the chaos. Three glarings surrounded her and waited for instructions.

"Torok, stay with Emily and secure the throne room. Togaro, follow us to the top of the stairs and wait there. Kinaroko, you're with me!"

The bears marched up the stairway from the subterrain, confident that they still had the element of surprise. Sahra, the sly cat, led her glaring to hide in a side passage. They waited for the bears to pass and surrounded them.

"They said no one comes down here!" cried one of the bears.

A grizzly fell sideways, his throat bloody. Two cougars fell to the ground, broken and unconscious. A group of lynxes leapt onto a black bear and wrestled him to the ground. Sahra twisted through the frenzy of bodies, and Miriam warned her of any animals sneaking behind her.

Back and forth they raged in the narrow stairway, but Sahra's cats couldn't hold them. The bears pressed into the first floor and dispersed through the hallways.

Miriam felt like her brain had been torn in half. "Aah! I can't follow them all!"

CHAPTER SEVENTEEN

"Try to keep on them!" said Sebastian.

Frustrated, she hopped onto her good foot and concentrated on one group of bears as they slipped through the perimeter of the building. She locked the scene onto the wall in front of Sebastian. She flew back through the halls until she found another group and cast that scene into the panel next to it. Again and again she did this, and each new image took more effort to keep on the wall. She was desperate to show Sebastian see as much as she could.

"I don't know how you're doing this but keep it up!"

She could only focus on one at a time, so Sebastian called out when he saw trouble in one of the panels. She soared anywhere he told her to go.

A line of bears with glowing eyes controlled a mob of rodents. They cornered a family of bobcats in a dead-end hallway. "There!" said Sebastian, and she found cougars who could rush to their aid.

Then Sebastian warned her that grizzlies were approaching the nursery. Miriam warned the doula cats, and they retreated into the chamber and sealed the entrance shut. The squad of bears marched past it unaware.

Miriam caught her breath. "That was close!"

"Miriam!" said Sebastian. "The front! Get to the bridge out front!"

She pulled back and zoomed in. She was dumbstruck — Copernicus and his front-line troops were unaware that there was a battle raging inside the temple.

Copernicus! They're already inside!

He hissed at the air and spun to face the temple just as the thick slab of obsidian that was the door began to slide down. He shrieked and ran with his cats toward the shrinking opening, but it sealed shut just before they reached it.

Miriam shouted. "Aah! I can't find how to open it!"

She could tell that Sebastian was running around the sphere to watch the scenes on the walls, as they now wrapped all the way around the chamber.

The Battle of Doyadu-khani

"All right, forget about the door. They're flanking over here — where is this?"

"Um . . . uh . . . northeast corner!"

"Tell them to watch their backs!"

As she did what he suggested, a whoosh and skitter attracted her attention back to the subterrain stairs. Sahra and her cats fought a deluge of smaller animals — the muskrats and porcupines, the raccoons and badgers, and the marmots and mice — backed by the bears who possessed them. Miriam screamed as Sahra screeched. Her vision clouded over as the rodents attacked in a muddle of incisors and claws and beady eyes. She lifted her mind from the fray and didn't know where to look.

"It's too much!"

She was dripping with sweat. Her hands slipped off the sphere, and she caught herself with her shoulder to avoid stepping on her injured foot. She gasped for air and pushed herself upright again.

"Stay on Sahra!"

"I'm trying!"

"Wait! No! The bears!" he said, and she knew what he meant. She flew to the prison and found the guards under attack. Every Doyadu-khani cat was occupied. She couldn't find anyone to help.

She let out a shout and tried attacking Lucifur's bears, which distracted them, but there were too many to ward off. They reached the lever that opened the prison door.

"No!" said Sebastian.

"I'm sorry!"

"No, not you! It's just — stay on them!"

Lord Nagus stomped and roared. His presence was huge, as large in her mind as he was in person. He bowled through the defending cats, stopping to cripple one here and snap the neck of another there.

NO! she yelled, attracting his attention.

"Where are you, you cowardly chimp? Show yourself!"

She jabbed at his mind. He flinched and jabbed back. It felt like he'd

353

Chapter Seventeen

stabbed an icicle through her forehead. They traded barbs as he and the freed bears stormed the narrow entrance of the throne room.

Emily was there with the cats of Sahra's inner circle. The attacking bears fought with a relentless fire behind their eyes, driven to near madness. Emily struck a commanding stance and swung her tusks through the enemy while the cats protected her sides.

Lord Nagus ignored them. He searched only for Miriam. She felt suddenly exposed and tried to retreat into her thoughts, but he looked up at the blue glass in the ceiling.

"HA!"

"Sebastian?" she cried.

"I see, I see! Get some help up here!"

Miriam moaned and slumped forward again. Her hair was soaked and clung to her forehead. Her clothes were drenched. Her hands slipped on the stone, so she strained to keep them in front of her.

Sebastian roared from halfway around the sphere. Miriam dropped to her hands and knees so she could crawl toward him.

"Sebastian?"

Two husky pumas pinned him down. Lord Nagus entered the chamber and swatted Sebastian across the face. Frightened and enraged, Miriam reached a hand toward him, wanting to blast the cats away, but her strength was gone.

Nagus barged past and shoved Miriam onto her back. His girth filled the space between the sphere and the wall and blocked her view of Sebastian.

He growled at the Palacemind. "This human junk doesn't belong here!"

Miriam scooted backward around the tight chamber to get away from him. He marched forward, and when she reached for the Palacemind, he smacked her arm down.

"None of that!"

She was too terrified to focus. Her attacks were feeble. She kicked at him as she scuttled and dragged her scalded foot. He batted her kicking

The Battle of Doyadu-khani

foot away each time like it was a pestering fly. With a snort, he pinned her bandaged foot to the floor.

Her vision went black with pain.

"I'm going to devour you."

Miriam felt a sudden spark. Sahra was crouched just outside the door. Nagus released her foot and reached his enormous paw toward her face. She blasted her energy at the ground to shoot backward.

Nagus pounced. Sahra leapt onto him and sank her fangs into his blubbery neck. He twisted and wrapped his arms around her. She looked tiny. He dug his claws into her back and wrapped his mouth around her throat.

Miriam smacked her hands onto the Palacemind, found him, and shot into his brain. She yelled and pushed with all her might until all his synapses fired, until he released a short and sickening squeal and slumped to the floor. Sahra got out from under him and collapsed against the curved wall.

There was so much blood. Miriam crawled to her.

"There's a brave little girl," Sahra whispered.

Sebastian ran from around the sphere with his mouth and back and sides stained with blood. He stopped short at the sight of them.

Sahra's tongue pulsed with quick, alarming breaths. She paused to swallow to wet her throat.

Miriam felt a flicker of coldness. "Oh no."

Sahra opened her eyes and let them close again.

Miriam scooted onto her knees and cradled the cat's head in her lap. Her healing energy swelled, but Sahra's body rejected it.

"Miriam. Here is my time."

Miriam pressed, but Sahra's warmth vanished.

"Beauty," she whispered, and she was gone.

Miriam cried. She squeezed the folds of the cat's furry skin and buried her face into her.

"No," whispered Sebastian.

Miriam looked at the Palacemind. Filled with a rage to stop the

Chapter Seventeen

fighting, she stood and jammed her hands against it again. It has to end, she thought, and she mustered her strength to scream "STOP IT!" throughout the temple. The animals flinched, spun, growled, and roared. Some of them were stubborn and continued fighting. "I SAID STOP IT!" she yelled, knowing full well that her words carried a sharp edge, a slip of force that hurt all who received it. She didn't care if it was harsh. They stopped.

Now that she had their attention, the words poured out. "Why are you fighting? Sahra is dead! Do you hear me? She's dead! And Lord Nagus is defeated. Are you happy? Is that what you want? What do you WANT?"

The bears and cats cowered from the force of her voice. Copernicus wailed, drawing her attention to him. He looked around the bridge — still trapped outside where there were no enemies — and stumbled forth, delirious.

Miriam ignored him.

"GO HOME."

Her words carried the psychic ingredient Lucifur used, the power of persuasion. The attacking cats turned from wherever they stood and headed toward the exit. The bears wavered. Older, more experienced bears stood their ground and growled. Their resistance pressed like a hand against her forehead, so she leaned into it, muscles tense and hands warming on the stone, until she reached a breaking point.

Snap.

She connected with the primitive part of their minds. They were hers to control.

"Go home."

"Miriam," said Sebastian. "If they leave, they'll regroup and attack again. Guide them into rooms until we can figure out what to do."

She nodded and shifted her focus. Commanding their innermost processes was disgusting. This was Lucifur's way, not hers. She led them to the second level where several empty rooms were big enough to hold them. When they were secure, she pulled free and collapsed onto

The Battle of Doyadu-khani

Sebastian.

She couldn't speak. She couldn't even cry. She stared at Sahra's calm face and wondered how everything had changed so quickly.

That evening, Doyadu-khani was filled with caterwauling. Sebastian carried Sahra's body to the throne room and up the steps to her dais. Copernicus was waiting there and fell onto her, weeping. Several cats looked on. Emily cried at the bottom of the pyramid as Miriam climbed with her crutches, one step at a time, not because she had to, but because she wanted to be there.

"Jiya," said Sebastian, "fly to the Mesa and tell Ze'eva what's happened here. Then come find us again. We'll be hiking south tomorrow."

Miriam felt a storm of emotions inside him. Sadness and anger clashed for which was the most dominant, and she knew that he was struggling to contain his temper.

"Copernicus," he said, "We're leaving at daybreak to find John and Millicent."

The big cat lay curled over Sahra's body and didn't respond.

"Copernicus!"

He lifted his head, his eyes wide and weary like he was only half there.

"Who will lead the cats?" asked Sebastian aloud to the rest of them.

Copernicus's expression devolved from lost to despondent. Another cougar stepped forward.

"I am his second."

"What's your name?"

"Putamah."

"We need a safe room to sleep in tonight and provisions for tomorrow."

"You dare to dictate to us?"

Miriam felt Sebastian's anger peak.

"Cat, I am one wrong word away from ripping out his throat. Do

357

Chapter Seventeen

you understand me? He brought this upon us."

"There are some who would say that *you* brought this upon us. You could have handed the human children over to your brother at any moment and spared us all."

The fur on Sebastian's hump and shoulders bristled. "Your queen *died* protecting this child! Even when she was reluctant, she leapt to the fore and protected them one-on-one against Lucifur himself!"

The throne room went silent. The air shifted under the scrutiny of a hundred cats. Miriam realized that the same cats she helped to defend could decide to turn on them, which made her feel even more lost without Sahra. It was déjà vu. Emily and Ze'eva had welcomed them into the Mesa and treated them like guests of honor only to be vilified and thrown out. A few hours ago, she was sitting on the very same platform as a guest of the queen. Now the queen lay dead.

Sebastian seemed to sense the shift in the room, too, because he pulled back his anger.

"Tell me this. Your queen fought to protect the children. Your king fights for power. Which would you follow?"

"The queen is dead. The king is all who matters now, and his wishes will be granted."

"I see. So, are you letting me take the girl tomorrow?"

The tension between them felt like a finger on a trigger, and Miriam thought Sebastian was eager for the fight. But Putamah hesitated in a meager way, as though he hadn't considered what his master's wishes might actually be.

Copernicus rolled to stand. His tail whipped back and forth, and he staggered toward Sebastian with crazy eyes.

"WHAT WOULD YOU HAVE ME DO? Hah? Let this little girl go? Fall into his grip so he can rule us all?"

"No. You let her find her siblings and find her way home."

Copernicus sneered and whimpered. "She *was* home. Remember? Then they came back . . . They came back and destroyed everything."

He looked down at Sahra.

The Battle of Doyadu-khani

"But for her. All but for her, I stumble in the hunt, clawless, with hunger, never to feed again, for the daylight is dark and the night will be darker. Go. Find a room. Sleep. Take what you want. Then leave. And never come back here again."

"My lord?" said Putamah.

Copernicus swiped a paw across his face.

"Those are my wishes! Now grant them!"

To Miriam's dismay, Sebastian continued to press, though she felt it came from genuine concern instead of anger this time.

"But you can't let your guard down," he said. "You need to keep those bears and cats under close watch, keep up your defenses, and seal the temple shut after we're gone. Emily can help barricade the subterrain before we go, so no one can get in that way again."

"My wishes, my wishes," said Copernicus. "I wish to end this conversation. Grant me that. And get out of my sight."

He returned to Sahra and lay down next to her.

The next morning, Miriam's face was grim as light from the sunrise streamed through the seams between the closed shutters. She wore dry clothes, a backpack full of supplies and food, and a new dressing on her foot. Her crutches were lashed beside her on Emily's back. Without a word, they followed Sebastian out of the temple, and the thick, black obsidian gate slid shut behind them.

Eighteen

Tumo Nataquinde

As they hiked through the mountain pass from Doyadu-khani, Emily lowered Miriam onto Sebastian's back, so she could be closer to him. They shared a somber mood and were content with not making conversation. The woods were empty, and the absence of birdsong created an unnatural silence. Miriam guessed that every living thing in Caldera was somehow involved in the conflict now. The rhythm of Sebastian's stride comforted her. The two animals walked all day and reached the Norris Geyser Basin by evening.

Miriam's foot hurt the entire way. She kept willing it to feel better, and she supposed it did, compared to the day before, but the incessant stinging and throbbing was impossible to ignore. Sometimes, instead of fighting it, she tried to embrace the pain and imagine the burn going all the way up her leg, up both legs, and covering her entire body. She knew that burn victims suffered incredible pain, and she couldn't understand how someone with burns over large parts of their body could endure it.

Emily commented that they weren't far from where Miriam scalded her foot, which made them nervous, as though another army of bears and cats could arrive any moment and start the whole thing over again. They quieted their steps and studied every stand of trees and cluster of boulders for signs of ambush, but nothing came.

Miriam scanned the steaming ground that spanned to the right, but nothing looked familiar. She wanted to spot the rock formation where she fell. She wanted to see where the accident happened and wondered if she would be able to find the hole where her foot went through the crust, or if the boiling gumbo had reclaimed it and erased the evidence. She shook her head, just to herself. She was okay with never seeing it

Chapter Eighteen

again. *But it's nearby,* she thought, as though the rock was calling to her. She didn't believe in superstition, but rock didn't behave like rock should in Caldera.

It isn't well-behaved at all.

She replayed the injury. She'd been scared but confident a moment before Emily fell. Riding on her back and warding off the cougars almost felt natural. Then they fell. They climbed. And John blasted the cougars away. She couldn't blame him for defending himself, and she hoped that he knew that.

But it occurred to her that they needn't have climbed the rock in the first place. It felt like the only choice at the time. Had they surrendered, Copernicus would have sent all three of them to Abatakai. But then, she wouldn't have ended up in Doyadu-khani to use the Palacemind, and the battle would have gone much differently. She was sure of that.

Sahra might have lived.

"Darn it," she said. She looked skyward and choked back another urge to cry. Her emotions had sneaked up on her throughout the day. She didn't always stop them (because her parents convinced her it was unhealthy to bottle up her tears), but she was tired of crying. She wiped her eyes.

"You okay, kiddo?" asked Sebastian.

"Not really. I was just thinking, if everything really does happen for a reason, then I'm still waiting for the reason."

"Ha. Yes. Best laid plans. Death steps in and blows it all away, doesn't it?"

"Yes."

Out of nowhere, the image of Sahra's startled eyes and open mouth when they arrived at the Mesa made her chuckle. She always thought it was strange how a person could go from sorrow to humor in the same moment.

"Emily, I just remembered the look on her face when you gave her all those blankets. Gah, this sucks."

"Yeah," said Emily. "I did that accidentally on purpose. And, boy, was it worth it."

"She was hard to get to know," said Sebastian, "but she became one of my closest friends. Our relationship was yin-yang in that she kept me serious when I needed to be, and I tried my darnedest to get her to relax from time to time. She said it annoyed her, but I think deep down she appreciated it. It meant a lot to me when she agreed to find you and Millicent when you first got here. I know she didn't want to."

"I'm glad it was her."

"You were very dear to her, Miriam. I think you reached her in a way that I never could."

She kicked him with her good foot. "Okay, you can stop that."

She inhaled mightily through her nose. The cold air was refreshing despite the smell of sulfur.

They made camp next to the Gibbon River, and the stars twinkled brighter than she'd ever seen in her life. She found the Summer Triangle, imagined her parents looking up at it, and wished she could talk to them through the twinkling points of light with a mind power more magical than the ones she already had.

I'm looking. Are you looking, too? I just wanted you to know that I'm okay. Well . . . I burned my foot, but I'm okay.

I wish I could tell you that I'm okay.

The sudden ripple of blue light shimmered across the sky and startled her. She'd forgotten about it.

"Do you know what that is, Sebastian?"

"No. It started after you arrived. More specifically, after Lucifur forced his way back in. That's when Caldera started to change."

"Like he put a crack in it?"

He nodded. "Like he put a crack in it."

"And then Nidever broke it?"

"Maybe. Maybe he's the one who broke it."

Her mind was spinning. "Then maybe there's a way to put another crack in it? You know? Break it open again?"

"I hope so. But let's get some sleep, kiddo."

Chapter Eighteen

Sebastian and Emily fell asleep, which left Miriam alone with her thoughts. She lay on her back with her hands draped across her tummy and waited for the dazzling light to return. It reminded her of the nights when her parents would drive her, John, and Millicent into the countryside, away from Chicago's light pollution, to watch a meteor shower. She never knew when the next one would streak by.

In the same way, she waited for another swath of blue to pass in front of the stars. She started counting as soon as the next one appeared.

"One Mississippi, two Mississippi, three Mississippi, four Mississippi, five — ."

It took five seconds to traverse the sky.

It was a reminder that the mystery of Caldera kept getting deeper and taking them farther off course. It made her feel lost, and she didn't like feeling lost. She hated the feeling as much as she hated being confined to her crutches. She wished they'd never left the Mesa, because by the time Copernicus sprang his trap, they'd already been swallowed by the conflict between the animals. Now they were so far flung from the search to get home that she wondered if they'd ever get back to looking.

Put a crack in it. Break it open, she thought. *Going home is more important than anything happening here.*

Yet, each new discovery gave her more to care about, and a scary thought occurred to her. For the first time, she felt that she might hesitate if an opportunity to go home presented itself. She wouldn't want to leave until she knew everything was okay. For Sebastian's sake. And Emily. And Gabriel.

No. Don't be stupid. You'd jump at the chance to go home.
Wouldn't you?

She snuggled closer to Sebastian.

When she woke up, the pain in her foot was almost tolerable for the first time in four days, and she found herself sighing with relief every few minutes. It still made her nauseous, and with the nausea came the icky cold sweats. The nightmare from the previous morning had put a genuine fear in her that she'd never walk again. So, she took up her crutches and put pressure on her foot, just to test.

Pain seared up her leg. She bent her knee and leaned hard against the crutch handles. The pain was so sharp that it forced her mouth open as she waited, waited, and waited for it to go away again.

You stupid idiot!

Emily was sucking gallons of water from the river to quench her thirst and paused with her trunk still in her mouth.

"Wha — ? What'd I do?"

"Oh, no, not you. I was talking about me. I just tried to step on my foot."

"Oh, whew! I mean, I may be a needless mountain of flash and worry, but I'm no idiot."

Sebastian quirked his head. "Waitaminute . . . Who said that about you?"

Emily's tone turned regal, like she was the herald at a Victorian party who announces the names of arriving guests. "Why, 'twas Sir Rodney, Dombul of Groscorn, Representative of the Northern Bighorn Sheep. He's the one who said it."

"That's right. I mean — it wasn't right of him to say that — I just remembered it from Miriam's memories. He was very harsh."

"Well, he'd been through a lot, I guess."

"It isn't true."

"Please. You're being kind. I understand. I'm boisterous and proud."

"Ugh," said Miriam. "I just realized, if we ever see him again, he earned the biggest 'I told you so' in history. He basically told us we were stupid for leaving the Mesa."

"Hey now," said Sebastian. "You left the Mesa to come look for me, so I, for one, thank you. I'm supposed to be the one protecting you, and you've had to rescue me twice."

Miriam climbed onto his back for the day's hike. "Well. Stop getting

Chapter Eighteen

yourself captured, and I won't have to rescue you anymore."

"Wow, you're on fire this morning! Hopefully John and Millicent were able to retrace their steps. We'll just keep heading this way till we hit the Yellowstone River."

"Okay," said Miriam. "I'll keep an eye out for them."

They followed the winding river. The tight S-curls carved across the grassy landscape seemed like an impractical way for a river to flow, and Miriam wondered how it could have ended up so loopy. The strong current babbled past them looking quite blue under the clear sky and was speckled with sheaths of white where the water churned over the rocks in the riverbed. A pod of trout slipped past below the surface in a brown blur.

Fish! she thought. *I haven't spoken to any fish! I wonder if they can talk. Ah, Caldera, you are questions on top of questions on top of questions. I'm kind of over you, you know. I'm sorry. It's not me. It's you.*

The river led them from the meadow into a thick forest where the bank straightened through the trees, and the dimness offered relief from squinting in the sunlight. Emily maneuvered through. She enjoyed the rough bark against her sides.

Miriam pictured herself and shook her head. She was riding a grizzly bear while watching a mammoth rub against a tree, and it seemed like such a strange thing to be doing.

They left the forest and arrived at the northwest corner of Hayden Valley, and its bright, green expanse was warm and inviting with pockets of crystal water and patches of yellow brush, all surrounded by the misty, blue ridges of the mountains beyond. Miriam closed her eyes and let her mind wander as far as she could but didn't sense John or Millicent. She did this every few minutes over the next hour, each time with a rush of hope that they might show up.

"It's so crazy."

"What's so crazy?" asked Sebastian.

"We looked at Hayden Valley from our van when we first got here.

Tumo Nataquinde

Who'da thought I'd be crossing it like this?"

Emily plodded along. Her legs swung like four, long clock pendulums. "Wow. Yeah! Must be surreal. This hasn't quite been the vacation you thought it'd be, has it?"

"Ha-ha! Nope!"

She felt a far-away speck of warmth through the ether. She sat up taller on Sebastian's back to concentrate. Millicent's voice cheered into her mind.

Miriam! We can see you!

She squinted across the valley. A tiny shape was waving at her.

"There! Sebastian, they're up ahead!"

"They are? Where?"

"Straight that way! Go faster!"

"Faster?"

She laughed and wrapped her arms around his neck. "Yes, faster!" she said, and he broke into a full run. She shouted with joy. Her grip was tenuous. Emily gaited to keep up, and the feeling of flying across the landscape with them was exhilarating.

When they met, Sebastian skidded to a halt and tilted so Miriam could slide off, and she landed on her good foot with her body leaning against him as John, Millicent, and Gabriel plowed into them.

The siblings hugged. John couldn't believe how good it felt to hug his little sister, the girl who was always there for him and kept him running, the one he'd been so mad at that he broke his father's thermos. They'd been reunited in Caldera before, but it felt different this time after everything they'd been through.

Millicent cried, overcome by waves of panic or anxiety or something she couldn't quite describe, a horrible feeling of abandonment and happiness mixed with a paranoia that something was tricking them.

Miriam shook her by the shoulders to snap her out of it. "It's okay! You're okay!"

Millicent squeezed the flesh of Miriam's arms. "This is really you, right? You're really here?"

Chapter Eighteen

"Yes! Oh, Milly, yes, it's really me!"

Gabriel pranced and barked and stood on his hind legs with his forepaws on Miriam's shoulders to lick her face. Emily made delighted, squeaky, elephant-like sounds.

John and Millicent smothered Sebastian. They couldn't and wouldn't let go of him, and John bounced his fist on the bear's head, wanting to punch or pet or yell at him.

"You left us," he said breathlessly.

"I know."

"Don't ever do that again."

"I won't!"

"You promise?"

"I promise."

Druck and Arthur approached. After John and Millicent made introductions, Miriam fawned over them. "A vulture and a tarantula are perfect companions!" she proclaimed.

She was thrilled to speak with Arthur as he sat on the palm of her hand. She marveled at how he gazed back at her. It seemed normal to share eye contact with the rest of the animals, but the spark of intelligence behind his eight, spidery eyes seemed more magical. He asked about her foot. Then he hopped from her hand and skittered off into the forest.

"I'll be back, brutha!"

"Huh? Did he just call me *brother*?"

John shrugged. "He calls me Captain."

Sebastian called for them to find a less conspicuous place where they could rest and catch up and led them onward to a cozy stand of trees that grew near the shore of a flatland marsh. He sniffed around the water's edge and seemed wistful.

"This is one of the Cygnet Lakes. There's a series of them up ahead. I remember being here with my mother. Just . . . roaming around and being a bear. So strange to be back here."

"Heh," said Millicent. "Cygnet Lakes? Cygnet means 'swan.' This is

Swan Lake!" She performed a dreadful, flat-footed version of an *en point* spin and sang an off-key phrase from Tchaikovsky. She did this without a stumble, so she deemed it a success and curtsied for no one in particular.

Miriam hopped off Sebastian and untied her crutches. Emily and Gabriel drank, and John plopped to the ground and took off his sweatshirt.

They could sense that they were stronger than when they last saw each other. And there was the matter of the strange, black and glowing-purple objects that John and Millicent carried. Miriam had an inkling that they were the Obsidians, but she had a better idea than asking.

"Okay. I wanna try sharing my memories with you two, and you can share yours with me, okay?"

"Oh?" asked Millicent.

"Yeah. Sebastian? You should join, too. Heck. Everybody circle up. It's easier when we're touching, so, um, reach out and touch your neighbor."

They sat on the ground in a circle. Sebastian sat between John and Millicent, so they could be near him. Gabriel sat on the other side of John and next to Miriam, so he could be close to her. Then Emily lowered to her knees, Druck sidled up to her, and Millicent put her hand on Druck's back at the base of his neck to complete the circle. She gave him a friendly scratch, which made him trill and coo.

John looked around the circle. "Well, here's something you don't see every day."

"Yeah," said Millicent. "Feels like a setup for an elaborate joke. 'A mammoth, a vulture, and a German shepherd walk into a bar . . . with three kids and a bear.'"

"Mayhem ensues!"

"All right, are we ready?" asked Miriam.

"Actually . . . " said Emily. "I'm not too sure about this. I'm a little nervous here."

Druck looked around like he was the new kid in school. "Yeah.

Chapter Eighteen

Oy'm not sure what we're even doing!"

"It's hard to explain. A lot easier just to show you. Here, let me start."

Her eyes glowed, and her stories from the past few days flowed out. Her experience with Sebastian and Sahra taught her better control, and her memories transferred outright, complete with emotion, sound, scent, and temperature. The speed of the transfer increased until they were all in a trance with glowing eyes.

She hid the news of Sahra's death because she didn't want them to find out unexpectedly.

"Okay," she said. "That leads us up to now. Everyone good so far?"

"Oy!" said Druck. "Me noggin' is overflowin'!"

Emily gave a trumpet bleat and shook her head, so her little ears fanned around like two skirts stuck to the sides of her head. "I was there for all of that, but it was *crazy* to see it from your point of view! Crazy!"

Gabriel hooked his head under Miriam's arm and pressed against her. "I should have stayed with you! I could have helped!"

Millicent was white. Experiencing the battle of Doyadu-khani through Miriam's eyes, through the Palacemind, was overwhelming. She doubted that she would've been able to do anything Miriam did. But something stuck out to her. Sahra was missing.

"Oh no. Miri . . . I'm so sorry."

John was puzzled. "What's wrong?"

Millicent stared past Sebastian into Miriam's eyes. "She died, didn't she?"

Miriam nodded.

John fell quiet. He hadn't gotten to know Sahra and wished he could have been there — but was glad he wasn't there at the same time.

They were quiet. It was a lot to absorb.

John looked around at the group again. "Okay. Our turn."

The memories of their journey — meeting Jiya and Arthur, and then Mort and Druck; seeing Süütakkan and hearing Lucifur's speech; racing the army to Abatakai and all that happened on the way to meet Robert

Tumo Nataquinde

Hume — swirled between them in a torrent.

They reached the point when they touched Robert's memory wall, and a surge of new energy flowed through them as they retransmitted, with startling clarity and recall, his story. They finished with the flight of the eagles and caught up to the present.

They sat in silence again.

"I don't know where to begin," said Sebastian. "Lucifur's speech was . . . I still don't know whether he actually believes everything he's saying or if he's just manipulating his followers."

"Maybe it's both," said Gabriel.

"And those freaking water-bears!" said Emily. "Wow! Wow!"

Miriam closed her eyes and replayed the flight with the eagles. Both of their journeys had been fraught, but that was one part she wished she could've experienced in person. And the waterleaf. And meeting Robert. Lucifur's speech terrified her.

Nowhere in their memories was there news about their parents. They'd gone to the opposite ends of Caldera, Millicent remarked, yet they were no closer to finding a way home.

"It's been over a week since we've talked to them. Eight days! I've never gone this long without talking to them! Ever!"

John reached over and squeezed her leg. "None of us have."

Miriam dismissed these thoughts. She wanted to stay calm and focused. Their memories included the keystone. The thin, smooth hexagon lying at the bottom of Robert's chest was a part of her memories now, and the thought of it put her on the verge of tears.

"I want to see it. The keystone."

She raised her hand and levitated it from Millicent's backpack as though she'd placed it there herself. It was such an innocent-looking thing.

"Why did he have it?"

"I don't know," said Millicent. "To keep it safe?"

John watched numbly as Miriam rubbed the keystone's smooth surface with her thumb. "Is that it then?" he asked. "We take it to the

Chapter Eighteen

falls and see what it opens?"

"Yes," said Millicent. "Follow in his footsteps to Tumo Nataquinde. He said it meant *the written story*. I guess we'll have to find out what that means."

"And why it's worth all this killing," said Miriam. "Nothing could be." She nodded at the dark hammer connected to John's backpack. "And what about these?"

He held in front of him. "I named it *Grelyxir*."

"Oh?" said Millicent. "When did you decide this?"

"While we were walking this morning."

"I like it."

He smiled. "Yeah. I just like the word."

He handed it to Miriam. She held it gingerly until she felt its power and lightness. The energy that flowed up her arm made her feel strong.

"Oh, this is awesome! *Grelyxir* is a perfect name!" She held it aloft with her right hand. "Behold! I have the power of *Grelyxir*!"

John panicked because he hadn't called dibs on it, and he wanted it to be his. And now she was doing cool things with it. He wished she'd taken one of the staves instead.

"Yeah, isn't it cool?" he asked with an obvious tone.

She rolled her eyes. His approach to getting what he wanted always became more pathetic the more he tried to hide it. Sometimes she liked to toy with him to see how contorted his logic and lies could get. But today, she wasn't in the mood. She liked the look of the staves.

"Here. It's all yours."

She walked on her knees to Millicent and detached the staves from her pack. She spun one in each hand like two batons, and they made humming, circular blurs.

"That sounds cool!"

Sebastian sniffed the hammer in John's hands. "I've never seen anything like them."

Miriam tossed the other staff two feet away to Millicent. "Catch!"

It hit Millicent's fingers and bounced on the ground. "Grr. You

Tumo Nataquinde

know I can't catch!" She picked it up and rocked it in a blurry bowtie shape. "It does feel cool, though, doesn't it?"

Miriam tapped their staves to be playful. There was a blinding flash with a loud *ZAP!*

Millicent fell flat on her back. "Dang it, Miri! We're not together an hour, and you're already wrecking me!"

His curiosity overriding common sense, John reached over and tapped Miriam's staff with *Grelyxir*. Predictably, it zapped him, too, and he yelped.

"Um, children?" said Sebastian. "Can we err on the side of caution with these things, please?"

Miriam offered to pull Millicent up. "You did miss me, though, right?"

She huffed. "I miss you more when you're gone."

They continued walking east. They hadn't gone far when Druck called out, "Mort!" as the turkey vulture glided in. They greeted each other by rubbing beaks and tangling necks.

"Mort, look at me! Oy've been a guide!"

"You 'ave! And Oy've been a scout!"

"To think: we were just buzzards the other day."

"Oy told you! Stop sayin' that 'bout us!"

Jiya darted past the vultures and landed on a branch in front of them. "Sebastian! We bring word to you from Ze'eva. Abatakai has fallen, and Lucifur's army at Süütakkan is dwindling."

"Oh, Jiya, you little gem," said Sebastian. "She made it back to the Mesa?"

"Yes, but she is not strong. I do not know what is wrong with her. She requests your presence! She is gathering the animals for an assault to strike Lucifur while his forces are weak."

Mort perked up. "Kick 'im while 'e's down, oy say!"

Sebastian lowered his head.

"We're so close," said Millicent.

Chapter Eighteen

"I know," said Sebastian. "I know we are. Jiya, we can't go back. Not yet. Please, will you stay with us for now?"

"Yes I will, silly-silly."

"Take your bandage off, brutha!" called Arthur. He crawled from the forest dragging a folded leaf. He opened it to reveal a dollop of foamy, white poultice. "Lo and behold, this should help your foot!"

"What is it?" asked Gabriel, sniffing the stuff.

"Ah, you're a curious yeoman! Well, I mixed plantain with sage bundle, oxeye daisy petal with ground nettles, added ten drops of venom, and then bonded it with pine sap. *Voila!*"

Gabriel quirked his head. "Did you say venom? As in *your* venom?"

"Yes! Rich in peptides, don't you know?"

"Huh. I had no idea spiders were so handy." His broken ear flopped from back to front over his forehead as he looked on.

"There is much the world doesn't know about us," said Arthur with profound gravity.

Miriam was amazed by how he'd whipped up the salve and was touched by his thoughtfulness. She unrolled a blanket from one of Emily's saddlebags to sit on and to keep soil away from the wound. Her nine companions circled to get a look at her foot as she unwrapped it.

"Oh, my goodness," said Millicent, horrified.

John made a retching sound. "Oh man! That looks terrible!"

Though it was ugly with redness and dirty, dead skin, it looked better than Miriam remembered. Most of the blisters had popped. One on the side of her heel was calloused and dark yellow. "Could be worse."

Millicent's face pinched like a prune. "How? How on Earth could that be worse?"

"At least it's not infected," said Emily. "You've taken good care of it."

Mort and Druck whispered about something, but their conversation grew heated.

"No! Oy'm not gonna ask 'er!" said Druck.

"Well, it would be nice to know," said Mort.

"It don't seem like good manners. Let's see if it falls off."

The pair noticed that everyone was looking at them and stopped talking.

Miriam recognized that vultures will be vultures and gave them a shrug. "Hey. If my foot falls off, then it's all yours, but I think it's safe for now."

"Most generous, girlchick!"

"Yes, most thoughtful."

Arthur pulled the leaf to her foot and with dexterous skill applied the salve. It stung madly at first, but then the concoction soothed and cooled it. The pain vanished.

"Oh, Arthur! Ohmigosh! That's amazing! Thank you!"

"My pleasure, brutha!"

As the group followed the Gibbon toward Yellowstone's Grand Canyon, Millicent declared it absurd that the three-mile hike ahead seemed short after their long journeys. Gabriel scouted by patrolling ahead and circling back. Arthur rode atop Miriam's head, she and Millicent rode atop Emily, and John rode Sebastian.

Millicent used her hands to pantomime how the river would plummet a hundred feet over the Upper Falls and then flow a quarter-mile to drop three-hundred feet over the Lower Falls. "It's twice as tall as Niagara," she said. "Getting there is the easy part. I don't know how we're gonna climb down."

"Jiya?" asked Sebastian. "You said Lucifur's army is dwindling?"

"Yes! Ze'eva thinks his animals are losing morale after their loss at Doyadu-khani."

"I thought that might happen. He's persuasive, but the animals must be able to see through it once they're away from him, right?"

"See through what?" asked John.

"His vision. It's empty. There's nothing there."

"That's what I've been thinking. It's like he's the only one who cares

Chapter Eighteen

about what he's doing, you know? You don't think they're buying it anymore?"

"Maybe not."

"Or, they just don't trust him," said Millicent. "Copernicus played along until he double-crossed him."

"Madness is considered sane if enough people agree with it," said Emily, "and Lucifur wanted everyone to hop aboard his crazy train."

Sebastian nodded. "Hopefully they realize how dangerous he is."

They reached the Yellowstone River and followed it north until they found a clearing with a breathtaking view of a bleached and yellow canyon that sprawled to the horizon. Another hike along the river brought them to the brink of the Upper Falls. The water rushed past, over the edge, and into a giant plume below.

At John's request, Mort and Druck took to the air to circle the canyon as lookouts.

"Oy wish we were applyin' for jobs, eh!" said Druck.

"Ya! We'd 'ave so much to put on our resumes!"

"Guides!"

"Scouts!"

"Lookouts!"

"Oy tell ya, Druck me old mate, we've done well for ourselves. We've done well." They glided through the canyon and out of sight.

Sebastian laughed. "I don't know where you found those two, but they're delightful."

"Yeah," said John.

"Hey," said Millicent, "speaking of them . . . how's my face?"

John peeled back her bandage and cringed. The slice across her cheek was scabbed over and sported a shiny bruise around the puckered skin.

"You might have a scar from that."

"Ya think?"

"So, it's a lovely view and all," said Emily, "But how are you getting down? I'm not getting down, just so you know — there's no way I'm getting down there — nope-no-way."

"Ahoy!" said Arthur from atop Miriam's head. "Methinks I have an idea. Do you trust me?"

"Yes," said John.

"Then let me see what I can see."

Miriam set him on the ground, and he skittered over the edge of the cliff.

"Oh, I don't know about this," said Millicent.

As though she'd given him a cue, Arthur arrived on a tube of water from beyond the edge of the waterfall. He brought it to rest on the riverbank in front of them and pointed into the open end.

"*Passez par ici*. It is a water slide, no?"

"Oh no," said Millicent. "You've got to be kidding me. I can't do that."

"Gabriel and Jiya," said Sebastian, "You'll stay with Emily."

"But — " said Gabriel.

"Before you start, I don't want any of us left alone. Jiya can fly down to us if anything happens. Arthur, is this thing strong enough to hold me?"

"Yee! We'll find out!"

"Ha. Wonderful."

Miriam crutched toward the slide. "Are we doing this? Is it ready? Yes? Then see you at the bottom, friends and family!"

She swung on her crutches feet-first into the opening. Her stomach lurched and flipped. The tube curved over the bowels of the waterfall and deposited her at the side of the river. She landed on her good foot and swung off her momentum on the crutches. She stopped with a pivot to gape up at the shimmering, translucent tube.

I'm down! I made it!

"You're next," said John to Millicent.

She burst into tears. "No! I can't! I'll find another way down!"

Emily wrapped her trunk around Millicent's waist and tossed her

Chapter Eighteen

into the chute.

"There. She's down."

John's eyes bugged out. "What the *heck*, Emily? Wow. I mean, just, wow!"

"She'll forgive me later."

"Don't count on it!"

He ran and jumped with a long shout. Sebastian followed and landed behind him. Arthur arrived last and let the slide collapse into the falls.

"You're amazing, Arthur!" shouted Miriam over noise. She scooped him up to sit on her shoulder.

"Aye-thank you!"

Millicent shook with anger. *EMILY! I know you can hear me! I can't believe you did that! I'm never trusting you again!*

Arthur turned to John. "Will she be okay?"

She'll be fine. His face was already dripping from the spray. *Let's head downriver and get away from this.*

The canyon towered over them with steep, jagged walls. They hugged the tight space next to the water's edge until they reached a natural overlook at the brink of the Lower Falls. A ceaseless gush of water poured into the three-hundred-foot drop.

Sebastian stepped to the edge. "Yikes. Arthur, I don't suppose you can create another water slide, can you? Not that I'd want to use it."

"Ah, no. This is beyond me."

"Okay, then we'll hike along the rim till we find a way down."

"What if I do it with you, Arthur?" asked Miriam.

Millicent groaned. "Miriam, we can find another way."

"You already went down one! We'll curve the slide nice and shallow! I promise!"

"What do you know about it? You've never done anything with water!"

"Your memories are my memories. I felt what you did with the waterleaf."

Millicent made an exasperated, isn't-that-amazing face. "Wow, look at me! I watched a surgeon on TV, so now I can perform surgery!"

"Brutha," said Arthur, "you're one crazy human. I'm willing to create it with you, but failure would surely mean death."

"Let's try, at least!" said Miriam.

Millicent turned away and swore under her breath in a masterful string of profanity that made Sebastian do a double take. John feared a mighty fight would break out between the twins and dared to rub her back. Fortunately, she didn't hit him.

Miriam got on her hands and knees to reach the river. Her fingers skipped on the rushing current. Arthur climbed down her arm to sit on the back of her hand.

"Together now!" he called out.

The knowledge from the memories worked. She connected with the water as though she'd done it before, and together they lifted a tentacle of it from the river.

"We've got it!" she said. "Now what do we do?"

Arthur grunted. "Let one end slide over. We shall hold the other end here!"

"Oh! Like a giant Slinky!"

"Eh?"

"Nothing. Never mind."

They let the tendril elongate down the face of the waterfall. It was more water than she'd ever be able to carry physically, but the energy coursing through them made it feel like an extension of her mind. She and Arthur hollowed it into a tube until it was wide enough for Sebastian to fit through.

"Okay. Okay. Okay. OKAY!" said Millicent to no one in particular. She swiped John's hand away and ran headlong into the opening with her eyes pinched shut.

Miriam screamed. The bottom of the tube pointed straight down at the rocky plunge pool.

Chapter Eighteen

There was no thought. John launched his mind in with theirs and helped to curl the slide downriver as Millicent slipped through. She landed on her hands and knees on the riverbank.

Sebastian teetered. "John — "

John cast his arms open. "What! First, she had to be thrown down a chute, and now she leaps into one three times longer that wasn't even finished yet! I'm tellin' you! Ya can't win with her, Sebastian, you just can't win!" He turned and jumped down the water slide.

"You're next," said Miriam. Her eyes pulsed yellow.

Sebastian rocked back and forth. "Hoo boy. Here we go. This is it. The big one."

"You're stalling."

"Yes, I am."

He bounded into the tube and slipped out of sight.

Miriam set Arthur on her shoulder and sat on the ground.

"It's been fun, brutha," he said.

She nodded and scooted into the slide.

At the bottom, they decided not to tell Millicent about her near-death experience. It would only cause panic. The slide had carried them downriver to dissipate their momentum, so they hiked back to the base of the falls. They searched for the spot where the woman used the keystone.

Millicent's eyes flashed when she saw a place that matched.

"Here," she said, and she traced the cliff with her fingers until she found the trigger spot. An empty hexagon sank into the rock. "Wow. It sure is a lot easier to find things when you know exactly what you're looking for."

"Yeah. It feels like we were just here," said Miriam. She pulled the keystone from her pocket and slipped it into place.

From behind the waterfall, a plank of rock jutted to split the water like a curtain and revealed an ancient, mossy passageway. Smooth, dark stones rose from the riverbed to create a path to the entrance.

Tumo Nataquinde

"Here we go," said John.

"Into the darkness," said Miriam.

Millicent nodded. "Tumo Nataquinde. The Written Story. I hope it's a good one."

They walked across the slippery stepping stones. Miriam showed off her skill with the crutches by traversing the gaps. A purple glow beckoned at the end of a tight corridor, and they entered a monolithic dome lit by grelyxir torches.

John rested his hands on his hips to survey the empty room. "Boy. The people who lived here sure liked building strange and confusing structures, didn't they?"

Millicent nodded and ran her fingers along the wall until she felt a jolt of energy. There came a loud crack. The ground rumbled, and a column rose from the center of the floor.

They felt a lurch of vertigo with the realization that the column wasn't rising; the floor they were on was sinking around it. They teetered and leaned toward the column as they descended through solid rock. They passed into a black space where the open air was cooler.

Miriam stepped close to the edge. "It's so dark in here. Ha-loo!" Her voice bounced several times to come up behind her again. "This place is huge!"

"It smells okay," said Sebastian, "for a secret, underground chamber."

"Aye. There are spiders here," Arthur reported from the top of Miriam's head.

"Spiders?" asked Millicent.

"Nothing to be afraid of. We spiders are everywhere there's a food and water supply."

Millicent put her hand against the rising column to feel the rock glide past. It helped to assuage her faintness. "I wish there was a way to turn on some lights," she said. At her command, streams of sunlight poured in through a thousand tiny openings to illuminate a vast, conical chamber. The platform they were riding was still a hundred feet from

Chapter Eighteen

the floor. Carved artwork covered the walls.

Miriam shoved Millicent's arm. "Nice! Look what you did!"

She wished she hadn't — the platform seemed abruptly small.

After a minute of gliding down the column, they landed on the floor with a soft thud. The first thing they saw, slumped against the distant wall, were three human skeletons sitting in a row.

Millicent went bug-eyed. "Are those real skeletons? Those are real skeletons!" Her forehead wrinkled. The giant chamber seemed abruptly small now, too. "What is this place?"

"That's what we're here to find out," said Miriam. "Why don't you stay here with Sebastian while we look?"

Sebastian nodded. "We'll be right here." Millicent grabbed his fur.

The floor was covered with colorful stones that formed a pinwheel design and each blade stretched a hundred feet from the center to the wall. Miriam and John walked across the expanse toward the skeletons.

John shook off the chills that ran up his back. "You see them all the time in movies and on Halloween . . . "

"But these were real people . . . "

"Do you think they got trapped in here?"

The skeletons wore remnants of ancient clothing, and their hair lay in clumps down their shoulders and in their laps because the flesh that once anchored it was long gone. The one in the center clutched a stone tablet the size of a coffee table book.

John crouched to inspect the tablet. "There's nothing on this side. Should I turn it over?"

"Be gentle," said Miriam. "The arms might fall off. They always fall off in movies when people pull ancient manuscripts from the hands of the dead."

"Ohmigosh, Miriam. Be quiet!" He lifted the skeleton's hands off the stone. "Okay. Yeah. I can't believe I'm doing this." He lifted the heavy stone, and the skeleton's arms remained intact. "Huh. The other side is blank, too, but — "

It's holds memories, doesn't it? asked Millicent from the base of the column.

Think so. Yeah.

They left the skeletons to carry the tablet back to her, so she could investigate it with them.

"Wait," said Millicent. "I bet we can bring Sebastian with us, so he can see what we see."

Sebastian lifted his brow. "If you think it will work, sure."

They joined minds with him. It felt natural after all that they'd shared. They activated the memory, which also felt natural, and they found themselves standing in the same spot when the chamber was new. The woman from the keystone memory stood near them and surveyed the artwork. She was joined by two young men.

We're finished. We set out to collect and preserve every memory we could find, and our work is complete. We transferred everything into these walls.

We created this place where only humans can go. It was Gareth's idea for me and my brothers to seal the memories so that only siblings can unlock it. A lock of siblings. He reasons that three humans are easy to assemble. Requiring three *siblings* ensures that some element of family still exists in the world. It's a brilliant idea. Establishing the lock took some experimentation, but we did it.

Meanwhile, the Hunters know we're here. They can't reach us, but they'll lie in wait until we either emerge or starve to death. There's nothing left but sadness and ruin out there. We choose to die here.

The spiders, being helpful, bring us water, but we won't last long without food. So be it.

Gareth volunteers to hide the keystone. He's brilliant and cunning, but his chances of making it back to the Mesa are slim.

I have just said goodbye to my husband for the last time. We'll never know if he's made it.

The humans in Caldera are almost extinct. I don't know how many remain. I don't know when anyone will discover our work, but if one

Chapter Eighteen

thing is clear to us, it's that humans always find a way into Caldera. History will repeat itself as it has for thousands of years. We rest knowing the history is safe.

I'm looking at you, future visitor. I am Shori. My husband is Gareth. My brothers are Tulin and Brom. We existed here, and our memory lives on through you. Let these walls be your guide. Let these walls be your warning.

Good bye.

Sebastian looked around the chamber, which returned to its present, dustier condition. "She recorded this tablet right here! It felt like she was right next to me!"

Millicent held her hand over her mouth and had tears in her eyes. She was too young to know what it was like to have a husband, but now she knew what if felt like to lose one. It was horrible. Noble. Proud.

"Gareth volunteered to lock them in," said Miriam, "and they volunteered to stay."

John nodded toward the skeletons. "At least we know they didn't get trapped in here."

A shiny, new piece of the puzzle sprang into Millicent' mind. "They were the original siblings. That's why Lucifur went after us — he somehow knew that he needed siblings!"

Arthur tapped the top of Miriam's head.

"Yes, Arthur?"

"Could you set your course for where that lower sunbeam comes in, brutha?"

"Aye-aye," she said, and she swung on her crutches to a bright spot in the wall. John followed close behind them.

Something obscured the sunlight as they approached. Eight, hairy legs splayed out of the hole. Miriam dismissed the spook in her gut. A gray, weathered jumping spider twice the size of a tarantula peeked out at them.

"How are things done around here, Admiral?" asked Arthur.

Tumo Nataquinde

The gray spider's voice was faint. "I'm not sure I understand your question, friend."

"Has anyone ever read these carvings?" asked Miriam.

"Why, yes. Three boys."

How long ago? asked Millicent from afar.

"Time . . . time. It flows swift and slow. Maybe it was yesterday. Maybe it was a long time ago."

"Do you remember their names?" asked Miriam.

"No. They were young boys, but they didn't see me here. Never said hello. Oh, I wished they would have."

Millicent's mouth dropped open. *That spider is over a hundred years old.*

"How old are you, Arthur?" asked Miriam.

"Hm. Admiral said it best: time flows swift and slow. *Je ne sais pas.*"

"To your question," said the gray spider, "they poked around and made the walls move. I didn't know the walls could do that. Curious thing. I tried to activate them after they left but nothing happened, so I crawled back here. I think it was a while ago."

"Do you know how they started?" asked John.

"Yes. Stood in three places, as I recall, if I can recall that. I'm not sure what I recall."

"Thank you. You've been helpful."

The spider rubbed his mandibles. "Have I? That's nice." He inched forward and blocked all the sunlight. His hairy abdomen was heavy and scoured. "You smell nice. May I feed on you?"

John stepped back. "Um, no. No, you can't. Sorry."

The spider considered John's refusal and sighed. "Very well. I thought you'd be a nice meal." He slipped backward into the hole.

"Stood in three places," said Sebastian. "What do you suppose —"

Millicent was already walking toward the perimeter.

"An-nd there she goes again."

"I found a handprint!" said Miriam.

Judging by where she was standing, John ran a third of the way

Chapter Eighteen

along the circumference of the wall and scanned the artwork until he found a handprint.

"I found one, too!"

Millicent estimated the distance and approached the third spot, expecting new skeletons to pop out at any moment.

Yes, there's a handprint here, she said.

Ready? asked John.

Ready.

Ready!

One . . . two . . . three.

They placed their hands in the adult-sized prints, and a loud rumbling sounded above. Grelyxir poured down the walls from the ceiling. It filled every line and nook in the artwork with purple flame all the way to the floor. The room blazed triumphantly. A dizzying miasma of animation began as thousands of tiny figures — humans and animals, trees and grass, water and clouds, windswept fields with herds of mammoths, soaring birds, and pennants that furled above human villages — came to life in the rock.

"Well, Sebastian," said Miriam. "You wanted to see the walls move in the Mesa. This is a thousand times bigger than anything we saw there."

"It's amazing. How do you — how do you know where to start now?"

The grelyxir drained into the floor and out of sight, but one scene flashed purple before it was gone.

John chuckled incredulously. "Well! At least they left us a clue! That's better than the other places we've seen."

"I'm nervous," said Millicent.

Miriam took her hand. "I'm nervous, too. Let's see what this is all about."

With Arthur standing vigil atop Miriam's head, they linked their thoughts with Sebastian and plunged into the memories. The whoosh that transported their minds bumped and dipped like a mine car

Tumo Nataquinde

switching tracks. This first memory was recorded elsewhere and farther back in time than any other they'd experienced. It was copied here, and Shori's journey as she carried it to Tumo Nataquinde was imprinted on it. They could sense that the memory was as ancient to her as it was to them. A new woman's voice spoke into their heads as they looked through her eyes.

I'm standing in my village of tall grass tents. My people wear animal skins and rugged fabrics as they carry camas root and gooseberries in baskets and water in earthen pitchers that our grandmothers made and decorated. Our oxen bellow, and the mountain goats bleat. My friends pull a sled of crops in front of me — we've been working all day, so our muscles are sore, and our skin is hot. I smell the soil and smoke and pine. The babies are hanging on their cradle boards, sleeping. It's summer. The air is warm. We fish the bountiful and abundant streams. It's my favorite place and my favorite time of year.

This memory sprawled and seemed to last forever.

"This — " said Sebastian standing beside them in the village. "This is a memory?" He looked around, bewildered. "Hello!" he called to a passing woman. She nodded at him but kept walking.

"They'll kind of react to you," said Millicent, "but you can't change what happens."

"It's so real!"

The sun slipped across the sky as though the author of the memories had pressed a fast-forward button.

It's after dark. We gather around racks of bison roasting over fires. Shaman spins his tales for us, skilled at bringing to life our fears of the cougars, bears, and wolves, and I'm delighted to hear the old stories. The sleepy children laugh at a turkey gobble in the woods. What a funny sound, they say. As the fires die, we salute the moon with song and look

Chapter Eighteen

forward to the sun's return in the morning.

It's midnight. A strange sound draws us from our slumber, and we gather in the center of the village to search for the source. A brilliant flash of blue light explodes in midair. It expands as a cascade of energy through us, through our huts, and beyond our village in all directions.

We don't know what's happening. The blast of light knocks us out.

Some time later, we're awakened by a whistle. The whistle grows into a shriek, and in the spot where the blue light exploded appears a new light that looks like the sun, yet we can look at it without hurting our eyes.

It's the most beautiful thing I have ever seen.

It descends into our midst, a golden gemstone whose light touches every living thing.

We cannot approach it. Anyone who tries must turn away. When I attempt to touch it, I discover the sound, like a chorus, grows too loud and terrible and the light too dazzling for me to reach it. I turn away like all the others.

In the weeks to come, we go about our lives around the strange stone. The song it emits seems to draw sap from the ground as though the Earth itself is weeping. Purple and flaming, it is everywhere, yet it doesn't burn to the touch. We harvest it to light the village at night.

The animals are speaking.

The owls in the trees, the otters in the river, and our sheep — we stop eating our sheep. We can't slaughter them now that they can speak to us. They beg for their lives, and we spare them.

Now, we can speak without opening our mouths.

We mold stone and water by touching it and build our permanent home, a modest dwelling of rock we have coaxed from the ground.

This is my life for the rest of my days. The Stone is with us forever.

Tumo Nataquinde

The memory ended. The echo of dripping water was the only sound in the chamber, and Miriam and Sebastian staggered away from the wall to rest, certain that a lifetime had passed.

She looked up even though she couldn't see the tarantula on her head. "Arthur, how long have we been here?"

"Hmm?" he asked. "We talked to the Admiral a moment ago, yes?"

"But," said Sebastian, stunned, "that was weeks — months — years!"

Arthur wiggled his pedipalps in thought. "Maybe, but I don't think so. I would have gotten hungry and bored, no?"

"It's okay," said John. "We thought the same thing when Robert showed us his memories. It's like a dream; it feels like it lasts forever, but it only takes a minute in real life."

Millicent tapped her fingers on her lips. "What was that stone? Sebastian, have you ever heard of it?"

"No, never," he said. "But it changed everything."

She nodded, deep in thought. "That was the beginning. We just watched the origin of Caldera."

There was her amazing insight again, thought John. She had to have been right.

Arthur drummed his legs on Miriam's head. "Will you look at more?"

"What do you mean?"

"Only this part of the wall moved," he said, gesturing toward the artwork in front of them, just one vignette among thousands of friezes that spanned the rest of the chamber.

"Oh, my goodness; there's so much!" said Millicent.

Miriam wrapped her arm around her. "This is what we came here to do, right?"

She took a deep breath and blew it out sharply. "Right."

The next memory had them looking through the eyes of a man in his thirties.

Chapter Eighteen

All I have left of my mother is her memory. She was one of the first to record her memories, and now it's my turn.

The cats have invited us to follow them into the valley on their hunt.

Look! They're pulling their prey from the air!

There is a flash of blue light as they strike. I ask how this is possible, but they don't know. And the prey animals cannot speak. They are mindless, as mother described the animals before the Stone arrived.

With practice, we learn to hunt this way, too.

It is a week later. I am a guest of the carnivore leaders as they convene to develop the Code of Cognizants, so that no thinking being may prey upon another. The elders of my village are pleased.

A new memory: The council of animals was a year ago. Today, my closest friend, Puth, invited me to his burrow to share grave news. There is a rumor that the carnivores are questioning human dominance. They resent what we can do, our abilities that elude them.

It is nighttime, and it is cold. We sneak into the cats' caves. Certain they will detect us, we creep close enough to read their minds and confirm Puth's rumor.

They plan to kill us. No, please. Don't let this be real. Let this be a scattered few. We rush back to our village.

It is three nights later. I wake to the sounds of yelling. Screams in the commons. The cats are attacking, but thanks to our warning we have prepared weapons and barricades against them. We fight all night and push them back into the cold. Their minds are clear: they are after the Stone.

To what purpose, we don't know.

Puth is dead. My sister is dead. The ground is littered with the bodies of the dead.

The Animal Revolution has begun.

We must fortify our home. We are no longer safe.

This is my life for the rest of my days.

Tumo Nataquinde

Millicent wiped tears from her face, surprised to find she'd been crying. They all were. The onslaught of this man's memories filled them with dread and hopelessness. There was no closure; he spent the rest of his life in constant fear. Groups of animals remained loyal to the humans and were appalled by the motives of the revolution, but the betrayal made it difficult to maintain trust.

"Are you okay, brutha?"

"Oh, it's awful, Arthur," said Miriam. She reached up and stroked his hairy abdomen. "We'll be okay. It's just a lot to take in."

The next section of memories struck them with a youthful vibrancy. They looked through the eyes of a young woman.

My grandfather's memories! I've wanted to learn how to record mine (which is forbidden for some inane reason) and finding his (and my great-grandmother's) has taught me how to achieve the recording. My mother has always claimed they didn't do this, but today I found their tablets beneath the shelter. I'm angry that it's taken this long. How different would my life have been had I found these when I was younger?

So much has happened since my grandfather's time. They had no idea how good their lives were at the beginning of the Revolution. Since then, animals have been quieted, converted, or killed as the carnivores covered Caldera. They hunt us. The chase is relentless. We stay close, back to back, and fall into smaller camps. I refuse to bring a child into this world, as do most of my friends. Not until we find a way to make it safe again. Now I have proof that it once *was* safe. It *is* possible!

It is my idea to wield the "Stone." The majority disagree with me. They cling to the notion that it's divine. No! I refuse to deify it! But I do believe that it's a source of unlimited power. If we can harness it, it could turn the tide.

But publicly, I agree to leave it alone.

Chapter Eighteen

The purple sap that bleeds from the earth allows us to get closer to the gemstone than ever before. I have named the sap Elixir of the Grey, for its neutralizing properties lie between the golden and violet hues of the stone and sap, respectively. The Grey is where complimentary colors meet.

We scour the country side in search of more memories. From what we cobble together, I can't ignore that the first appearance of Elixir of the Grey coincides with the gemstone's arrival. They must be related. I believe it's a byproduct of the stone's power.

Our hypothesis is that it's the key to reaching the gemstone. If we can find the right tool . . .

The wolves defend us as we harvest grelyxir, as my companions have taken to calling it. I suppose it's a better name. It's certainly easier to say.

We test hundreds of combinations of materials. Weeks pass. We work in secret. We work at night.

At last! We discover that it binds with molten obsidian. The mixture is stable! With our bellows urging the hearth, we forge a staff with tines in which we plan to set the stone. I don't often fall to prayer, but as the horde of predators presses ever closer to our settlement, I hope this alchemy will work.

Holding the staff fills me with strange energy. It feels like a living thing. My partners celebrate our creation and bestow upon me the honor of making the attempt. We wait until nightfall, after the fires have turned to ember and our neighbors have retreated to their rooms.

I approach the bright, singing star in our midst. The staff vibrates in my hands; it's modulating its frequency to match the gemstone. I am standing closer to it than anyone ever has. How can I look at it? Why does this brilliant point of light not blind me? It should burn my eyes out!

I thrust the staff.

The tines lock onto the stone like a powerful magnet.

Tumo Nataquinde

The light dims, the singing subsides to a delicate hum, and I know that the energy coursing through me has changed me. I am the light. I am the song. I drive the butt of the staff against the ground, and it causes the air to bend.

The stone has not moved since it arrived two hundred years ago.

Now it's ours.

The entire village surrounds me in the plaza, drawn from their homes by the commotion. "We brandish," I say to them, "so we can protect ourselves!"

The next morning, for the first time in two generations, we march to meet the carnivores. I batter them with wind. I crush them with water. I bury them with the earth. A few of them break through, and I swing the staff, and the stone's energy slices through reality and sends them flying away like ants from a stick.

This is my life for the next few months. We are the Liberators. We push the Hunters back with every engagement. We reestablish the Code.

This is my life for the rest of my days. We have found peace.

Sebastian turned slack-jawed to the children. "This woman speaks like a scholar! They devoured history, geology, and physics thousands of years before the Greeks!"

Millicent nodded. "Yeah . . . They were even using scientific method, kinda."

"Arthur?" asked John. "How long did that one take?"

"About ten minutes, Captain. Don't worry about me. The chamber's been quiet."

The next memory began with immediate bitterness through the eyes of a middle-aged man.

Chapter Eighteen

Ignorance is bliss. Grant power and destroy freedom. Elora, the Great Liberator, the Wielder of the Stone, was right about things, but she couldn't have foreseen what's happened in my time. Here's what I know: not all humans were as united as they thought. A group seeking total domination over Caldera, in alliance with the carnivore Hunters, attacked a village.

Turns out this attack was a distraction to draw the warriors away, so they could infiltrate the main city and steal the Stone.

Nightmare. For the first time, humans wield the Stone against other humans. They lay waste to any who oppose them. I don't know how I've survived this long.

Abomination. They've used the Stone to combine the carnivore leaders into a being of pure evil. He is a misshapen beast of bear, wolf, and cougar. He commands legions of animals, and his intention is clear: he will wipe out the last of us. The fools have created their own destroyer.

I am a Preserver sworn to protect the Stone, and this is my record. The Preservers will carve a new chamber deep underground, a shrine for the Stone if ever we reclaim it.

But, oh, the beast has been cunning. He kept the insurgence alive. He advocated patience. He lulled us into a false state of comfort while his army grew.

The beast drove us out of Dragon's Mouth and claimed it for himself. We're going to the Central Plateau to create our final stronghold. It will be our masterpiece.

It will be the end of us.

Sebastian and the children stood in shock. Their brains pulsed with the influx of lifetimes.

Millicent scanned the remaining vignettes. "That leads up to the memories in the Mesa. It looks like they're stored here, too. Look. There's the creation of the Mesa. My gosh, what are all the others?"

"So," said Miriam, "our powers come from that gemstone?"

John nodded. "Everything came from that gemstone."

Millicent hugged herself. "It has to be what Lucifur is after. He could do whatever he wanted to. He could make himself like the Asaquatzi. At least we know we can hide in here if we want to."

"What, and end up like them?" asked Miriam, pointing at the skeletons. "No, thank you!"

"We came here for answers," said John, "and wow do we have them." He pulled *Grelyxir* from the loop on his backpack and swung it around. "So, we were right. Obsidian and grelyxir."

Miriam meandered on her crutches, deep in thought. "Our staffs are like the one Elora used. But when did they make the hammer?"

"Yeah. And why?"

Millicent bit her nails and stomped her foot. She disagreed with John's appraisal. "Do we, though? Have answers? We know a lot more of the story, but we have no idea where the Stone is. I didn't recognize anything when they made the shrine to protect it. I bet they did that on purpose." She frowned.

"I can't believe it," said Sebastian, startling them.

"What?" asked Miriam.

His emotions were erratic. "My brother is out there. Ze'eva is waging war on him. I know I've been quiet about this, but it's killing me! How do you reconcile? How do you reconcile the pain when somebody you cared about is doing bad things? This is what he's after? Do you get that? Everything that's happened and everything that's about to happen is because he wants that . . . *thing*? My brother! Some of my closest friends have died because of him."

The kids were silent.

"We have to stop him."

Nineteen

The Asaquatzi

The climb out of the canyon was slow and treacherous. They hugged the steep walls and paused often to catch their breaths while Sebastian scouted ahead for good footing. His instincts led them well, as they only had to double back once when a route proved impassable. Miriam rode on his back when she could, but there were a few spots where she had to crawl and climb on her own, always mindful of her foot. A rainbow cut through the powerful mist and spray of the Lower Falls and followed them as they zig-zagged up the cliff.

Emily and Gabriel waited near the top of the Upper Falls and greeted them happily. John hugged Gabriel extra tight, and the girls retired to the security of Emily's back. Mort and Druck circled overhead after John asked them to keep up their good work as lookouts, and knowing they were there was a comfort.

Sebastian's voice was subdued. "Where's Jiya?"

"Flew back to the Mesa to see if there's any news," said Gabriel.

"I see."

The kids shared all that they saw in Tumo Nataquinde with Gabriel and Emily. For Emily, the story of the Stone was revelatory. This, she said, explained why mammoths existed in Caldera while they were extinct in the homeworld. Once the Stone arrived, the families of mammoths in Yellowstone were protected from whatever killed off all the others.

"We should get back to the Mesa," said Gabriel. "Tell Ze'eva about everything you've learned."

"Yes, I think so," said John.

"Another long trip," said Millicent. Her legs ached, but she

Chapter Nineteen

acknowledged that the two weeks of exercise had improved her endurance. "*Improved my endurance* was not a phrase in my vocabulary before this trip."

"Yes, thank goodness for you, Emily," said Miriam, patting her back. There came a wave of appreciation, but then Emily returned to her thoughts.

"Do you have any idea where that shrine they made for the Stone could be?" asked Gabriel.

"No," said Millicent. "I've been racking my brain for clues, but I think they left out the location on purpose. We know it's somewhere deep underground."

"What do you mean?" asked John. "Where did you get that it's underground?"

"From the memories. Did you miss that part?"

"No, I saw it, but he said the Preservers hid the Stone in a 'wall of rock'."

"Well, that's interesting," said Miriam, "because what I saw was a diagram with three circles, all cryptic-like."

"So-o," said Millicent. "It's another puzzle, and we each saw a different piece. Great."

"Three circles, a wall, and somewhere deep underground," said John. "How is that useful?"

"I'm sure it's *very* useful. We just have to figure out what it means."

As dusk settled into darkness over Hayden Valley, Arthur rode on Gabriel's back and shared the Legend of the Spiders of Tumo Nataquinde that his mother had told him — and his 140 siblings — when he was young, and how the gray, wizened spider reminded him of it. The spiders who lived there were sworn to protect the walls and would fight off anyone who tried to harm them. Most spiders dismissed it as a fairytale, he said.

"I didn't know spiders could live to be so old," said Gabriel. "I wish I could've met him."

"*Oui*, it is true," said Arthur. "There are rumors of spiders who are even older."

"I have to tell you — what you did for Miriam this morning was amazing. You really helped her."

"It was nothing. Maybe someday people will not underestimate spiders so much?"

"Maybe. Can I ask you a question?"

"*Oui?*"

"Why all the strange nicknames?"

"Admittedly, I am terrible with names."

"Ah. Do you even know my name?"

"Uh . . . No."

"Ha!"

"Is it Floppy? Because of this ear? Pincushion? Lucky?"

"It's Gabriel."

"I shall call you Floppy. Your ear amuses me," he said, and he tapped Gabriel's broken ear with the tip of one leg.

"There we go. That's all I was after."

The temperature dropped as night fell. John joined the girls atop Emily, and they donned sweatshirts from one of the saddlebags and wrapped themselves in a blanket. Swayed by the rhythm of her tireless march, they leaned against each other and slept.

"Kids, wake up!" said Sebastian.

"Huh! What?" asked Miriam. It was early morning.

"The vultures spotted smoke. Look there."

A thick plume of black smoke billowed over the treelined horizon.

"What is it?" asked John. Millicent was already wide-eyed and sitting stiff with her fingers digging into Miriam's sides.

Jiya chirped from a branch. "I would say good morning, but it is not! Süütakkan is burning! There are fires all around it. Ze'eva's animals arrived last night, and there has been a terrible, terrible battle!"

"Ohmigosh! Are they still fighting?" asked Miriam.

"Yes, all through the morning."

Chapter Nineteen

"We need to go to them!"

Millicent couldn't believe her sister's tenacity and gave her a shove. "We've done enough! We're not fighters!"

"Yes, but — I know. It's — "

"You can't even walk!"

"Girls," said Sebastian.

Miriam twisted to snarl at her. "I couldn't walk in Doyadu-khani, either."

"Stop it, you two," said John. "We can't go, and you know it."

"He's right," said Sebastian. "We stick with the plan and get back to the Mesa."

Gabriel whimpered. "I'm with you no matter what, but part of me wants to be there, too."

"I know. But there's no way. We can't put the kids in harm's way or bring them anywhere near Lucifur."

"Jiya," said Emily, "did the mammoths go to Süütakkan?"

"Yes. All of them! They carry the Banners of the Wolves."

Emily's gait quickened, heaving the children backward. She moved so fast that Sebastian and Gabriel had to run to keep up.

"Emily, wait!" said Sebastian.

The plume of smoke grew larger. Millicent slapped Emily's thick, hairy hide. "Stop! Stop!"

John ducked, and Miriam yanked Millicent sideways to avoid a passing branch.

"Emily, what are you doing? Slow down!"

"If you want to go, then go," said Sebastian, "but leave them here!"

They plunged through the end of the forest onto a plateau that overlooked Süütakkan and the oxbow valley surrounding Dragon's Mouth.

"*You will stop now!*" said Sebastian with the jagged edge of persuasion. Emily obeyed and stopped at the edge of the plateau before it descended into the valley.

They stood speechless. Süütakkan, the colossal blade of white, stood in contrast against black smoke that furled from countless fires around its foundational terrace. Several sections of the tower were broken off and lay in heaps about the grounds as barricades. Hundreds of big cats, wolves, bears, and rodents tumbled over each other, wrapped in combat. Elk swung their antlers. Bison charged through defensive lines. A row of mammoths stampeded through the center of the fray and thrashed their tusks against the throngs of Lucifur's army. Dead animals littered the plaza.

Miriam dropped her crutches to the ground and slid off Emily's back, grabbing fistfuls of coarse hair to slow her descent. She took up the crutches and swung to the edge of the plateau to watch the battle. Her chest heaved.

Cougars phased in and out of sight. Shoals of rodents attacked groups of bears. Giant birds of prey swooped to snatch the rodents and carry them away from the battle. Ze'eva, the great silver wolf, fought deep in the clash surrounded by her wolves and the line of mammoths as they marched toward the base of the tower. A glaring of mountain lions tore down one of the mammoths. They leapt to attack the next in line and fought until a pack of wolves jumped to save it.

Miriam's eyes brimmed with tears. She had no power to stop this.

Sebastian stood beside her. "Do you see now?"

She slid her staff from the makeshift holster on her backpack and cocked her jaw.

John climbed down Emily's side, copying the way Miriam had done it.

"I'm sorry I took off like that," said Emily. "My family's down there. I have to go."

Millicent beat her fists against Emily's back. "No!"

But Emily pulled her off with her trunk and set her next to John. Millicent sobbed as she took off down the hill.

Miriam knew that no kid in their right mind would run into a battle between such powerful animals, but now, with Emily and Ze'eva down there, she felt hopeless. She clung to Sebastian and wished that they had

Chapter Nineteen

some greater power to do something, like a giant Palacemind that they could use together to stop the fighting.

Ze'eva's line met the ruined plaza that surrounded the foot of the tower. Lucifur's animals were outnumbered wherever they attacked. The individual fights were savage. On and on they fought, and it was clear that they would fight to the last animal standing.

John saw that Lucifur's animals were retreating into smaller groups and edged closer to the tower. "I think — It looks like Ze'eva is winning!"

"I think so, too," said Gabriel.

"Oh, Sebastian," said Millicent, "why won't they stop?"

"Hold on," he said. "Look!"

Lucifur walked out of the tower through a gothic, peaked doorway and stood at the top of the grand stairway where John and Millicent had watched him deliver his speech. He roared, but the sound wasn't savage or threatening. It was mournful.

His animals turned to face him, and the fighting stopped.

The sudden silence was jarring as Ze'eva's animals disengaged from their enemies. A low song filled the air, sung by the mammoths and bison. The elk joined at a higher pitch to create a harmony that grew louder until the air vibrated even where the kids were standing on the plateau. The singing stopped, and the valley echoed into silence.

Ze'eva climbed the steps to stand before Lucifur, who lowered his head in her presence and led his animals to do the same. She howled a long and sorrowful howl.

"Oh, my word," said Sebastian. "They did it. It's done."

"It's over?" asked Miriam.

"Yes. Lucifur just surrendered."

They walked into the valley. The Yellowstone River flowed nearby. Birds cleaned themselves and rested on rocks in the valley, and the number of dead and wounded on the ground increased as they approached. There was a wounded badger and a limping elk, and there was a black bear with a nasty head wound. Wolves ran between animals to check their condition and siphon pain wherever they could, but the casualties outnumbered them. The cries and moans of the mourning and injured were overwhelming.

Ahead of them lay the dead mammoth surrounded by a dozen survivors, including Emily, who grieved in silence with them. They sniffed and caressed their fallen friend with their trunks.

Lucifur sat with his head low and didn't look up as they approached the bottom of the stairs. He seemed smaller and slouched next to Ze'eva, who sat with her head high and an eye on them as they climbed.

John tensed. This was the bear who attacked him and his mother, and this was the bear who attacked him again in Hayden Valley, who hurt Rodney and betrayed Sebastian at the geyser — and the image of the massacre in the keystone tunnel hit him. This bear did that, too.

Millicent walked with her hand on Sebastian's neck. She closed her fist around a clump of fur. She never felt as well-protected and vulnerable at the same time, and she couldn't believe after everything they'd been through that they were walking toward the red grizzly on purpose.

They reached the top of the stairs, yet no one spoke, which seemed odd given the many reunions. John petted the back of Gabriel's head, waiting, and realized that this was the first time they'd seen Sebastian and Ze'eva in the same place.

Ze'eva addressed the crowd.

"I'll make this short. Today will be marked as the day Lucifur and his armies surrendered. We will walk with our enemies without rejoicing, for those who have died were us, and those who are living must face this crime as one species. We are the species of life. We'll heal and rest today, but tomorrow at daybreak we'll leave for the Mesa. What's important here and now is that all of you act. Lives on this battlefield can still be saved. Go now!"

She turned to Sebastian and spoke quietly. "You have one moment with him. Then I'm locking him away." She turned again to sit facing

Chapter Nineteen

outward.

Sebastian was boiling. He walked to Lucifur with the silence between them broken only by the lamentation from the valley. His emotions built to a point where Miriam was sure that he would strike him.

"Two days ago, I would have embraced you."

"Hm," said Lucifur. "If only it were two days ago. What's changed?"

"What's changed? What's changed! I can't stand the sight of you. What you've done . . ."

"What I've done is keep Caldera safe. We've had this conversation. You think I should've read more literature instead of history. Be like you and pretend that life is poetry and fiction."

"I don't care what you've read. Look at me."

"Oh, I am looking at you. If you've perceived my intentions as hostile, then I — " he said in a casual tone, but Sebastian cut him off.

"I know about the tunnel."

"The tunnel? Which tunnel are we talking about? There are so many tunnels."

Sebastian paused. "No. I won't allow you to insult every life you've taken by denying it."

"I see. Well. Since I'm not allowed to argue, then tell me. What *is* your plan when the humans get in?"

"There you go again! It's like you're reading from a script. This is the part when you twist it around and tell me that we're fighting over a definition of peace, right? 'If only you could see what I've seen, then you'd understand!' Right? I've experienced the memories! I saw the Stone and what you wanted to become and the world you wanted to create, and I still don't care about your cause."

Lucifur scoffed. "Then what are you doing here? Why speak with me at all?"

There came a painful buildup of anger in Sebastian that made John,

Millicent, and Miriam shake with empathy. It poured like a burst dam as he spoke.

"I want you to know that I know what you've done. You're not as cunning as you think you are. I want you to know that I feel something that I never thought I could. They're going to kill you tomorrow, and I think you deserve it." He paused. "You deserve to die. I want you to know that."

He walked back to the children in silence.

"Secure Genesius," said Ze'eva to her wolves. "We have a lot of wounded to attend to."

Lucifur was taken into Süütakkan, and the remnants of his army either fled into the woods or surrendered to captivity in solidarity with him. Many of the smaller animals who'd been held in his thrall woke in confusion. Many were horrified, and in their realization came shame, and they fell into two groups: those who were inconsolable and those who hurried to help the wolves with the wounded.

The children rested with Gabriel and Arthur on stone benches in a nook along the grand terrace at the base of the tower while Sebastian spoke with several animals not far away. The floor of the terrace was a beautiful mosaic of colorful stones. The ground was twenty feet below over the railing next to them, which gave them a commanding view of the valley. The afternoon was hot and breezy with a cloudless blue sky that turned the landscape into a postcard vista, were it not for the dead bodies and lingering smoke from the defensive fires and barricades.

Ze'eva approached them.

"Children. You've traveled far and wide. I'm so happy to see you again."

"My Lady," said Gabriel.

Miriam hopped up and hugged her. "You're okay! Are you all better?"

"Now that this has ended, I'm feeling much better, yes. What about you? You've been taking good care of that foot! And I detect the scent

Chapter Nineteen

of an impressive ointment? Who was the chemist?"

"*Je l'ai créé*," said Arthur. "I cannot believe that I am standing in your presence, Lady."

"This is intricate work, spider. Thank you for taking care of her."

"*Bien sûr!*"

"You left so suddenly," said Miriam. "I talked to you, turned around, and then whoosh, you were gone!"

"I know. I hated doing that to you. Please understand; the less you knew the better. Copernicus confided in me his plan to imprison the bears once you reached the temple, so I trusted that you'd be safe. Can you imagine the panic when I learned you were under attack? I thought I'd sent you to your death!"

"It wasn't your fault."

"Miriam, word of your actions has spread. You are the Hero of Doyadu-khani. And you, John and Millicent, making it all the way to the top of Abatakai! I trust that your journey was easier once the birds scared off the cougars?"

"Yes," said John. "Jiya told us!"

"Thank you for sending them," said Millicent.

"Ah, and you don't know yet, do you? Robert Hume escaped Abatakai. He's looking forward to seeing you again."

"He's alive?" asked Millicent, brightened by this news.

"Yes. He's resting in the Mesa with barely a scratch on him, the scoundrel."

"What will happen with Lucifur?" asked Gabriel.

Ze'eva took a breath. "Tomorrow we'll hold court at the Mesa to determine his fate. But be prepared. The citizens of Caldera are after his blood. There's a chance he could be imprisoned, but I suspect they'll ask for his death."

Miriam hugged her again, sat down, and took a big breath. "You know about Sahra?"

"Yes, Miriam. My heart aches with you. She was a great leader for her species. And my thoughts are with her husband — I think he's just starting to understand his role in his own downfall. The cats would be decimated if it weren't for you."

Sebastian rejoined them. Seeing him next to Ze'eva was surreal, as it demonstrated again just how large she was. Her pointed ears and straight posture made her tower over him. She stooped to nuzzle under his chin, and the size of her snout compared to his made him look like a teddy bear.

"My heart breaks for you, too, my friend" she said. "Lesser animals would've collapsed by now, yet you continue to lead in everything you do. Thank you for showing discretion with him in front of everybody."

"I'm not a leader," he said with a hint of impatience.

"I know. And that's what makes you exemplary. You teach restraint. Kindness. Thoughtfulness. Just by doing. I would never ask more of you, but these traits will be the strongest antidote to the poison we've been forced to endure."

Sebastian seemed to ignore her praise. "So. Tomorrow. Will Lord Nagus face trial, as well?"

Ze'eva straightened and returned to her formality. "Yes. What's left of him. I'll send an envoy to Doyadu-khani to retrieve him and his lieutenants. They'll likely arrive the day after. But I know first-hand the depth of his depravity, and he cannot go unpunished.

"We walk a thin line, morally speaking, by threatening to break the Code in order to uphold it. I have to admit that Copernicus posed the hardest question: what are the consequences for someone who breaks the Code? Yes, your brother did much more, but it's never been put to the test in my time. I suspect the conversations will be terse."

"I just want you to know," said Sebastian, "I'll stand by whatever decision is made. We keep our chins up. We rise above. And we keep going."

John chuckled, which drew everyone's attention to him. Sebastian gave him a stern look.

"I'm sorry. Totally not laughing at this. I was just lost in my thoughts."

Chapter Nineteen

Ze'eva smiled with her eyes. "Please. A little levity would be nice. What were you thinking about?"

"Well, Rodney said our wounds today strengthen us for tomorrow, right? So, I was just thinking, if that's the case, then we should be frickin' superheroes by now."

Miriam teared up and sniffled and guffawed at the same time.

Millicent snickered. "Yeah, I'm not sure how much more of this strengthening I can take."

They felt Ze'eva's chuckle and a pang of bittersweetness from Sebastian.

She straightened again. "Remember when I told you to close Pandora's Box? Well, as you may know, that's impossible to do by definition. All I really came over here to say is that the three of you have performed heroically, superheroes or not."

"Thank you," said John.

"So. Tell me. What did you learn at the Falls?"

Inside the gothic doors of Süütakkan was a grand lobby. While the outside was white alabaster, the interior was made of polished obsidian. Tall, thin, peaked windows ringed the lobby so they could see out in every direction. Delicate, white stonework lined the window frames and trim along the floors and ceiling.

Sebastian led them to a spiral staircase. Though he tried to be informational, his usual zest was gone.

"These stairs spiral all the way to the top of the tower, so no two rooms are on the same level. An interesting design, but a little impractical."

They bathed and ate dinner, and then collapsed into one of the rooms with Gabriel, Arthur, Mort, and Druck.

Miriam combed her fingernails through the fur on Sebastian's head. "You were right. Ze'eva told us what's going to happen tomorrow. How are you doing?"

"Oh, Miri. I'm just sad. Sad and numb. Glad this is over. I know what has to happen, but it doesn't make it any easier. Get some sleep if you can. Tomorrow's going to be a long day."

The morning brought rain that pelted the windowsill of their room. They tightened the drawstrings of their hooded sweatshirts knowing they would shield against the annoying patter on their heads but do nothing to keep them dry. Millicent wondered how many umbrellas were sitting useless in the Den of Antiquities.

A poncho would be nice. Just a garbage bag would do.

The piazza around the tower was braced by a stone palisade that followed the oxbow curve of the Yellowstone River. The animals in Ze'eva's army formed lines according to species and flanked the prisoner animals. The beavers presented a wooden pillory that they attached to a harness suspended between two mammoths.

As Ze'eva escorted Lucifur through the crowd and drizzle, the animals stomped and hooted. The prisoners watched their leader. They gasped and murmured when they realized what he was meant to do. He reared to stand on his hind legs and slipped his head through the open pillory, and the rodents clamped the cuff around his neck and bound his front paws. He was stoic before the jeering mob and the pleas from his followers.

"Are they gonna make him walk like that the whole way?" whispered Miriam, horrified. "How far is it?"

Millicent flashed a map into her mind. It was ten miles and mostly uphill.

"Get on," said Sebastian to Miriam. He stared at the ground. She climbed onto his back and secured her crutches in a sling next to her obsidian staff.

"Sebastian?"

"Let's be quiet for a while, okay?"

"Okay."

Ze'eva walked to the western edge of the plaza and howled. The thousands of animals followed her from Süütakkan in a cacophony of

Chapter Nineteen

paws and hooves through the mud. Everyone was soaked. Sebastian had warned them that the day would be long. The wind and rain made it cold and miserable, too.

The gradual but relentless uphill hike proved too strenuous for John and Millicent, so Ze'eva let Millicent ride on her back and summoned an elk for John. While they waited for the elk to arrive, and despite the circumstances, he couldn't hide his disappointment that he had to ride what he imagined to be a deer. It was an annoyance, he thought, and he acknowledged his own peevishness.

The elk towered over him with a splay of antlers that looked both majestic and deadly. John gazed in awe.

"I'm Hucklebuck. Climb on up, son."

Riding a full-grown male elk was pretty cool, after all.

Walking on his hind legs, Lucifur stumbled a few times but never protested. His followers begged Ze'eva to release him, to stop humiliating him, but her emotions when she ignored them revealed that the decision wasn't hers to make.

Can you hear me? asked Millicent.

Yes, said Miriam.

Yeah, said John.

How do we get home? Now that this is over?

I don't know, said Miriam. *I've actually stopped wondering.*

What? said John.

I'm not giving up. I'm just tired. I'm tired of this, and I don't know the answer. So, I've stopped wondering.

We keep looking for the Stone, said Millicent.

John sighed. Cold rainwater dripped from the tip of his nose. *Three circles, in a wall, and deep underground. Any ideas?*

No, said Millicent. *None.*

It took four hours to reach the Mesa. The plants in the garden drooped from the weight of the rain and in the mist blurred into rows of gray. Sunlight slanted through a break in the clouds and struck the face of the Mesa. It was blinding in contrast to the gloom. The sky rolled clear as the city of rock came into full view.

Murphy's Law, thought Millicent. *Now it's sunny.*

Ze'eva led the procession down the center aisle, which reminded Millicent of a Roman triumph approaching the temple of Jupiter, a detail from history she was surprised to remember.

They realized how many animals Ze'eva had kept in reserve. Members of every species waited for them in the muddy, cobblestone plaza before the main entrance. The younger animals who hadn't been allowed to go to battle peeked around their caretakers from the doorways and windows. Guards were stationed at every opening, and lookouts stood on every tower and terrace.

Millicent squinted up at the main tower and gasped so sharply that all the animals in her vicinity turned to look at her. The tower's three circular openings yawned. Her mind raced. *Three circles! The Stone could be inside the Mesa! There are plenty of walls. But deep underground? Maybe it's even deeper than the keystone tunnel. Maybe —*

"What's wrong?" asked Miriam.

Stricken with anxiety and a desire to keep the idea to herself, she swallowed hard. "I'm not sure. I was just thinking about something."

The mammoths carrying the pillory with Lucifur between them stopped at the outside edge of the plaza. Ze'eva, carrying Millicent, led Sebastian with Miriam and Arthur, Hucklebuck with John, and Gabriel up the center aisle. She left Millicent with them at the base of the main stairs and went inside. A moment later, she reemerged on the balcony above them, where they'd first seen Emily.

Her voice resounded through every mind in the plaza.

"I am not one for speeches. I am not your leader. No animal is. After weeks of senseless bloodshed, we bring before you the one who would stake a claim as your leader, your protector, and your savior. This evening, we will convene in the Amphitheater to hold court and decide what — "

Chapter Nineteen

Lucifur interjected. "Why not hold court now, Lady? We've come all this way. Why delay the inevitable?"

A murmur of gossip and protest rose from the crowd.

"Is that what you want, Genesius? Swift justice?"

"Yes."

After the long hike, one could have expected Lucifur to be hanging from the pillory, but he stood as strong and proud as when they left. His voice was loud and clear.

"And since we all know what your decision will be, let's skip the deliberation. I accept your judgement."

"You don't know that."

"Yes, I do. And I have one last request."

Ze'eva paused. "Which is?"

For the first time since seeing him again, he looked directly at the children, a hundred feet across the plaza. "I want you to retrieve the Stone and bring it to me."

They froze. This was the moment they feared the most, and it was happening in front of every animal in Caldera.

"Genesius . . . " said Ze'eva.

Lucifur furrowed his brow, his eyes blazed with yellow flame, and his words ripped through the kids with barbs of persuasion. "You will bring the Stone to me. Now."

Compelled to complete an impossible task — because they didn't know the Stone's location — their brains seared in a paradox. Miriam grimaced and clung to Sebastian. Millicent fell to her knees. John dropped from Hucklebuck and landed on the ground next to Sebastian.

Out of desperation, he reached behind him to grab *Grelyxir*'s handle. Its energy surged up his arm. It washed into his brain and suppressed the burning conundrum. He reached up and yanked Miriam's hand to her staff, and, seeing this, Millicent grabbed her staff and hugged it.

"You think you don't want the Stone," said Lucifur, "but you will."

A distant chant turned every head to the northwest.

The Asaquatzi

"Hrah, rah, RAH! Hrah, rah, RAH!"

Lucifur's glowing eyes pulsed. "You will want it very soon."

"Hrah, rah, RAH!"

Beyond the border of the gardens, at the top of the ridge that surrounded the Mesa, up the slope of Mary Mountain, appeared hundreds of bears. Their glowing eyes formed a line of bright light. They stomped their forepaws on the final beat of their chant, so their eyes flared, and the strength of their numbers echoed down the hill. They were too far away to see details, but something seemed odd about them.

"Form ranks!" called Ze'eva. "Stay agile and watch your backsides." She vaulted from the balcony over the kids' heads and raced down the center aisle to Lucifur in his pillory. She growled in his face. "Let this be over, Genesius! Let it be done!"

He looked at her coldly. "Yes. Let it be done."

On his cue, the captive bears and cats — who had marched peacefully and unbridled — attacked their captors. Ze'eva leapt to avoid a charging grizzly, but the kids lost sight of her as the plaza erupted into chaos.

A gang of cougars and bears split from the main group and raced toward them. Miriam recognized their movement like it was a soccer play. This was planned. This was rehearsed. From Sebastian's back, she grabbed John's and Millicent's hands on either side of her and cast a shield around them.

A bear smashed into it and stumbled backward. The rest slowed their approach and clawed, rammed, and pounced against the energy, causing it to shimmer and buckle.

The shield faded.

Hucklebuck ran in front of them and flourished his mighty antlers. Mort and Druck swooped down on either side of him. They screeched and brandished their claws to help him keep the animals at bay.

Sebastian crept backward toward the Mesa. Miriam held her staff ready, and John and Millicent clutched Sebastian's sides. Millicent

Chapter Nineteen

hyperventilated. Her eyes spilled tears and yellow light. She held her staff against her body, terrified of using it.

Gabriel barked next to John. The cougars phased to get around Hucklebuck and the vultures while the bears stormed through the middle.

"Milly, duck!" cried Miriam, and she swung her staff. The blunt end cracked against a cougar's skull. The tined, crescent end whistled through the air and struck another cougar, and the power of it magnified her blows. Arthur flattened himself into Sebastian's fur in front of her.

"Hrah, rah, RAH!" came the chant from the ridge. Lord Nagus appeared there, looking massive, and led a thunderous charge down the slope. As they approached, what looked odd about them became clear. They were wearing the pelts of mountain lions. Two of the bears ran with a wooden spit lashed between them, and from the spit hung Copernicus, hogtied and looking dead. He strained to keep his head off the ground.

A mountain lion leapt at Hucklebuck, who sprang to the side and swept his antlers to scoop the cat and throw him into the garden. Druck swooped past so close that his feathers flicked across John's cheek. He and Mort landed and hissed at three cougars who were sneaking behind them.

"They're behind us!" said John, and Hucklebuck spun to ward them off.

A grizzly struck the elk from the opposite side. As the bear opened his mouth, John swung *Grelyxir* and hit his hindquarter with a tremendous crack and burst of light. A cougar took the bear's place, and then another, too many to fend off. They attacked from every angle and dragged Hucklebuck down. They pounced on John and pinned him to the ground.

Emily stood tall and mighty in the center of the plaza with her family of mammoths. Her legs braced wide, she swung her tusks to fling her enemies aside. Her sides bore dark streaks from where the animals

The Asaquatzi

had wounded her. Wolves and cougars fought by her side, including a large mountain lion who stood on her back to protect her.

"Emily!" cried Sebastian. "Get John!"

John felt the ground rumble.

"Get off him!" yelled Emily, and she whipped her tusks through the pile of carnivores. John gulped the open air. Emily wrapped her trunk under his arms, and, as she hoisted him from the ground, he saw Hucklebuck in the mud with his neck bent in an unnatural position.

Lord Nagus's army of bears was gone. The children had expected them to crash into the battle, but they were nowhere to be seen. Nagus arrived at the plaza alone with a cat skin flapping along his back like a primeval coat. He scanned the battlefield until he saw Miriam and bolted toward her with a roar.

Sebastian backpedaled faster. Millicent screamed and grabbed Miriam around the waist, and they projected a new force field as Nagus was upon them. He swiped at the shield. Pain erupted in their heads each time he hit it. In anguish, Millicent faltered. Nagus pounced and knocked Miriam from Sebastian's back. Her crutches flew to either side and skidded across the stone.

She released a shockwave to repel him and scooted backward along the ground. Sebastian seized him from behind. She screamed, frightened that he was about to repeat Sahra's sacrifice in the Palacemind chamber. She blasted again and again, but Nagus advanced with a blinding, yellow rage in his eyes.

Panicked, she leapt to her feet. The pain in her scalded foot forced her to crumble. She thrust her hands down to catch herself, and a burst of energy launched her into the air. Nagus watched in disbelief. She gritted her teeth and strained to hover, and she rose so high from the ground that the height became terrifying. Her strength faded, and she descended toward Nagus's open mouth.

Something stopped her just out of his reach. She floated in place for a second and then was pulled higher, as though she was attached to a hot air balloon. She floated all the way to the balcony above the

Chapter Nineteen

entrance, where somebody grabbed her.

She twisted and kicked. "Get away from me!"

Miriam! Stop! It was Robert Hume. His strong, bony hands held her tightly.

She recognized his voice from John and Millicent's memories and collapsed into his arms.

Mort and Druck plunged to the ground in front of Millicent and Gabriel and stood with their wings spread and beaks open to protect. In a rage, one of the cats swatted Mort across the ground.

Sebastian ran to put himself in front again. "Emily! Help!"

Emily broke through the melee with John on her back, but the animals jumped onto her hind legs. John flew over her head. He crossed his arms to brace for the impact with the round but found himself floating instead. He dropped the rest of the way and landed hard on his hands and knees.

He spun as he stood, afraid that his attackers would climb over Emily to get to him. They writhed on the ground as though an invisible force was pinning them there.

Get the mammoth! said Robert. *Get out of there!* He stood with Miriam on the balcony thirty feet above with his arms outstretched to hold the animals in place.

"Come on, Emily!" said John. With his mind, he reached under her ribcage to help prod her up. He couldn't lift her, but the pressure was enough to encourage her to move. She ran with him to Millicent, Sebastian, Arthur, and Gabriel, and the group retreated into the Mesa.

"Bar the door!" said Millicent.

"We can't!" said John. "Everyone will be trapped outside!"

"Then what's the point of — "

"We need to hide!"

Emily groaned and stumbled backward. Her hind legs bore terrible, bloody scratches. "I'm in a bad way here, folks."

Lord Nagus approached the entrance at the fore of several carnivores. They crouched and bared their fangs.

The Asaquatzi

"My brain! That little blonde brat stewed my brain! Get her down here!"

Emily charged at him. He reared and wrapped his arms around her head. She dropped to her knees. Sebastian bounded toward them, and John readied *Grelyxir*, but they stopped short as she threw her head back.

Lord Nagus's full weight sank onto her tusks.

John! said Millicent *They're coming up the stairs! Blow them away from the door! Blow them away from the door!*

But John stood in shock watching Nagus's gruesome demise.

John!

He caught his wits, extended his arms, laced his fingers, and blasted the carnivores away.

From the doorway, they watched Ze'eva and her wolves fight around Lucifur, who was still standing in the pillory. Bozhe arrived from outside the gardens with two other bison and bowled through the animals. They rammed the mammoths from both sides.

"No!" said Ze'eva.

"You are no master!" said Bozhe. "He is the master!"

Frightened, the mammoths separated to avoid the bison and wrenched the wooden trap enough for Lucifur to pull free and drop to all fours. He bit through the binding around his forepaws.

Ze'eva crouched low to the ground, her tail tucked between her legs, ready to pounce. "Look at what you've done! You're outnumbered. Again! How many animals must die for you?"

The remaining wolves and mammoths, elk and bison, rodents and badgers formed a hasty platoon behind her.

Lucifur cocked his head in a curious way, looking like a giant, ragged, blood-red puppy. He scraped his claws through the soil to draw a line and sat behind it. His followers gathered behind him.

He lowered his head. "You've done well against the first wave, Lady Wolf. How about the second?"

His eyes sparked to life again and sent a current through eyes of the

Chapter Nineteen

bears around him.

Ze'eva and her animals braced. The forest outside the gardens rustled to life, and the foliage rippled like a wave of grain in the wind until it broke at the edge of the brush. Hundreds of possessed rodents poured around Lucifur and his followers and flooded the plaza. They overran Ze'eva and her animals like a colony of ants.

"No!" cried Miriam.

Robert shouted and resumed his attack to trap swaths of them flat to the ground. Miriam leaned against the banister and raised her hands to help. She felt the slippery and bristling furs, a miasma of tiny claws and incisors, and scrapes through the ground and over the flesh of the bison, elk, and wolves. It was horrifying, but she pressed harder, desperate to protect them.

From the main entrance below her, John tried to scoop the invaders away from the sides. The sensation of touching them mentally was sharp and horrid. *How is Miriam keeping this up?* He fell against the doorframe and strained to bend them away.

Ze'eva and her wolves fought to incapacitate the rodents but not to kill. They hummed in unison with their eyes glowing to break the bears' possession.

She glowered at Lucifur. "*Rodents?* You think I can be felled by rodents?"

"No, Lady. They bought time for the third wave."

There came a shriek. Animals to the northwest screamed and howled. The Doyadu-khani bears, still wearing their cat skins, had sneaked around the back of the Mesa and marched in a line of glowing eyes. Behind them, a thick, white mass approached from the shore of Lake Mary, a thrashing, undulating army of giant tardigrades. The grotesque creatures gnashed their way past the bears and into the plaza, leaving thick trails of slime. Ze'eva stood in horror.

Millicent assumed that the tardigrades would die out of water, and she knew that Lucifur didn't care. They were pawns to him. She looked at the staff in her hands. It was powerful . . . and useless. She felt

The Asaquatzi

powerful and useless. She watched Ze'eva flail among the writhing, white bodies like a swimmer drowning in rapids, with her eyes to the sky. She reached for help before disappearing beneath the surface. The mammoths were falling. Lucifur's line crept closer to the stairs, and John was crumpled on the ground from pushing them away.

Millicent turned and ran. Sebastian called after her, but she ran as fast as she could down the main hall, past animals and their young who were cowering inside, and dashed up a staircase to the Amphitheater. She ran all the way to the entrance of the main tower.

Robert's voice entered her mind. *No, child! Not until we've defeated him!*

She tilted her head back to look at the vast interior and three circular windows four-hundred feet above.

It's up there, isn't it?

Yes, but it requires three. Siblings. I couldn't tell you before.

She hoped to find the Stone on her own, but she'd forgotten that it would probably require three siblings to retrieve it. The lock of siblings, the ancient security system. This was Lucifur's plan all along. This was why he brought the three of them to Caldera. She covered her face.

We can use it to stop the fighting, she said.

Millicent. Everyone wants to use it to stop the fighting, and everyone ends up dead. You've seen the memories!

She looked up again, her eyes a brilliant blue from crying. *It'll be different this time. I know it will be!*

With no other choice, John closed the main doors shut and slid the bar into its bearings before the tardigrades could reach them. It wouldn't hold them for long, and there were countless other ways to get into the Mesa, but it gave them a moment to breathe.

He realized Millicent was gone. *Where are you? Where did you go?*

I'm here, she said, flashing an image of the tower to him.

He gasped. *Three circles, in a wall, deep underground!* The third clue was misleading. On the wall opposite the three windows was the cross-section diagram of Yellowstone's caldera, which was deep

Chapter Nineteen

underground. He raced down the main hallway.

"Sebastian, come on!"

"Where are you going?"

"Millicent's found the Stone!"

"Then why are you running toward it?"

Gabriel barked in agreement.

John stopped. "To end all this."

To wield it! said Miriam, breaking into their thoughts.

Sebastian's voice spiked with disbelief. "You're playing right into what he wants! You know this, right?"

"What choice do we have?"

"John! You always have a choice. We can leave it hidden. We can run."

We'll never get out of here alive, said Miriam.

"Even if we could," said John, "where would we go?"

Miriam raged with tears and clenched her teeth. Her thoughts came in a flood. *Abatakai. Doyadu-khani. The keystone tunnel. Sahra! Sebastian, he's never, ever going to stop!*

John's voice broke in pain. "We need you to be with us!"

"I'm always with you. Of course, I'm with you."

"As am I, Captain," said Arthur, startling them. "Yes, I'm still here." He waved from Sebastian's back.

"Emily?" asked Gabriel.

"Go on! Go with them," she said, and she leaned against the foyer wall.

Up two flights of stairs they met Miriam and Robert, who had come in from the balcony. Miriam's hair was frizzy, and there were dark circles under her eyes and sweaty streaks of dirt down her face. She collapsed onto Sebastian's back, and Arthur climbed onto her shoulder.

"Bob," said Sebastian, "it's good to see you alive."

Robert knelt and quickly embraced Sebastian's head. "It's good to see you, too. That brother of yours is a real bastard, do you know that?"

"We're heading to the tower. Can you keep them off us?"

"I can try. This isn't going to end well, you going after that thing with him still loose."

"Keep thinking happy thoughts, okay?"

Robert walked back toward the balcony and called over his shoulder. "Go!"

They entered the base of the tower. Far above them, up the dizzying flights of stairs that hugged the walls, Millicent stood on the landing below one of the giant, open circles. She studied the caldera mural across from her. In the center of the image was a simple diamond shape etched in the rock that they hadn't paid attention to.

The Stone.

They could hear the battle rage on as they climbed the steps. John peeked over the edge to ensure that nobody followed. He hoped Robert could keep them away long enough.

As they reached the landing, Millicent waved her hand over the wall to reveal three handprints.

"I found these."

Miriam slipped from Sebastian's back with her staff and balanced on one foot. "Help me. Oh! My hands are shaking."

"So are mine," said John. He put his arm around her to help her balance.

Millicent's teeth chattered. "My whole body's shaking!"

"Kids," said Sebastian. "Are you sure about this?"

"No," said Millicent, "but yes."

They placed their hands in the prints. A narrow bridge of rock extended from the landing and ended in the middle. It led to nowhere but pointed at the mural. The lines of the artwork glowed, and the ethereal song they'd heard in Tumo Nataquinde filled the air.

In the diagram, from the magma chamber below Yellowstone, the carved diamond shape rose through layers of earth to break through the ground and hover above the surface. From that spot on the wall, an imperfect, yellow gemstone the size of a pear materialized and floated

Chapter Nineteen

toward them. It ignited with light brighter than the sun, yet they could look at it without squinting.

It was, Millicent agreed, the most beautiful thing she'd ever seen.

Their staves and *Grelyxir* vibrated harshly. Millicent stepped onto the rock bridge. She reached back to grab John's hand and extended her staff toward the Stone as they shuffled toward it. She aimed the forked end at the bright spot, ignoring the vertigo, the screams in her head to flee the precarious walkway, as her feet knocked loose pebbles from the edge. A complex harmony blared from the Stone to an unbearable volume. She turned her head and thrust the staff at it like the woman had twenty thousand years before. A vacuous whoosh sucked the light and sound into a single, delicate *clink!* as the Stone attached to the tines of the staff.

It hummed and glowed warmly. The air inside the tower pulsed with a heartbeat. She was afraid to look at what she was holding and turned to John and Miriam, who pulled her back to the safety of the landing. When she worked up the courage to look, she laughed and wept from its beauty and simplicity. She wanted them to experience it, too, so she held the staff for them to touch. Once their hands were on it, their eyes burned yellow.

Everything became clear. The Stone's energy flowed through the air and into the rock. They saw Sebastian, Gabriel, and Arthur as beings of light, as they saw themselves. They felt the gush and ebb of grelyxir flow like blood through a circulatory system, where they were the heart at the center, and the paths branched throughout the Mesa and beyond, past every creature and tree, along every river and stream, until the energy reached its limit and cascaded back into itself at Caldera's boundaries, where the Unreachable Trees encased the perimeter. Space bent to look like the edge of water viewed through glass along the silver seam. The intelligence of the animals was connected to it via thousands of individual strands of light.

Sebastian stepped closer. "Kids? Remember your purpose here."

Millicent nodded. Sebastian was wise to caution them, she thought, because she could have basked in it forever.

The light and serene view turned black. The connection crashed into a pit of limitation that jarred her vision back to normal. She looked at her empty hands no longer holding the staff. A giant, dark, and headless raptor had snatched it from her and was flying toward one of the circular openings.

The sky darkened with countless silhouettes of headless birds of prey. They swarmed into the tower like a plague of locusts, and their enormous wingspans blocked the sun. The kids cowered into Sebastian and Gabriel and used their remaining strength to form a protective bubble against the bizarre creatures. They made no sound except the whoosh of air across their wings, and as soon as the raptor with the staff cleared the window, the rest followed.

"No!" screamed Millicent.

Miriam dropped her staff, pushed off with her good foot, and blasted her energy against the landing to propel herself up to the bevel of the window, so she stood on one foot at the bottom of the great circle. She stared in terror down the four-hundred-foot drop along the outside of the tower. The chaos of animals in the plaza and gardens sprawled below. The dark flock of headless birds spiraled toward Lucifur with the staff.

She jumped after them.

As she fell, she formed a powerful sphere of yellow energy around her. She reached for the raptor with the Stone and pulled on it with her mind. But the birds had too great a head start. Lucifur caught the staff in his teeth.

In a flash of panic, she knew that she wouldn't survive.

Robert launched straight sideways from the balcony, He collided with her in midair and wrapped a cocoon of energy around them that reinforced hers. They tumbled across the plaza grounds. The bubble of energy fizzled, and they scraped across the stones before coming to a stop at the edge of the plaza.

Robert rolled off her and lay broken and bloodied like they'd been

Chapter Nineteen

in a motorcycle accident. She leaned over him and searched his eyes for some sign that he was okay. Then she noticed the silence.

The animals were motionless as Lucifur set the staff on the tiles of the plaza. Ze'eva lay beside him under a pile of half-dead tardigrades. Her breathing was labored.

"Bring Copernicus," said Lucifur.

Two grizzlies dragged the exhausted cat forward and snipped his bounds with their teeth. Lucifur studied Ze'eva and seemed to consider something for a moment.

"No, not you," he said. "One of your lieutenants, someone weak of mind."

He scanned the animals and nodded at a gray wolf. The wolf resisted and backed into the crowd until two bears shoved him forward.

Lucifur looked around the plaza at the animals, at Robert and Miriam, and at the main tower. Miriam felt his heart pounding. He was nervous and uncertain and full of adrenaline. He pressed his forehead against Stone.

It screamed like an angry kettle and shook the grounds. Loose debris fell from the Mesa walls. His back arched and his fur bristled. Spirals of yellow light erupted from the Stone and wrapped around his neck and shoulders. It formed tendrils that streaked to Copernicus and the wolf and dragged them to him. The sky plunged into darkness. The three animals were engulfed in a maelstrom of light with the flock of headless birds circling overhead and the horrible, flopping tardigrades around them.

Lucifur bellowed as all the animals looked on in awe. While they were distracted, Miriam pulled Robert from the ground. She reached and summoned Millicent's empty staff with her mind to use as a walking stick. Robert slung his arm around her waist to keep her upright as they hobbled toward the Mesa. The tip of the staff sparked each time it hit the ground.

Miriam! said John.

Yes.

The Asaquatzi

Are you crazy? What were you thinking?

It's too late. Lucifur is —

A beaver scurried past her leg. She turned with the staff, ready to fight, and saw that it was joined by other rodents who stormed past into the Mesa, followed by the black bears and grizzlies, cougars and elk. She and Robert stumbled to the side of the mob.

John? she called.

What happened?

The animals are going crazy!

Find a place to hide. We'll come down to you!

With her head on the landing next to Sebastian, Millicent glowered at the mural, overwhelmed with regret. She wished she'd never revealed the Stone and wondered how she ever thought it was a good idea. She knew it was Lucifur. His command compelled her to that decision. But it had felt like her own.

The lines of the mural glowed like neon, and parts of it stayed brighter as it faded. She pushed herself from the ground and stood on shaky legs.

"Milly, let's go!" said John.

"No," she said, and she stepped toward the mural.

Gabriel ran to block her from the edge with his body. "Look out!"

"What is it, Millicent?" asked Sebastian.

"Something . . . " She touched Gabriel's head as she walked around him and onto the narrow rock bridge. He whimpered and looked down through the tower at where she would fall were she to slip.

John caught up to her and put his hand on her back to let her know that he was there. She stepped to the end, so the toes of her sneakers hung over the edge, which made his stomach turn. He didn't want to watch another sister fall.

"Milly! What are you doing?"

She needed to touch the mural. She looked over her shoulder. "Arthur, can you find water?"

"Lieutenant?"

425

Chapter Nineteen

"For a bridge. I want to touch that wall."

"Nay, there's none near enough."

Sebastian hummed in thought. "What about grelyxir?"

"*Incroyable*! I've never attempted such a show! Lemme see. Ah — oh my. Yes, there we are."

He flopped to the ground from Sebastian's back, crawled to a recessed tract along the stairs, and stuck a leg in. The flaming, purple oil rose like a tentacle, and Arthur guided it to meet the end of the stone.

"*Mon Dieu*! It takes it! It takes it from me!"

The grelyxir snapped into place and became solid. The new half of the bridge looked like it was made of the purest, glowing amethyst.

Millicent and John walked to the wall. She ran her hands over the rough surface and traced the carved lines with her fingertips, and, as she anticipated, it was a memory wall. They entered it without hesitating.

They looked through the eyes of a woman. They were famished but strong, young but haggard in appearance.

We've dwelled among gods on Earth. Perhaps it was not meant for the Shoshone, but we will rest knowing that our final purpose is clear: we must hide the Stone again.

We were not the first. We traced the history back twenty millennia in Tumo Nataquinde, and the memories we discovered there have divided us. We want to wield the Stone. The others plan to destroy it.

We beg them not to. There are other stories, we say, more recent than Tumo Nataquinde. We found memories in Tihuzaveh, the Hourglass. We found them in Doyadu-khani and in Si'aka, the Great Tree. We found them here in Pentigoi.

One thing is clear. Anyone who attempts to destroy the Stone dies.

From what we've pieced together, there have been at least four Asaquatzi. Every time humans wield the Stone, another Asaquatzi is formed.

The others don't listen to us. Inspired by the Staff of Elora, they

The Asaquatzi

forge three new objects of grelyxir and obsidian: two staves to secure the Stone upon the altar in the Atrium and a hammer to destroy it. It was there, where the roundtable now stands, where the Stone first appeared.

We have altered too much. Over the past hundred years, we inserted our language into these memories as though they were ours to retell. Our people were arrogant. And we'll pay for this arrogance with our lives.

We are down to twenty. Twenty humans remain in Caldera. We decide to erase all traces of our presence, so the animals will forget. No one must know we were here. We scour the memories and destroy every human figure and conceal every handprint. But the Spiders of Tumo Nataquinde protect the walls there. They won't let us near. So, we bury the keystone deep beneath Pentigoi.

We are down to seven. My two sisters and I remain to secure the Stone with the lock of siblings. At least that much we believe in. The others will sacrifice themselves, so we can complete this task.

The Asaquatzi knows. She is coming for us. We must kill her if we are ever to hide the Stone. She is coming.

She is here.

John reeled from the haste and despair embedded in the wall. He looked at Sebastian, Gabriel, and Arthur on the landing, and his heart ached with fear. He and his sisters were responsible for the Stone falling into Lucifur's possession and the creation of a new Asaquatzi.

They didn't speak. They hurried down the stairs and found Robert carrying Miriam in the main hallway. Animals ran in every direction.

"Bob," said Sebastian, "we need a safe place."

Chapter Nineteen

"We can hide in my room," said Emily from behind them. She was caked in mud from head to toe and looked like she was about to fall over. "We don't have much time; that creature out there is almost whole."

Her room was still empty from when they cleared it, so they shoved milk crates and a wooden trunk from the hall to block the doorway.

Emily lay on the ground. Blood seeped through the mud where her wounds were deep. "Don't mind me. I'm just gonna rest my head here for a minute or two or twenty."

Millicent held Miriam by her forearms and transferred the Shoshoni memories from the mural, and she pressed too hard on purpose.

"Ouch, Mill! That hurt!"

"Serves you right! I can't believe you jumped off the tower!"

Miriam hugged her. "I can't either."

John paced with Gabriel. "What do we do? Once the Asaquatzi's formed?"

"He's going to come after us," said Miriam, holding Arthur. "Lucifur did exactly what he set out to do when he kidnapped us, and now he doesn't need us anymore."

Millicent felt sick. "Sebastian, where can we go?"

"The only place I can think of is Tumo Nataquinde. It's the only place he can't get into."

Miriam threw her hands in the air. "We can create a hole in the ground anywhere! And then what? Sit there till we die? Every memory ends that way! The people were either wiped out or trapped somewhere talking about how they were okay with dying — all to protect the Stone. Well, I don't care about the Stone! I'm not going to become a skeleton for someone to find a thousand years from now!"

John stopped pacing and turned *Grelyxir* in front of him, transfixed by the violet energy that pulsed through the veins set into the obsidian. "So, we destroy it. We destroy the Stone."

Millicent scowled. "Did we see different memories again? They said destroying it would end all life, and anyone who's tried to destroy it has died! Didn't you see when we held it? It's connected to everything!"

"Everything in Caldera," said Sebastian.

"Yes — "

"Maybe it's time for Caldera to end."

The effects of his idea flooded her thoughts. She saw the thousands of stands of light severed. "There has to be another way."

"Millicent is right," said Robert. He stood with his hand braced against the wall with the southern landscape carved into the rock, the direction Abatakai once stood. His other hand hung by his leg and trembled. His bony shoulders slumped. He looked like he was made of old newspaper that would blow away in the slightest breeze. "Everyone who tries to destroy the Stone ends up dead."

John looked again at the hammer in his hands. "You tried, didn't you? You and your brothers? I mean, you knew where everything was. You gave us these weapons — these things — whatever they are."

"Yes, we tried. I wanted to tell you before. Now, it seems, that I can. Whatever he did to me is gone."

"What happened? With your brothers?"

"We followed the same path you have. We had everything we needed. Before we could pull it from the wall, a group of animals learned that it required the three of us, so they killed Sam."

"See?" said Millicent, her voice shaking. "The thing is cursed!"

"No!" said Robert. "I said you were right; people die when they attempt to destroy it." He turned with yellow fire in his eyes, stood tall, and stepped toward them. "But Miriam is right, too! You will not become another memory here. And Sebastian and John are right — it's time for Caldera to end, and to do that we must destroy the Stone!"

A hundred and fifty years of longing crashed into them.

Millicent cried. "What if we're wrong? What if destroying it kills everybody?"

The commotion in the hallway grew louder. The animals were frantic.

Chapter Nineteen

"Captain, how will you get this Stone away from him? He's partial to it, methinks."

"I don't know, but that memory said we need to bring it to the Atrium."

"And since he's coming after us . . . " said Millicent.

"That's where we need to go," said Miriam.

Citizens of Caldera, came a vibrant, booming voice that was a harmony of Lucifur, Copernicus, and the wolf, that shook loose stone from the walls around them. *You will never know fear again. You will never know hunger. I have fulfilled my promise and will breathe the strength of life across our world.*

The children cleared the doorway to Emily's room, covered her with blankets, and used their power to seal the room with rock.

The Humans of the Other World are a danger to our existence. They will end our tranquility when they break through. Today I make a new promise. They will never enter Caldera, and the ones who remain will never leave with the knowledge of our home.

Miriam vaulted onto Sebastian's back with Arthur. John, Millicent, and Gabriel ran in front of them through the crumbling hallways choked with dust, and Robert followed. Smoke clung to the ceiling and burned their throats. Grelyxir flared in every tract and basin. Every animal they passed was listening to the voice.

Calm yourselves, beavers and marmots. Calm yourselves, bighorn, elk, and bison. Be at peace, lions and wolves. The fighting is over. We have won the day.

As they approached the wooden doors outside the Den of Antiquities, John spotted the copper sculpture of the diversity of life and realized in a fleeting moment that the empty section at the center would have contained humans.

With no time to dwell, he pulled the doors open. The Den was ablaze. Thick, noxious smoke billowed from the piles of clothing and junk and funneled out through the holes in the ceiling. Heat seared through the doorway.

The Asaquatzi

"Back up! Back up!"

"This way!" said Sebastian, and he led them down another corridor.

The thunderous voice grew louder and shook the Mesa harder. *For too long we have lived in their dwellings. My followers have already begun the cleansing: we have toppled their Abatakai back into our lake; we have crumbled their Doyadu-khani to our travertine terraces. Join us now and wipe out the pestilence of Homo Sapiens here in Pentigoi, and it, too, shall be destroyed!*

At the end of the hallway in front of them, the doors to the library had been blown off their hinges and lay broken on the floor. Fire exploded from the entrance and cast smoke into the hall. Through the swirling darkness, the endless rows of hanging books blazed with fire. They dropped like beads of molten metal down giant wicks.

"We're running out of options here," said Sebastian.

The nearby animals turned. All their attention was on the children.

"*Back off!*" commanded Sebastian with the rasp of persuasion and a flash in his eyes, and most of them cowered.

"I can create a mind-sphere!" said Miriam. "Something small and quick. Arthur, I need grelyxir!"

"*Laisse moi en trouver.* Closest is that way!"

They ran to a fountain of grelyxir in a rotunda intersection of two hallways.

Sebastian counted the animals approaching down each hall. He roared. The animals recoiled, growled, bleated, and squawked. They pressed forward again. John and Millicent cast a shield around them to keep the animals out.

Sebastian roared again and then lowered himself so she could hop off. "You said quick, right, Miriam?"

"Yes!"

She dropped to her hands and knees and rubbed the floor with her palms to coax up a lump of rock. She swirled her hands around it like a sculptor, expanding and smoothing it to form a hollow sphere the size of a grapefruit. She left a small hole and dunked it into the fountain to let it fill with grelyxir before she sealed it.

Chapter Nineteen

The animals clawed at the forcefield.

Gripping the mindsphere with both hands, she connected with the Mesa. It wasn't as powerful as the Palacemind, but it was better than she'd hoped for.

Stay back! she cried. *Go outside and leave us alone!* They obeyed her without protest. The hallways cleared, and John and Millicent dropped their shield.

"Brilliant, Miri," said Sebastian. "All right, follow me!"

She rode on his back with the sphere in front of her and projected her mind as far ahead as she could to clear the way of animals. The Asaquatzi's control over them was powerful. She grimaced and squeezed to push through until they reached the Atrium.

The cavern was as dark as night even though it was midday, and it glowed with a rainbow of bioluminescent colors. Gabriel ran down the hill ahead of them. He crossed the bridge to where the stone roundtable was waiting. Rodney sprung from the foliage with his horns low and rammed into him. Gabriel yelped and slid under the table.

"You must not proceed," said Rodney with his one eye glowing. "I cannot allow you to destroy Caldera."

Miriam located him through the mind-sphere, but her thought projection shattered against a visage of the Asaquatzi. The sphere slipped from her hands, rolled down the hill, and popped onto the table, where Rodney stopped it with his hoof.

"Now, now, young lady," he said. "What did I tell you about reading minds? Tut-tut, naughty-naughty."

Dark shapes flew past the glowing plants on the walls and ceiling.

"John," said Robert, "hit the hammer against the ground!"

John wound back and struck *Grelyxir* against the hillside. A shockwave of light lit the Atrium and revealed the swarming flock of headless birds of prey.

Millicent screamed. The raptors clawed at her staff and lifted her from the ground until she repelled them with an energy blast. John swung *Grelyxir* wildly, and every bird it touched turned to ash. Robert ran between them to cast a shield, but the raptors continued their attack and disintegrated against it.

"You know, Fisherman," said Rodney. "The peculiar thing about birds is how long they can live without their heads. I struggled for days to break them, but they resisted me until I decapitated one. It was a simple solution: If you can't control the head, then remove it. I believe you know Quan?"

A giant, headless bald eagle flew into the Atrium and dove at the forcefield.

"No!" cried Robert, and he fell to his knees and let the shield collapse before Quan touched it. His massive talons plucked Millicent's staff from her grip.

The Asaquatzi arrived behind them at the top of the hill. The Stone was embedded in his forehead, and yellow flames trailed from his eyes. His pointed wolf ears stood tall and fanned out with jagged edges. His grizzly hump bristled with gray, red, and tawny fur from the three animals that comprised him. His long, broad snout was a snaggle of fangs and five misaligned nostrils. And his powerful legs ended in monstrous paws of many toes and an array of claws.

"I knew seeing Rodney again would confuse you," he said.

Quan swooped to drop the staff. The Asaquatzi caught and levitated it the tines pointing at the children like a harpoon ready to launch.

His voice reverberated through the cavern. "Remember that day by the river, boy? I asked you to come with me. All of this suffering could have been avoided had you listened."

John didn't know how these words were meant to affect him, but he didn't feel guilty. *None of this is my fault —*

The Asaquatzi yanked the hammer from his hands with his mind, almost pulling him over. Then he plucked Miriam's staff away from her. They flew up the hill and hovered next to the other staff.

"Brother, please," said Sebastian, stepping along the path in front of the group with Miriam on his back. "You've done everything you've set

Chapter Nineteen

out to do. Caldera is safe! Please spare these children! They can't harm you now."

"They can destroy all we know. Now is their time to die."

His mighty telekinetic grip seized the children and Robert and lifted them into the air. Millicent trembled. Miriam thrashed against his will but couldn't break free. Sebastian charged up the hill at him, but he flicked him aside like he was a gnat.

"Wait!" said John.

The staves and hammer launched toward them. Millicent winced for the impact. Miriam watched the tines rushing toward her, but they veered into the ground with bursts of light.

The Asaquatzi shook his bear-wolf head and thrashed his long cougar tail. The children dropped and landed on their feet. Miriam shouted and collapsed because of her injury, and, fueled by her pain and fear, she lifted her staff with her mind and launched it at the monster. It struck him deep in the chest.

He bellowed with a horrid, grating roar. The ceiling showered the cavern with debris.

In his shout was command. Rodents poured through smaller openings into the Atrium, and his army of bears, cougars, and wolves entered through the doorway behind the him. Lucifur no longer needed his army of bears to control the animals. The energy from the Stone pulsed from him through all of their eyes.

Robert scooped up Millicent, Miriam climbed onto Sebastian, and John stooped to grab the hammer as the five of them retreated down the hill.

The animals advanced and forced them against the table. Standing over them, Rodney raised his front hooves and brought them down to crush the mind-sphere, forcing grelyxir to squirt from between the pieces like yolk from a broken egg.

John summoned *Grelyxir* to his hand, whirled, and threw it at the ram. With a crack, the hammer knocked Rodney off toward the ancient well. They scrambled up to take his place on the table as the animals encircled and snarled and hissed and scoffed. They formed a sea of glowing eyes.

The Asaquatzi thrashed like a broken automaton with the staff sticking out of his chest. He reached up with a dexterous paw and yanked it out. Rays of light shot from the wound as it sealed shut.

What do we do? asked Miriam.

"Nothing," said the Asaquatzi. "Your thoughts are mine."

Millicent held her fingers to her mouth and looked around at the glaring, hungry animals. She looked at the dark holes where the sunlight was supposed to be streaming in. She looked straight up at the blue-glass window set into the ceiling. If they could get — STOP THINKING, she thought. *Stop thinking, stop thinking, stop thinking!* Desperate to keep her mind jumbled, she turned, ran across the table, and leapt into the crowd of animals.

"Millicent!" said Miriam. She slipped off Sebastian, hobbled in agony to the edge, and jumped from the table to follow her.

John looked back and forth between the Asaquatzi and where his sisters disappeared and leapt after them.

"Stop!" said Lucifur's voice.

"Go, Sebastian!" said Robert.

Sebastian ambled off the table with Arthur on his back.

Robert spread his arms wide and turned with a crazy look in his eyes. "Come on, Red Bear! You got me out of my bird house! You destroyed my Abatakai! Come finish me!"

The Asaquatzi advanced down the hill.

"No!" said Lucifur's voice. "I said NO!" He lashed out with his mind and smashed rock, scooped water from the stream — anything he could grasp to push himself backward. "He wants it, so it's a trick! We can't!"

"Yes, we can," said Copernicus's voice.

Lucifur's voice roared. He levitated one of the staves and speared it into Robert's torso. "I SAID NO!"

Hidden among the animals, John clamped his hand over Millicent's

Chapter Nineteen

mouth to block her scream. Robert staggered with a shuffle to the edge of the table with the staff sticking out of his belly, tipped an imaginary hat, and fell into the crowd.

"Bring the children to me!" said the Asaquatzi as he stepped onto the roundtable. Up close, he was gigantic, a twisted, muscular mass of fur, double limbs, and compound features.

Pronghorn antelopes moaned with their eyes glowing and shoved the children forward. Miriam grabbed Sebastian's fur and climbed onto his back.

"Yes, good," said the harmony of voices. "Bring the bear."

He quirked his head. Millicent knew that he detected her thoughts among the fray. He roared. The Stone and his eyes flashed. His long, cougar tail whipped back and forth as he strained to get off the table — but he couldn't move.

Copernicus wouldn't let him.

Millicent grabbed *Grelyxir* from John's hand, and, in a single motion, she ran onto the table and hurtled the hammer upward with a telekinetic push. Her movement was awkward and desperate. Her knees buckled under a confidence that was foreign to her. Her aim was born out of luck and a torn shoulder, and she was certain the hammer would stray and hit the ceiling next to the window in a useless exertion. With a spectacular crack, it struck the center of the blue glass, and the massive, shallow dome dislodged from its bearings and fell in pieces.

Miriam screamed and blasted Millicent from the table before the pieces crashed and shattered. She rebounded like a thrown doll from the side of a bison into a bighorn sheep and fell to the ground between them.

The Asaquatzi lay buried under a ton of volcanic glass.

John grabbed a staff and walked around the table to study the pile of glass from every angle. He wiped the tears and sweat that stung and clouded his vision with the back of his sleeve. He climbed onto the table. Shaking, he held the staff like a spear fisherman and prowled forward. He used his mind to roll aside the massive chunks of debris.

The Asaquatzi

The Asaquatzi lay broken and bloody. It struggled to shake its head.

John paused in the moment of eye contact. How was it possible to feel sympathy after everything Lucifur had done? The sadness in the Asaquatzi's eyes shifted to fear, and through those eyes John saw himself reflected as the monster, he and his sisters. And the monsters had won. He pressed the tines of the staff against the Stone in the creature's forehead to collect it.

The Asaquatzi — Lucifur, Copernicus, and the unnamed wolf — died.

Twenty
Aftermath

Rosy light from the sunset streamed into the Atrium. The animals looked around as though they were awakening from a dream, unsure of how they'd gotten there or why. Some collapsed, some fled, and many leaned against each other and wept.

"Miriam, help Robert!" said Sebastian. Robert had pulled the staff from his gut and lay bleeding, slumped beneath the table. Gabriel crawled over to him and put his head in his lap.

Miriam hopped from Sebastian's back. She slipped off her hoodie, lifted Robert's tunic, and pressed her garment against his wound. He helped her to hold it with one hand and cupped her face with the other, smearing a bit of blood on her cheek. His dark, calloused hand made her face look tiny and cherubic.

He tried to push her hands away. "I don't think it's fatal."

She shook her head no and searched around the fabric to be sure she wasn't leaving any part of the wound uncovered.

Seeing her now in her cami, John winced at how gaunt she'd become — as thin, he guessed, as he was himself.

Millicent lay flat on her back in the crowd of animals and gaped at the hole in the ceiling she'd created. The bighorn next to her bowed his head to offer his horns to help her up and pulled her to her feet. She stumbled in pain not from any specific injury but from the overall toll her body had taken. She gripped the edge of the roundtable with both hands to steady herself and looked around the cavern at the melancholic crowd of animals. She watched Ze'eva enter through the doorway at the top of the hill, and her heart swelled. *She's alive!*

"It's over," said Ze'eva. "We've won, yet we have nothing to show

Chapter Twenty

for it but death. We who survive . . . must again tend to the dead and injured. Go now, please. Help where you can."

The animals who were able to respond dispersed or stayed to help the ones who couldn't.

Ze'eva limped down the hill, raggedy and blood-stained. "Children, are you okay?" she asked as she reached the table.

John and Millicent nodded. Miriam stared at her bloody sweatshirt. Ze'eva circled to find her with Robert.

"How is he?"

Robert lifted his head and grimaced. "I'm doing fine. I'll eventually need a better bandage than a shirt."

Sebastian climbed onto the roundtable and crossed to stand with John before the Asaquatzi's body. He sniffed the creature's deformed face and moaned. John set the staff with the Stone on the table and wrapped his arms around Sebastian's neck and cry into his fur.

"I'm so sorry!" he said.

"I'm sorry, too."

Ze'eva nuzzled against Miriam's shoulder. "Here. Let me have a look."

But Miriam wouldn't let her heal him alone. She closed her eyes and helped to siphon his pain. She felt a stronger connection than ever before, as though she could knit him back together cell by cell just by imagining it. She was disappointed, then, when she opened her eyes and the wound remained unaltered.

"Don't despair," said Ze'eva. "You do wonderful work."

Millicent walked along the curve of the table to them.

"Can I help?"

"We've done what we can. I'm worried about the effect of the grelyxir in the staff, but we'll keep an eye on him."

"Thank you," said Robert, and he pulled Gabriel closer to him.

"*Bonjour*," said Arthur. He'd crawled out of nowhere and rested on Gabriel's torso.

"Hey, little spider," said Gabriel.

Aftermath

"I may just change your nickname to *Le Chien Misérable*."

"No. I liked Floppy. Floppy was perfect."

"Hmm. All right. Perhaps it is representational of your greater strife."

"Perhaps."

Millicent continued to watch the animals around them and felt their fear, sadness, and confusion. She wondered how many dead lay outside. She didn't want to go near the plaza after walking through the battlefield at Süütakkan. The images there would haunt her forever. She knew it was selfish, but she hoped that the wolves could take care of the injured. She couldn't imagine absorbing so much pain. Miriam could spend an entire afternoon just healing animals and be perfectly happy. Millicent squeezed her pigtail buns almost to verify that they were still there and that she was, in fact, still herself. She could never be like her sister, she decided, no matter how many miles she walked or windows she smashed.

Or monsters she slayed. She glanced at the hulking form on the roundtable and couldn't believe she had anything to do with its death. But she did. Her shoulder sang with pain from throwing the hammer. She was relieved that nobody was approaching her or hoisting her into the air as a hero, because it wasn't that kind of victory. This victory centered on a glowing rock that rested on the table with nobody paying attention to it.

How bizarre is that? All this trouble to get it, and now it's just sitting there.

John looked down at the staff. She was right; he'd set it aside as casually as if it were an unneeded umbrella. Seeing it uncoddled startled him. This was the staff that Miriam had leapt off the tower to retrieve, after all. He thought it ought it be treated with more reverence, so he stooped to pick it up again.

The phantasma of awareness swept over him for the third time. The coursing energy. The flow of grelyxir. The thousands of strands of light connected to every animal. The first time he experienced it was

Chapter Twenty

overwhelming. It was like suddenly seeing frequencies of light beyond the visible spectrum and being unable to process it. This time, it reminded him of the view from the Skydeck at the top of Willis Tower. He remembered the awe of the first time, and it never lost its wonder, but going with visiting relatives for the fourth or fifth time allowed him to see the patterns of traffic, focus on a tree on a rooftop, find a new building he'd never noticed before, look for the highway that led west to Naperville and home, imagine the lives and shoes and pets and food and coins of the people down below, and never quite comprehend how the city came to be built in the first place. It was a matter of becoming familiar with something so complex that it could never be memorized, only marveled at. That's what holding the staff with the Stone felt like, only with a network of light and energy instead of steel and concrete.

When he looked up from his thoughts, he discovered that all eyes were on him. "So. What do we do?" he asked.

Robert pulled himself up despite Miriam's protests and leaned against the roundtable with the sweatshirt pressed to his wound. Gabriel stood, too, and shook his fur. Arthur climbed to his head.

"The way I see it," said Robert, "we have two options. We can hide the Stone again, and the three of you live in Caldera for the rest of your unnaturally long lives like I have, or we destroy it, and you go home."

Millicent slapped her hand on the table. "And Caldera disappears, and all the animals lose their intelligence? That's lovely! What a lovely, lovely choice!"

Miriam pet Gabriel's neck and Arthur's abdomen at the same time, unable to settle her thoughts long enough to form an opinion. This was new. She always had an opinion.

As the power of the Stone coursed through John with its connection to everything, he wondered if it would offer an opinion. He searched for a sign, some glimmer of knowledge, but the Stone was mindless. It was agnostic unto itself.

He shrugged. "Maybe we just hide it again and find another way home."

Aftermath

"John. Kids," said Sebastian, "there's no decision here. You're going home."

"But what about all of you?"

Ze'eva eyed the Stone and then looked at John.

"Tell me more about your plan to destroy this thing."

"Well . . . Can I show you?"

Her eyes widened. "Show me?"

He lifted his chin. "Yes. Let me show you the rest. Then you can tell us what you think."

"All right. Show me."

He joined his mind with hers. They'd already shared with her all the memories from Tumo Nataquinde; he just wanted to catch her up on the final memory from the wall in the tower. He showed her that several Asaquatzi had been formed over the years. He revealed that they were standing on the same spot where the Stone had first appeared twenty thousand years ago. And he showed her the purpose of the staves and hammer.

Two staves to secure the Stone upon the altar in the Atrium and a hammer to destroy it.

Then, he offered her the staff.

She stared at it horrified, as though it would burn her if she touched it. She shook her head and backed away.

"No . . . I don't know enough . . . I don't trust myself!"

He held the staff across his upturned palms and extended it toward her. "I trust you."

"John . . ."

"I trust you. And I think you should know what this feels like and — oh my gosh — see what I can see right now."

"Maybe." She nodded to the side, still unsettled. "Retrieve that hammer of yours first. Just in case something goes wrong."

He couldn't imagine wielding *Grelyxir* against her. He wouldn't.

"No. Just . . . take it. Please."

The great silver wolf approached and took the staff with her teeth.

Chapter Twenty

Her eyes burst with light, both yellow and blue without mixing into green. She dropped the staff to the table and howled.

She placed one paw on the Asaquatzi's shoulder and proclaimed, "Here lies Lucifur the Arrogant! Bender of Wills! The Asaquatzi of the Shortest Reign!"

The remaining animals bowed. There came a flood of relief that eased the sadness and confusion in the air. Her words couldn't take away all their pain, but she inspired the crestfallen to stand.

"Please, leave us," she said, and the animals filed out of the Atrium.

She picked up the staff and gave it back to John.

"What's clear to me is that the creation of Caldera also created a cycle of destruction that has repeated for twenty millennia and will continue to do so until it's broken. I must thank you for trusting me. My lineage is far grander than I suspected. I'm still not entirely sure what created the spark or when that spark was forgotten, but I know that my kind was born of light as well as flesh. Caldera was never meant to be permanent. Its relevance has expired. And the three of you have a greater future than being trapped in it. You will be the Children of the Stone."

"But," said Millicent, "if we destroy it — aren't you scared?" She was scared enough for all of them.

"No, Millicent. I'm not afraid."

"But, this seems so sudden! What about all the other animals?" she asked, pointing at the exit. "How can we just take it all away from them?"

"We're not taking anything away. We're giving it back."

"I don't understand!"

Miriam climbed onto the roundtable and balanced with one hand on Sebastian's back. She pointed at the Stone. Her face was deadly serious.

"Look. I don't know what that thing is, but none of the other people who lived here did, either. Ooh, it came from the sky! It came from the Sun! Heck, maybe it's an alien meteor rock, or maybe some shaman

Aftermath

conjured it twenty thousand years ago. Who knows? Whatever it is, everything will go back to normal when it's gone."

"Please," came Rodney's voice from behind them. "Help an old sheep understand what's happening." He limped to the stone table and sneezed. He looked a mess.

John felt awkward, having just hit him with a hammer. "Are you okay?" he asked.

"I may have a few broken ribs . . . some internal bleeding . . ."

"I'm sorry. I didn't know what else to do."

"John, I wasn't myself. But I'm reticent to admit that my life would be far less dangerous if you were to go home!"

Though there was a smile in his voice, John crumpled under the sarcasm. He handed the staff with the Stone to Miriam, and while the entire universe opened before her eyes again, he hugged the ram.

"Ze'eva?" asked Sebastian. "I think what Millicent was trying to ask was what will happen to us, the animals? I'd be lying if I said I wasn't a little scared."

"I would never lead you into darkness, Sebastian. Take the staff from Miriam. You, Rodney, Gabriel, Arthur . . . It's important that you understand."

One by one, they touched the staff, even little Arthur. They each reeled in turn. Rodney shook his head and swung his horns. Sebastian and Gabriel panted.

"*Je suis perdu!*" said Arthur. "I had no idea the world was so . . . *l'univers est beau!*"

"Yes," said Sebastian. "Beautiful. Beauty. Sahra said — I wonder if she saw — I wonder if she saw it in the end!"

"May I?" asked Robert, gesturing humbly at the staff. "I never got the chance to."

"Please," said Ze'eva. "You deserve it more than any of us."

With one hand on his abdomen, he picked up the staff. His eyes blazed. He caught his breath, laughed, and cried all at once. It was as though he'd finally been told the punchline to a joke to which he'd only

Chapter Twenty

heard the setup for over a century.

He gave the staff to Miriam and backed away to wipe his tears.

Ze'eva nodded. "I hear the humans have wonderful hospitals these days."

"I hear they do." He smiled at first, but then his face relaxed into solemnity. "I hear that they do."

Millicent was alarmed by the image in his head. He was imagining himself lying in a bed for the first time in over a hundred and fifty years. The linens were crisp and white. The room was white and plain, as he had no frame of reference for what a modern hospital might look like. But it was clean and comfortable. While he looked eighty years old now, in his vision his features were aged beyond any living person Millicent had ever seen. All his muscle mass was gone. His skin was thin and gray like tissue paper. And his eyes were glazed over foggy white. Once he left Caldera, he knew that his true age would catch up with him, and he was wide-awake dreaming of dying.

And while it was sad to imagine him dying, his sense of peacefulness filled her with heart-wrenching joy.

Ze'eva addressed all of them again. "Remember this: Caldera has fundamentally changed this time. The boundary is closed. And though I can't explain how I know, it will remain closed. It may open someday long after we're gone, but who has time to wait for that?"

She gave a sly wink, though John and Millicent couldn't see the humor in the situation.

Miriam smiled at her. "Yeah. I don't wanna wait forever," she said.

Ze'eva pressed her forehead against Millicent's chest. "You don't belong here, Millicent. None of us do. It's time for us to go home."

Millicent nodded. She trusted Ze'eva more than anyone. Her mind filled with more questions and — she clapped her hand to her forehead. "Emily! She's still trapped in her room!

They collected the hammer and the other staff and walked back to Emily's room, past the carvings that held countless memories from eons ago — most of which they hadn't touched and would leave unseen —

Aftermath

and opened a doorway through the rock, so she could leave once she woke. They watched her sleep, still caked in mud, and could hear the echo of her boisterous voice in the room. It was easiest to let her sleep through what was about to happen, though they weren't certain what that would be.

Each step back to the Atrium felt like another choice, yet they walked as though they were on a conveyor belt and wished it would slow down so they could say goodbye to every mural and tract of grelyxir. They wished they could see the library and the Den of Antiquities as were before the fires.

Millicent wiped away tears as they walked. She froze when they reached the entrance to the Atrium, unable to take another step at what she saw as the point of no return. And all her worries poured out.

"What's going to happen if all the mammoths appear in our world? How will we find our parents? How do we get Robert to a hospital? What about all the memories — "

"Millicent," said Sebastian, "you'll figure it out."

Her voice cracked. "How?"

"You're the smartest person I know; you'll find a way."

"But what do you mean? I don't know what I'm supposed to do!"

"Listen to me. You're going to be okay. We're going to be okay. I know that now."

Say it again, she said. She needed him to mean it.

"We're going to be okay."

She threw her arms around his neck. John grabbed him, and Miriam hugged him from atop his back.

The children climbed onto the table. Robert sat beside the animals on the Atrium hillside that led up to Ze'eva's garden. The Stone hummed and pulsed with a buttery yellow light at the end of Miriam's staff. She aimed the tines at the center of the table, and when Millicent touched hers against it, the two staves locked together with the Stone between them. They looked to Robert and the animals. Ze'eva nodded. Arthur sat on Gabriel's head. Rodney stood stoically. Sebastian's golden

Chapter Twenty

eyes regarded them warmly. John shared a final look with his sisters and swung the hammer.

CRACK!

The air felt green.

Warm. Easy.

John lay flat on his back with *Grelyxir* lying next to him. At the center of the table lay the broken pieces of the Stone. The fragments were dark and crumbly. With a start, John looked to the animals on the hill. Ze'eva was gone, but the rest of their companions were there.

Sebastian bound to the table. "Are you okay?"

"I think so . . ."

Miriam shook herself awake and rolled onto her hands and knees to investigate the broken Stone. She touched a piece, and it collapsed like ashen embers.

"We did it," she said.

Millicent sat up straight. She looked around the Atrium, at their friends, and at her hands. Everything felt the same. "But . . . did we *do* it-do it? Are we home?"

The air swirled. Gabriel barked. Sparkles of blue light appeared above the center of the table, and from this spot emerged a wolf made of pure, blue energy. It was Ze'eva. The light pulsed through her in waves, like a heartbeat. She was larger than she'd been as a flesh-and-blood wolf, and the air bent around her in a vaporous shimmer. She threw her head back and filled the Atrium with an unearthly sound, a chiming rasp, like a symphony of celeste and bassoon.

The children's eyes glowed in response. They saw the stone table, the Atrium and the Mesa. Their vision zoomed back so far that they flew out of Caldera and could at last see the dimension they were in as a bead of dew trapped on a string that wove into a tapestry of stars and galaxies and a bright, white —

Their vision returned to normal.

Aftermath

"No," said Ze'eva. "You're not home yet, but you will be soon. I understand this place now."

"And?" asked Sebastian.

"The Stone did not create Caldera."

Millicent bounced her hands in the air like an excited toddler. "The Stone didn't create Caldera — Caldera was created to hide the Stone! It was all in that first memory we saw! The blue light came first, and then the Stone appeared! The blue light when we go trough the geysers, the blue light in the sky. *That* is Caldera, and it has nothing to do with the Stone. Well, except to hide it."

Miriam stood on her knees and gawped at Ze'eva's bizarre form. "What are you talking about? Why was it hidden?"

Ze'eva's eyes narrowed, and she lowered her ethereal voice to a delicate wind. "There are many who've sought it. The Sojourner especially seeks the Spectra." She said this knowingly, as though this was supposed to mean something to them. "Energy, space, and time. They're all connected. The Stone was hidden to protect all of reality."

"Huh?" said John. "And now?"

"Now that you've destroyed it, Caldera is a hiding place with nothing to hide. I can close it now. Dissolve it. Shut it down. I can send you home!"

"What is the Sojourner?" asked John.

"I don't know yet, John! I'll find out. In the meantime, once you're back in your homeworld, I'll do my best to conceal you, so you can go about your lives. But, eventually, your journey could turn treacherous. So, be on your guard."

Millicent's head wobbled like a bobblehead. "Don't worry. I think I'll be on guard for the rest of my life after this."

Ze'eva nodded. "Good. Don't worry. I'll be watching over you. Sebastian, Gabriel, and Arthur? You'll come with me."

Nobody moved.

"Please," she said patiently. "Say your goodbyes. I promise everything is going to be all right."

Chapter Twenty

They hugged Sebastian again, unsure of what was about to happen.

"Well," said Sebastian, "if our time together has proved one thing, it's that there's no such thing as a real goodbye between us."

Ze'eva nodded. "My friends? Caldera is at an end."

THOOM.

John heard his mother's voice as he opened his eyes. His parents smothered him with hugs and kisses in his hospital bed. It was real, they told him, and he had the cuts and bruises and scars on his body to prove it. They escorted him to the next room where Millicent and Miriam woke soon after. Miriam's foot had a new dressing. Their mother had let Millicent's very curly hair out of its pigtail buns, and it sat on her head like a bundle of silk tubes as she looked around and realized where she was. They all piled into Miriam's bed and hugged and cried. There were tears of happiness, tears of disbelief, and tears of loss. But mostly, there were tears of happiness.

CNN played on the television on the wall. The sound was off, but the screen showed talking heads next to helicopter footage of the Mesa. The bold caption at the bottom of the screen read:

Strange New Structures Appear in Yellowstone National Park

The image cut to a shot looking up at Tihuzaveh, the Hourglass, one of the sites they'd never visited during their time in Caldera. The next shot was more helicopter footage, this time of Süütakkan.

Then the program cut to a shot of a herd of mammoths walking across Hayden Valley. The kids wondered if Emily was one of them.

Or if Ze'eva had taken her. They wondered many things, but the endless coverage of the Yellowstone Incident could wait.

They were home.

Appendix I
Glossaries

Abatakai
AH • **BAH** • TI • KAI
"The Great Fish" (Shoshone)
Abatakai is a 400-foot-tall tower in the shape of a trout standing on its tail. It's anchored to Frank Island in the middle of Yellowstone Lake.

Doyadu-khani
DOY • AH • DOO - **KAH** • NEE
"The Cat House" (Shoshone)
Doyadu-khani is a trapezoidal pyramid resembling a Mayan temple. Made of black and yellow stone, it sits on the Upper Terrace Area of Mammoth Hot Springs. It connects to the South Passage by a long, curving bridge.

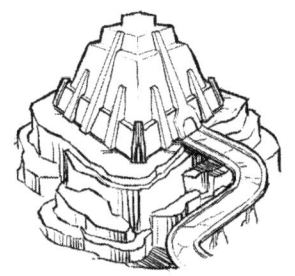

Süütakkan
SOO • **OO** • TI • KAHN
"The Basket Knife" (Shoshone)
Süütakkan is a 300-foot-tall white tower that looks like a giant blade. It stands near Dragon's Mouth Spring on the Yellowstone River.

Tumo Nataquinde
TOO • MO NAH • TI • **KIN** • DAY
"The Written Story" (Shoshone)
Tumo Nataquinde is mysterious site rumored to be hidden near the Lower Falls of the Yellowstone River.

Arthur's Phrasebook

s'il vous plaît	if you please
Scélérat!	Villain!
Sacré bleu!	Exclamation of surprise, exasperation, or dismay
Comment ça va, puppy dog?	How are you, puppy dog?
Heavy beasts! Envoyez-les loin!	Heavy beasts! Send them away!
Fermez vos gueules!	Shut your mouth!
La réponse est claire.	The answer is clear.
Passez par ici.	Go through here.
Oui, it is true.	Yes, it is true.
Je l'ai créé.	I created it.
Bien sûr.	Of course.
Incroyable!	Incredible!
Mon Dieu!	My God!
Laisse moi en trouver.	Let me find some.
Bonjour.	Hello.
Le Chien Misérable	The Miserable Dog
Je suis perdu! I had no idea the world was so . . . l'univers est beau!	I'm lost! I had no idea the world was so . . . the universe is beautiful!

Appendix II
The Yellowstone Sketchbook

The idea for Yellowstone: The Bears of Caldera started with a single drawing in 1995. I was searching for an idea for a comic strip. At the time, I was inspired by Bill Waterson's Calvin and Hobbes, Berkeley Breathed's Bloom County, and Lynn Johnston's For Better or For Worse. I admired their artistry, the fully-realized characters, and, especially in Waterson's case, their desire to test the boundaries of the medium.

One of the first attempts was about a newlywed couple who move to the suburbs. Their middle-aged neighbors would provide advice on marriage, which would usually be detrimental to the optimistic main character. I decided not to pursue it, deciding that the genre was already crowded. And at 23, I felt that I didn't have the necessary experience to write it. One of the neighbors was a fisherman named Bob, though.

On April 27th, 1995, I drew the image below. This misshapen girl was one of several ideas on a page full of doodles. Something about her crossed arms, judgemental pout, and curly little pigtails struck me. I wrote the name Millicent next to her. I drew another girl and named her Miriam, and I knew at once that they were twin sisters. I finished the page with a boy named Michael.

The next day, on my birthday, I kept drawing these new characters. Michael became Matthew and then, because I didn't want three M names, he became John.

I had the main characters, but who could be their foil? Who would be the Hobbes to their Calvin? The Bill the Cat to their Opus? I drew a big bear with forelorn eyes and thought it would be interesting to put them together.

That night, I drew this image of the three kids and the bear. This was the dynamic I was looking for. The kids would get into shenanigans, and the big, brown bear would be there to guide them, pull them out of trouble, and generally be a big, cuddly playmate. There would be humor and tenderness. I wanted to create something gentle, oddball, and fun.

I thought of setting it in Yellowstone National Park, and Yellowstone was born as a comic strip. Four of the strips that I created appear on the next two pages.

Amazingly, a few of those moments survived all the way into this novel.

But comic strip writing wasn't for me. I didn't enjoy the format of setup-to-punchline, and I felt like there was a bigger story that I wanted to tell. While I was deciding what to do next, I drew the characters constantly. I drew them on forms at work or in the margins of calendars. I drew them on napkins and on the backs of paper placemats at restaurants.

Miriam had long hair until recently. I decided that she cut it short when she turned eleven and donated her hair to Locks of Love.

For a time, I thought Yellowstone could be a graphic novel. The script I wrote and the sketches from this period became the basis of this novel. Early drafts of the story spent more time with the family at the campsite at the beginning. These scenes had great character moments, but I decided that they slowed the plot.

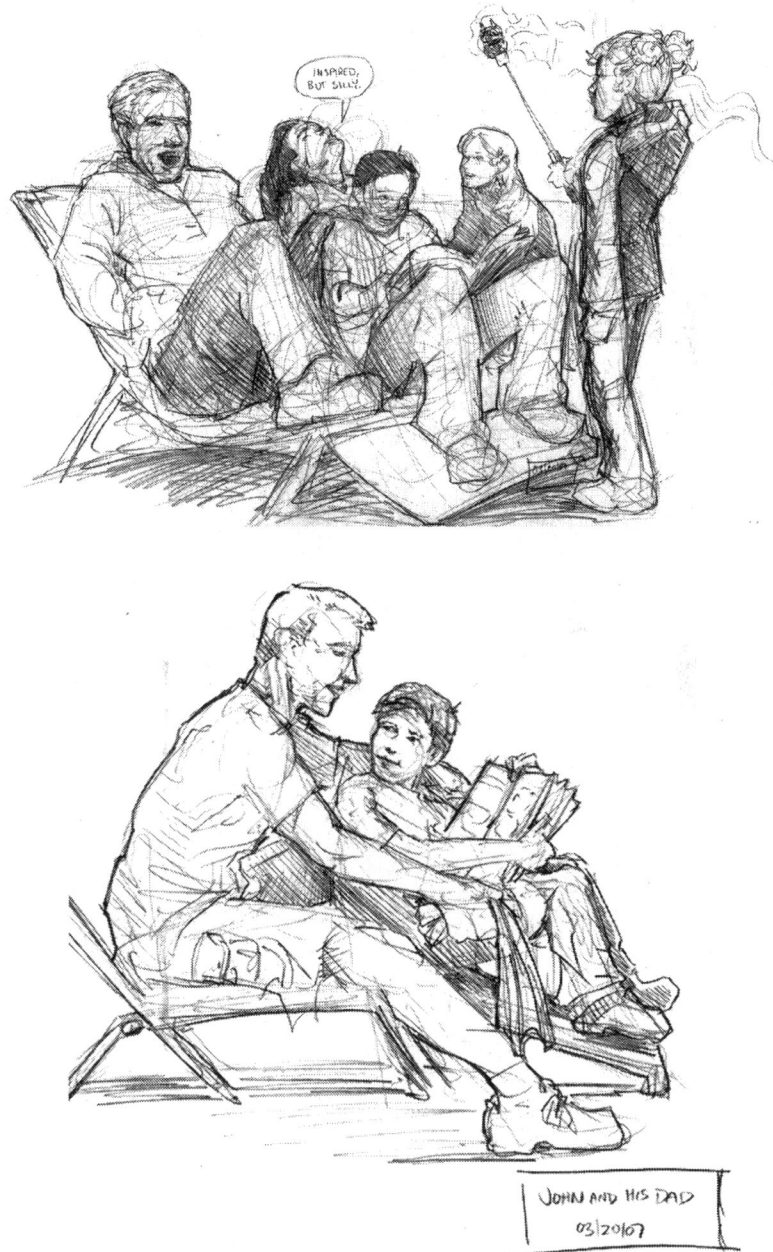

John and Ana encounter Lucifur on the Grizzly Lake Trail

Millicent and Miriam at the Lake Clinic

John meets Benjamin

Rough sketches from the Mesa:
Copper sculpture, the library, and the Amphitheater

Some sketches inspired entire sequences in the story. I had no idea where the kids were sneaking into or why when I drew this, but it became the basis for the end of Part I.

The kids rescue Sebastian from Nidever's lab.

Miriam and John experience a memory wall for the first time.

This is another sketch that inspired a pivotal moment in the story.

Two rough sketches of Miriam helping Robert Hume

Note from the Author

I must take a moment to caution young readers. Real dangers exist in Yellowstone National Park. Remember that *The Bears of Caldera* is a work of fiction, and although meeting a talking bear like Sebastian is a great fantasy, we must respect nature and the rules that are posted in our National Parks. All wildlife and the geothermal features in the Yellowstone region can be harmful . . . or deadly! So, stay away from the animals, don't go off the established paths and boardwalks, and always, always stay close to your parents or guardians.

Best,
Chad-Michael Simon

Made in the USA
Lexington, KY
09 May 2019